Today is
the first day
of the rest
of your life

THE JESUIT

THE
JESUIT

John Gallahue

STEIN AND DAY/*Publishers*/New York

First published in 1973
Copyright © 1973 by John Gallahue
Library of Congress Catalog Card No. 72-94911
All rights reserved
Published simultaneously in Canada by Saunders of Toronto, Ltd.
Designed by David Miller
Printed in the United States of America
Stein and Day/*Publishers*/7 East 48 Street, New York, N.Y. 10017
ISBN 0-8128-1531-9

SECOND PRINTING, 1973

To *Martha, Fiona, and Sean,*
without whom naught.

ACKNOWLEDGMENTS

Renni Browne contributed in so many ways to the strength of this novel that no expression of gratitude here can do justice to her work. This book is equally a tribute to her enthusiasm and perceptions.

To my agent, John Hawkins, I am grateful for a personal interest and astuteness about the book that transcended business conventions.

Limitations of space prevent my acknowledging all the friends who encouraged me during the writing of this book. They know who they are, and the depth of my appreciation of their support. My debt over the years to Preston and Emily Waddington, Bernard Murphy, and Filippo Galluppi goes beyond this acknowledgment, as it does to Bert Pollens.

As for my publishers—Sol Stein and Patricia Day—and their remarkable staff, no author could have been better served.

CONTENTS

BOOK ONE: *The Summons*   11

BOOK TWO: *The Competition*   61

BOOK THREE: *The Mission*   145

BOOK FOUR: *The Truth*   271

BOOK

I

The Summons

1

One morning in 1931, in early June, the pious routine of the rector of a sleepy seminary in Maryland was spectacularly interrupted. A young priest from the office of the Apostolic Delegate in Washington, D.C., personally delivered a sealed message from Rome to the Superior of the House. He did not wait for a reply; indeed, as he informed the rector of Woodstock Seminary, he had no knowledge whatsoever of the contents. He was simply a courier. The Vatican had communicated with its representative now in Washington, Archbishop Francisi, and the young priest had been commandeered to ensure an unhampered relay to the rector. Saying no more, the priest departed, leaving Father Dillon to peruse the brief message.

> Dear Father Rector:
>
> We request your immediate cooperation in the reassignment of one Alexander Ulanov, S.J., from his present residence at Woodstock College to the Gregorian University in Rome. Your superiors have also been advised of this request. There is, therefore, no reason for delay in the matter.
>
> Mr. Ulanov, S.J., shall be tendered all prompt assistance in order that he be aboard the *Mauritania* in three days' time. It is berthed in New York City. A stateroom has been reserved for him on said liner at said port. Your facilitation

of this request without delay will, of course, be deeply appreciated here.

Your servant in Christ,
Eugenio Cardinal Pacelli,
Secretary of State
Vatican City
Rome, Italy

Father Dillon read the telegram three or four times. Finally, he delegated one of his seminarians to fetch his confidential house consultant—Father Sullivan, a former rector now eighty years old. Together, they tried to comprehend the import of this extraordinary communication.

"Very unusual, most unusual indeed," Sullivan said after rereading the message. "Ah, but that is the price of office. Administrators like ourselves must expect these little collisions." He limped over to the window, tapping his blackthorn stick as he went. "You know as well as I that we are the Pope's shock troops. Who else in the history of the church has been as closely sworn to his service as we? So if Rome slights us a bit now and then, it is we who must give."

"All very well," said the rector, "but why wasn't this letter sent through direct channels?"

"Don't be headstrong, Jimmy," said Father Sullivan, quick to take advantage of the fact that he had been the rector's teacher twenty-five years ago.

"We are an ancient community and we have our prerogatives," Dillon said, "not to mention our power. The cardinal can't order Jesuits about as if they were parish priests. I myself only accept commands from our own father general."

"Do you think you should take it so seriously as all that?" asked Sullivan.

For an answer Father Dillon seized the telephone and called his own superior in New York, who turned out to be equally resentful of the cardinal's intrusion.

"And why this young scholastic?" Father Dillon asked him. "Who the devil is he to merit this kind of treatment?"

"You really know him better than I do," said the provincial.

"I've only met him a time or two on my visitations. After all, I have eight hundred subjects and a few colleges and high schools to worry about. You only have two hundred and fifty, and can see them every day."

"Yes, well, I do *not* have a complete record of this Ulanov's years in the Society," said Father Dillon. "Those are at your headquarters."

"They wouldn't be of much help to you, I'm afraid. As soon as the telegram arrived, I had the dossier brought up. I could find very little that would bring Mr. Ulanov to the attention of a man of Pacelli's stature—the right hand of His Holiness, they say. It's quite baffling! Obviously, we have missed something in his record."

"Should you not call the general in Rome?"

"No, I don't think so. I rather think you are on your own, Father Rector. Should any mistakes be made, it is better that they arise from confusion—rather than, let us say, resistance or possibly disobedience."

"I see," said the rector.

"Yes, well, let me know how it turns out. You can send me the resolution by mail. Since I have not been consulted by Rome in the ordinary way, I am really only a bystander. In any case, I have great confidence in your abilities." The provincial offered a subdued chuckle. "We'll see you soon. *Deo gratias!*" And with this cheery farewell, the line to the provincial seat on Fordham Road in the Bronx went dead, and Father Dillon was left in the Maryland countryside with his jurisdictional conundrums intact.

His first decision was to send Father Sullivan to the vaults for the young Jesuit's dossier. Whatever he might have indicated in the phone call to New York, he did have a duplicate file on all the scholastics in his house. The provincial surely knew that, but Father Dillon had fished in hopes that there might be something more to be found out. As it was, he was still left to his own resources.

It was probably true, he thought, that there was little more information on Mr. Ulanov in the provincial archives than there was in Dillon's own vault. A nuisance, sometimes, this gathering of information on their young men, but it was in crises like these

[15]

that all the trouble could turn out to be worthwhile. There was always the possibility that some apparently innocuous point recorded by a sharp-eyed priest might yield an important clue.

As he waited for Father Sullivan to return, Dillon glanced around the walls at the portraits of a few of his spiritual forebears, sixteenth-century generals of the order—St. Ignatius, the Jewish Diego Lainez, and then some recent rectors of Woodstock. From a variety of baroque backgrounds, their gazes seemed to follow the rector.

Dillon could not decide exactly what the severe pursuit of their eyes meant. They were forbidding old men—these Spanish, Italian, Irish ancestors of his; and while he celebrated masses in their name and publicly preached their virtues, in his heart of hearts he still felt uncomfortable with their ascetic poses.

He turned and looked at a bust of St. Ignatius. "I would rather command the odd ones than be commanded by them," he announced to that Christ-intoxicated wise old face carved from the death mask of their Spanish father before God. "I mean, if it comes to that."

A discreet knock at the door was followed by the reappearance of the house consultant, who swept in with the documents.

"I thought you were lost in prayer somewhere," said Father Dillon, spreading out the material on the rectorial desk. "What's your opinion?"

Father Sullivan understood the question. "I just took a very quick look, James, very quick."

"Now, Andy, that's not what I asked you."

"All right," said the other, "but there is really not a thing in here that will tell you more than you already know."

The rector turned toward the window. "Well, let's see, what *do* I know? After all, as our provincial has so nicely put it, I only have two hundred and fifty subjects in this house. It stands to reason I should know this young man better than anyone else, does it not?"

Father Sullivan let the sarcasm pass.

"Mr. Ulanov," said the rector, "is a second-year theologian. He has been in the order twelve years. He will be ordained next year, am I right?"

"Go on!" Father Sullivan was quick to encourage; already

they both had a definite sense of where they were going once these necessary preliminaries had been cleared away.

"He looks to be, would you say, six foot three, six foot four—about two hundred and ten pounds?"

"That's close enough."

"I believe he was born in Youngstown, Ohio. In, let's see—in 1896, which would make him thirty-five years old."

Father Sullivan looked up from the dossier. The rector had a knack of amazing even his closest friends with details he squirreled away and then sprung at the moment of maximum impact. "The way you spoke to Father Provincial," Sullivan said, "one would think that you had no knowledge of this scholastic."

"You never know," said Father Dillon. "Anyway, it is better to find out than to tell. Now isn't that true?" The shrewd Irish eyes twinkled at the lovely disguises of his rectorship.

He paced the floor, trying to pull from some mental compartment impressions of Mr. Ulanov. So might he achieve a kind of rational ecstasy whereby the scattered pieces fell into place, hopefully in some sensible frame. "Our young man," he told Father Sullivan, "did not enter the Jesuits at the average age, nor did he graduate from a Jesuit high school. He worked in a steel mill in Youngstown for four years before he joined us at St. Andrew's on Hudson. Both of his parents are dead. He has no living relatives that I can make out, except for a younger brother."

"How do you know there are no others?"

"No one else has ever come to see Mr. Ulanov on our visiting days. If there were someone else, surely in the last two years, eight visiting days in all, they would have put in an appearance. At least once!" No, there's no one—besides that other boy, I mean, and he's an odd type. You know, the brother."

"How so?" asked Sullivan.

"Well, not at all like this man of ours. A kind of pale fellow, always hanging on the older one. A weasel type, they would say in Ireland."

Father Sullivan nodded.

"And, there's another thing, Mr. Ulanov only sends one Christmas card a year. To that one brother."

"Jimmy, you don't miss a trick!"

"When I was appointed rector," Dillon said quite seriously, "I took it as my job to know all my men and really know them, and I enjoy it."

"I never told you," said the consultant, "but I was one of those who voted for you. And for precisely that reason."

"What reason?"

"Any theologian, I said, who was as interested as you were in knowing what went on downstairs in the kitchen had all the qualities to be a good rector."

"Well, that's something!" Dillon laughed. "All these years I've known you, and I never gave you credit for half that intelligence." Then he sobered. "You know, Andy, some public choices are worth the weight of your soul. This scholastic is being removed from my jurisdiction by what I can only call, well, the strangest means either of us has ever—"

"It *is* unprecedented."

"And if it is as important as it seems, there is all the more reason to proceed with caution."

"And you're usually so easygoing!" said Father Sullivan.

"Nine things out of ten don't require any more," the rector said simply. "A man is a fool in any walk of life if he doesn't know the difference. Now let's take a look at these papers and see what we have missed."

For twenty minutes the two of them studied first the master of novices' notes, written after Ulanov's two years in the novitiate; next the report of his two years of classical studies in the juniorate and three years of philosophy; finally, the assessment of his three years of teaching in the Regency period. Each of these represented ascending grades through which every member of the order had to pass. Only after sixteen years or so did the confidential reporting on each Jesuit's spiritual progress cease. Ulanov's dossier was thus not yet complete; he still had ordination before him and the completion of theology.

"Rather what one would expect," said Father Dillon, laying aside the thick packet.

"Exactly," said Father Sullivan. "Fine marks in every category, mature sense of prudence, exemplary observation of the rule. Ulanov is a likable young man, I've thought so myself in my few dealings with him. He seems to be intelligent, responsible, a very hard worker."

"I understand all that," said the rector. "What is it we *don't* know?" He unfolded his hands and stared at his friend. "Out with it, Andy! Over the years I've found that your common sense can be invaluable if somebody acts as a dentist and pulls it out."

The old priest hesitated. "Well, I don't like to criticize, Jimmy, and I won't. This is a fine young man. I know him to be generous. He has always struck me as . . . as deeply Christlike as anyone I ever met."

"Yes, yes." The rector nodded. "But would you make him a superior?"

"Oh, no."

"Why not?"

"Well, because I don't know him. I mean, there is a way in which you can't grasp him. I couldn't go that far."

The rector stood up. "Exactly! And neither do *I* really know him." He lifted one sheet from the pile on his desk. "Your old friend Father Sweeney up at St. Joseph's in Philadelphia has a few lines here."

"Father Sweeney's a saint."

"He's an unholy shrewd judge of men," corrected the rector. "He wrote a couple of paragraphs to the effect that he found Mr. Ulanov the most socially conscious Jesuit he has ever met, isn't that interesting? Socially conscious!" He turned the words over and over in his mind. "It seems that he has spent his Saturday free time attending labor union meetings and marches, and he apparently tried to lead a campaign to turn St. Joe's into a half-free school for the poor."

"And just a young scholastic!" said Father Sullivan.

"Yes, well, it says a lot for him. I wouldn't have gone about it that way myself, but there's an obvious commitment in this that might be revealing."

"You don't think the Vatican heard and—" Sullivan stopped as though the thought, once articulated, collapsed from its own weight.

"Hardly. In my opinion, the Vatican sounds better in the

encyclicals than it ever intends to be in the real world. I don't really believe they want a young social reformer in Rome. Anyway, the point is that Sweeney ends here by saying the scholastic is 'more hidden' than any young man he has ever met in the Society. He notices that Ulanov seldom drinks even on feast days, and that this seems out of keeping with his general masculine style. Very good point, don't you think?"

"What are you driving at?" asked Sullivan.

"The control, the control! It's out of the ordinary."

"Surely you are making too much of this. You know, Ulanov's remoteness may simply be due to the fact that he is older than the others, or that he has suffered some tragedy that we know nothing about. Perhaps the years in the steel mills—"

"But you would not make him superior?"

"That is different."

"Why?"

"Because then I *must* know. An absence of negative factors is not good enough, not for that position."

"Well said," replied the rector, "and that is exactly what I am about. I must treat a request from such a position as Cardinal Pacelli's as tantamount to a very important recommendation. Something extraordinary is afoot, and I cannot for the life of me fathom what it could be. But if it is an assignment, some post, some career of importance, I cannot be a part of it."

"They never asked you, Jimmy!"

"No, they didn't. But I am responsible wherever and whoever I am for things that come in my range. They can depose me, I don't care, but no man can deny me the right to exercise my authority if I have been given that obligation."

The consultant said nothing.

"Think of it," Dillon insisted. "Out of the many hundreds of Jesuit houses around the world, out of the thousands of Jesuits, out of the hundreds of thousands of Catholic priests, nuns, and seminarians in the world, this young Russian-American is the subject of a command from the Secretary of State. It really seems—well, the point is that I shall not release him under these conditions."

"But that is disobedience!"

"Perhaps."

"What shall you do?"

"I shall do nothing."

"They will be angry."

"*We* are surprised at *their* request. *We* are affronted."

"It is the Vatican, James."

"And we are the Society of Jesus."

"Pacelli may become Pope."

"Only I would be hurt. In any case, they must explain and then *we* will advise."

"But it may all be for nothing! There may be nothing wrong."

"Probably not, but no chances will be taken. You will support me when I meet with the rest of the consultants this afternoon?"

"Father Rector, I support your instincts."

"Instincts are good enough. *Gratias,* Father Sullivan."

That afternoon, however, the support of Father Dillon's friend proved insufficient. The rector could not bring that aging convention to say yea or nay. They were far too impressed by the stature of Cardinal Pacelli—who, it was already rumored, would follow Pope Pius XI in the Apostolic Succession. The Jesuits had once been persecuted by the church itself, they reminded the rector, for just such conduct. There was too much at stake for the Society and its small empire of schools in the United States to risk this display of independence.

And then, finally, the *coup de grâce.* As an old theologian put it, "We do not understand your misgivings about the scholastic, Father Dillon. We really should be quite gratified that one of our young members has been selected by his Eminence himself for something extraordinary, we sincerely hope so. He is a young man of great intelligence, piety, character—and it is your misgivings, it seems to us, which are quite peculiar. That he does not fraternize in the ordinary way, that he does not indulge in beer parties or display the boyish zest of our less mature seminarians—it seems to me that these are strong points in his favor rather than black marks. I suggest that you examine your own perspective. Very strange . . ."

Out of courtesy to their house superior, the group did not record their disapproval of the rector's announced course. As for

Father Dillon, he felt that he had done a very poor job of presenting his case to the consultants; had found himself incapable in that formal convention of articulating these small anxieties of his about Mr. Ulanov.

"Damn, damn, damnation!" he kept repeating after they had left. "Why couldn't they grasp the distinction? Are they so stupid?" he asked the painting of Loyola in his study.

The rector was still left with his power of decision, and more than ever he meant to exercise it. It wasn't that he found anything bad in the young man. No, that would represent a loss of balance, and if there was one virtue the rector prided himself on possessing, it was perspective. He simply sensed in the young Jesuit an empty spot. But even that wouldn't have mattered much if Rome hadn't been so insistent on his promotion.

His sense of fairness forced him to admit that there might be an easy unmysterious reason why Ulanov kept himself so aloof— and, after all, no one had ever asked him. Despite the famous scrutiny which the order exercised over its members, there were areas never probed.

The rector realized that he was hoping to put himself more in line with the conventional wisdom of his colleagues. And, yes, there was still a way out in which without sacrificing his integrity he might yet save himself from a decision that would send repercussions to the Eternal City and back.

He would tell Ulanov exactly what had happened. He would explain his own peculiar reservations and ask the scholastic himself for help in laying them to rest.

While the community dined in silence that evening, the rector looked over the heads of his subjects. The seminarians sat in sextets at the heavy tables arranged the grand length of the refectory. From his position at the head table, Father Dillon had a fine view of the room and its several hundred inhabitants. His eyes checked the youthful black-habited ranks, from the lay brothers' tables all the way up to the older, prouder eleven- to thirteen-year members. The arrangement of the enormous room reflected an *esprit de géométrie,* a sense of order through the various grades of members that appealed to the rector's feeling for hierarchy and command.

The medley of types was gladdening evidence that the range of personalities responding to Christ's call had not been limited by the Society's regimentation. There was no problem with being different, as long as they all obeyed the important rules and followed, unquestioningly, their assignments.

Ulanov never violated any rule, never informed, and then again was not a "strict observer," not one of those formal fellows who to Dillon's eyes looked to be in rigor mortis.

Studying Ulanov's features at a table far removed from his own, Dillon marveled at his exceptional size and strength. "Of course, this is no boy," he thought, "he's thirty-five. It shows in that quiet command he has of himself." The scholastic also communicated a sense of joy, a happiness in "the life," as Jesuits called their existence, as though he were saying to everyone, "I am realizing my purpose perfectly here."

The rector noticed also that the people seated near Ulanov tonight were not those of last night or the night before. "Particular friendships" were, of course, frowned upon in the order—not that one couldn't have brothers in Christ closer to oneself than others, but many scholastics could not help forming small cliques. Ulanov, on the other hand, seemed just as happy with one member as with another. Apparently it made no difference who sat next to him, even on the official "speaking" nights—which reminded the rector that he was going to surprise the community with a dispensation to speak.

"The Martyrology, Mister," he called through the hall and up to the pulpit. The history of those martyred for the faith through the centuries on this particular day cued the community that pulpit reading was at an end, and that a relaxed meal lay ahead.

The rector gestured at the ninety-year-old priest next to him and announced that it was his birthday. In point of fact, Dillon had hauled the old Jesuit out of his comfortable infirmary room, where he always ate alone or with the voices of death and angels, and brought him down for the birthday celebration. The rector had designed the whole charade to soften up Mr. Ulanov, believing that even this imperturbable scholastic would be less guarded after conversation and roast beef than after an ascetic meal.

After declaring *Deo gratias,* Father Dillon patiently endured the silent contempt of the ancient Jesuit while the rest of the community enjoyed their dinner. When it was finally over, Dillon waited in the rear while his subjects filed out. As his quarry was leaving, the rector touched him on the sleeve and asked him to follow.

Ordinarily, when a superior wished to interview a subject, he did so apart from the prying gaze of the rest of the community. Father Dillon, however, chose to walk conspicuously around the grounds with the scholastic. Such a departure might mean any number of things to the others—that Ulanov was in trouble, that he was a special friend of the rector, that he had been selected for a major position in his class. Father Dillon felt that if Ulanov had worked at maintaining an inconspicuous role in the community, this experience might be so painful as to be revealing.

Surprisingly, it was Ulanov who opened the conversation as soon as they started to walk outside. With a smile he complimented the rector on the fine meal and the permission for conversation. "I did not know," he said, "that our Father Stocke was so beloved. He is so rarely seen. Most people here do not know his name."

"Then you know him?"

"Quite well. I visit him from time to time."

"And he talks to you? What about?"

"About history, about Europe."

"You know," said the rector, "Father Stocke doesn't tolerate me more than half a minute. Thirty seconds after I am in his room he asks me my business and then tells me where to go."

Ulanov laughed with or at the rector, who could not tell which. "Well," he said, "he knows a great deal about Europe. He was born there."

"I was aware of that," said the rector.

"It is interesting that he was sent to the United States as a *missionary.*"

The rector chose not to pursue this tack. "Why are you so interested in Europe?" he asked. "I mean, that's going to a great deal of trouble. You might easily have read about it in place of visiting the sick."

"Why not do both, Father Rector? Europe is the intellectual capital. The cultural tides generally reach us ten or fifteen years later, and Father Stocke knows the various levels of their society. His comparisons between America and Germany are very instructive."

"You are that interested?"

"I would like to go over there for studies."

"I'm sorry. The chances are slim."

"Perhaps!" said Ulanov, and then recovered quickly. "I mean, you never know what Mother Society will do. She may decide that it is not right that the church here is so divorced from the church in Europe. It is unfortunate, I believe, that the Great War increased our isolation. It will not last."

The rector was happy to hear Ulanov speaking so easily about his ideas, expressing his hopes and opinions without restraint. Nevertheless, he felt disturbed at the lack of any opening into what for his purposes he thought of as the "real person." The man seemed mature, self-confident in a life where a certain childlikeness characterized the scholastic; where, in fact, awe of authority generally produced a bubbling naïveté or adolescent formality. Mr. Ulanov had even surprised the rector at one of his own tricks—had he not intimated that he did not believe the "birthday party"?

"A penny for your thoughts!" Ulanov said with an easy smile.

Father Dillon took that stock question of the twenties in good humor. Ulanov obviously had no intention of sounding ambitious with regard to Europe, which would almost certainly result in his being sent somewhere else.

"I was thinking that you have a very interesting name," said the rector.

"Well, it isn't Irish!"

"I didn't mean that," said the rector, laughing. "I was wondering if you were related to Lenin."

"Someday," said Ulanov, "the world will have a hundred books about him. But right now it is unusual to hear him mentioned here."

"His real name was Ulanov, and his older brother was called Alexander—just as you are."

"No relation," said the scholastic. "Still, one hardly expects a Jesuit rector in this time and place to know those details."

[25]

"I meant that it was an unusual *coincidence* of names," replied Father Dillon, reddening slightly from this gambit of inversion to which he had been suddenly subjected.

There ensued another difficult pause, which the young man seemed at no pains to relieve. The rector looked sideways for a few moments at his very independent inferior. Ulanov was a good six inches taller and broader than the aging Dillon, and there was simply no comparison as to physique. He really is a damned impressive religious, the rector thought. The well-pressed habit, the total cleanliness, the smooth straight manner in conversation, all seemed to fit together. The rector considered his own rumpled habit, his falling belly, his rambling speech, and knew himself to be personally prejudiced against men who were so totally of a piece, so very conscious of the whole effect of their looks and voice.

"Well," he said, as much to break his train of thought as the silence, "I have been told that when you were teaching, you were interested in the poor children of Philadelphia. I think it's wonderful, and also that work of yours with laborers!"

"I achieved very little," said Ulanov.

"That's not what I heard. And you had your own heavy schedule in the school."

"I'm afraid the real reason for our failures is the order's aristocracy, Reverend Father."

"I think so, too, but we need influence among the upper and middle classes."

"They are doomed!" announced Ulanov.

"I beg your pardon?"

"I only meant," said Ulanov, "that Christ loves the poor. That is where Christianity came from—St. Paul knew that the destiny of the poor is to trouble this world. If we follow him, we belong to them."

"We have our hands full with the children of immigrant families, and they are working people. We are trying to advance them into the middle class of this country."

"Yes, indeed. *Oh,* yes. Poverty is something to be ashamed of. Jesuits are the image of elegance. Bringing them up through education, from shameful places—"

[26]

"What else can we do?"

Ulanov shook his head. "The order's drift is toward alliance with Americanism and its system. I swear we'll end up as the holy servants of this economy if we aren't careful."

"You didn't answer my question," said the Rector, sure he was about to reap a windfall.

"I only know that we should be 'the poor people's people' and think it out from there. It is not a doctrine, like communism or something of that sort." Ulanov enunciated these last words with particular care. "It's an attitude of mind, Reverend Father. There's to be no compromise with the world's ideas, no forgetting where we come from."

"Whew-w-w," breathed the rector. "For a moment it sounded very revolutionary."

"No, no!" said Ulanov. "The communist revolutionaries succeed because they have stolen something of Christ's."

"Oh, I don't know," said the rector. "This sort of talk is rather new to me."

"Well, perhaps I misinterpret Christ."

Ulanov seemed reluctant to go on.

"It is true that economic issues are very much in the air these days," said the rector, "but we must be careful how we treat them."

"Yes, I would like to get more advice from you on the subject, Father Rector."

Father Dillon sighed and put his hand inside the pocket of his habit. "By a strange coincidence, Mr. Ulanov, considering the interest you manifested in Europe a few minutes ago, this telegram arrived today concerning just that." He handed the open page to the scholastic, who read it quickly and then gave it back to his superior with the slightest trace of a smile.

"Aren't you surprised?" the rector was compelled finally to ask.

"What will be, will be."

"I don't understand."

"God decides all."

"God and the rector."

"God alone! You are his instrument."

"But this letter, do you know where it came from?"

"From his Eminence, Cardinal Pacelli. And, therefore, the Pope."

"That is all you have to say?"

"I would like very much to obey his Holiness."

"Do you have any idea why he would send for you? There are a million religious in the world, and he found you—for what?"

"I have no idea."

"Have you ever spoken to anyone about an assignment?"

"Nothing more than what I have said to you tonight."

The rector, smarting over the man's coolness, waited for his own pique to subside. Then he said, "I can't assent to it, my friend, that is final. I'm sorry." The ultimatum sounded more blunt than Dillon had intended.

The rector was not actually looking at him, but he could sense the slight jerking of Ulanov's head—up, straight ahead to the horizon, the lips pursing and releasing. Father Dillon, tempted to pursue his advantage in the midst of the scholastic's small panic, could not bring himself to that kind of exploitation of the other's sensitivities. In any case, Ulanov had by now regained, if not his usual sangfroid, at least presence enough to maintain his interests. When he turned to face the rector, his efforts at control showed only in the set of the jaw and the hurt querulous eyes.

"Why would you not honor the Pope's request?" he asked.

"Because I don't know you well enough to recommend you for an unknown position."

The scholastic shook his head. "What is it you wanted of me?"

"You're too careful, Alexander. You've been planning something. It may be some innocent ambition, but whatever it is, it leaves a bad taste. I am sorry to disappoint you."

As if he had planned it, the rector found himself ending his dialogue with the scholastic just as they reached the door they had walked through a half hour before.

As the rector reached for the knob, Ulanov said, "You will not win this gamble."

"I *beg* your pardon?"

[28]

"I do not wish to hurt your feelings either, Reverend Father. But I believe that I am entitled to express an opinion."

"Yes-s-s."

"I will not quarrel with your instincts, or the judgment they lead you to. But I rather think that you will not win."

The rector felt the heat in his face as Ulanov stood calmly shaking his head. There was no gloating, no denial of authority, no shadow of personal vindictiveness. His attitude seemed to manifest only the sad matter of fact—as if he felt quite sorry for the rector and wished to advise *him* of his predicament!

"We shall probably not meet again, Father Rector," said Ulanov, "not like this, anyway. So I want to tell you now how much I have appreciated serving under you in this house. You have fine sensitivities. You are a kind of Irish statesman—two feet on the ground, the better to serve the spirit. I want you to know that I hold nothing against you! You have done what you thought best. Now, as we say in Russian, *do svidaniya.*" With that he bowed, turned, and hurried away.

The rector had held onto the doorknob throughout this extraordinary farewell, his features as frozen as the fingers touching the half-opened door. Somehow, there had been another move in the game. He had not seen it, had not thought of it before or during, but there it was. In the very throes of defeat, he had found Ulanov judging *him*, telling *him*, "No."

As he labored up the stairs on the way to his room, Father Dillon could not help relishing the personal challenge. He knew that in the first few rounds of sparring with an unfamiliar opponent, he tended to be caught off guard. Sometimes he blamed his easygoing ways for these initial blunders; it was only by concentration and planning that he ever managed to even the score.

The match had been uneven from the beginning. As soon as Ulanov read Pacelli's telegram—Dillon's honest gift—he had concluded immediately that the rector was disobedient. Ulanov had gambled, then, that Rome would win.

Once inside his room, the rector did not immediately turn on the lights. Perhaps, he thought, the order might be merely a vehicle for his strange subordinate's grand designs. That would account for the man's solitary ways. He could really trust no one, for who would understand the far-reaching nature of these schemes? They were locked in one self-confident brain, and were, for that reason, all the more dangerous.

"Years in the steel mills," Dillon said aloud, tapping nervously at his desk. That would make his man a different kind of missionary. "But what is he really planning? And whatever does he want of the Jesuits?"

There had to be clues in Ulanov's past. Orphaned at fourteen, he had raised his younger brother by himself. In the gloom of his study, Dillon leaned back in his chair and recollected from the recesses of his experience every orphaned man he had known. They all seemed to live their lives bound to the dead mother in a bizarre unity, their feelings frozen at a certain stage of youth. Intolerant of disagreement, they seemed able to relate only to those who shared their own rage.

For the moment, Dillon could press his thoughts no further. Few of these details could he connect, and even fewer would make sense to his consultants or superiors. And yet, more than ever, he was strengthened in his resolve to deny Ulanov passage to Rome.

Kissing his crucifix that night, especially the wounds of Jesus, and meditating a little longer than usual, the rector laid all his qualms in the hands of God, and slept more soundly than he had expected to.

The date for Mr. Ulanov's departure on the liner in New York Harbor had come and gone. Nobody had called Reverend Father Dillon and he, in turn, had called no one.

The conversation in the recreation room was so strained that Father Dillon took to leaving early and walking with the seminarians. The *cognoscenti* had grown so nervous over his decision not to obey Cardinal Pacelli—and, most probably, the Holy Father—that some of the elderly ones were dropping cups at the table and visiting the infirmary at odd intervals.

They were all convinced, Dillon knew, that whirlwinds were gathering secretly in all corners of the globe. Roman fury, any moment now, would break suddenly upon Woodstock, and the destruction would scatter its inhabitants to the winds. From time to time one of the consultants, drawn and ailing, would lean over to the rector's table and murmur, "But the Holy Father . . . It is the Pontiff, after all." Father Dillon would pat him on the arm, smile, and manage a show of enthusiasm for his dinner.

His nemesis, Mr. Ulanov, was the only other principal in the drama to give no indication of worry. During the "conversation meals" Ulanov laughed and talked and listened. No one would guess that he lived, as he must, under a terrible strain.

His destiny is waiting in the wings, and he's a lot cooler than I am, thought Dillon. Well, Alex, old boy, you do impress me but, as usual, the wrong way. Now if *you* just looked a little sick, I'd be a lot happier with you.

The rector hoped his thoughts might find their telepathic way to Ulanov. The scholastic, however, never so much as glanced at his superior's table.

Father Dillon knew that the silence which now enveloped him was a bad omen. Ordinarily, assuming a disagreement in which a decision could reasonably go either way, he would have been approached within a day of the telegram's delivery. The problem surely could have been hammered out pro and con before the ship sailed.

No, he thought, they expected my complete obedience, and they were caught by surprise. So now they're circling, checking everything out completely.

At nine thirty the next morning, Father Dillon was astonished to see his door opened without a knock to admit a figure wearing the deep red cassock of an archbishop, a scarlet zapata on his skull, and a black cloak draped over his shoulders. The man moved toward Dillon with intimidation in every step.

"Do you know who I am?"

An Italian accent, quite pronounced.

"I'm afraid not, your Grace."

The rector made no move to kiss the gleaming plain gold ring. "Usually," he said softly, "visitors are announced before arrival in my house."

The prelate took no notice of this rebuke. "I am the Apostolic

Delegate to the United States of America," he said. "I am Archbishop Francisi."

"Ah! And I am pleased at your visit."

"I doubt that."

The rector let his hands part agreeably.

"I have already sent for Mr. Ulanov," said the archbishop.

The rector's expression showed more surprise than he actually felt at this usurpation of his authority.

"By the rights vested in me," continued the archbishop, "and acting as representative of the Pope, I have come for Mr. Ulanov. He will leave with me this morning."

"You did not send for my objections?" The rector handed him a piece of paper from his desk; a single typewritten page on which he had formulated as best he could the reasons for his veto.

Archbishop Francisi glanced at the sheet, holding it at a distance as though it were contaminating. In a few seconds he looked up. "I have already spoken to your consultants. They told me all. They disagree with you almost to a man."

The rector shook his head, rueful acknowledgment of the fact.

"You forgot your place, Father," said the archbishop.

"I remembered my duty."

The archbishop looked at Dillon with the pity of one whose worldly dealings were clearly beyond explaining to this simple person. "It was such a small thing for you to be excited about," he said.

"Since when," said the rector, "do you consider papal orders small things and your presence here so unimportant?"

The archbishop stiffened. Before he could reply, a knock sounded at the door and he threw it open. Alexander Ulanov stood outside in his habit, accompanied by the young priest who had delivered the message from Rome some six days earlier.

"You will come with me as you are, Mr. Ulanov," said the archbishop. "Immediately! But first . . ." Leaving Ulanov just outside the door, he walked back into the room and addressed himself to the rector. "We have all his reports, and they are remarkable. Yes! You have called him brilliant and generous. So be it! You have said nothing concrete to justify your disobedi-

[32]

ence." He removed from his cloak pocket a small sheaf of letters. "You may deposit these documents from his Holiness and his Eminence, Cardinal Pacelli, in your files. They are the final dispositions from the Vatican on Mr. Ulanov. And these"—he handed over two more letters—"are also for you. You are hereby deposed as rector of this house. To preserve the equanimity of the community, your removal will not take place for two months, but your replacement is mentioned, and your new assignment will be . . . I forget . . . as curate in some parish in southern Maryland." He bowed to the rector and turned to go. "Send his clothes, books, anything else, to the address on that paper," he added over his shoulder. "We have no time to lose, he will go as he is. He will not be returning."

As the archbishop reached the door, the rector saw Ulanov, waiting. He had heard everything!

Father Dillon searched his victorious adversary's face. Incredibly enough, he thought he found there a genuine concern for his superior, possibly even admiration.

The door was closed, rather forcefully, and Alexander Ulanov, S.J., was on his way.

2

The Apostolic Delegate and his charge sailed out of New York Harbor on a French liner that same day. Both of them lingered at the railing long after the other passengers had gone below. Ulanov, though tired, wished to watch to the last the skyline of his native land.

Archbishop Francisi was sympathetic. "It may be some years before you see this sight again," he said.

Years later, the archbishop could still recall Ulanov's rejoinder: "It may be never."

After Woodstock, the day had turned out to be quite ordinary. The scholastic had pleased Francisi by not once inquiring during their trip to New York what might be the reason for his extraordinary summons. He did not refer to the Pope, to Cardinal Pacelli. The archbishop sensed, however, that this commendable restraint did not signify a pious naïveté, as he had at first suspected. Ulanov's acceptance of the morning's drama seemed purposeful, as if it were the scholastic who was guided by some inner gyroscope, not by the Vatican.

When Francisi made a remark about the "mad" rector of Woodstock, he was instantly corrected. "It is my opinion," said Ulanov, "that the Vatican did great wrong in removing Father Dillon, your Grace. He was a good man, and very shrewd. I only hope I may be able someday to make him understand."

Ulanov's tone preempted dispute. The archbishop was unaccustomed to being addressed in this way—and by an inferior whom he had saved from that very rector whom the young man now praised. Francisi could not exploit this ridiculous reversal because he felt compelled to keep the seminarian happy for some reason which no one in Rome had made clear to him. In fact, being commanded by Eugenio Cardinal Pacelli to chaperon a young Jesuit across the Atlantic was hardly Francisi's idea of how the rank of *episcopus extraordinarius* should be employed.

As they left the first-class deck, Francisi's mind drifted back to the rector of Woodstock. Was not Father Dillon's fate in fact a warning to the archbishop himself? The cardinal's message to Francisi had read in part, "Your prime function on this journey shall be the protection of this valuable young man. You shall be as a hen to a chick . . ." If it came to a showdown, Francisi had the feeling that the Cardinal Secretary of State would sacrifice his prelate.

"I will not argue with this young religious," he told himself. "I will breathe no word of discontent, I will not involve myself unless he compromises me in some way." If, indeed, Francisi's diplomatic career—which was otherwise faring quite well and had occupied these fifty years of his life—would be finished were this mission to miscarry, he had no intention of jeopardizing himself.

When Francisi returned to his cabin, he found a note posted on his door. That was quick work, he thought, expecting an apology.

> Your Grace,
>   I am embarrassed by the luxury of our compartments. Is it possible that we—or at least I—might change them for third-class accommodations tomorrow?
>   In Christ,
>   Alexander Ulanov, S.J.

The nuncio, tempted to tear the sheet into unrecognizable pieces, was prevented by a reflex of restraint; the fruit, he told himself, of long diplomatic training. He whispered a sign to heaven, then cursed the door of the adjoining stateroom. His distress, as he had suspected on the bridge, was just beginning.

As he undressed, he begged intercession of the Virgin and the saints that he would be faithful in prudence.

[36]

At breakfast the next morning he saw his ward decked out in pressed white linen trousers and a blue blazer, a dashing scarf carefully folded around the neck inside the coat.

"A gift from the captain—for the duration," Ulanov explained jauntily.

"What about the clothes I left for you in your cabin?"

"Two sizes too small."

"But this pious note you left me last night—you aren't consistent!"

"To be honestly poor," said Ulanov, "is one thing. To dress like a clown, quite another. Those clothes are out of the question here." His wave took in the mirrors reflecting lighted tapers and enameled ceiling cherubim, interspersed with fake Renaissance murals. "We poor can't afford to look foolish."

Francisi sighed and blessed himself, than gave his attention to a cup of tea and a hard-boiled egg.

"I am moving this morning," his ward announced.

The archbishop closed his eyes. "We are all servants," he said wearily, "and the Holy Father expects us all to do as we are told. I am an ambassador from one sovereign state to another. It is required that I travel in such a manner as does honor to both of these states, the Vatican and the United States of America. It has nothing to do with my personal preferences. It is for the glory of God, as we say. And, as you just reminded me, the humble are not to look ridiculous or call undue attention to themselves by outlandish acts. Amen!"

The Jesuit smiled. "I am no novice, trying to be fervent, your Grace. And I have no desire to cause you distress. Your own position is understandable, but I am a different sort of ambassador. I must therefore insist that I exchange my room with one or two poor families in third class. Some of them, I saw this morning, are very cramped for space. They need it, I do not."

"You really are in disobedience, young man."

"How so, your Grace? This is no spiritual matter, you know that. You would be commanding me to sin, to go against my conscience. Christ would not live as I do. You may report me when we arrive, if you wish."

A shudder ran through Francisi. He was certain his reaction showed on his face. He comforted himself by considering the

[37]

incongruity of the Jesuit's spiritual ideals with his smart secular outfit. But then the radiant face made the clothes out to be what they really were, a disguise.

Ulanov bowed to the Apostolic Delegate, apparently wishing to convey that Francisi's decision to remain in luxury had cost him no diminution of respect in the eyes of his inferior.

As good as his word, Ulanov transferred within an hour one family of Russians and another of Italians into his first-class suite.

The archbishop emerged briefly from his stateroom to confirm the source of the babble that had disturbed his reading. Both he and the Jesuit had been allotted a master bedroom and a large sitting room each. It was possible, Francisi calculated, to squeeze a family into each room. "But they shall be crowded all over again," he concluded, and smiled for the first time since breakfast.

Worse than the next-door noise was the fact that Francisi could not now adequately chaperon his charge. His watchful eye could hardly penetrate two decks. If something untoward happened, the archbishop might find himself ending his days as a chaplain to cloistered nuns. But if he interfered too much with the young Jesuit, the latter might report *him*.

"Absurd as it may sound," Francisi told himself, "it is a possibility. There are more than a hundred archbishops, and perhaps only one Ulanov."

As Francisi turned to go back to his cabin—a prospect he now contemplated with an unaccustomed sense of guilt—he heard the deep voice of his scholastic rising amid the mixture of Slavic and Mediterranean sounds. If his ears attested rightly, Ulanov was speaking both languages fluently. The nuncio glanced through the door—there was the Jesuit, immensely happy, directing the moving operations of the families, both of which were ignoring him.

He means well, but he's doing a bad job, Francisi thought. They must be allowed to settle it themselves. Damned idealist, that's what he is. If he could, he would rearrange the world according to Assisi and Loyola, get crucified in the bargain, and still manage to leave the world even worse off than it is!

[38]

Francisi called out in Italian: *"Signor Ulanov, per favore... per favore..."*

The Jesuit came quite readily. "Your Grace?" He gave Francisi his customary curtsey of the head.

"Lei parle italiano?"

Ulanov smiled and answered in English, "Yes, I do."

"Why did you not say so? That is my native language, we could have conversed much easier."

"You speak English so perfectly, your Grace. There is no need. I use these tools of language only when I must."

"Really? And how many languages do you speak?"

"Six or seven, your Grace."

"How remarkable for an American! How—where, that is—did you learn them?"

Ulanov smiled again. "A private hobby. Over the years in the seminary, I spent most of my afternoon recreation with those who spoke foreign languages."

"But why?"

"To be prepared!"

"But for what?"

The Jesuit shrugged. "For anything."

"Diplomacy, perhaps?" The episcopal features, so visibly stamped with the character of administrative intrigue, were suffused with a glow. "So, against all the rules of your order, you have planned a career after all. So, you have plotted your own biography. What has become of the great command to be 'as a corpse,' as an 'old man's staff' for your superiors?"

"You misunderstand totally! To be prepared for all eventualities, yet accept unquestioningly what is given—*that* is the obedience you refer to."

"Ah, but such studied brilliance must force superiors to its utilization. His Eminence will be glad to know that you have, let us say, 'prepared' your career."

Francisi turned away. Perhaps something could be done with his discovery inside the closed circles of the Secretariat of State in Vatican City. It was not that he disliked the young man, but he certainly did not want to see him go very far. A word in the right ear about a certain ambitious youth intent upon an international career might serve nicely to jostle this Mr. Ulanov off the track.

As the archbishop put his hand on the knob of the cabin door, a finger touched his shoulder. "You forgot one thing, your Grace."

"Yes?"

"The whole world doesn't share *your* ambitions. I learned these languages to better serve the poor immigrants in my country who do not speak English."

The archbishop squinted at him.

"I must tell his Eminence in Rome," said Ulanov, "how his servants are maligned by innuendo! Thank you, your Grace."

Francisi spent the early part of the afternoon working. There were confidential reports to be completed—by hand, since no secretary could be trusted with their dictation. These files Francisi would hand personally to Cardinal Pacelli. Many of the reports were delicate assessments of the American hierarchy, bishops and well-known cardinals. A number of negative judgments on outstanding church figures had to be not only kept absolutely secret, but also phrased with fine distinctions as to what was faulty and what was good so that the Secretariat would not waste time and prestige in vague condemnations.

Francisi, having completed two of these reports shortly before dinnertime, could not help contrasting his adroitness in this area with his handling of the Jesuit scholastic. The position Pacelli had placed him in with respect to Ulanov was too poorly defined for him to act with his customary expertise. *"Per favore Christo!"* he exclaimed to the absent Pacelli, his superior and friend. "I can't do justice to you if you insist on treating me as an inferior to this fellow—he isn't even ordained, and I am your archbishop to America! *Buono Dio,* it makes no sense. He will tell you that I have insulted him. I dare not report to you my feelings about this man. Your plan might be ruined, and I might find myself . . . well, never mind, but I remind you, you must not trust young saints. They look beautiful, the beautiful thoughts are in their heads, a very private vision, no? And then they think they can—*con miracolo,* by wishing it—change the world to fit a

[40]

dream. It isn't so, Eugenio. We are, all of us, cursed with the world."

Whereupon Pacelli's archbishop executed that cleansing motion of the hands made so famous by Pontius Pilate—though, in his case, it had a Mediterranean origin. *"Finito,"* the gesture proclaimed, *"finito."*

Yet the nuncio still could not rid himself of the visage of the cardinal. And so, as an exercise, he focused intently on Pacelli's face. The ascetic lines he took for granted, but the eyes seemed to see further than ever. "Oh, he is careful for the organization," Francisi announced, "but he isn't like me, a true administrator. He is a mystic at heart. I should have remembered."

Francisi thought about it all the way down the corridor, not liking at all the conclusions he was coming to. Was his Eminence off again on some half-brilliant plan so outrageous in its scope that it could not be breathed to his trusted advisers? It was Francisi's experience that when Pacelli had visions, he was likely to go off on his own—as if the Secretariat that he himself headed might contaminate his ideas with its routine ways.

Confronted with the dinner menu, the archbishop felt only distaste for the meal ahead of him. He told himself to cheer up. Nothing terrible had yet befallen the church at the cardinal's hands. "God will look after us. *In manu Dei sumus,"* he murmured in what the other occupants of the captain's table took to be a devout offering addressed to the divine by a professional.

As it turned out, that first night at the high table and the next few evenings proved relaxing for the archbishop. Mr. Ulanov, S.J., made every effort to be pleasant to each of the archbishop's hosts and guests. The panoply of rich and famous figures from both sides of the Atlantic invited to join the clerical couple at dinner seemed to thoroughly enjoy their company. Francisi was surprised to note that both sexes seemed equally mesmerized by the Jesuit. The men thought of him as a man's man, while the women, married or not, delighted in his athletic good looks, his air of authority, even his distance from them.

The archbishop had to admit that he was impressed by the way Ulanov handled all this attention. He accepted none of the invitations offered him; his unvarying reply was that he had work to do and that he was subject to headaches at parties. The letters of refusal were written with a certain graciousness. The archbishop, midway into their voyage, finally complimented Ulanov on a tact so nicely combined with integrity.

"Those people are no temptation to me," said Ulanov. "In my heart I despise everything they stand for."

"Surely that's too strong a word."

"I said everything they *stand for*. There is nothing personal about it."

"I must remind you, young man," said the nuncio, "that many, many of these people are exemplary contributors to the church, to its schools, orphanages, its seminaries."

"To save their souls, I should think."

"So much the better for them!"

"Why should you defend them so?" Ulanov's gentle, perhaps Christlike tones contrasted with the archbishop's shrill assertions.

"Do you not think," Francisi went on, "that in a world so materialistic, their choice to devote a good part of their riches to noble purposes suggests that they have surmounted some of the temptations of greed?"

"Ill-gotten riches," Ulanov said, and then stopped. "I don't think we should pursue this topic any further, your Grace. From my point of view, I think it unchristian that the working people of the world support luxury with their sweat." He held up his hand to stay his superior's rejoinder. "I'm sorry if that offends you. You have your work, you pick up the crumbs—for a good cause. It's just that I find the principle of, well, trafficking with such wealth difficult to square with the Cross of Christ."

"The real world is not your forte," Francisi said softly. "We did not make the world, nor did they. We salvage what we can in the redemption of it."

"It's too bad we can't change the world," said Ulanov.

"If we could, we should not be the church."

Mr. Ulanov, S.J., unmoved by the older man's wisdom and experience, had obviously decided not to reply.

"Well, I hope you do a better job in your life with the poor than you did next door," the archbishop said with an air of fatigue over *that* particular situation. "Instead of one family you brought in two. And now they quarrel all the time—very angry, very loud. They do not speak the same language. I'm sure they are more unhappy now than when they were below."

"That," said Ulanov, "is because they are still too crowded."

"Well, *I* shan't move out," the archbishop said, and closed the door to his first-class suite.

After this conversation, Ulanov absented himself from the episcopal table. Since he was under no order from Francisi or anyone else to join the nuncio at meals, his departure could not be viewed as disobedient. And yet, the archbishop knew, no other cleric in the whole of America would do such a thing. As far as Francisi was concerned, his young Jesuit was independent, impertinent, dangerous.

He hesitated on the last count. That might be exaggerating the case—to state such a thing upon his arrival in Rome. *Qui nimis probat, nihil probat,* he repeated to himself. He knew, however, that he would inform Pacelli of the Jesuit's bizarre behavior. Moving people into cabins, insulting donors, sleeping in third class—he continued the list of Ulanov's activities—imprudent idealism, denying the archbishop company without apology or excuse. In the inner sanctum of the Curia, any two of these accusations in a cleric's dossier might place the culprit forever in a rural limbo.

Unfortunately, the archbishop was not sure but that the very actions he would enumerate might not turn out to suggest just the virtues Pacelli was looking for.

On that despairing note, the nuncio abandoned his dress rehearsal with Pacelli. When the time came he would behave in the diplomatic fashion, simply noting that Ulanov was "unusual," letting drop some of the more disturbing peccadilloes, and for those who had ears, let them hear. He personally would not commit himself.

Having arrived at this decision, he felt that he was within a whisper of grasping precisely what and who Mr. Ulanov was— that, in fact, it had been handed to him on a plate; that he had but to turn the card over, or simply translate it. That the information was all in and it was he, Francisi, who had a blind spot. Behind Ulanov's random acts ran a logic. And the oddest thing about it, whatever it was—it never intimated a black mark against Ulanov himself.

The insight never came. In his failure to find it, the archbishop, for the first time in his life, found himself fleeing the consequences of a train of thought.

3

The afternoon before the ship was due to dock in Marseilles, a large number of party invitations arrived at Francisi's suite. He was well aware what his presence meant to a hostess. There would be the posed shots with Mr. and Mrs. somebody or other, he would autograph a picture of the Pope or the flyleaf of a book, "To my dear friends on the Crossing, 1931," or he must write out a card recommending the petitioners "to all concerned in Rome" for a *bacciamano* audience with his Holiness. His name, Francisi realized, would be dropped in the most inappropriate places, and the character of his relationship with these nameless couples exaggerated a hundred times over.

There were other reasons why his presence might be solicited, but he fervently hoped that one or two of them would not come up tonight. He became short-tempered when asked to interfere in annulment proceedings in Rome on behalf of some relative or other. The hint of a heavy contribution to the church if he succeeded was enough at times to trigger a barrage of subtle Neapolitan insults.

Out of the trayful of cards he selected three or four for serious attention. Two were ranking diplomats of major nations. He would listen attentively for news that might be of importance to his Eminence. Four more he set aside in the category of a quick polite appearance.

When he had so arranged his affairs for the evening, he gave a few moments' thought to Mr. Ulanov, whom he had not seen for several days. "Will he be at these parties?" Francisi wondered. "I suppose not. He must be up to something. He probably won't come out of hiding until we land in Naples." With this thought the archbishop departed on his evening rounds.

He had not gone far along the deck when he stopped short. There, less than thirty yards ahead in a semicircle of chaises longues, were three women and the Jesuit, all talking animatedly. The archbishop paused only a moment before moving toward them.

As he approached the small circle, every head turned to study Francisi's scarlet-and-black-robed figure. He quickly felt the burden of being a most unwelcome intruder.

"Good evening, ladies," he said.

The Jesuit proceeded to introduce his companions; a contessa now living in France, a titled English lady, and the very rich wife of a well-known Spanish banker—none of them under fifty, and all arrayed in shining extravagances: pearls, diamonds, and rubies that reminded the forgetful of their station.

Francisi raised an eyebrow and smiled at Ulanov. "It is a beautiful night. So soon to end, how unfortunate!"

There was no response from the quartet.

The archbishop bowed to the inevitable. "Well, I do not wish to interrupt this spiritual cabal."

"It's not that Roman, your Excellency," said the English lady. "It is a spiritual dis-cus-sion."

"The Lord will be displeased if I interfere with such a noble pursuit. I beg your leave, ladies. Perhaps I shall see you at one of the parties."

"Hardly," said the bejeweled señora.

The archbishop, after a small flourish to the group, had not gone fifteen or twenty yards before he heard again the resurrection of those subdued voices. Why should his presence be so distasteful to the gathering? Ordinarily, people of this class greeted him as a fellow member of their elite ranks; standing, as he did, for the legitimation of privilege before the Most High. Could Mr. Ulanov have so breached the code of religious ethics as to denigrate him behind his back? If not, then whatever could have caused their reaction? Of course, these women had no intention of showing up at receptions where their own husbands would be in attendance. "At least I am not the only target of resentment," the nuncio concluded with a sigh.

His relief was short-lived. Within the space of an hour and a half he had fled from the third party in perfect haste, and now stood grasping the ship's railing and gazing into the dark swells of the sea. Despite the acceptances he had already sent, Francisi had neither the courage nor the patience to attend one more of these farewell-and-happiness gatherings. At each of the three parties, he had been forced into a corner by the husband of one woman or another demanding from the archbishop an explanation as to the "causes" his protégé Mr. Ulanov, S.J., represented. The archbishop had been forced to proclaim total ignorance of any of Mr. Ulanov's doings.

The facts, as they emerged from this series of confrontations, seemed to be that the Jesuit had received from a number of their wives—six or seven—amounts of money totaling perhaps thirty thousand dollars! The checks were made out to the League of Christian Working Class Unity in Rome. What, the enraged gentlemen wanted to know of the archbishop, was this organization they had never heard of?

The archbishop confessed he didn't know. Did they not believe him? And why did they not have their wives recall these checks, which undoubtedly were still on board?

The husbands could not understand how Mr. Ulanov could solicit for projects without the permission of his superior. If this Jesuit was not yet ordained, then how came he to dispense priestly advice with such authority to their women? And without supervision? Was there someone in Rome they could settle this matter with? Couldn't the archbishop command the young man to let the ladies be, or, at least, return their money? On and on . . .

Turning away from the ship's railing, the archbishop was startled to see the captain.

"I did not want to interrupt your thoughts," he said.

"You have a problem, Captain?"

"Yes, Excellency."

"A complaint?"

"I do not wish to embarrass you, Excellency, but—"

"Ulanov?"

The captain stared at him, astonished at the prelate's uncharacteristic directness.

"Well, Captain? What has Ulanov done now?"

"Very Christian, your Excellency. You understand."

"Yes, yes, I'm sure."

"But difficult for the discipline of the ship." The captain took a deep breath as though imploring heaven to guide him on a stranger voyage than he had ever known. Then he said, "Your Excellency, please come with me. You will see for yourself."

The archbishop followed the captain through a number of labyrinthine corridors and then down into levels of the ship Francisi had never seen. They made their way through steel-plated passageways, until, at the end of the last tunnel, the captain twisted open a heavy sealed door and pointed.

Below them, shoveling coal alongside two sweating laborers, was the Jesuit.

The archbishop stood at the top of the iron ladder and stared in disbelief at the sweltering men twenty yards below him. The three bodies were streaked with rivulets of sweat and black coal dust. The pit itself seemed to Francisi the incarnation of a nineteenth-century engraving of the mills of Manchester.

The captain touched his arm. "You will be all right, Excellency?"

Francisi was unable to mask his distress for the sake of an impression. Such manual labor was so absolutely forbidden to clerics that he found it hard to believe even such an odd one as Ulanov could so blatantly violate it. For Francisi it was as though the Jesuit had slapped the whole hierarchy of the church.

"Of course," said the captain, "you understand, I did not want to bring you here."

"Yes, yes, you were quite right to do so. How long has this been going on?"

"A week, or close to it. The night shift, I believe."

"Why was I not told before?"

"Because I was not told before."

"You do not have very good control of your ship, Captain, if strange people can take over jobs for a week without your knowledge."

"That makes two of us, Excellency, who did not know. Still, he must be quite a fellow to get those men to cover up for him. Ordinarily they would throw someone into the furnace who tried to give them a sermon—"

"A *sermon?*"

"Why yes, that's why he's going through all this. I have been given to understand that your man is instructing them on the teachings of the church. Frankly, I am touched."

"It's disobedience, pure and simple. Why else did you call me here?"

Before the captain could answer, Ulanov suddenly appeared at the bottom of the stairs. The archbishop had lost sight of him for a few minutes while he talked with the captain; assuming, all along, that the darkness of the shadows above the grim pit protected him from observation. Yet Ulanov it was, hardly recognizable in his stoker's pants and boots, the muscles of his shoulders and arms half black and gleaming beneath a ragged undershirt—standing with one foot on the rung of the ladder, laughing up at his superior, sending positive waves of joy through the semidarkness.

"Must you follow me around, your Grace? I'm all right, really! I enjoy this!" He laughed uproariously, apparently having just realized himself how incongruous the situation must seem to an observer. From his comrades back at the furnace Ulanov's laughter found an answering echo, resounding off bars and pipes and metal plates into corners from which a variety of human shapes began to emerge like a mob moving into a square on the eve of a revolution.

The archbishop stood paralyzed by this display of collective madness: the backdrop of tongue-red flames and smoke, the distorted noises from this patchwork horde, the eerie squinting of the faces in this below-sea-level boiler room.

Francisi made an involuntary motion of retreat.

From below, the Jesuit's commanding voice called to him: "Don't be alarmed, your Grace. It's good work, and I'm not a boy. You don't have to check up on me. No sin involved at all!

See?" He waved at the scattered group behind him. "My brothers in Christ, your Grace!"

Ulanov's use of the phrase reserved for priests and other religious appalled the archbishop as much as anything he had done. He backed away from the top of the ladder and into the passageway.

"Get him out of there!" he instructed the captain. "And confine him to his cabin. Immediately! Well, isn't that what you wanted? Isn't it?"

As the nuncio turned to flee the tiny corridor, he mumbled, "I have him now, this is it! *Finito!*"

The captain delayed. He gazed down on the mysterious employee on which he had informed. "He's a damned fine stoker, and they say Jesus was a good carpenter. Isn't that something? Probably as close as I'll ever get to meeting a saint."

For the remainder of the voyage, Francisi neither saw nor spoke to Ulanov. Indeed, the turn of events had caused the Apostolic Delegate to confine himself as well as the Jesuit.

After the stop at Marseilles, the ship lost no time in picking up speed. As they cruised on through the Mediterranean the archbishop began to feel more comfortable. His confidence further increased as they crossed the Tyrrhenian Sea, between Cagliari and Palermo. He was coming home.

If his feelings and his position had been hurt—well, no matter. There had been profit in the encounter. Mr. Ulanov had been revealed to be a madman.

From time to time, Francisi felt a twinge of shame at his reactions on that infamous night. The frightening scene, he believed, surely excused him. He hardly gave a thought to his presentation of the Ulanov problem to Pacelli. There would be no difficulty now. He would simply have to take steps to ensure that he spoke with the cardinal before Ulanov did.

Archbishop Francisi suffered so little internal argument on that score that his customary equanimity was all but fully restored by the time the ship eased into its berth in his native and beloved Naples.

For Francisi to land in Naples after such an absence and leave without so much as a word to his family was unheard of. Yet when he and the Jesuit disembarked, that is precisely what happened. The archbishop and his charge proceeded immediately to the railroad station for the trip north to Rome. Neither spoke to the other except in extremity.

The traditional black limousine, chauffeured by a lay brother, met Francisi and his ward when they arrived in Rome. It sped quickly to its first stop, the old Collegio di San Roberto Bellarmino on the Via del Seminario. This ancient building housed most of the Jesuits in the Italian capital. In answer to a quizzical look from Ulanov, who was wondering why the driver was holding the door open at this particular juncture, Francisi said, "This is your order's residence here. Further directions await you inside." He then dismissed the scholastic with a curt gesture and signaled to the brother; they were gone before Ulanov had begun to approach the large doors.

Following a swift passage through the hectic Roman streets, the car slowed down to enter Vatican City. Through the Borgo Pío and down the Via di Porta Angelica, and the archbishop was delivered to the Vatican palace.

The nuncio felt little trepidation as he walked through the bronze door of the Secretariat. Before his appointment to America, he had spent a great deal of his working life in this great gray building, and he was very well known inside.

He had no sooner gained the ground floor than he encountered two monsignori from his own class at the Gregorian University. The *ciao*s and the embraces were effusive. The archbishop managed, however, to cut off any further conversation within a couple of minutes. In a world where indirection had been developed to so high an art, it took very few signals from the nuncio to convey that he was on delicate business requiring immediate attention.

Having climbed 294 steps without stopping, Francisi immediately entered his superior's offices. A young monsignor sat behind the main desk in the cardinal's antechamber, acting manifestly as both secretary and protector. He rose and bowed with the minimum of deference. He was, no doubt, used to the comings and goings of archbishops, and, as an assistant to *the* cardinal, he

[51]

could hardly be intimidated by the presence of any member of the hierarchy less than the Pope.

"You are?"

"Archbishop Francisi."

"Ah, yes. But"—and the monsignor began to thumb through a number of pages in a large ledger—"you are early. I believe—yes, here it is! Four days to go. Why have you not waited for your conference date, Archbishop?"

"Certain developments, of great importance to his Eminence . . ."

The monsignor lifted out a blank white sheet of paper from a side cupboard and dipped the end of an ancient quill into the ink. "Yes? What is it in reference to?"

"I'd rather tell his Eminence personally."

The monsignor shook his head. "You must tell me, and I will tell the cardinal. Then, if he consents, very well."

Francisi looked at the young man in astonishment. "There are so many details, I—" The environment of the room mitigated against a long explanation of his troubles. Such a humiliating scene would never have occurred with Pacelli's predecessor, Gaspari, but . . . "Well, write this, Monsignor, that it is regarding a Mr. Ulanov and that the problem is disobedience."

Only two words had been scratched down by the secretary, who obviously was waiting for more. "That is all?" he asked finally.

"That is all."

It was now the monsignor's turn to be perplexed. He considered first his meager information and then this eccentric prelate.

"Yes. Well, I shall inform his Eminence of your request."

"Now, if you please."

The monsignor shrugged and shook his head. "The cardinal sees no one—no one—*súbito.* If he decides it is important, he will summon you outside the hour of your appointment. Otherwise, it shall be as it was."

Francisi contained with difficulty the surge of emotion that threatened public revolt against this treatment. This young monsignor was unimportant in himself; he merely reflected the wishes of the cardinal. Any umbrage over his conduct would be taken by Pacelli as a personal affront. Francisi therefore made a great show of obedience as he said, "Of course, I understand. Very good!"

Francisi spent that hot June afternoon and evening in full expectation of a summons from the Secretary of State. He waited the next day and the day after that. No message, one way or another.

Not until the fourth day of his stay in Rome did the Apostolic Delegate appear again at the Secretary of State's office. As he waited again in the antechamber, it seemed as though his previous intrusion had been bracketed in some limbo of nonexistence. The monsignor-receptionist made no reference to it, and this time welcomed him effusively as if he had never before set eyes on him. He even remarked on how privileged he felt to receive such an outstanding personage as the Vatican representative to the United States. In those fifteen minutes or so of waiting, Francisi was accorded every possible courtesy while his judgment was solicited on all sorts of international questions.

As the inner door opened at precisely ten thirty, that perfectly still and gaunt figure appeared in the starkest of black habits relieved by a single ribbon of blood-red color about his waist and a tiny scarlet skullcap. The dead-white skin struck an enormous contrast with the brightness of the eyes, so much so that even Francisi was unnerved for a moment. The visage left no doubt of sanctity, but—and this was rarer in their world of administration and government—the holy man was also the diplomat *par excellence*. Power had been wedded to holy duty in the incarnate wraith of Eugenio Cardinal Pacelli, who in that instant seemed to be touching in one drawn-out stare the very soul of his visitor. Francisi stared back.

Finally Pacelli stirred. A gentle motion of the hands; the familiar Italianate gesture of outstretched palms escalating upward in the sign of welcome and signal of entrance. Francisi walked toward him and kissed his ring as the door closed behind them.

For two long hours and a half the Secretary of State asked pointed questions about the American church and state and

[53]

various personages in both the sacred and profane orders. The archbishop was well prepared, though he was surprised at his interrogator's remarkable perceptivity and store of information. It was as though one expert were asking another. The cardinal wrote constantly during their conversation, and the entire dialogue took place in an aura of formality that was annoying to Francisi, searching for an opening to inform the cardinal about Ulanov.

"Just to be heard, that's all I ask," he told himself, while murmuring a few prayers for supernatural intercession. He could not believe that the cardinal would terminate the interview without a single reference to the young man whom he had ordered Francisi to accompany four thousand miles. The moment never came.

As the clock chimed one o'clock, Pacelli arose and extended his hand. "You are a very capable workman," he said. "If you stay within your assignment, be assured of our pleasure."

Francisi kissed the cardinal's ring, then bowed his head. *"Grazie, eminenza."*

They both moved to the door, and then, as Francisi grasped the knob, he turned very hesitantly toward his superior. By the time his eyes met the other, he had managed a very deliberate tone of voice, befitting in his own mind this act of professional courage. "I am puzzled, *eminenza,* that you did not ask me about the—the protégé, Mr. Ulanov. I have something to say."

The lines around the cardinal's thin face tightened noticeably. "I already know what you have to say, Nuncio."

"I am your servant, *eminenza.*"

"Then you should be intelligent enough to know when you are interfering. Without being told."

"I thought my opinion—"

"Not in this matter, Francisi. You simply do not know what you are talking about!"

"As you wish, *eminenza.*"

"So you do not approve?" Pacelli could not restrain himself from pushing the very topic he wished to crush.

"I am sorry, I . . . you must understand that in my conscience . . . No, I do not approve."

[54]

The ordinarily pale countenance of the Secretary of State now seemed pink with fury.

"I apologize for any embarrassment, any hurt I may have caused you—unwittingly, *eminenza*—but we have known each other thirty years."

"Tell me, Francisi. Do you know the first requirement of all who would be statesmen?"

The archbishop shook his head.

"A sense of their own limits."

"*Sì, eminenza.*"

"In this case you must understand what you do not understand, what is beyond your comprehension. Certain personalities frequently appear odd to one whose training belongs to an office in the Curia."

Francisi did not reply. The irony of the situation was too ridiculous to dignify with assent. After all, Pacelli had trained for thirty years, just like himself, in the very bureaucracy he was now patronizing. And then a more incredible irony struck the archbishop: if one were untrustworthy outside his field of training, what did that portend for any plan of Pacelli's that bypassed his own State Department, the cardinal's only domain of expertise? Was Pacelli attempting something that would have dumfounded his former colleagues? If so, then the scheme lay perhaps in an area where Pacelli was not at home.

"Ah, I think you understand," murmured Pacelli. "I do not wish to censure you. *Unless,* of course, you persist in your attitudes or intend to make an accusation in my hearing or submit a report or opinion on the matter. To anyone."

"I accede completely to your Eminence's wishes in this matter. There shall be no word mentioned on the subject to *anyone.*" With this Francisi gave a slight bow of the head.

He realized all too well the importance of that one word. The "anyone" went far beyond the influential professionals of the Curia: the monsignori, bishops, and cardinals, whom, it was true, Francisi could prejudice against the young Ulanov, or else encourage to a powerful curiosity about the grand designs in Pacelli's mind. No, the "anyone" really referred to his Holiness himself, Pope Pius XI. Pacelli knew that Francisi would probably see the Pope at some reception within the next few weeks. His Holiness, who must know that the archbishop had brought this Ulanov to Rome, could be expected to inquire as to what impression the young man had made on the nuncio during the crossing. And though the Pope and his Secretary of State must have planned this Ulanov affair together, Pacelli clearly felt the most urgent responsibility for shielding the Pope from any flaws in the scheme.

The diplomatic intelligence of Francisi formulated these considerations during the few seconds in which the cardinal left him in order to return to his desk. He fumbled quickly through a couple of drawers until he found a small wooden box. Picking it up, he carried it to his visitor, beaming like an uncle with a surprise treat for a child. When he reached the nuncio, he opened the box very carefully, as though to keep the anticipation alive for a few more seconds. First, he pulled out a medal of Pope Pius XI. "This piece has been most carefully struck for our Holy Father—a most magnificent specimen of the art of bronzemaking in medallions. There are but a hundred of them in the world. It is my gift to you, dear Francisi, a symbol of my great confidence in you, and of our friendship."

The archbishop took pains to simulate the enormous gratitude for this present he would, under ordinary circumstances, have genuinely felt.

The second item in the little box was a scroll. On being handed the parchment, Francisi dutifully untied the ribbon and quickly unrolled the scroll to its full length. Rapidly glancing down the page, he gathered in short order that he had been appointed to one of the major commissions in the Vatican, the Congregation for Religious.

"No words of mine can express to you the sentiments of gratitude I feel in my heart, *eminenza.*"

The cardinal gave him a pat on the wrist which translated, "I understand. You're quite right. Say no more, it is only your due." The gesture also signaled the immediate end of the conference, as if to say, "We have reached a high point. Let it end now, and let us remember this peak of leavetaking."

The archbishop feigned obtuseness to the urgency of this

unspoken message, projecting a gratitude that could not be satisfied with brevity. "Be assured, *eminenza*, of my everlasting debt to you for such marks of favor, and of friendship . . . No, I must say more, I must assure you that I will remain utterly faithful to my promise, will not mention to a living soul these misgivings of mine over the young Jesuit's presence in this city, nor that I have ever warned you of placing any trust in him."

The cardinal, who had himself moved to open the door as the quickest way to dispatch his troublesome visitor, stopped short. His eyes searched Francisi's features for some clue as to whether the other really understood what he was saying. Had he planned or blundered his way into this move? Francisi, who could read these confusions in his superior's face, hoped that his own would remain safely beyond Pacelli's comprehension.

"Yes, yes," said Pacelli, "he is quite young. There are some faults, but he errs in the right direction. And it is good, *dignum et justum*, for youth to be so wholeheartedly committed to Christ, before too much responsibility stains the soul, robs it of spontaneity."

"There was an incident," Francisi said, "with some women, with the workers on the ship, the captain . . . the husbands, they . . ." Francisi spoke in a soft halting cadence, hoping by its gentleness to establish himself not as an antagonist, but as a simple flowing feature of Pacelli's own internal dialogue.

Pacelli waved his hand.

"Yes, yes, those women. They came here for an audience with the Holy Father and myself. Mr. Ulanov has strengthened them in their faith. They have contributed so heavily to our charities . . ." The Secretary of State's eyes moved admiringly upward.

"And the League of Christian Working Men?" injected Francisi in a most soothing uncontroversial manner. "I have heard they are socialist. And Ulanov had these women write their checks to—"

"Oh, yes, he did not know about our Italian politics." The cardinal laughed. "Can you imagine? The name of the group sounded quite wonderful to him! Apparently in America they are truthful when they christen their organizations. He is young, and—"

[57]

"He is thirty-five, *eminenza.*"

"We have time to watch him mature . . ."

"And if not?"

"There are others, we have brought others here. We shall select which one we wish. And"—the cardinal held his hands up in a calming gesture—"in due time, in a few years, perhaps, I will apprise you of our reasons for this secrecy and the kind of person we were looking for."

Francisi felt at once close to an opening and at the same time unable to find that one sentence, that perfectly phrased sentiment that would strike just the right chord of conspiratorial resonance in Pacelli's soul. "You do not think my advice could help?"

"You must not think ill of yourself or me," commiserated the cardinal. "Very few know, but that is the way it must be. It is no fault of yours that you are not a party to these conferences. I delegated to you the very important assignment of bringing this man here. You may take that delegation as a sign of my continued esteem for your competence, which this morning's transactions have only augmented."

"I had thought, *eminenza,*" replied Francisi, "that the exercising of such a responsibility would be concluded by a report on all aspects of the assignment. I misunderstood, apparently, your design in this affair and I must apologize. Simply intending to follow the normal procedure in such a case, I have in my seriousness studied the various facets of our subject Ulanov with earnest care—perhaps overearnest—in the expectation that you would wish as complete a résumé as possible of his behavior from one who has been trained to mature judgments in these kinds of matters by the Vatican and yourself."

The cardinal stared at him for a long moment, then pulled open the door of his office. "Yes, yes, of course," he said. "You mean well. Of course, you must! Remember now, dear Francisi, how many souls there are in your care, and remember how much we depend on your great powers of discretion, and above all, trust your silence. Now goodbye, goodbye, good Francisi. *Deus benedieat tibi.*" He kept patting the nuncio on the shoulder, ushering him all the while from the office and even the reception room, granting him a final little blessing with a swift motion of the fingers above his forehead.

The archbishop, walking blindly through the corridor and down the hundreds of marble steps, kept his eyes fastened on the stone patterns beneath his feet. His mind and feelings were numbed by the weight of his defeat, intensified greatly by the now certain knowledge that Mr. Ulanov, S.J., was to be a most important figure in the history of the Catholic church.

Later that afternoon, Archbishop Francisi finished typing out a secret report on the Jesuit scholastic. He paid a notary a handsome sum to seal and stamp carefully the date of the packet's closure. Shortly thereafter the document was deposited in a personal box in a very private bank vault in Rome—to be opened, so the label indicated, solely at the discretion of its owner. The future date was unspecified. The Latin words appended could be translated as: Only when the occasion demands.

BOOK

II

The Competition

4

Father Paul Marais, S.J., took advantage of a short spell of solitude to avail himself of the wall-length mirror in the first-floor reception room of the Collegio di San Roberto Bellarmino. His colleagues, Fathers Nimsky and Ulanov, had retired for a few moments to their cubicles upstairs. Marais was aware that this compulsion to Narcissuslike contemplation of his image was a vice. Other members of the Society would certainly condemn him out of hand if they ever caught him walking up and down, beholding himself in front of a mirror.

Marais found himself in this predicament simply because he liked to concentrate while looking at his reflection. It was not that he was that interested at present in his physical appearance. "After all," he thought, "how much can you do with black? Oh, with a black suit perhaps, but this eternal wearing of lumpy black habits has rendered me absolutely insensitive to the nuances of a tailored suit." On that cue his passionate hatred of Roman clerical customs gathered in a cloud of temper, paralyzing momentarily those Gallic mental processes in which he took such pride.

As he paced the length of the tapestried, carpeted room, Marais concluded that many of his mannerisms were bound to alienate Cardinal Pacelli. Even without the slight mustache he'd worn in those "worldly" days in Paris, before he entered "religion," he still resembled a dapper Frenchman. He could swear that there were times in this afternoon's interview when the

[63]

Secretary of State's distaste for him had seemed tangible. Well, for that matter Marais did not particularly care for a number of Pacelli's own mannerisms. "In that sort of thing," he thought, "it's all a matter of nationality."

At noon, the three young Jesuit priests had been informed that the Cardinal Secretary of State expected them for a private audience in his apartment at the palace. The abruptness of the summons was its only surprising feature, for out of all the seminarians and priests studying at the Gregorian University and the Collegium, the cardinal seemed to take a special interest in these three only. He had invited them to various dinners over the past two years. He had himself, in a rarely granted privilege, ordained the trio together in the Sistine Chapel last year.

Now, glancing at his figure from a three-quarters angle, Marais allowed his imagination the stimulation of a possible papal decision involving one of them. There seemed no doubt that the purpose behind this afternoon's meeting had been further scrutiny of the three men. The cardinal had not even tried to hide this design from them. He had let each of them know how pleased he was with their theological and language studies over the past three years. He had even commented on how odd it was that the very three he had selected out of so many students should turn out to be close friends. "I hear that you are inveterate companions," he had said, laughing. "Does the Society permit *amitiés particulières?*"

"Oh, indeed," Marais informed his reflection. "We are friends, closer than your Eminence would ever allow. How bizarre the three of us together must seem to you! Nimsky, the convert Jew born in Russia, myself, the Frenchman with a Russian princess for a mother and an agnostic surgeon father, and Ulanov, the American—worker?" The very correct and pious Secretary would indeed have his problems trying to comprehend such an alliance.

"The whole affair," said Marais, bowing to an imagined reflection of the prelate in the glass, "can be resolved very easily. It's all a matter, your Eminence, of trust and fun. That's it!" He paused. On reflection he added one further item for complete satisfaction. "And intelligence."

As he back-pedaled from the mirror, Marais noted the continental bearing reflected in it. French, liberal, intellectual, all were there for anyone with eyes to see, despite his enclosure in that damned black habit. Slim and impeccable—one day, he vowed, he would grow that mustache again. "Cardinal Marais," he dreamed. A credit to the modern French church. Quickly he dismissed this vulgar temptation and scolded its demonic source.

He could not so easily rid himself, however, of other feelings arising from the tacit competition which Pacelli had set up between Marais and his dear friends. Implicit in some of the Secretary's statements this afternoon was the notion that only one of them would be chosen for the arduous mission, whatever it was. Though this sentiment was just perceptibly implied, degrees of subtlety were unimportant. Very soon the three years of waiting for Marais and his comrades would be over, and one of them—only one, yes, he was sure of that—would embark on this crusade or adventure.

Marais wished with all his heart to be that *one*. He felt in his marrow that what was about to happen would be historic. As a son of Vercingetorix and Joan of Arc, Rimbaud and Malraux, he yearned for that action which would give his intellect its true milieu, and raise his sensibilities to a new plane. Since childhood he had dreamed of his soul placed forever on some fully imaginable horizon of destiny.

"It is a holy ambition, Lord," he said, very close to the mirror now. "But, we have been such friends that this present situation is deplorable!"

He reconstructed the beginning of the friendship; the trio's finding one another amid the clerical hordes sitting in the amphitheater of the Gregorian, listening to the dreary incantation of medieval Latin, or, in the afternoon, embroiled in Slavic tongues at the Russicum. The great quality each possessed for the other was silence—in an atmosphere where so little was secret and so many reported the least infraction or impious sentiment, the three could trust each other completely. Perhaps it was because they were older and more mature, but each of them disdained most of the other seminarians and priests. They regarded the Italians as unstable in serious matters and the Americans as naïve observers of the rule.

And then, of course, the three had enjoyed such good times together. Nimsky was an uproarious fellow, forever laughing at the cruel absurdities of life while nonetheless remaining a mystic of rather profound depth. Ulanov, often silent, could be very funny in a sarcastic way about the Vatican and Mussolini. Indeed, he seemed to loathe the whole established world, whether liberal or Fascist, and was quite ingenious at exploiting any opportunity to have fun at its expense.

Contrasting himself with his friends, Marais felt that he was cleverer, more intellectual, less theologically inclined, than either of his politically simpler colleagues. His command of the necessary language, he knew, was as unaccented and fluent as theirs. Indeed, his knowledge of the literature was ten times vaster. How could Pacelli then turn him down? And yet, he was all but certain that the cardinal would do so.

Nimsky was impractical, an artist and a utopian who romanticized the peasants terribly. He really was the product of the cities, Marais had told him repeatedly. The peasants would not understand him at all, and if they did, they would crucify him.

Ulanov, on the other hand, had the knack of appearing very practical to everyone, superiors and colleagues alike. Somehow that remoteness of his, together with his muscular self-confidence, gave off the air of unity with God. He must be the real competitor, Marais had decided. "Still," he said aloud, "I don't think there is very much in his head except a few ideals, and misplaced ones at that. He is sturdy, very tough. So? He isn't clever, I don't think, maybe not even deep. He resembles an empty sky—no birds in it!"

In the few moments left before his friends returned to claim him for the rare treat of a dinner out, Marais wrestled with the urge to go to Pacelli and unburden his whole mind on the subject. His awareness that such a strategy might actually succeed influenced him more than he wished to admit, but the only motives he would consciously allow were honorable ones.

He turned as the door opened with force to reveal the dwarfish hairy form of Nimsky, grinning delightedly at having caught Marais posed before the mirror. He moved inside around by the wall with a great show of delicacy, parodying the movements of a ballerina. "How beautiful you look, *tovarishch,*" he said in Russian. "And what beautiful clothes. Whom are we addressing, your Highness? I can't see them."

"I'm *thinking,*" said Marais. "It's my way, you know that. It . . . it helps." He gestured toward the glass as though it were a trivial instrument of his spirit.

Nimsky was still laughing when Ulanov appeared at the door and called to them both. "Has either of you thought of a place for tonight's celebration?"

"Any place with a good piece of meat," shouted Nimsky, who had lost thirty pounds on the ascetic diet of the Bellarmino residence.

"A spot with a little elegance, please," said Marais.

Ulanov laughed. "No names? Well, then, there is a workingmen's cellar with good food about half a mile from here."

Marais groaned. "What kind of a change is that?"

"It will do you good, you old exploiter," said Nimsky.

"You're outvoted, Paul," said Ulanov. "Anyway, we're being treated, so save your allowance for some other night at one of those capitalist dives."

"Very well, a workingmen's cellar it is, then, *narodniki.*" But as they walked down the hall together, Marais stopped. "How will these workers take a black habit coming in? A lot of them are anticlerical."

"You're always afraid of embarrassment, Paul," said Ulanov.

"More of being killed by butcher's knives," Marais said quickly.

"Fear not, my timorous spirit. You will not die, you will not be thrown out."

"Do you run the place, then, Alex?"

"They are friends of mine."

"Pacelli will not hear?"

"No one hears about La Casa degli Esclavi. It would not exist long if they did."

"The Slaves' House? What a queer name."

"I like it!" said Nimsky.

"Who is paying for the meal, Alex?"

"A friend."

[67]

Marais stopped and stared pointedly at the other. "Why are you being so secretive? You are usually so open with us."

"When we get there, he'll show you," said Nimsky. "A hell of a place, right, Alex?"

"That it is," said Ulanov.

Marais surrendered to the momentum of Ulanov's leadership.

As they moved along the crowded streets to the heavy swinging rhythm of their habits, Nimsky bantered good-naturedly with Ulanov. The Frenchman did not join them but noticed, instead, the reactions of the people they passed. A good many were indifferent, deluged as they were by the sight of so many clerics. Some would shout, *"Ciao, padre,"* and a few would kneel for a blessing or bring some ancient article out of their pockets for a prayer and a sign of the cross. There were others, however, who spat as they passed the Jesuits, proclaiming their bitter hatred for all things Catholic, most of all her priests.

Suddenly the three of them veered off the broad light avenue into a narrow alleyway. "Surely we can reach this place by the main streets," said Marais.

"This is a shortcut," said Nimsky.

"I believe you." Marais fingered his throat. "It might be *very* short."

"Jesus," said Nimsky. "I swear, the French aren't happy unless they're living in fear."

"No one would dream of hurting you here," Ulanov said in that incredibly authoritative way of his.

"You can vouch for that? Personally?"

Ulanov laughed. "I know many of the people."

For Marais, this statement raised more questions than it answered. In three years he had never once heard Ulanov mention this section of the city. And, now, he was throwing salutes and kisses to people gathered by the windows or inside dim hallways! Ulanov would have had to spend hundreds of hours here to be on such terms with the people, yet Marais could not remember his being away that often from the house. Had another person set him up as a beloved figure in this quarter? But what for? And why, even now, was Ulanov revealing to his fellow Jesuits this well-kept secret? It seemed a pointless Palm Sunday.

[68]

Another fifteen minutes through the back streets brought them to their destination, signaled by Ulanov's sudden halt at a dead end formed by a cluster of small warehouses. Then, as though on cue, a door swung open on their left, rattling like something of incredible age.

"Come!" said Ulanov.

Marais did not move. "What's happening, Alex? Why all this mystery?"

Ulanov did not answer.

"You spoil the adventure," said Nimsky.

"Merde!"

"You will be no good for our mission," he continued. "I mean it, Paul. You want the reason for things laid out before you begin, so you are never surprised in life. No? Yes?" Nimsky laughed in the dark hallway.

"The day of the sage, Jewish or otherwise, is over, my friend," said Marais.

Ulanov pointed to the open door.

"Make up your own mind, Paul, but I don't want to miss this," said Nimsky, walking through the door. Without glancing at Marais, Ulanov followed Nimsky. Marais hardly knew what alternative existed but to move toward the dim cave ahead, where he stumbled into a hanging curtain that seemed to be made of tarpaulin coated with layers of black paint. Ulanov led him through a slit on the right side of the canvas.

Emerging from this tunnel, Marais found himself in the rear of a low-ceilinged room whose ten or so round tables were filled with men wearing cloth caps and a variety of old mixed suits and coveralls. Through the gray shifting banks of smoke, Marais saw Saul Nimsky already sitting at a table, playing an accordion. The Jesuit habits, Marais thought, looked absurdly out of place here. A few men glanced at the trio from over their newspapers or past the faces of their companions. This masked concern intrigued Marais, who sensed here the same hostility he had found on the streets. He deduced that this cafe was not a spot for random visitors but a local meeting place for certain like-minded individuals—of just what mind, he did not know.

Ulanov and he had sat down on either side of Nimsky, who

was entertaining the crowd with soulful melodies out of Tuscany, the Piedmont, Naples, any part of Italy that offered a few notes adaptable to the concertina. Marais, bored with these vulgar tunes after hearing them for three years, turned around to inspect a second room that was separated from them by a half partition of brick jutting out from the side wall. The men inside, their heads close together, were talking animatedly, like peasants in front of a cottage fire.

Ulanov touched Marais's arm. "Don't stare!"

"Why not, *Father?*"

"These workers have pride, Paul, they feel that you may be slumming. You do look very bourgeois, you know."

As Marais sat back, astonished at getting this kind of ideological rebuke from so long-standing a friend, the waiter-proprietor came from behind the bar at the opposite side of the room with a large pear-shaped bottle of unlabeled wine. He placed the decanter in the center and smiled at Nimsky, who had just finished his concert. "You played wonderfully, Father," he said softly. "Enjoy. Your meal will be here in a moment, gentlemen."

"Not 'Father,' " said Ulanov. "Not 'gentlemen,' Giuseppe. Fellows, fellow workers, brothers . . ."

Giuseppe gave an obedient nod to Ulanov, then said, "My politics are important, but I am still a Catholic, and to me you are not like the others. To me you are 'Father.' " Having spoken these words with great dignity, he disappeared into the small kitchen.

"Still brainwashed by this system of master and slave," said Ulanov.

"Well," said Nimsky, "the slave just talked back."

Marais, laughing, caught a look of disgust from Ulanov. "I'm surprised you don't see the joke on yourself, Alex."

Nimsky chose this moment to fill each of their glasses. "One thing I am very happy about here," he said, "there isn't a sign of Mussolini in the place. Now that's something to drink to. *N'est-ce pas?*"

"*Mais oui,*" answered Marais, very conscious of their switch into French. "*À bas il Duce.*" They clinked glasses. "Amen," said each in turn.

Marais pursed his lips. "Surprisingly good."

"Goddamn those middle-class remarks!" said Ulanov. "What the hell did you think these people would drink—sewer water?"

"He didn't mean that, did you, Paul?" asked Nimsky.

"I meant every word! I never expected good wine down here. Nor did I expect this kind of performance from you, Alex."

"Performance?" Nimsky asked.

"Now, now, Saul, Alex has tried to do something, and it hasn't worked, whatever it is, and—"

"But we are all *friends!*" said Nimsky.

"Real friends are not to be manipulated," said Marais. "Even for a cause."

"Everything was done for *your* sake," said Ulanov. "Not for anyone else."

Marais, touched despite himself, sat back in his chair.

During this last exchange, the waiter had placed before them their dinners, with a small salad and dessert. "Veal a la francese," Ulanov said softly. "I took the liberty of ordering for you beforehand, Paul. You will pardon me?"

The Frenchman waved aside Ulanov's apology for what, in Marais's mind, was the least of the evening's usurpations. Besides, he liked veal. "Where is our host, Alex?" he said. "I should like to thank him."

"He isn't here at present, but never mind, I shall thank him for you."

For a few moments they ate the "surprisingly good" meal in silence. Then, at the same moment, Ulanov and Marais looked up and met each other's eyes.

"Well, Alex?" asked Marais. "Why have you brought me to this socialist meeting house?"

"I wanted you to see another world that exists alongside the liberals and the Fascists."

"Why?"

"Well, you might be the one of us picked for the mission. And it has to be one of us, wouldn't you say?"

"Yes. But I don't think you really believe I'll be the one. So why did you bring me here?"

"Saul is my friend, he understands. You are my friend. And I wanted you to understand, too, something important about me. I had no idea you would carry on like this over some rudenesses committed against your sensitivities. I apologize. Nothing was intended."

"You really are a socialist, then?"

"Yes," said Ulanov.

"But this is serious. Are these people communists?"

"They think so. Because there is no alternative, or because the church has forced them into the party."

"They are trapped between the capitalists and the Fascists," Nimsky said. "And as far as we're concerned, the liberals belong with the capitalists."

"Who's 'we'?"

"Christian socialists, I guess."

"Not communists, Saul?" asked Marais, who had stumbled into a logic that he never intended.

"We've had to play a game with them," said Ulanov. "We believe in the socialist ideals, we don't believe in Russian communism. The important thing is that the church must not cross off the whole collective revolution that is taking place in the name of communism. The church's truth is necessary for the fulfillment of socialism, don't you see that?"

"My sympathies don't lie that way at all, Alex."

"All right, but whichever of us is chosen for an important mission that has something to do with Russia—it has to be Russia, or we wouldn't have been studying at the Russicum for three years—we must not let ourselves be used against the socialist experiment. Otherwise, we are just a mouthpiece for exploiters in the capitalist countries."

Marais stared at him.

"What's wrong with you?" asked Nimsky.

Marais shook his head as if with that gesture the talk during the last few minutes would rearrange itself into a semblance of sanity. "We're three little priests, Alex. You and I and Saul, we're members of an organization. We obey orders. It isn't we who make decisions, and we certainly don't bring world powers together like parts of a sentence in our head. But you, now—you assume we can unite Christianity and socialism. Who do you

[72]

think you are? We don't have the authority, the machinery, the people."

"Then we make do with what we have. No man can abdicate the little responsibility he has."

Marais sagged in his chair, unable to argue any longer. The three of them finished their dessert without conversation; even as they sipped their wine afterward, no one spoke.

The hum of voices around them began to ebb and then ceased. Their own silence was absorbed by the quiet that flowed through the rest of the room. Marais, following the direction of everyone else's eyes, settled on a young man who had just entered through the tarpaulin slit. He seemed to be sizing up the occupants of the room; his gaze moved slowly from table to table, then stopped at the Jesuits.

Of all those in the room, Ulanov alone continued to face the wall. The stranger's eyes seemed fastened on his back.

"There's a man over there who just came in," whispered Nimsky. "He's staring at you."

Ulanov's fingers caressed the outlines of his wineglass.

"The whole place is looking at us," said Marais.

The stranger took cigarettes from his jacket, knocked one out of the pack, and lit it without relaxing for an instant his scrutiny of Ulanov's back.

"We're in trouble, I think," said Marais.

The fellow removed his jacket and for the first time looked away from the priests. He made his way between the tables and over to the bar, where he called for whiskey in a rough voice.

"Those arms!" said Nimsky.

The man's cotton shirt had no sleeves, and nakedness drew attention to his unnatural biceps and forearms. Just under six feet, and slender, his body seemed dwarfed by muscles which might have belonged to a much larger man.

"A driller?" Nimsky said.

"Saul, look closer."

The man's profile as it caught the light at the bar seemed uncannily familiar.

"I'll take the bottle, too," he said quietly as Giuseppe handed him his glass.

[73]

Marais looked at Nimsky. The stranger spoke Italian with an American accent.

The man turned and without hesitation made for the priests' table. He circled behind Ulanov, and, bending over him, set down the bottle and glass. Then he put his hands on the Jesuit's shoulders and pressed down. Ulanov immediately leaned forward in his chair, but still the strong hands gripped him.

"It seems our host has arrived," Ulanov said in Russian.

The man relaxed his grip. He pulled another chair up to the table, turned it around, and straddled it so that his arms rested on the back.

He raised his glass to the others and drank half the contents before setting it down again. "It's nice to see you here, Alexander," he said in Russian.

"I wish I could say the same about you."

The man licked the edge of his mouth for a few seconds and then returned to his whiskey. He finished what was left and lifted the bottle.

"That's enough," said Ulanov.

"You and your friends can sip your wine. I'll drink."

"I know you when you drink. I'd *prefer* you didn't."

"That's better." The man smiled and filled the glass slowly.

Again Marais and Nimsky exchanged glances. Neither of them had ever heard anyone talk this way to Ulanov.

"What's your names?" asked the man.

Ulanov held up a hand.

The stranger turned to the priests. "Anyway, I'm Nicholas."

They held out their hands, but he ignored them.

"Did you enjoy your meal?" he asked.

"Of course," said Marais.

"Very much," said Nimsky. "Your Russian is excellent, my friend."

"But from your Italian," said Marais, "I take it you're an American."

"You two should be spies."

Nimsky turned to Ulanov. "He's Russian, and American like you, Alex."

Nicholas laughed. "That deserves a toast," he said. He gulped several swallows of whiskey, then stared at the glass as though suddenly overcome by depression.

Marais studied the man, trying to pin down the resemblance that had disturbed him. It was a hard face with little decipherable character in it. The eyes, however, were amazingly bright, blue, and clear. They and the fine forehead seemed to contradict the pockmarked cheeks and swollen biceps, as though the prince and the mechanic had been inexplicably crossbred.

"I don't want to hurt your guests' feelings," Nicholas said, "but since when do you bring habits in here? I didn't know this dinner was for them."

"You offered it," said Ulanov, "and you didn't ask for whom."

"What made you bring *them here?*"

"To show them the working-class socialists of Rome."

"You must be crazy!"

"No harm done," said Ulanov, laughing. "If only you hadn't shown up."

As Nicholas finished his glass and reached for the bottle, Ulanov pushed it just beyond his grasp.

Nicholas shook his head, as if clouds of alcohol had backed up on him for a very bad second. "Goddamn you and your cronies!"

"What have we done?" asked Nimsky.

The man turned instantly, reached down, and jerked off the rosary beads that dangled from Nimsky's cincture.

"Coming in here with this, that's what you've done!" He held the beads up in front of Ulanov's face. "How will I ever explain it to our people?"

"Please give those back to me," said Nimsky.

Ulanov put a cassocked arm across Nimsky's chest, signaling that his presence stood between Nimsky and the intruder. "You've treated my friends very badly," he said. "You must apologize."

"You'll see me in hell, first.'

"You *will* apologize, Nicholas."

"I really don't want any apology," said Nimsky. "Why don't we just leave, Alex?"

"That's right," said Nicholas. "You just leave."

[75]

"No," said Ulanov. "He is finished with me, unless—"

"You would sacrifice me to these people? So. Now we know where you stand." The voice was curious, a self-pitying, hurt sort of whine.

For the first time Ulanov's expression registered uncertainty. Nonetheless, he took out a watch, paused for a few seconds, and put it on the table. "Sixty seconds," he announced.

"Really, Alex?"

"Fifty-five seconds."

"For what?"

"To make amends. Or get out of my sight."

Nicholas got up. "I'll go," he said.

Nimsky and Marais heard each other's sigh of relief.

"Not until—" Ulanov, again.

"Then never!"

Ulanov, rising from the table for the first time that night, carefully undid his cincture.

"You have no right!" screamed the younger man.

Ulanov kissed the cincture, laid it aside, and began to undo the hook that held the black collar of the habit in place.

"Please," Nimsky said finally. "Not for me."

"Look at all these people," said Marais. "They're not friend-ly."

"All these years together, for nothing?" said Nicholas. "Don't you see you need me? You can't handle things alone."

Ulanov said nothing.

Seeing Nicholas's expression, Marais leaned over to catch a closer glimpse of the man's features in the light, then turned to Nimsky. "Do you see it?" he demanded.

"Stop staring, you," said the man. And he ran two large hands down his cheeks. "Only pockmarks and scars, see? A lousy face—nothing like *his!*"

Pity and revulsion gripped Marais at the knife scars barely visible around Nicholas's lips and nose. Worse than the scars, an obscene drama seemed to be played out in that terrible face, as if a mistreated changeling inside were screaming for the world to recognize him; expecting, somehow, that some midnight event might transform him. It was hopeless, of course; that weasel character so ingrained in the hating face doomed its owner to forever remain a child of the streets. What, Marais wondered, could conceivably drive such a man to make any kind of claim on greatness?

"There must be something else between you two, Alex." Nimsky's tone was frantic. "It isn't for *us* that you do this."

"That's irrelevant now, Saul," Ulanov said gently.

"No, no, please. What's going on? That man said, 'All these years together.' What does it mean, Alex?"

"Nothing." Ulanov smiled and removed his habit. Having kissed it, he laid it carefully on his seat. Standing there in his black trousers and a thin wisp of an undershirt, he looked more like a gymnast than a priest. Marais—never having seen Ulanov in the flesh, so to speak—was astonished. Where, he wondered, could that kind of extraordinary physique come from, other than some incredibly arduous kind of labor during adolescence or early manhood? The shoulders were remarkable, but it was the size of the Jesuit's arms that really surprised Marais. They were massive and, if such a thing were possible, larger again by a third than those of his blond opponent. How came two men with such a pair of arms to be here in the same room together? Could they have done the same kind of work?

Ulanov walked slowly around the table to the stranger's seat and stood over and behind him. "Your time is up, Nicholas!"

"Please be peaceable, Alex," said Nimsky. "This is a personal quarrel now. I wash my hands of it."

"Saul is right," said Marais. "There is something here that we don't belong to, he or I. You haven't explained yet, Alex, and you must. Please! Think of *us,* if Pacelli ever hears of it. What then?"

Ulanov began to pull Nicholas out of his seat.

"What are you doing?" muttered the other in a low breath meant only for the figure above him.

"You tried me. You wanted to know something—well, now you know. You've had your day."

Nicholas jumped up to one side of the table.

Ulanov was actually laughing as he tugged at his black trousers and then moved slowly forward with his hands clenched loosely into fists in front of his face.

Nicholas backed up to an empty table against the wall and shoved it aside. "Stop!" he shouted.

Ulanov moved within striking range of Nicholas, but instead of throwing a punch, he began to weave in closer, covering himself neatly with the hands clenched before his face. Clearly he did not wish to be the first to unleash a blow.

His opponent pushed the Jesuit away with a violent shove that nonetheless displaced him no more than two or three feet. It was enough. As Ulanov came back toward him, Nicholas let fly a fast right hand which caught the forehead above the left eye. Ulanov began to sag; another blow caught him on the right cheekbone with a sound so harsh that the reverberations of the punch seemed to be echoed by the gasps of the onlookers.

Ulanov, sinking, hooked one arm about a chair. The blood was starting to pour from the wound above his eye. He seemed to be hanging on to the back of the chair by a very slim margin, working desperately to keep from sliding off and away. Nicholas, surprised himself by the effect of these blows, assessed the damage and then, convinced that little was needed to finish off his work, moved in closer and closer to Ulanov, savoring his advantage a little longer, perhaps for the admiration of the crowd. But in the instant that his right hand poised to come down on Ulanov's left temple, Ulanov's free left arm shot up and gripped the other's wrist.

Nicholas's attempts to free himself, falling backward, thus succeeded only in pulling Ulanov to his feet. Ulanov leaned against his trapped opponent, who could neither free his right hand from Ulanov's grip nor gain sufficient windup room to use his left. And so they ended up against the wall; Ulanov letting his body rest heavily down against the other's, pinioning Nicholas to the wall while he regained his strength.

It happened so quickly that Marais could hardly follow it. In the same instant that Ulanov released the stranger's hand, he drove his right fist into the other's midsection with such force that the head slumped. As it fell forward, Ulanov's left hand

[78]

drove an uppercut to the jaw, driving his opponent's skull against the brick wall. A sickening gurgle from Nicholas's throat was matched by the flinching moans from the watching crowd. Another quick right hand struck the barely conscious victim on the cheekbone as he began to topple, but it seemed a follow-through from Ulanov's natural movement rather than unnecessary brutality. With that, matters were at an end. His opponent's crumbled hulk lay at the feet of Ulanov, who stood frozen in his last position.

The cellar crowd seemed as motionless as did the Jesuit. The shock of the reversal seemed to congeal the underground space; clouds of smoke shifted about in the mean narrow atmosphere like traces of an exhausted event.

"Do you believe it?" Marais asked Nimsky.

"Luck!" Nimsky whispered. "But what will happen now?"

"No one seems to know."

"We shouldn't wait for them, Paul."

"Can *we* really act? Would it really set the tone if we went out there?" Even this hushed exchange seemed dangerous in the confines of the cellar.

The silence was ended by a hoarse cry from the rear, followed by the appearance of the waiter. "A raid . . . the police . . . a raid! They are on their way. Go, everyone . . . Please . . . out, out, out! There is no time to spare, gentlemen, please, if you are caught . . ."

Before Giuseppe had finished, the room's occupants were moving through every available exit. Some ran into the kitchen, some to the rear, others through a second door in the front. The crowd had almost disappeared when Ulanov, bending with obvious difficulty, picked Nicholas off the floor. Balancing him over his shoulder, he staggered toward his Jesuit brothers. He signaled impatiently for his habit and cincture, and, once Nimsky had them tucked under an arm, led his comrades out a rear exit. In the background they heard the screeches of police whistles, laying to rest whatever doubts Marais had about the "raid."

In the darkness of the street, Nimsky and Marais touched Ulanov's back every ten seconds or so. From time to time he would stop and lean against a wall, moaning softly while he sucked in air with desperate breaths. His friends, huddled close, tried to speak to him, but every time they began, he would put a finger to his lips.

Marais, astonished that Ulanov could carry the unconscious victim, was even more at a loss as to why he was doing it.

How far they trekked through the unlighted byways the priests could not guess, but it was clear that Ulanov knew where they were. They stumbled along until they began to see knots of people, at which point Ulanov set down his burden—very gently, almost tenderly—and changed into the habit. Having used Nimsky's and Marais's handkerchiefs to wipe as much of the blood from his forehead as the cloth would hold, he said, "I am going to leave you here. Nicholas and I will find a place nearby."

"But why don't you leave him?" demanded Nimsky. "He will wake up eventually, and then—then he can be sorry all he wants!"

Ulanov gave Nimsky a look that inspired him to turn to Marais for reinforcement. Before the Frenchman could begin to think of a response, Ulanov had rendered their resistance useless.

"Would *you* treat your brother that way, Saul?"

Marais and Nimsky stared down at the bruised face of the victim and back up at Ulanov.

"Why did you never tell us?" asked Nimsky.

Ulanov shrugged. "He drinks sometimes. He's difficult."

"Vicious, I'd say," said Marais. "But why is he here?"

"He lives in Rome."

The other two continued to stare at the form on the sidewalk. "He's a bit of a disgrace, isn't he?" asked Nimsky.

"He has a bad temper sometimes. It's settled now. He's my brother. We had a fight. I'll tell you about him sometime."

"Now!" said Marais.

"No, Paul." Nimsky put a hand on the Frenchman's arm. "He'll tell us sometime."

"This creature is his brother!" Marais shouted.

Nimsky understood his friend's desperate attempt to pin down the meaning of what he saw. "I wish you could leave him here," he said to Ulanov. "He gives me the feeling of an albatross."

"I would leave you before him," said Ulanov.

The echoes of what sounded like groups of men stumbling in the dark and slamming doors, cursing perhaps over their bad luck in the night, seemed to be coming closer.

"They're hunting *us!*" said Nimsky.

"That was no ordinary raid," said Ulanov. "Someone has tried to give us away. But there's no evidence if we are not caught. Believe me, nobody in that room will ever talk. Give me your word, both of you—that this . . . incident will not be mentioned. Marais? Nimsky?"

"Of course!" The two men answered together. Ulanov, it seemed, would play out his advantage to the last possible second before their pursuers reached them.

"Well, now, it is time to go." Ulanov put his arms under his brother and expertly threw the body over his shoulder, then disappeared into the house behind them. His companions followed him through a dark hallway and into an unoccupied apartment. They climbed out a rear window onto rows of flowers and vegetables, feeling stalks crumple beneath their feet as they walked. On the other side of the garden, they made their way into a cobblestoned alleyway and then stopped beside a door with a dimly lighted pane at its top.

Ulanov knocked a few times in an odd rhythm. A minute later, the door opened and an old man peered out at them. With a small wave and only the suggestion of an arched eyebrow to express his surprise at the bundle on Ulanov's shoulders, he let the Jesuit pass.

"I'll be back for you," Ulanov called over his shoulder. "Stay there!" The door closed quickly.

Marais and Nimsky stood still, listening for their pursuers.

"We've lost them," Marais said with a sigh.

"But why should *we* be in these situations? Fugitives—look at us!"

"I saw it coming, Saul."

"This is no time to congratulate yourself."

"Be fair." Marais felt his confidence returning. "I *did* have suspicions before, during, after this whole thing. You and I could have outvoted him if you—"

[81]

"Forget your justifications, will you? Just look at us now, hiding in an alley. And why didn't he take us inside? It would have been much safer. This is dangerous."

With that they both paused again to study the stillness beyond them.

"We aren't trustworthy enough," whispered Marais. "That's why he left us here."

At that moment, the light in the pane above them went out. The door opened quickly, and Ulanov pulled the two of them out of the alleyway. Inside the vestibule, he had them remove their habits and put on scarlet blouses over their shirts. He then wrapped their habits in brown paper, tying the packet up with old string.

This done, Ulanov stared at them for a long moment. He seemed to be shaken by the prospect of parting from them. Tears—Marais had never known him to have any—showed in his eyes. He grasped both their hands. "This man will see you safely home. Count on him. Do what he says." He gave them each a great embrace. "God bless you, Saul. God bless you, Paul." Then he was gone, quite suddenly, around a little corner.

They gave themselves over to the old man's guidance and were safely back in their house before midnight.

5

On the afternoon following the brawl in the Slaves' House, Marais fled from the Bellarmino. The confines of his room had exacerbated his nervousness until he could hardly bear to remain in the same position longer than a couple of minutes.

The plan he was formulating could, he knew, seriously damage both himself and Nimsky. The idea seemed so extreme that he backed away from it even as he worked out its details.

In this state he could not bring himself to answer the repeated calls from his father, who had come to Rome to see him. As a doctor, Marais senior was quick to spot abnormal signs in his only son and would probe relentlessly for their cause. Marais hoped to delay the annual encounter until he had settled what he should do about Ulanov.

He had awakened from a troubled sleep more frightened than he had been during the fight. While he slept, an overwhelming sensation had seemed to focus all his energies on the danger incarnate in Ulanov. Its command over Marais was so immediate that Marais could not question it. Quite simply, every instinct he possessed dictated that he try to prevent Ulanov's selection by the Pope.

Marais, believing that he was experiencing a deeper truth than he had ever known, nonetheless felt himself unnerved if not unmanned by the act to which he was being drawn. The intentions of his soul were so pure, while the execution seemed so stained, that he spent hours exhausting himself in an attempt to reconcile the two.

Time and again he had opened his door to walk the short distance to Nimsky's room. He needed desperately to talk to someone else, to expose his conviction along with his dreadful plan. The one person who would understand it all was Nimsky. Pacelli's order, of course, stood between them. The cardinal had made them swear that they would not speak to one another during the period of decision which had begun this morning. This order now struck Marais as a perverse piece of idiocy. It was in fact preventing a loyal Jesuit from helping the church.

And so the Frenchman sought release from his dilemma in the streets of Rome, walking aimlessly through quarters he had never glimpsed during the previous three years. For hours he drifted along with the crowds or sat in the cafes. He tried to relax by studying a hundred different dramas being enacted on the streets; by participating imaginatively in the odd fragments of conversation he could overhear at other tables. These tactics succeeded in distracting him for no more than a few minutes; and so he turned toward home at dusk, his fear at the decision before him stronger than the morning's fear. Crossing a street, he happened to notice that an old woman was keeping pace with him.

As he stopped, she stopped. When he began to move, she followed, always keeping at a distance of half a block. He found himself looking back at her repeatedly—her wizened face and the stare she fixed on Marais drew his eye like a magnet. As he neared home, he began to hurry his pace. Every hundred yards or so he would pause and look back only to find that, despite her age, the old woman had not lost ground. Marais finally ran the remaining few blocks, and actually flung himself through the door before he felt safe. "Why me?" he muttered to himself. "Why me?" As he climbed the stairs, he wondered what on earth had kept him from pursuing the woman and demanding the reason for her behavior. There was no sense in the thing; she had terrorized him and he had accepted it.

As he put his hand on the doorknob of his room, he found himself unable to enter. His fears had brought on a spasm of trembling at the prospect of living alone with his thoughts one more evening. He spun around and lost no time moving through the corridors to Nimsky's room, which he entered without waiting for a response to his knock.

Nimsky was lying on the bed, staring at the ceiling. "Finally, brother Paul," he said.

"I had no choice, Saul."

"Who cares about Pacelli's orders?"

"I didn't know what to do."

"It was a hell of a night, wasn't it?" Nimsky tried a laugh.

"What shall we do, Saul? It can't go on."

"Do? Do?" Eyes closed, Nimsky pulled a bottle of wine from under the pillow. "This and rest, *nyet?*"

Marais moved to the bed and stood over Nimsky. "I'm ready to go to Pacelli," he said.

The Russian slowly opened his eyes, his easy smile changing by degrees to a glare. "And who are you to report anyone?"

"I'm convinced Ulanov will ruin us all. Look, Ulanov isn't like you, he doesn't play games. If his brother is in Rome, it is important to him, you may be certain of that. The fight, the cryptic remarks—it was clear that everyone in that cafe knew them as a team, that's why they couldn't react. Admit it, Saul."

"Of course I admit it. Of course!"

"Then we have a duty to report them. Who knows what they're up to?"

"On what real evidence would you turn Alex in? So far, I've heard only speculation."

"Let Pacelli be the judge of that."

"If you report what happened last night, Paul, you've already made an accusation. It's your opinion these events amount to more than just an embarrassment. But suppose they don't? The effect is still the same. Ulanov will be so compromised in the cardinal's eyes that he couldn't possibly remain a candidate."

"But we saw enough last night to make anyone suspicious," Marais shouted. "Naturally the brothers Ulanov didn't spell everything out, but they didn't have to."

Nimsky, pouring from the bottle of wine, eyed Marais quietly over the glass. "What really makes you want to betray Alex?"

"My loyalty to the church."

"But you've always been the cautious man—"

"That's all the more reason to trust my instincts now, Saul!"

"And where did you come by this kind of spirit? You, the rationalist. It's my opinion you're deceiving yourself. Personal ambition, hatred of Alex—"

"No!" And then Marais stopped still. "*Oh*, no—isn't that odd? You've been so antagonistic to me from the start. No matter what, you can't believe anything bad about Ulanov. You've made an act of faith in him, and that isn't like *you*, either." Marais started to laugh. "You can't be my witness, and I can't go alone. We shall never stop him. No one can stop him. *He is really meant to go!*"

Marais was gone before Nimsky could reply. Walking through the corridors, he did not take the turn toward his own room but moved instead to the entrance of the house. He felt a vague need for a breath of fresh air. As he walked down the steps and out on the pavement, he came face to face with the old woman from whom he had fled not an hour before.

"What do you want?" he asked her.

"Who would want anything from you, Father?"

"Madam, I don't know you. So why are you talking to me like this?"

"I recognized you this afternoon!"

"How? Who sent you?"

"God spoke to me. He said to me, 'That weak priest there, help him, Theresa.' But you kept running away and stopping and I couldn't approach you at the corners. So I've waited for you."

"How did you know I would come out here?"

"God said—"

"Stop saying 'God'! You're a madwoman, or possessed by the devil."

"Then why are you afraid of me?" The old woman gave him a soft, ghastly smile. "You, a gentleman priest, believing in an old woman possessed by a devil?"

Marais put a hand over his eyes for a moment, as if he thought she might be a hallucination. "Who sent you after me?" he asked.

"The Lord has said his will is to be done, and I obey it. I see

[86]

the strong march with Alexander." She gave him a final glance of contempt, then closed her eyes for a moment and limped off.

Marais watched her until she was out of sight. An agent of God, or some shrewd enemy? Alexander would never send such a creature. He walked into the house and through the monastery gloom of the house to the chapel. "God," he whispered, "you may not be responsible for these acts but you have allowed them to happen. Nimsky's heart is turned to stone. I, the man of reason, know that if Ulanov wreaks harm, then you're not the God I pray to. I have tried to stop him and I am being defeated— from on high?"

He genuflected and made his way back to his room. Before lying down, he took two of the sleeping pills his father had left on his last visit. As he waited for them to take effect, he let the meaning of the day's events ease into his mind. One thing seemed certain—his carefully built rational approaches to life were done for. The spiritual prize belonged to an adventurer; that was the message of the day.

The next morning Marais called his father. During the next few days, he found himself grateful for the chance to escort the doctor around Rome. Without his companionship, he felt his nerves might collapse. He could not concentrate on the simplest material, and he had no desire to remember recent incidents. Waiting for the decision of Cardinal Pacelli and Pope Pius XI only intensified the already intolerable strain.

The notion of denouncing Ulanov continued to assert itself with no warning. Just as Marais was describing some event or pointing out the details of some Baroque construction, he would feel the voice: "You must tell all, no matter what the cost. You must! Now!"

Marais had devised various ruses to conceal from his father the effects of these sudden inner directives. "It's the suspense about that damned assignment," he explained time and again. "A different place, a different job, always stirs my imagination..." This little *règle de jeu* enabled the two of them to play out a game that never embarrassed Marais, and at the same time amused and presumably deceived his father.

"Where was it just now, Paul?"

"The Russian colony in Paris. I am their chaplain."

"Where then?"

"Warsaw . . . mediation . . . Poles and Russians."

"Before?"

"Scholarship . . . writing books . . . the archival materials . . . collating . . ."

"*Ah, oui,* I prefer that for you, Paul!"

"Government work, international affairs . . . diplomacy."

"Even better!"

His father now seemed delighted at Marais's anxiety. "They've not killed holy ambition in you yet," he would invariably say at some point after dinner together. As for Marais, any fantasy seemed better than the demands made on him by an overworked conscience.

And so he focused his energies on making his father's holiday in Rome memorable. It was unprecedented for Marais and his father to have a vacation like this. They had never spent more than two days together over the past sixteen years; even then his mother, the princess, had come along, totally dominating their conversations. Thankfully she had remained home on this occasion, fearing that the hot Roman summer might bring on some kind of attack.

The estrangement between son and father was, for the most part, a consequence of the Society's rules which so severely limited family visits to three or four afternoons a year. This regimen had deeply discouraged the doctor, who had already been forced to stand by as his son developed under the Jesuits in a direction he deplored. To an agnostic doctor, the son's choice of a career constituted a terrible rejection. Fortunately, Marais's advance during the last few years to the final grades of the order had caused him to shed most of his self-righteous pietism. With the order's permission to spend a number of weekends at home during the year, the family wounds had nearly healed.

On the fifth day of his father's visit, Marais said mass, by extraordinary permission, on a side altar of St. Peter's Basilica. The doctor was the lone communicant. Surprisingly, this congregation of one betrayed an intense if silent pleasure in witnessing the ancient ritual of the church as celebrated by his son.

After breakfast and on through the early afternoon they perused exotic collections of coins and stamps, ancient and modern, in the Vatican. Dr. Marais, who had made a lifetime hobby of numismatics, was overwhelmed by the treasures unlocked for his personal attention.

Around three o'clock he insisted on treating his son to early cocktails at the Excelsior Hotel—the favorite watering spot, so he had heard, of worldly clerics and foreign businessmen. He made a point of adding that he was gratified to see his son recovering from his nervous condition. "Who knows, maybe I'm a tonic for you, Paul."

Marais declared that this was indeed the case.

As they were approaching the Excelsior's entrance, his father even admitted to a certain admiration for his son's vocation. "It took a long time for me to come around, and you understand, Paul, that I can't say 'God bless you' and feel in my heart that there really is one up there to do it, but . . ."

Marais gave the old man's hand a quick squeeze as they settled into the comfortable chairs of the cocktail lounge. They discussed for an hour the sad character of events transpiring on the world's stage. Dr. Marais was surprised that his own son was not more distressed by the Depression, nor by the sway that Mussolini and Hitler held over great peoples like the Italians and Germans.

"The Vatican will act," Marais murmured tiredly. "She is never desperate, she never hurries."

"But this is the hour! The catastrophe is coming, I tell you."

"If it comes, she will meet it. She is not Fascist, she is not liberal. Each has certain values which appeal to her. If one or the other goes too far, she reacts."

"What a holy dispassionate bastard you've become, Paul."

Marais laughed. "Ah well, you liberals always want things to be corrected immediately. And if they aren't, you blame some authoritarian institution. There is a fundamental weakness in attacking whatever values the church has—and then expecting her help to prevent this catastrophe you see coming."

"I must say, Paul, it's strange to hear you talking so dispassionately."

"Politics isn't the ultimate to me. Very important, but secondary."

"You have changed, then. Politics is all you used to talk about."

"I have *evolved.*"

"Since when?" The doctor turned toward the bar and gestured dramatically at a sleepy Italian waiter who apparently had no peripheral vision.

Marais took advantage of the distraction to formulate the answer to his parent's question. Since when, indeed, had he changed? Since five nights ago. That response would surely infuriate his father, and to no purpose.

The doctor finally rose, emphasizing his discomfort with a groan, and confronted the waiter in a voice so loud that the poor fellow ran for the drinks.

A long pause ensued as Dr. Marais swilled the good whiskey appreciatively. "An elixir, a home healer, a gift for all seasons all rolled into one," he murmured finally.

"It's very good."

Marais was searching for some further neutral point of conversation, and with no promise of success, when Ulanov entered the lounge.

Neither the Jesuit nor the two ladies accompanying him looked toward Marais and his father. It was an admirable if strange characteristic of Ulanov's—that he hardly ever looked around him. He was dressed in a cleric's street clothes, not in the habit as was usual. He found a table that suited him and signaled to his companions, who followed with alacrity. The movements of escort and entourage could not but attract attention. The ladies' overgraceful walk, their jewels, their dresses, reminded Marais of his mother's friends, connoting station no matter what the hour. Even the afternoon. Especially the afternoon. Ulanov claimed his seat at the end of the small table, stood while the waiter ceremoniously seated the ladies, and then, with a graceful little bow, sat down.

The group, seated three tables away, was directly opposite Marais and his father. Studying Ulanov's profile, Marais saw no sign of the cuts and bruises suffered that night in the Slaves'

House. Perhaps it was the other side of Ulanov's face that bore what was left of the telltale scars.

"You know the fellow?" Dr. Marais asked suddenly.

"Quite well, as a matter of fact. I wondered what he was doing here with those women."

"One of your boys?"

"He's a Jesuit."

"Handsome chap. What is he?"

"American . . . Russian-American."

"Ah, yes, they say that males grow big over there—with the prairies, factories, milk, and all."

"Confidentially, I think he's a socialist."

"A Jesuit socialist? What next?"

"I'm not sure," Marais said carefully. "So if we should meet them, you won't say anything—"

"Of course!" The old man smiled.

"I'm not supposed to talk about other Jesuits to an extern, that's the point. I could look very bad if you—"

"I delivered you into this world myself, and I'm an . . . extern, is it?"

"It's like being a doctor. You keep some things even from your wife."

"Very little, I'm afraid. You shouldn't use examples you don't know anything about."

Marais lightly applauded the retort, hoping that this concession would distract the doctor from any irritation he might feel with "socialists." He wondered why he had even mentioned that piece of scandal to his father.

Dr. Marais, seated sideways to Ulanov's table, could study the Jesuit simply by leaning an elbow on his chair's arm rest and inclining his head. "When are we going to say hello, Paul?" he said.

"Let's wait a bit."

"What for? I love to meet charming women. The Jesuits I can take or leave."

"You can't have one without the other."

"No, no, you talk to him and gossip about old times. That will leave me free to enjoy myself, you understand?"

[91]

"I understand that. But I *don't* understand what someone so dedicated to the working class is doing in a plush bar with women like that."

"That's another story, Paul. I believe I taught you a long time ago never to mix up categories. Of course, from where I sit, they're too old for him. Young for me, though—just the right age."

Marais caught himself in time. He could not explain his concern without emphasizing the seriousness of Ulanov's social convictions.

Fully ten minutes had passed while the ladies gazed into Ulanov's face. The Jesuit, for his part, seemed to be expounding some difficult point or other to the two women, whose expressions suggested that they were partaking in a mystical experience.

Marais realized that his father was growing restless. Nothing would do but that he meet "interesting" people, should the chance be offered. As Marais tried to think of a plausible excuse that would prevent matters from taking their natural course, the doctor began. "Do you know that fellow or don't you?"

"Of course I do."

"Well, come on, then."

"I can't."

"What kind of nonsense is that?"

Marais hesitated.

"Paul? You aren't afraid of him, are you?"

Marais laughed. "Do I look afraid?"

"Not particularly, but why this reluctance to simply say hello, to a friend. And, I might add, indulge your old father?"

Marais sighed. "All right, Father. We're not supposed to talk, that priest and myself."

"Who says?"

"His Eminence Cardinal Pacelli."

"I never heard of such a thing. For what conceivable reason?"

"I can't say."

"Oh, this is going too far! Anyway, I am not supposed to know about your cardinal and his damned restrictions." With that the doctor rose, and, before his son could say a word, began making his way between the tables. The better part of discretion, obviously, was to follow him.

"Pardon me, you good people, but I am Dr. Marais and my son here, Father Paul, tells me that he is acquainted with this young priest. May I treat you to a round or two? It would afford me the deepest pleasure to do so."

The two ladies looked up in amazement. Even Ulanov seemed unable to handle this sudden intrusion. It was not until he caught sight of Marais coming up rather sheepishly behind the older man that his face regained its usual composure.

"Hello, Alexander." Yes, the marks were there; one particularly noticeable bruise and a narrow scar.

"Hello, Paul." Ulanov's eyes went from father to son.

"I couldn't stop him, Alex. I merely mentioned to him that we were friends, and he . . ." Marais shrugged.

"Well, then! Won't you join us, Doctor?" said Ulanov.

"I've explained to him, Alex, that we are not supposed to talk to each other."

"Isn't that foolish?" Dr. Marais asked the ladies. "Whoever heard of such a thing? Friends who meet by accident, not allowed to speak?" He signaled to the waiter, who redeemed himself by appearing instantly.

"A round of the same for everyone," said Dr. Marais, without consulting his guests.

Ulanov was quiet. Dr. Marais had apparently exhausted his conversational resources with the bravado of his entrance, leaving his son with the task of making sociable waves in a motionless pond.

"My name," he announced to the ladies, "is Father Paul Marais. I too am a Jesuit, and I have been studying with Father Ulanov here in Rome these past three years. I apologize for this invasion by my father and myself, but we will leave shortly. After our drink, I promise you."

One of the women gave him a slight bow of the head; the second managed a smile, but her eyes begged him to hold to his promise of a quick departure. The doctor stiffened perceptibly, knowing the apology was for his own behavior.

"This beautiful lady," said Ulanov, "is Lady Orrin Bowe. And her equally beautiful comrade is the Countess Grimaldi."

Marais murmured and smiled, subtly conveying the impression of being greatly honored by the very mention of those names. His father said nothing.

"We met on shipboard three years ago," continued Ulanov, "when I was on my way to Rome. These noble ladies were so kind as to offer me their hospitality and friendship."

"And he, of course, has given us such spiritual food for thought that we are his eternal debtors," said Lady Bowe in what sounded like an antiphonic response.

"He has almost singlehandedly put us on the road to salvation," said the countess.

"That *is* edifying," said Marais, looking at Ulanov. "Well, you must have much to talk over about what has happened these past three years."

"Oh dear, no, not at all," said Lady Bowe. "We meet with Father Ulanov every six months or so to discuss things spiritual and political."

"Oh, really." Marais turned to Ulanov. "You are a busy person, Alexander, what with the slaves of the cafe *and* these fine ladies."

Ulanov seemed less discomfited by this remark than by those of his flock. Evidently the women felt compelled to praise their mentor before one of his own. They also thought—quite incorrectly, it seemed to Marais—that they had given away no significant content in so doing.

When the waiter brought the drinks, Marais senior threw the lire on the tray.

Marais held his glass high. "To the most charming ladies I have met these past three years, and for the sake of whose company my father has performed a most courageous deed . . . for which he, too, received this testimony of most cordial esteem." He clinked glasses with Ulanov; the ladies nodded politely while his father tossed off his drink, a double.

Marais sipped slowly from his fragile glass. Ulanov, never concerned about such matters, now seemed aware of a shift in

[94]

their relationship. The Frenchman's own feelings were that he himself had inexplicably grown, while Ulanov somehow seemed less complex, much diminished from the figure he had presented over the last three years. Marais even felt grateful to his father for the pleasure of this discovery and wished that he could find a way to break the older man's grim silence and tell him so. What he could not understand was why his father had made no overtures to these women, considering the grand point he had made of it not so long before. They had done nothing to hurt his feelings that badly. It was inexplicable—unless, of course, the doctor had never intended his quarry to be female company in the first place.

"Where did you get that bruise on your head, son?" Dr. Marais suddenly asked Ulanov.

"Your son is over there," he said.

Dr. Marais amiably pointed to his forehead, as a sign that he would still like an answer to the question.

"In a fall."

"It's a nasty crack! Well touched up, though, whoever did it. Good job. Forgive me, I'm a doctor. Where did it happen?"

"On some steps . . . down the stairs."

"It really is quite high for that, you know. And you suffered a cut as well, I see."

Marais was appalled at his father's none too subtle probing. Ulanov, in turn, threw a quick glance at his colleague, surprised at this puzzling attack and wondering, quite obviously, what secrets had been given out. Marais raised his eyes to the ceiling.

"Let me see," said Dr. Marais. "Perhaps I can be of some assistance."

"Thank you, but no. I've had it attended to."

The doctor, not dissuaded in the least, rose so quickly that he was already inspecting the bruise before Ulanov could fend him off.

"Ah . . . and you have a nasty lump there on your cheekbone, too." The doctor moved slowly back to his seat. "That was no fall . . . on steps," he said offhandedly, as though his inner concern were elsewhere.

[95]

"I beg your pardon!" said the Countess Grimaldi.

"Sometimes fighters look like that, afterward." The doctor covered his face with his hands for a moment.

"You had better go back to medical school—or retire, sir," Ulanov said lightly, keeping up his end of a bad joke.

"Is that so?" The doctor was now massaging his eyes.

"You heard Father Ulanov!" said Lady Orrin Bowe.

"I heard, and it's not the truth. He lies, your father."

Marais closed his eyes at this latest challenge to Ulanov's rectitude. Surely one of the ladies would rise in outrage—but no, they were all obviously caught so off guard that even Ulanov stared at the portly doctor and waited for the inevitable jest and the wave of relief that would follow it. Marais could have told them that neither would come.

"You were in a physical engagement of some sort. That is my diagnosis." The doctor's even tones did not disguise the undertone of malice.

"You've been drinking quite a bit, sir," said Ulanov. "That is *my* diagnosis."

Marais shuddered. If ever there was a wrong tack in handling his father . . .

"My son can vouch that my sobriety varies with the requisites of the occasion."

Marais injected into his glance at Ulanov a warning to leave—now.

"I further surmise," said the doctor, "that you two are in competition."

"Really?" said Ulanov.

"You're pushing things too hard, Father," said Marais. "Anyway, why should you be interested in that sort of thing?"

Dr. Marais ignored both questions and addressed himself to the ladies. "My son has been talking all week about some vague assignment. I suspect that he and his colleague are up for the same job, whatever it is, and that this is part of the reason why they can't speak. It makes sense, does it not? Here we have two fellows who study together for three years and yet pretend, sitting in the same room, that they don't know each other. Then, when they do meet, it's apparent they're just going through the motions of friendship. Now what can that mean? I can't be sure, of course, but I suggest that their orders are only an excuse. They would just as soon not talk anyway. And why not? Perhaps because this blood descendant of mine claims to be a liberal, and he gives me to understand that Father Ulanov is a bad actor of a socialist?"

Ulanov turned immediately to his colleague. "You really are trustworthy, aren't you, Paul?"

"The fact that my son is not in the least surprised by your head wounds, my friend," continued Dr. Marais, "would indicate he knew about them, let's say a week ago. And the fact that you are lying about what happened leads me to surmise that you received your wounds in some sort of fight which you would just as soon keep quiet—and so would my son. Perhaps he was present. I doubt that you would tell him had he not been."

Ulanov burst out laughing. "What an imagination!"

"And you may be a very ardent socialist, young man," the doctor went on, "but not so bright as ardent, I would guess, if you're trying to convert these two."

The ladies turned immediately to Ulanov. A mistake, thought Marais. They should counter the accusation immediately on their own. As it was, they were for all practical purposes admitting the justice of the charge.

Ulanov's eyes never left Dr. Marais's face, nor did he move to satisfy the ladies' wordless request for help. "What kind of person," he asked, "what guest by sufferance would take it upon himself to make that sort of remark about things that are none of his business? A boor and a drunk—I apologize to you, Paul, for having to say that. And, sir, my dear friends here must tolerate your rudeness in return for their kindness." Ulanov nodded to the countess and Lady Bowe, who were only too relieved to exchange head bows with him.

Marais had to admire Ulanov's ability to stand his ground in the face of an attack so surprising and shrewd. And yet, how much more intelligent it would have been to retreat from this room! Could he not see that the doctor's attack was fueled by some uncanny sense of dislike or distrust? The older man had picked up half-invisible threads of suspicion and woven them

[97]

together with such swiftness that his son was stunned. Yet Ulanov, who had the most to lose, continued to sit through the contest as though he could wear the old man out and triumph.

This peculiar confidence of Ulanov's no longer awed Marais. Such a performance simply uncovered the secret of his strength these past three years: an unquestioned faith in his own powers of understanding. It was impressive but not, in the final analysis, intelligent; and Marais felt surer than ever that no matter how much the world of action belonged to people like Ulanov and not to himself, the premises were savagely wrong.

Marais's father stood up, laughing. His face, however, was a heavy red, and any geniality in it was pierced by bright hating eyes that needled not only Ulanov but the women and, finally, his son. His standing posture seemed calculated to emphasize his role as solitary judge over the others, all of whom sat as if awaiting sentence.

As the doctor's laughter subsided, he leaned over the table and fixed every one of them with those eyes. "May your God have pity on you fools," he said. "You *are* fools, do you understand? A man like me, having to sit here listening to you all as if you had knowledge and power! A man like you"—he pointed to his son—"instructing me on nations and states of affairs, you who never had to earn your bread—what do you know of the world? What have you had to do with materials, yes, *matter,* my friend, do you have any idea how tough the real stuff of this planet is? In medicine you pull a human through, you pull a life out by conforming to the laws and the way things operate and if a patient dies, why everything goes with him, his brain, his love, his talk. So before you start, you've got to get materials straight. But you people spin out your webs of wishes and prayers and dreams ... It's a waste, you're talking to yourselves, and you think that kind of head magic will change this earth—you've *got* to be lunatics! If a body can't be saved by that kind of nonsense, then how can a soul? Presuming that it even exists?

"Now you, young fellow"—the doctor turned to Ulanov—"are supposed to have all the answers and yet there are four or five important things about you that even a nonprofessional detective like myself can discern. I figured you to have been in a brawl, I learned with no trouble that you are a socialist and deduced that you hated liberals, such as my son used to be. I'm sure that you're converting these ladies and using their money for some stupid socialist cause and that their husbands probably don't know that they're here and neither, most likely, do your superiors. It's a master game you're playing, son, all alone in your mind, and if, for a fraction of a second, a fraction of your ignorance about how the world operates could be displayed before you, you would fall into a coma.

"Oh, yes, it's true. If a drunken boor, as you say, can pick these things up in half an hour, how smart can you really be? And *you* are going to reckon with the powers of this earth? Well, I've had a share of respect for the Vatican in my time, but if they are thinking of selecting either of you two Jesuits for a mission of any importance whatsoever, they can't deserve respect. It's unbelievable. The two of you, whatever you touch, I warn you, whatever you two put your hands to is bound to end in folly or . . . tragedy! That's how it ends. As when a knife slips in the hands of a senile surgeon. Death, not just foolishness.

"And you, ladies, you've been cultivated by this socialist because you *have* these jewels that you display. If you didn't have them, you would be out there somewhere, the object of a millennium once upon a time but not here, not the object of this man's personal attention in this lounge, in this life—believe me! And where did you obtain these marks of distinction that entitled you to such attention? From your husbands, who are no doubt despised."

He stood up and reached for his coat. "I'm wasting my breath on you people! Who is there to see and hear sanity in this place? To whom can I appeal? Is there some kind of God's eye that records the truth, or are you to be the sole judges of what you don't know? And what happens if *my* judgments turn out to be true? Will you remember?

"Goodbye, son. You have joined these people, and you have gotten worse with that sickness you call spiritual. I leave you to them—and it."

Marais, standing up to stop the old man as he turned, grasped his coat. "You can't leave, not like this."

The hand was thrown off. "I am right."

"You overshot the mark!"

"I am right."

"You are partly right."

"How will you ever know that?"

The father departed like a stranger, without looking backward.

6

Four days after the incident in the Excelsior Hotel cocktail lounge, a limousine bearing the license plates of his Holiness Pope Pius XI arrived at the residence of Father Alexander Ulanov, S.J. Stopping before the door of the college promptly at eight o'clock in the evening, it lingered there less than a minute. Its guest had obviously been prepared for this rendezvous; he came down the steps very rapidly and was settled in the rear seat before anyone in the neighborhood could really take heed of the car's presence. The limousine sped with its passenger toward the Vatican palace.

Twenty minutes later the Jesuit entered the papal apartment and was escorted into the large living room, where he faced a group of four gathered about Cardinal Pacelli.

Cardinal Bataille, the Vatican's expert on Eastern affairs, stood slightly apart from the others. His patriarchal beard contrasted severely with his ancient gold and silver brocaded vestments. Cardinal Maglione, the nuncio in Paris, wearing the more sober ecclesiastical robes of the Latin rite, stood closest to Cardinal Bataille. To the left of Cardinal Pacelli stood the father general of the Jesuits, Father Vladimir Ledochowski. His plain black habit at once signified great humility and enormous influence. He, the "Black Pope," the commander of the most illustrious religious order in the church, required no outward marks of distinction.

Archbishop Francisi hardly needed to study each of these gentlemen to conclude that he was the least significant member of the quartet. His real interest lay in their reactions to Ulanov. Surprised at the Jesuit's bow to him, he had given in exchange a graceful nod of recognition.

For some time no one spoke. Pacelli, who had not looked up from his desk when Ulanov entered, continued to thumb through a sheaf of papers before him. The others, gathered around him in a semicircle, maintained their silence in homage to the second most powerful man in Catholic Christendom.

Francisi resented having to stand and wait upon the pleasure of any man, even one who would be the next Pope. Pacelli had enemies who would fight the inevitable, of course. Most of them were in the Secretariat of State; old professionals who had brought Francisi in as their protégé. The archbishop wondered whether that might not account for the invitation to join to-night's mysterious assembly. The cardinal could permit him to watch the consummation of a masterful coup, and, in the process, hope to win a convert from the camp of his detractors. Another distinctly unpleasant possibility occurred to the arch-bishop. Pacelli had never forgiven him his previous judgments about Ulanov's character; perhaps the cardinal now intended to humble Francisi with the spectacle of Ulanov's elevation. For all his mystical qualities, the Secretary of State was not above such tactics.

The cardinal finally looked up from his papers to the young man standing before his desk. "Father Ulanov," he said. "You have been selected by his Holiness for a mission."

Ulanov bowed slightly.

"It is the Holy Father's decision. As his servant, I merely submitted the requisite information on the candidates. You are his choice."

"I am not worthy, your Eminence," said Ulanov.

"We none of us are. Ever."

"I will do my best, Eminence."

"You will have to—in order to survive."

"The harder the better, Eminence. Whatever the assignment, I am ready to do God's will."

"Spoken as a true soldier, *o miles Christi.*" The cardinal seemed genuinely delighted. "It is the very severity of this

[102]

assignment that requires someone of your caliber. You bear the mark of one who could walk through the fires of Satan's hell and maintain his faith intact. You are beyond panic, and that, above all, is what this task requires. There cannot be the least doubt that you, praise be to Christ the King, give no evidence of such flaws as undue dependence on others. Your illustrious order should take pride in you."

The Jesuit bowed again with downcast eyes, as did the small birdlike man behind the cardinal, the Black Pope Ledochowski.

Francisi, watching the cardinal's exstasis of gesture and eye as he spoke, came to the disturbing conclusion that Pacelli had almost perfectly identified with his young subject and was actually praising those qualities he believed himself to possess.

"In the three years you have been with us, Father Ulanov," he said, "you have deeply pleased us by your conduct and demeanor. Not all, of course, have been satisfied"—this last phrase seemed directed toward Francisi—"but then, none of us are beyond criticism, especially from smaller souls or those prone to misunderstand. Yes, you have pleased us very much, my son, and thus without reservation his Holiness and I his servant lay the most extraordinary of foreign missions on your shoulders with complete faith that you shall carry it out *ad majorem Dei gloriam.* You may, of course, refuse."

"Never, your Eminence!"

"As I expected." The cardinal gave a nod, smiled, and began to thumb through the papers before him. "Now." He extricated a tiny packet from beneath the pile before him. "As to your mission."

The packet was unfolded slowly from numerous squares until it made a large blank sheet. Then, with a dramatic flourish, Cardinal Pacelli lifted up the top half and threw it to one side, revealing a map extending from Italy all the way to eastern Russia. "There," he said, laying a finger on the nearer regions of Leningrad and Moscow, "is your mission."

Francisi peered down at the orange-colored area, his imagination whirling around the circled letters:

MOSCOW

LENINGRAD

[103]

The others bent over the map with similar intensity, and Francisi wondered if this secret had been withheld also from them until now. It was difficult to tell.

The silence was punctured only by the staccato breathings of the group. Each of them kept his eyes focused on the map with its numerous crosses indicating roads and rail junctures. The associations conjured up by that dark and vast land held the feelings of them all as if in a vise. In every church in the world, prayers were daily offered for the conversion of Russia.

One by one, the members of the assembly lifted their eyes to the Jesuit, who did not look at them but kept his gaze fastened on the map from a distance.

"It is, of course, a very risky business," said the patriarchal Cardinal Bataille, to whom by virtue of his position really belonged the first right of comment.

Cardinal Maglione bent again to puzzle over the paper scene, monopolizing most of the space on Cardinal Pacelli's desk. A number of times his ring hand crossed his mouth and then fell. Those shrewd aged eyes, so experienced in diplomatic affairs, gave no hint of the questions that must occur to one so familiar with plans and disappointments. "Good luck," he murmured in Ulanov's direction. The group waited for a few more words, but that was the extent of Maglione's statement.

Father General Ledochowski bowed to Francisi. "And what do you think, Excellency? You are more knowledgeable than I about such magnificent undertakings."

"I doubt that, Reverend Father." Francisi turned to the Secretary, still not sure that he was the only person deprived of the facts. "Perhaps, *eminenza,* you should explain the exact nature of your plan."

"Yes, yes, of course," said Pacelli. "But I wished you to savor in these first few moments the very body, as it were, of our spiritual hopes. There is Russia itself . . ." The prelate laid the long smooth fingers of both hands, palms down, across the Western Soviet territory. He seemed, Francisi thought, nearly entranced; there seemed to pour from him silent raptures of prayer as he contemplated that divine moment when Christendom and Russia would again be joined. Francisi could not help feeling that in comparison to these great-souled aspirations, the reservations of himself or any others must inevitably appear rather mean.

"And you, my young father," said Pacelli, "do your feelings change now that you know the nature of your mission?"

The Jesuit stared directly into the eyes of the Secretary of State. "Changed? For this I could never have dared to wish. A dream . . . for this was I born."

Francisi was astonished at the eagerness that transformed Ulanov's noncommittal features. Surely the action of some force beyond and yet within had seized Ulanov.

"We each of us owe to Father Ulanov the witness of our esteem," Cardinal Pacelli said finally. "My own testimony is only too evident . . . dearest brother in Christ."

Each of the others immediately delivered a brief eulogy of the Jesuit, who—creditably, in Francisi's opinion—betrayed signs of increasing discomfort with each effusion. Francisi himself finished off the tributes by noting simply that Ulanov had certain propensities that were unique.

Pacelli then addressed himself to Ulanov. "I know how great must be your anticipation over the details of your destiny."

"I am ready to know only when and what your Eminence thinks appropriate," the Jesuit answered.

Francisi gave high marks to Ulanov for his shrewdness in limiting his response to the brief and formal. There was no need now for him to do anything but let himself be carried along. And, his modesty *was* convincing. Still, Ulanov was unlikely to be contained for long. He would doubtless wait his chance, and, when Pacelli pushed him, reveal himself . . . Francisi vowed he would climb the Santa Scala on his knees in his robes if he was *that* wrong.

The cardinal's expression changed rapidly to a professional mien. "As you know, Father Ulanov, there were untold numbers of Catholics in Russia before the Bolsheviks seized power in 1917. Many, if not most, are now dead or lost to us. Yet there are many thousands who at incredible risk to their own lives practice their faith each day. Their loyalty must be rewarded. They must have priests and bishops. We intend to deliver them from that need."

The cardinal's announcement, stunning in its breadth, touched Francisi deeply. The others, to judge from their expressions, were reacting similarly. The idea was too compelling to resist.

"They are calling to us," said Pacelli, his hands outstretched to the group. "Their plight has arrived at this extremity. Almost all of the priests who remained in hiding after the original persecutions have been destroyed. There is no bishop left in these centers to succor the faithful with the sacraments of confirmation and ordination."

"And whom shall you ordain?" asked Cardinal Maglione. "If there are no priests, then there are no seminarians. If there are no seminarians, you will be forced—even if you sent in a bishop—to ordain unqualified people. Is this what we want, to raise up a crop of ignorant men to dispense the sacraments and interpret the theology of the church? Despite their good intentions, this uneducated clergy could create a caricature of Catholicism."

After Maglione had finished, the Secretary of State waited for a moment before answering. A certain sign of confidence, Francisi decided. The question was left to resonate about the room as though it were inordinately profound—allowing, surely, a simple objection to develop into a giant balloon before pricking it. The effect, of course, would be to substitute that one uneasiness for any others that might be vaguely circulating in the mind of the assemblage.

The cardinal bowed at last to Maglione. "Very good, my dear friend! Your point is a worthy token of the seriousness you give all the affairs of his Holiness. But we have information that you could not have been aware of. It is so secret that only his Holiness, Cardinal Bataille, and myself are aware of it. The fact is that seminarians *have been trained*—in an unorthodox fashion, I grant, but nevertheless trained.

"I said that the Bolsheviks have immobilized all our bishops and nearly all of our priests. Still, a number remain active, privately instructing young men with a calling. It is a dangerous occupation, given the nature of the Bolshevik state. Yet these clerics have performed heroically over the last fifteen years, and their most recent communication informs us that many young men are in their opinion prepared to receive holy orders.

"I am sorry that this information could not have been divulged earlier. His Holiness decided otherwise until now. But it is happy news, is it not? The happiest! To imagine that in the pits of Satan's arena, so many Daniels still survive and grow and wait. Praise be to Christ!"

"Praise be to Christ!" the group murmured in response.

"Our informants in Russia tell us that there may be many more than these. We are not certain on this matter because many of the old families prefer to educate their children in the privacy of their home rather than risk exposure among the groups of students who meet in secret with a priest. Thus, we cannot determine how many of these faithful are still intact.

"It is for this reason, my dear brothers in Christ, that we are sending Father Alexander Ulanov to Russia, where the parched earth cries most loudly for that water of life which we entrust into his care.

"His Holiness and I his servant have every confidence that Father Ulanov is able to carry out this most dangerous and delicate of missions."

"But to do what you ask he must be . . . a bishop!" said Cardinal Maglione.

"Right!" said Pacelli, triumphant. "With the consent of his superior, Reverend Father General Ledochowski, and the rest of this assemblage, our Holy Father, who is even at this very moment waiting in his private chapel, will shortly consecrate Father Ulanov a bishop of the Holy Roman Catholic church. Our beloved servant shall then be empowered to ordain priests and also, in extraordinary cases, to consecrate one or more of these new priests as bishops. Russia must be self-sufficient in the near future—until the monster regime of the Bolsheviks be overthrown, as surely it must!"

"My permission I give with all my heart," said Father Ledochowski. It occurred to Francisi that Ledochowski, as a descendant of Polish royalty, had no doubt dreamed of the conversion of

Russia to Catholicism, which would at once safeguard Catholic Poland as a nation and create a proud Slavonic Catholicism capable of standing against the Eastern hordes.

"We are ever grateful," said Pacelli, "for your spontaneous charity, Reverend Father General, which responds with all it has to the needs of the Holy See."

Cardinal Bataille now addressed the Jesuit. "My dear son," he said, "do you have a clear idea of how different Soviet Russia is from Europe?"

"I believe so, your Eminence."

"Father Ulanov," said Pacelli, "has been a diligent student of Russian affairs since his arrival in Rome three years ago. His command of the varied dialects is superb. The knowledge of the culture, acquired at the Russicum here, in addition to his personal background—"

"To be sure, your Eminence," said Bataille. "*I* have no doubts on these particular points." He fingered the gold lacing on his vestments. "I merely wish to discuss with our young missionary some details that might have been overlooked in the classroom."

"We do not have a great deal of time," said Pacelli. "But we are grateful for any information our Master of Eastern Affairs can give us."

Bataille walked slowly around the side of the desk to the Jesuit. "I do not mean to be troublesome, Father Ulanov," he said. "Your desire to be of such assistance to the church is admirable, but in the heat of such desire one can easily blind oneself to the difficulties involved in such an exploit. It falls to me to be the devil's advocate and point out some things you can't possibly understand without experiencing them. If you were to say that you already understood what I will tell you, I would have to vote against your selection, for you would have shown yourself too overconfident to succeed in this mission."

"Anything you can teach me, Eminence, I will remember and use," answered Ulanov.

Bataille nodded, accepting the invitation. "Russia, my son," he began, "is a police state that beggars any notion you might have here in Rome. There is spying on every level and in every group. Children report on parents, colleagues on colleagues.

Every aspect of industry is organized so that workers can check on each other. The most innocent remark will be quoted to an authority and the victim executed or sentenced to a lifetime in Siberia, to their slave camps, to the coal mines, to the forests, where few stay alive for long.

"Nothing I am saying to you is meant to be melodramatic. It is the sheer truth of the situation, and I am duty-bound before God to warn you of the dangers awaiting you and any of those with whom you communicate. I am further compelled in virtue of my office to inform you that others have gone in before you and none has returned. Some have died the most hideous deaths at the hands of a secret service which knows neither mercy nor justice.

"It will not help that you are not going in as the agent of a nationalist power, or for some capitalist intrigue. Despite your spiritual purposes, they will treat you as the most villainous of saboteurs if they catch you. The more you resist such an identification, the more shall they torture you for it!"

Bataille had brought the room to a hush thick with fear, the matter-of-fact tone of voice rendering his words all the more effective. Francisi waited for some shift in ground that might relieve the unmitigated darkness of his description.

"I am reviewing these facts of life, Father Ulanov, not to break your spirit before you have even begun—no, not so. I am sure they sound appalling, as indeed they are, but you must know where you are bound and that the odds of your surviving are poor. You are, for all practical purposes, being called to martyrdom."

Cardinal Pacelli shuddered at the mention of this sanctified phrase of death, as though it were far too cruel to use such language in the present context.

Bataille went right on. "I say this advisedly, my son. Martyrdom? That is the only word for it! The chances are very slim that you shall ever come back to us. It is imperative that you understand this, for otherwise I and the others in this room are guilty of the most mortal of deceptions."

Bataille's candor so gripped the others that not even Cardinal Pacelli could take advantage of the caesura of silence that ensued.

Francisi, considering some of the facts Bataille had revealed, was finding himself increasingly astonished at the Vatican's recent attempts to deal with Russia. He had never heard so much as a rumor. In Rome, such successful concealment was unusual to say the least. He was even more struck by the chances that Pacelli and Ledochowski were willing to take in order to send a man in to Russia. He debated personally the morality of dispatching a representative under such apparently suicidal conditions. And if Cardinal Bataille, despite his professional love affair with the East, shuddered at the usual consequences of this kind of adventure, should not the group assert its prerogatives and negate the whole exploit?

Gazing around him, Francisi realized that this hope had the strength of a reed. None of those gathered in the room were really here to judge. While their countenances betrayed some anxiety as to Ulanov's fate, that hardly signaled rebellion. The Jesuit himself had never changed his expression once during Pacelli's entire soliloquy.

Francisi could not resist imagining an address to the young American condemned so soon to die: You worked so hard, my dear Ulanov, to look like the right man for the assignment. I do not believe you ever knew what you were preparing yourself for. God help you, I feel no malice toward you now, for if you take on yourself this sacrificial role that is your business! It is, after all, only the culmination of what you were unwittingly seeking all these years. You willed to play roulette, now your number has come up and it is red as well as Russian and it would not at all become you at this juncture, dear Ulanov, to back off from paying to the house the price of having played and lost. Therefore, I shall not object to your selection tonight, I shall pray for you and I shall make your safety an enduring intention in my masses—and hope that the will of God be not cruel.

Cardinal Bataille returned to his spot alongside the Jesuit. "I will finish what I have to say, Father Ulanov, very quickly. There is no question of my opposing the Cardinal Secretary on any question of callousness in sending you forth. I am simply emphasizing the need for the utmost caution in your dealings with others. You must trust *no one* to whom you are not recommended, and even then you must insist on the most extreme precautions. Only your hosts should know the working identity with which Cardinal Pacelli will supply you. None of the people with whom you speak should know your true residence. You must meet them at suddenly arranged rendezvous and then as quickly depart. A list of the kind of questions that you will ask potential priests has been devised so that your interviews may be brief and to the point. A short form of the ordination rite has been prepared and approved by our Holy Father—the entire ceremony can be managed while you are taking a Sunday stroll with your companion. There are many other strategies that have been devised for your safety.

"One last piece of advice! You must not allow yourself to wax confident because you have succeeded for a few weeks or even months in escaping notice. Your not being apprehended would not necessarily mean that you were not under surveillance by Soviet agents. They may be watching you at the very moment you feel most secure, and even if they aren't, the slightest miscue could mean detection. Some priests we know were doing good work until they relaxed their sense of alertness and then—well, they are dead now. Horribly!"

"Yes, yes, Cardinal Bataille," said Pacelli. "We are impressed by the practicality of your concerns for Father Ulanov. I am sure he also is grateful for your very direct advice."

"I shall remember your instructions to the letter," promised Ulanov.

Cardinal Bataille now stared at the floor. He had obviously been a member all along of the innermost circle. Bataille, Pacelli, Ledochowski, and Pope Pius XI had, then, constituted the quorum of legislators in this scheme. Yet Francisi surmised that something less than unanimity prevailed in the group. Certain fears had haunted their meetings, yes, and so Bataille had been delegated to give those fears public expression. But Bataille had thrown himself into the task with unfortunate honesty. He had frightened Pacelli, had run the risk of discouraging the young victim. If the evidence against success was as bad as he confessed, then precautions seemed all but irrelevant.

The Secretary of State now turned to confront the prelates,

his face shining. "My colleague has given you and Father Ulanov the very bleakest side of your calling. And it was well that you heard him first, for there is more than enough light on the other side to set against these darknesses. You will enter Russia, never fear, with the finest expertise at the Vatican's disposal—and with the advantage of past experience. We have not been remiss, you will see, in providing the most careful measures to ensure your safety."

The cardinal began again to thumb through the materials on his desk. "Here we are. You all understand that this is only the minutest portion of a large quantity of materials that Father Ulanov must digest over the next three weeks. He will use a passport in the name of one Dmitri Sherpovich, a telephone repairman. This occupation will enable him to escape the surveillance common in other sectors of Soviet industry. For the most part he will work alone." Cardinal Pacelli paused briefly, and a murmur of approval passed through the group. Even Francisi let out a small breath of relief.

"Do you know anything about repairing phones?" Cardinal Maglione asked the Jesuit.

Before Ulanov could answer, Pacelli intervened with a jocularity that put the company at ease. "And you did not know Paris before we sent *you* there, Nuncio. You learned."

"But I could afford to make a mistake," Maglione said good-humoredly.

"Of course, of course," the Secretary moved his outspread palms up and down, deflecting the point. "He shall be taught here in Rome within the next few weeks. It is not a difficult skill for an intelligent man to learn. There are duplicate facilities available to us."

"When does Father Ulanov leave?" asked Father General Ledochowski.

"In one month."

"And his contacts in the Soviet Union?"

"Arranged in such a way that when he has finished with one group, he will be supplied the names of the second, and so on."

"How long will he be gone?"

"That is uncertain."

"A month? A year?"

"Four or five months. If all goes well, longer. Perhaps from there into the Ukraine."

"Does that not indicate other purposes, *eminenza?*"

"Yes!" Cardinal Pacelli smiled at Ledochowski, who, Francisi now deduced, must have been only half an insider.

Pacelli motioned to Bataille. "Perhaps our expert in Eastern affairs can help us here."

"The Vatican," said Bataille, "maintains an interest in conversion possibilities among the Russian Orthodox. That church has let its people down severely during the last fifteen years. The circumstances, of course, are understandable. Still, the Roman Catholic church has not been tarred, as it were, with the same brush. We will ask Father Ulanov to survey the situation and give us his appraisal of what we can hope for there. We would also like to receive his opinions as to the effects on the Russian population of the spiritual starvation they have suffered. As you know, Stalin's religious purges have worsened. We are also interested in the sturdiness of the Soviet government and what kind of popular loyalty they can count on."

The Jesuit general seemed to contain his enthusiasm at Bataille's words only with the greatest difficulty. The excitement vibrated through his tiny ascetic frame—and was no less noticeable in Cardinal Pacelli. Despite their differences, the Secretary, Bataille, and Ledochowski shared the grand vision of a converted Russia.

Francisi and Maglione looked at each other, two men of Europe who distrusted the East.

"And have you established instruments to keep in constant contact with Father Ulanov?" asked Maglione.

The Secretary of State smiled. "That is my Maglione. He keeps us on the ground, keeps the windows locked—lest we fly away." Bataille and Ledochowski broke into a laugh.

"We have a plan that should work simply because it is so simple," Pacelli continued. "In each of the larger groups with whom Father Ulanov will meet there is one absolutely trustworthy person who, once a week, will meet the train that goes eastward from Moscow toward Poland and deliver to a trusted conductor all messages as to the progress of the mission. The trainman will give this news to a woman who sweeps out the station at the last stop, and a member of her family who lives near the Polish border will pass it to a courier who crosses the border at a certain unguarded juncture every week. From there it will be forwarded to us in Rome, quite rapidly.

"The opposite procedure goes into effect when for any reason we have messages to deliver to Father Ulanov. In this fashion we shall remain in constant communication with each other. It is difficult to conceive of any possible disruption in this chain of information."

"All very well," said Cardinal Bataille, "but I should like to add that this network hardly constitutes an underground. Our small chain is limited to three or four links. It is very fragile and perhaps that is why it is still intact." He pointed to Ulanov. "I want to disabuse you," he said, "of any misapprehension that a real underground can survive in Russia. From our every item of information it is clear that no antigovernment ring can last long in those spy-infested regions. The remaining Catholics exist only because they keep to very limited expectations. Their piety does not go much further than saying their prayers and performing discreet devotions. We prohibit you, therefore, from any extension of those activities to which you have been strictly assigned."

"Fear not," said Cardinal Pacelli, placing a hand on the Jesuit's shoulder. "The day is not far off when these restrictive fetters shall be cast off."

Francisi found this remark highly disturbing. Did Pacelli remember nothing of what Francisi had told him about Ulanov three years before?

"And you, Francisi," Pacelli said, disturbing the other's reflections, "you have hardly uttered a word since you entered his Holiness's chambers. We had expected surely the benefits of your much admired skills and wisdom to aid us in this most crucial and delicate task. Do come forward with whatever you wish to say. Be not too cautious before the prestige of your brothers in Christ. Here tonight we are all equals except for our Holy Father, who, for that reason, has chosen not to join us. He waits in the chapel for the results of this conference."

Francisi dismissed the condescension and said, simply, *"Eminenza,* Father Ulanov has not yet said that he would accept the bishopric. No one has asked him."

Francisi watched and enjoyed the effect of this remark. Pacelli, even, was flustered; Ulanov and Francisi alone kept their composure, knowing with how much more seriousness the comment was being received than it deserved. The group had simply failed to make sure of the obvious. Francisi hoped that this embarrassment might dissuade Pacelli from testing his mettle the rest of the evening.

And, yes, the Secretary seemed to be fumbling for some way to inaugurate an honored procedure that would sound neither too thin nor too sudden; that would maintain the dignity of the church as well as impress the prospective shepherd.

In the midst of Pacelli's discomfort, Ulanov stepped in with a gesture that Francisi adjudged to be pure genius. "Your Eminence," he said, falling to his knees, "I am not worthy of the honor you would bestow on me. Nothing in myself merits this gift instituted by Christ himself. Were it not for the needs of her flock who wander in the desolate places by night, there is no reason why such a one as Alexander Ulanov, priest of the church, should not remain content—no, happy, happier than he deserves—with the humblest lot in the clerical ministry.

"It is only the misery of the church's faithful that could lift him so far above his proper place. I beg, not in my own name, but for that people to whom I am bound by physical and spiritual kinship, that the will of God be done as is becoming in the eyes of his most proximate representative on earth, our Holy Father, Pope Pius XI, and his Secretary, Eugenio Cardinal Pacelli."

From the nadir of confusion, the group felt itself suddenly lifted as though on a cloud. The situation had not only been saved, its members had been edified. The decision was now appropriately reserved to the prelates.

Cardinal Pacelli recited from memory a brief history of the bishop's role in Christianity, then addressed a long list of questions to the candidate, culminating in a final one to the group: "Are any of you here aware of the existence of sinful or offensive characteristics on the part of Alexander Ulanov? No? Very well, then . . ."

There followed a litany of those ideal characteristics that the office demanded of the candidate. "Are those present aware of any impediment to progress in these virtues on the part of Alexander Ulanov?"

No one ventured to speak during the allotted thirty seconds.

"Is there a single item of significance that any member of this committee wishes to add? If he believes such information to be of consequence, now is the appropriate occasion to submit it. Otherwise he is derelict or hereafter bound to silence."

Finally the cardinal relaxed, and, glancing at his desk clock, signaled the Jesuit to stand. He next distributed five small pieces of paper to the group, keeping one for himself and excluding Ulanov. "You will write *certe* or *non* to the proceedings of this evening on your white slip. You are not to sign your name. Your act of voting does not bind his Holiness to your collective decision. It is simply a procedure by virtue of your positions as members of an advisory body. That is all."

With that, they separated, each of them looking for some hard surface to bear down upon. Francisi found an adjacent end table. With no hesitation whatsoever he scrawled *non* in large black letters across the slip and folded the paper in half.

Pacelli collected the pieces, shifted them in his palms, then opened them quickly. As chance would have it, the first three votes he declared were *"certe," "certe," "certe,"* and then the high reedlike voice cracked. "This ballot has nothing on it," he said, holding the virgin paper forward for all to see.

"That too is an option," said Cardinal Maglione.

A brief disbelieving silence succeeded this rebuff. The Secretary, not daring to ask Maglione what "nothing" meant, simply bent his head to ascertain the whereabouts of the remaining slip. Finding it, he opened it quickly, thinking perhaps to rescue himself from the previous violation of his sensibilities. *"Non,"* he whispered.

Maglione beamed a smile at Francisi. "In that case," he said, turning to Pacelli, "I can't allow my friend to stand alone. I must show a bit more courage, no?" He walked to the Pope's desk, pen in hand, and scrawled a highly visible *non* across the blank slip he had submitted a moment before.

Cardinal Pacelli and Father General Ledochowski stared incredulously at this incomprehensible breach of manners. Had Cardinal Maglione not possessed the purple himself, Francisi knew, his conduct would prove ruinous to his career.

Pacelli exchanged a glance with Ledochowski and then began to turn the ballots over and over in his hand. His glance at Francisi was unfathomable.

The archbishop knew that he was supposed to have been intimidated and even convinced tonight. The cardinal, he immediately concluded, had such faith in the efficacy of rhetoric that the present shock he suffered must be due to his failure to comprehend the limits of this ancient art. Despite his control of the evening's performance, he was now confronted with the spectacle of two professionals in open opposition to the plan.

And yet, watching Pacelli's light-struck face, Francisi saw that his superior had escaped the bonds of these immediate events. Everyone else, his expression conveyed, could cease to exist without his necessarily noticing.

Francisi was right.

"The vote of the ad hoc council," Pacelli said somewhat dreamily, "is three to two. The council therefore recommends itself as being in favor of the plan adopted by his Holiness and myself. That outcome is excellent. Our Holy Father, I am sure, is interested only in the final decision, which, of course, is favorable."

He beckoned to the Secretary of Eastern Affairs. "Cardinal Bataille, you may proceed to the chapel, where our Holy Father awaits us. His Holiness is semivested. Inform him of the result, only the result, of our discussions, and of Father Ulanov's willingness to offer himself for this mission. Tell him that we accept this candidate and commend him to the papal consideration for consecration to the bishopric of the One Holy Roman Catholic Church.

"When you have delivered this information, Eminence, you will stay to assist his Holiness in dressing—unless, of course, it is his decision to do otherwise than to raise Father Ulanov to the episcopal order. If you do not return to apprise us of such a change, we shall join our Holy Father and yourself in the consecration of this most worthy priest within the next few minutes."

Cardinal Bataille bowed to Pacelli and departed.

His superior lit the candle at the top of Pope Pius's desk and let the flame ravel the small pieces of white voting paper into ever darker and wispier filigrees. The charred scraps fell into an ancient iron pan holding up the candle; a small act from tenebrae, Francisi thought, quietly closing the gates of the past and opening the future space.

7

Each guest in the papal apartment wrapped himself in his own reflections. Francisi, who had already accepted the inevitable, relaxed and looked about the room. The chances were very good that he would never again be invited to these rooms—rather intimate, as Francisi saw them. The Pontiff moved professionally amid marble most of his waking hours, yet his sitting room showed that he remained at heart an old Milanese homebody. Stretched quilts covered the backs of the chairs, and the furnishings were not meant to compete with the aristocracy or even the upper-class bourgeoisie.

In one corner of the room, Francisi spied testimonials of those devotions for which Pope Pius XI was famous in the Vatican. Thirty or forty cards representing as many lay organizations covered a small busy table. Jesus with heart outstretched to reveal the symbol for the Sacred League of Reparation. The Blessed Mother in her sky-blue mantle, representing the Confraternity for the Conversion of Sinners. The Third Order of St. Francis and St. Dominic, Sons of the Madonnina Maria Bambina of the Duomo of Milan, the St. Charles Borromeo Society . . . Francisi knew that the Pontiff took quite seriously his membership in these three score societies and daily or weekly performed the duties required by each.

I am not now this pious, and would be less so if I were Pope, Francisi thought, struck by the enormous consumption of time this panoply of enrollments represented.

He stepped to a large window and gazed out upon St. Peter's Square. This empty plaza had symbolized, throughout Francisi's life, the center of . . . what? For him the Bernini columns were spokes, pointing to the farthermost ends of the earth. Upon those invisible ties the graces of Christ and the pontificate flowed ever outward as missionaries in all lands, celibate and poor, labored to convey a message of no self-interest but only salvation. And yet, viewing the square from the papal apartment, in this most important reflective moment of his life, Francisi found himself critical of the uses to which the Pope and his Secretary of State were putting their vast spiritual prestige.

Suddenly Pacelli snapped his fingers; in an instant the group was following him through the hallway and into a tiny chapel. Pope Pius XI, Cardinal Bataille at his side, stood looking out at them from the center of a platform raised slightly before the altar.

Cardinal Pacelli signaled Father General Ledochowski to prepare the candidate for the ceremony; Francisi and Cardinal Maglione stood apart from the Pope while Ulanov was quickly dressed in a white linen alb and cincture. The Jesuit then folded his hands in prayer and walked a few steps to the middle of the sanctuary, escorted on either side by Bataille and Ledochowski.

As Cardinal Pacelli assisted the Pope in the mass, it struck Francisi that Ulanov should be consecrated in the Byzantine rite, since this was the form of the Catholic mass used by Russians and the one in which the Jesuit himself celebrated every morning. Francisi now surrendered such trivial considerations in order to concentrate on the extraordinary sight of the Pope's consecrating a young priest by candlelight in his own chapel. Despite the spectator's role to which he and Maglione had been relegated, Francisi felt himself to be party to a historic transaction, the grander even as it was the more intimately conceived. Unlike secularists of his standing, Francisi knew that he could never leave memoirs for the world's perusal in his declining years. He had only the moment.

In an attempt to store up the significant, however, most of the visual aspects of the ceremony were lost to Francisi. His gaze shifted from the Pope to the young man he had brought to Rome only three years before. It still astonished him that this trouble-some person was the subject of the most extraordinary considera-tion by the Pontiff of Rome. Even as Ulanov lay before the foot of the altar—his arms folded beneath his head in token of humility, waited upon there by three cardinals of the church, an archbishop, and his order's father general—Francisi could not believe the triumph. To be sure, Ulanov would die soon enough; even now the ceremony seemed a ritual for a sacred lamb.

With the thought, Francisi shuddered. His eyes actually saw the alb turn into a bloodstained vestment. With no external disturbance whatsoever, he was watching a physical change from what he knew to be *white* into the color *red*. There was no mistaking that color.

Never in his life had Francisi's feelings found expression in that sort of mystical—or, at worst, superstitious—vision. Against magical displays his nature had, in fact, always rebelled; but then that could be taken as authenticating the sight.

Something else haunted him. Was it Ulanov's fate? Or was it a destiny greater than the priest's own, as it seemed to be? Yes, he felt that though the garment of blood was worn by the Jesuit, the blood itself was at some distance from him. Francisi probed his feelings more delicately: the blood belonged *on* Ulanov but was not, necessarily, his own?

Francisi, reaching for a distraction, forced himself to study the figure of his own sovereign, Pope Pius XI, the 261st Pontiff of the Roman Catholic church since Peter. Here was a man he truly liked. Despite the ever-present protocol around any Pontiff, Francisi knew this one to be a shrewd Milanese who could not abide pomposity. Achille Ratti before his elevation had been a librarian's librarian, an owlish scholar who on extended weekends and holidays turned into the greatest Italian mountain climber of the early twentieth century. He had conquered Mont Blanc; the Matterhorn, from its most difficult side; and many others. Francisi enjoyed imposing these images of Ratti's two worlds on this old man who looked and acted two decades younger than his nearly eighty years and who celebrated the mass as unselfcon-sciously as if he were walking alone in the snows.

Surely it was chance that had picked Ratti out of the Vatican

Archives and sent him as Benedict's visitor to Poland and later to Milan as archbishop, and, finally, on the fourteenth ballot on February 6, 1922, to the Chair of Peter.

Before tonight's revelation of this Russian adventure, Francisi had always thought of Pius XI as a decent, restrained superior. The man had a sense of limits nourished by an exacting subservience to ordering the truth of history. Accompanying his natural fearlessness was an inexhaustible reserve of patience. Francisi could not help but bow to those gifts which, interesting enough in their own right, were still more unworkable in such an office.

The Pope turned now from the bread and wine he had just consecrated to look down for a long moment upon the prostrate figure of the bishop-elect—as though, by sheer force of prayer, he could endow him with those graces needed for the mission.

In the midnight gloom of the tiny chapel, each of the standing figures, reduced to outlines by the high candles' wavering flames, seemed to be partaking of the same meditation, and with a sadness quite different from any earlier mood. The preparatory processes of judgment and decision were finished; the drama, cruel or holy, was about to begin.

Finally the Pope addressed himself to the body at his feet. "We are not adventurers, my son," he said. "We do not send you forth to Russia lightly. This is no game between states. You are not a spy, and we seek no worldly advantages from your mission. Russia with her intolerable exclusion of religious rights has forced us to these means of penetrating her wall and reaching our beloved brothers and sisters in Christ Jesus. They have a right to receive the satisfaction of their spiritual needs, and we must go to them, or we are derelict.

"And so we send you in our place to baptize, ordain, and consecrate. You are not the first nor the second to be sent, and it is your moral right to know this. The Cardinal Secretary has already given you this information and still you are willing to go. Please signify this choice, my son, by moving your hands together."

Without looking up from his prone position, the Jesuit moved his outstretched arms together until the palms clasped.

"Very well," said the Pope. "You are aware that death confronts you within those inhospitable borders. *In manu Dei, nunc vivis.*"

The Pope lifted his eyes to the figures standing before him, awarding each prelate a gaze that took account of his partnership in this act. "This is not the time for rhetoric, brothers in Christ," he said. "I am not very good at it anyway. Therefore, I shall not deliver the kind of exhortation common at the consecration of a bishop. For just a few moments before the elevation of Father Ulanov, we wish to tell you a little of the background of this action."

Pope Pius XI paused while Francisi puzzled over the discordant "I's" and "we's" in the papal self-references.

"Some sixteen years ago," the Pope continued, "when I was a nuncio in Warsaw, I watched with horror as the Soviets began the most cruel persecution against Catholics and Orthodox Christians. Bishops and priests were arrested. Archbishop Cieplak of St. Petersburg sentenced in 1923, his Vicar Budkiewicz martyred on that Good Friday. Archbishop Von der Ropp of Mohilew exiled with eighty priests, Bishops Sloskan and Matulis exiled to Siberia, priests in the hundreds sent to the labor death camp of Slovki. Other priests were rounded up and put to work on public projects under conditions so extreme that few have survived. None are free.

"We sent our first papal mission into Russia in 1922—twelve Jesuits and members of the Society of the Divine Word, who brought with them food, clothing, and medicines for hundreds of thousands, provided by the Vatican at a cost of well over one million lire. That mission operated against the greatest hazards until 1926, when the harassment by the Soviets was so complete that we were finished." The Pope paused for a moment. From this small audience he could ask only understanding, but the desperate plea in his voice had made it clear how related were past broken hopes to Ulanov's consecration.

He moved a few paces forward to the top step of the altar. "There have been other actions of the Holy See which you know, no doubt, only too well. In July of 1922 we begged the episcopate of the world for two and one half million dollars to feed the starving poor of Russia. In many addresses during the nineteen-twenties we begged the world to harken to the fate of Russia. And where in all this have been the liberal nations of the planet? Shall they rewrite history someday to their own pleasure, when we are dead, to say that this Pope did not know or care about Russia or persecution?

"Is it not a fact, brothers in Christ, that we are the only institution left confronting the nation-states with the limitations of their powers? Is it not we alone who deny to them the primacy of Mammon and Caesar, and shall they not hate us— liberal, Fascist, and communist state alike—for condemning their aggrandizement?

"I had, it is true, to negotiate with Mussolini, but I negotiated precisely to force the surrender of those religious prerogatives he was asserting. Insofar as he conceded these claims, he gave up his Fascism. That is the point! Of course, we now know that Mussolini has no intention of abiding by these agreements. He has killed priests who have stood up to his hoodlums and warned the populace where they are being taken. The church cannot substitute for a state. We are in no position to depose any leader.

"But with the few fragile weapons in our possession we do fight to prevent the people from being destroyed by their own leaders and to protect the true primacies of salvation and freedom. However inadequate we are to this task, who else is there? Who else can speak for mankind as a whole, for each individual's meaning, beyond a national destiny and economic success? Who else . . . ?" The Pope's voice trailed off, betraying, in that instant, the fatigue of one who was approaching eighty years.

As the leader of Catholic Christendom looked down upon them from the token elevation of one step, he seemed to want to share the burden. Then, he addressed his last words to Father Ulanov. "The hopes of Christ and the people of Russia now rest on you," he said, and, with that transfer of the task, turned back to the chalice and the Eucharist. Cardinal Pacelli and Father Ledochowski gathered around him; Maglione and Francisi lifted the Jesuit from his prone position.

Francisi watched as though dreaming the rapid sequence of acts by which Alexander Ulanov was consecrated a bishop of the church; received the Eucharist from the Pope, and the kiss of peace from all present. Then the mass ended, prolonged neither with last-minute sentimentalities nor with further prayers.

They all knelt as the Pope left the altar to disrobe in a tiny sanctuary. A few minutes later, he emerged with head down, and thus visibly caught in thought or prayer, walked down the small aisle and out the door.

Cardinal Pacelli led Bishop Ulanov to the sanctuary for disrobing. They returned quickly, and as they left the chapel, the Secretary of State signaled to Francisi to follow them. The archbishop was so surprised at the invitation that he hardly moved. When Pacelli repeated the gesture Francisi genuflected, leaving the two cardinals and the Black Pope, all of whom had been so much more a part of the proceeding than he, still kneeling in front of him.

Together the trio walked back to the living room in which they had spent so much of the evening. Pacelli closed the doors behind them and turned to Ulanov. "I will give you my blessing," he said.

"Thank you," said the Jesuit. "Please."

When Pacelli had given his benediction, he signaled to Francisi. The archbishop walked slowly to a position in front of the kneeling Ulanov and made the sign of the Cross. The blessing—*"Gratia Dei supra te veniat et te protegat et numquam in missione et vita tua te relinquat"*(May the grace of God come upon you and protect you and never leave you in this mission in life)—was brief and formal, yet the cardinal appeared to be satisfied.

Bishop Ulanov rose and stood before the familiar desk, obviously no surer than was Francisi as to what to do or say next. Where, Francisi wondered, was the Pope?

Pacelli sat down behind the desk and began to cross out various items on a list. "I believe," he said, smiling up at both of the bishops, "that a great deal has been accomplished this evening."

"And with such dispatch, *eminenza,*" said Francisi. "You must be pleased."

The cardinal's expression remained pleasant. "You are a good man, Francisi, an almost natural admonitor." He held up his hand to prevent the archbishop's demurral. "No, no, you must not apologize. I am not complaining. What sort of holiness would I be striving for if I could not tolerate a difficult critic?" He permitted himself a small laugh.

"I never envisioned myself in such a role," said Francisi.

"Ah, but that is your function, you see. You are valuable to us with your honesty and your resistance to superior plans. It is refreshing to have our own private *advocatus diaboli.*" The cardinal bowed to his inferior, then turned to Ulanov. "The archbishop," he said, "was not always so, shall we say, petrinely hard-grained. Before his chaperoning of you to these shores, I never noticed in him any problem with—"

"Do I understand, *eminenza,* that I am being charged with disobedience?" asked Francisi, knowing perfectly well that he was not.

"No, no, my dear Francisi, you do not comprehend. We were going to say 'routine obedience.' Nowadays your obedience is so much more complex, anything but routine, and for that reason all the more valuable to us. I can count on you for an honest disagreement with any number of policies. Of course, I always hear those objections with care and take them into account. It is your God-given function and of great worth. That is all we meant, there was no hurt intended in our remarks."

Francisi heard the levels of application in the Secretary's little discourse and deeply resented the judgments. He did take some comfort from Pacelli's unintentional communication that he, Francisi, had proved so disturbing that the cardinal could not overlook him. Francisi's presence in the papal apartment, Pacelli's finesse and sarcasm in addressing him—both testified, surely, to some pressure Francisi represented, and to Pacelli's own anxiety about this mission.

Francisi sighed. "I am only a poor archbishop who does his duty as he sees it before God, esteeming him higher than any human personage, *eminenza.* So faithfulness, which you honor in me and which does honor to yourself, belongs to God."

Pacelli waved one hand and smiled at Ulanov. "You see, our

new bishop—you are responsible for such fierce changes of life as our Francisi has undergone."

Ulanov laughed. "But I hold no hard feelings. The archbishop does his duty as I do mine."

A double knock sounded at the door, and a Franciscan entered the room with a decanter of wine and three glasses. He laid the tray down on a nearby table and left. The Secretary rose and poured out the wine, handing two glasses to the bishops and carrying his own to the desk. "This should only take a moment," he said, glancing again at his agenda. "Bishop Ulanov, you must remain for a few weeks in the Vatican." He looked up a little sheepishly. "I am afraid you will actually have to be trained as a telephone repairman. It will take a month's hard work, but we can't have you going into Russia unable to do what your passport claims."

"I like manual labor, your Eminence," said Ulanov. "I think everyone, of whatever position, should have a working skill."

Only the timing of the Jesuit's gratuitous assertion surprised Francisi.

"Manual labor as an occupation is forbidden by canon law to one who is a priest," said Pacelli. "You even need a dispensation, which his Holiness has granted."

"I think everyone should labor," Ulanov insisted. "Especially priests."

"You are now a bishop," Francisi pointed out.

"Bishops, especially, should work part time with their hands as an example of the dignity of labor," said Ulanov. "Christ was a carpenter."

"Monks do labor," Pacelli said smoothly. "If we were not in a world where such a confusion of roles would cause conflicts of interest and scandalize the faithful, why then we might well insist that all should labor daily."

Following Ulanov's reluctant nod, Francisi was amazed to hear the cardinal read from his small paper, "Our close assistant and liaison throughout Bishop Ulanov's stay in Russia will be Archbishop Francisi. The other details we have to mention are minor and can be delayed until tomorrow."

[127]

With that he grinned playfully and extended his hand to the archbishop.

"I can see I have much to learn about diplomacy," said Ulanov.

"It is not an American field," said Pacelli. He lifted his glass and the others followed suit. "God bless you, young Jesuit!"

"Amen," added Francisi, who was now more inclined to mean it. Each of them took a sip from the glass, and the archbishop slowly savored the bouquet. "An exquisite wine," he said.

"We were testing you," said Pacelli, "and the truth is quickly found. You are an unregenerate sensualist, Francisi! As for the wine—a hundred years old and a great vineyard. Perhaps once a year I take a glass to endow some holy occasion."

"A nice taste," said Ulanov.

"For that we should thank *your* friends, certain ladies that you and the archbishop met on shipboard a number of years ago."

The Jesuit and Francisi exchanged glances which only augmented the cardinal's enjoyment.

"I would like to ask a question, your Eminence," said Ulanov.

"Of course."

"What shall I say to them?"

"To whom?"

"To the Russian people. What shall I tell them?"

"What is there to tell? You are there to ordain, baptize, confirm. Sermons, oh, yes, sermons! Well, of course, you know how to give sermons, Christian piety is everywhere the same. But you must mean their situation. They are to bear up under duress, they will be blessed with the graces of the martyrs, for their sufferings are undoubtedly the most meritorious before God. Their torments can bring enormous benefit on the entire Christian world . . . Yes, perhaps it is they who can avert *our* possible tragedies here in Europe. God's plan for them is to act as the Old World's Redeemer—*that* can be the glory of their present crucifixion."

"I did not mean sermons of exhortation, your Eminence. I am familiar with the spirituality of the church."

"Then what *did* you mean?"

Ulanov sighed. "I have not been told some things, your Eminence. In fact, they have never been discussed."

"Very well, very well! Oversights are common enough here . . . so many preparations, something was omitted that you felt important. Ask anything of me, you deserve to be aware of everything involved." The cardinal's manner toward Ulanov was amiable enough—rather like a parent at the end of a long day's dealing with an inquisitive child.

"Thank you, your Eminence. You are very kind. But it's more serious, I believe, than you think."

"Bishop Ulanov, you are ruining our celebration. Preserve at least the decencies of sanity and allow us to sleep in peace tonight. Ask, please, ask whatever!"

"I shall." But Ulanov deliberated a few seconds longer by walking a few paces away from the desk, as though it were he who was the great figure of state about to make a decision of moment upon which the others depended.

He ignored Francisi, who was nearly dizzy with anticipation.

"Yes, I will phrase it quite simply, your Eminence. What shall I say to them about communism?"

"Ah, communism?"

"Well, yes, they will surely ask me—what do I think, what does the church think? They will want an answer."

"They will not ask you that question. They *shall not,* for the very simple reason that they are living under it. They are dying under it! Who knows better what a foul pestilence communism is than these future martyrs? You must have left your senses, Ulanov, to think for even a moment that the vaguest shadow clouds the church's teaching on this subject. They are barbarians, atheists, the cruelest tyrants in history. But" he paused—"I must have misunderstood—Francisi, did I hear him rightly? No, he really meant something quite different, I believe, and I too quickly misconstrued his point."

Francisi chose not to help Pacelli in his first hearing of what his archbishop had tried to communicate three years before.

"I shall answer for myself, your Eminence," said Ulanov. "My question was serious, and we must discuss it calmly. For the issue really is more complex than you may know among those Russians of whom you speak, and to whom I must attend."

Cardinal Pacelli sat down in the Pope's desk chair, quite obviously unwilling or unable to stand. "You see," the Jesuit continued, "the question of how we shall distinguish Christianity from communism is crucial, because the people, having tasted socialism, will want to know the relation between that belief and Christianity. I know that the people love both. But they will ask me if the church is antagonistic to their economic system, and whether the corrupted Russian Orthodox priests were really representative of Christianity, and—"

"You shall tell them," said Pacelli, standing, "that this experiment in Russia is a distortion, merely eighteen years old. That it shall pass as did the other torments of Eurasian history, as did Persia, Carthage, the Visigoths and Huns, the Mongols! You will tell them that it will all pass, every vestige of it, within— ten years. Yes, ten years."

"Every vestige?" asked Ulanov. "Even the socialist state? The economy?"

"Especially such!"

"I can tell them nothing like that, your Eminence. That is not part of my Catholic mission."

Cardinal Pacelli, speechless again, looked toward Francisi.

"You must explain your position more clearly to the cardinal, Alexander," said Francisi, thus compelled to mediate. The Jesuit priest was now bishop, consecrated and assigned. That made a difference.

"What is there for him to explain?" demanded Pacelli.

"You put yourself in this position, *eminenza*," said Francisi, pacing near the desk. "I am only trying to help in a situation created completely against my advice. This young man is hardly a protégé of mine."

"Enough, Francisi."

"Bishop Ulanov," said Francisi, "the Secretary of State has cause for concern. No organization, certainly not this one, can afford a representative going off with his own point of view in such a delicate matter. You should tell us what your intentions are so that some *modus agendi* can be worked out."

Ulanov bowed slightly to Francisi and addressed Pacelli with easy confidence. "Your Eminence, the church is concerned with the brotherhood of man under the one Father. Her values are universal, founded neither in blood like ancient Israel nor in nations. Since our function then is to serve the spirit in man, what we demand are the basic conditions of justice necessary to this mission. Therefore, Russia's economic system can in no way be our concern. I agree with you that other aspects of Soviet society are deplorable, and those we condemn."

He bowed to the Secretary and turned toward Francisi. When neither responded, he continued. "What I have said delimits the technical bounds of our authority. You are prevented from condemning the socialist economic system and you may not command me to condemn it. That judgment is not in the spiritual domain. Actually, any fair comparison between capitalism and socialism would show that the workings of socialism are closer to the ideals of the church than are the capitalist's. Surely there can be no debate on that point."

Again Ulanov delayed a few seconds, and again neither of his superiors answered. Francisi was surprised that Pacelli took no advantage of these opportunities to press a counterattack. The cardinal had unexpectedly sat down again and was studying the Jesuit with a dispassionate stare, his hands folded tightly over his purple cincture.

Ulanov went on. "Since any intelligent man is aware how loyal to their economic system are the people of Russia, I see no reason why I as a Catholic bishop should preach anything other than the end of their inhuman political and religious servitude. Certainly I have no intention of working against their innovations in ridding a society of exploiters, profiteers, and merchants. I will distinguish the economically good from the politically false, but that is all. There must be no base European motives in our going to Russia."

Ulanov ended this defense in a much stronger tone of voice than he had begun. His conviction had, it seemed to Francisi, grown in intensity the longer he had been forced to enunciate it without assistance.

The Secretary still had not spoken, and Francisi decided to

[131]

give him time to gather his reactions. "You really have deceived his Eminence," said the archbishop. "He did not expect this sort of thing from you, his trusted choice for a difficult assignment. Such a declaration of policy from a subordinate is unheard of here. Cardinal Pacelli brought you across the Atlantic and supported you in Rome—selected you over the opposition of many of us—and now you reward him by subverting his plans and telling him indeed how things shall be run. You have disappointed his hopes and confirmed the worst fears of *his* opposition, the very men who condemned *you.*"

Cardinal Pacelli turned his sharp gaze from Francisi to Ulanov.

"I deceived no one," said the Jesuit. "Least of all you, your Eminence!"

"Least of all his Eminence!" said Francisi. "Do you think you can say anything at all and think us foolish enough to believe it because it is cloaked in a show of outrage?"

"Did I deceive you, Archbishop Francisi? On ship I held none of my convictions back from you, nor before that from Father Rector Dillon of Woodstock College. So what is it you upbraid me with? You were free to tell his Eminence what you wished, what I did, what I thought."

"You did not hide anything from *me,* that is true! On the other hand, you most certainly did not come to me beforehand and ask for permission to work in that boiler room, with those stokers and what have you. On other occasions when you were denied permission, you went ahead anyway."

"Because, your Grace, you were out of the limits of your authority. There was no question of *sin,* but only 'impropriety,' some bourgeois notion of your own about what is fitting in a cleric. I prefer the example of Jesus Christ. In any case, it was up to his Eminence to decide what was or was not inappropriate in my actions, as it was up to him to pass over me in his selection. *And he has not done so.*"

Francisi, seeing Cardinal Pacelli's already drawn features tighten further under these ironic compliments, knew that he would not spare the man. "The Secretary of State did not approve of your actions," he said to Ulanov. "The Secretary refused to hear my reports on you, as he has refused to hear the reports of others. He made a mistake, the Secretary. He liked you too much and was too attached to your place in his plan to allow the exercise of his ordinary prudence . . ."

Francisi paused for a moment. The logic of events and circumstances had driven him far beyond his original intentions. He had expected to have to live another year before finding himself in a position to remind Pacelli of his folly; he had assumed the consecration to end forever his relationship to Alexander Ulanov. "You knew the Secretary could not possibly have taken the reports of his representatives seriously," he said. "You knew that—consciously or unconsciously, it makes no difference—as surely as you knew you would be here tonight! You abused this misplaced trust of the Secretary by concealing in his presence any manifestation of your true sentiments on socialism."

"I protest, I completely denounce this nonsense!" said Ulanov. "You have concocted a dialogue in your own mind and now claim that it belongs to me. I deny your charges, Archbishop!"

"Tell me," said Francisi, "tell me, Alexander, why you never said anything about these sentiments earlier this evening or at any time in the presence of his Eminence? After so many years in a religious order you must have understood the church's position toward communism, and you showed no surprise when Cardinal Pacelli explained his opposition to your beliefs. I appeal to your sense of honesty—how 'reckless' is it to suggest that you waited until you had the bishopric well in hand to announce your own policy?"

Ulanov put his hands behind his back and moved slowly toward the papal desk. "Your Eminence," he said. "It is really unworthy of your archbishop and myself to go on with this kind of discussion. I, for one, will participate in it no longer. Charity is not being served."

Ulanov seemed surprised and so too Pacelli when Francisi said, "I agree."

"There are two things I wish to say to you in my behalf, Eminence," said Ulanov. "First, I would like to make it clear that the premise of this entire argument is wrong. It is unimportant really whether I am subjectively guilty of some concealment—

unless what I am supposed to have hidden amounts to anything. With regard to what I have said about socialism, surely any number of medieval thinkers, Aquinas included, any number of church fathers, even Christ our Lord and Savior himself, can be quoted easily in behalf of my position.

"The Russian way of handling worldly goods being the people's choice, and more just than our own, I can hardly use the Catholic faith to destroy the barrel because of its bad fruits. I invoke no more than the common sense of our traditional beliefs. There is nothing very radical in that.

"My last point is this. If you disagree so violently with my simple beliefs, why don't you find another bishop to go into Russia? It isn't too late. You have Fathers Marais and Nimsky, I was only the first choice. I have been accused of concealing terrible opinions in order to obtain this assignment. But the assignment is not closed, and I have known this all along too. And what would be my motive in revealing myself tonight if what I had worked for all these years could be so easily destroyed? You have power over me, Eminence, up until the last day of my entrance into Russia. Considering the suspicions and charges your archbishop has made, why should you not revoke my powers? Amen. I shall say no more."

"Quite right," said Francisi. "Yes, that is very prudent of you, Bishop Ulanov. Considering what has happened, it is best for everyone concerned that you resign your appointment."

"You misunderstand, Archbishop. I did not offer to resign. I said, if his Eminence is so suspicious of these attitudes of mine, then let him revoke my powers and remove me from my assignment! But that would be his judgment. It would most certainly not be mine. It would be entirely against my wishes, and I would demand that it be so recorded, in the books of his department, in the presence of his Holiness."

The cardinal stood up. "Very well, Bishop Ulanov. Would you be so kind as to pray for a few moments in the chapel for divine enlightenment to resolve this conflict without impairment to your conscience? Meanwhile, I shall speak to Archbishop Francisi and perhaps together we can ascertain whether your position is irreparably hurt by these conflicts."

[134]

The Jesuit bowed to the Secretary of State. "I will be ready for your decision. Whatever it is." He looked into Pacelli's eyes for a prolonged moment, then left the room.

The cardinal rose from the desk. "God give us help, Francisi!" he said. "I have meditated so long on the murder of millions in Russia that I cannot believe there is anything salvageable about that barbarous ideology called atheistic communism. I burst out against that preposterous theory of our bishop's because it is unbelievable that an American Catholic Jesuit could cherish such naïve fancies. My temper, I hope, was a holy one.

"In any case, you did your best as an advocate, Francisi, in dealing with the situation. To be frank, I *am* quite disappointed in this young man's notions. Have Stalin and his hoodlums no murdered close to seventeen million kulaks? He admits to ten millions. And the numberless list of uncataloguable crimes? Our sheltered young Jesuit, does he think such inhumanity can be divorced from that system? And then he declares that Europe is decadent. If Fascist Europe continues to destroy Christianity, then we can expect that some of Europe will indeed resemble Russia."

"Yes, your Eminence," answered Francisi. "I understand this, but why did you not say it directly in that way, yourself, to Ulanov?"

"Hopeless, is it not? You tried! I did tell him, in no uncertain fashion, our feelings in the matter. But he is stubborn. Still, in his debate with you he revealed certain qualities of toughness which will serve the mission well."

Francisi felt sick. "You surely aren't thinking of allowing him to go, after what he said!"

"What choice do we have? In the first place, we can compromise on the issue of communism. He need not condemn it, but he must not praise it. That solution, I believe, is possible."

"But why should you even talk in these terms? Ulanov is right, there are the Fathers Marais and Nimsky—appoint one of them in his place! You can remove him easily."

"Can I? Can I really, Francisi?"

"In God's name, yes!"

"Think of our position, Francisi. His Holiness would have to be asked to consecrate another bishop for the same mission only a few hours or days after the consecration of Ulanov. The sudden deposition of our Jesuit friend would look ridiculous, since he is presumed to have passed the most stringent requirements."

"I beg your pardon, Eminence, but I wish that you would not implicate *me* in that decision to select Ulanov. You seem to forget that I have always opposed it, as have others."

"This is no time for recriminations, Francisi. The mission is too critical."

"And the same man? I do not concur!"

"You are supposed to be a diplomat, Francisi. Kindly apply your God-given diplomatic brains to this matter. The Pope would have misgivings, and there would be the whole matter of going through a commission again. The previous vote was very close, and with new developments it could fail to pass."

"Considering the nature of the man," said Francisi, "surely it is more prudent to risk an attempt to substitute Marais or Nimsky for Ulanov." He was trying, rather desperately, to modulate his tone so as not to appear overly adamant. His only hope remained in asserting himself as the sage councilor behind the throne.

"No, no," said Pacelli. "Think, Francisi, think! If I can bring Bishop Ulanov to accept my compromise, then we have not lost much. Yes, of course"—he gestured at the specter of an objection—"I am incensed at the Jesuit's attitude. You witnessed my outrage. Nevertheless, when we look at it calmly, and if he stays neutral on this question of preaching socialism in Russia, why nothing of any consequence has changed from this morning.

"As for Marais and Nimsky, I will tell you. Neither one of them is the kind of leader or equipped with the skill and resourcefulness of this Ulanov. That we are all agreed upon. Therefore, I would be placing the mission in far greater peril to substitute one of them for him. You see, we must free our feelings enough from the man to view the situation dispassionately. This is something, if you will pardon my saying so, that you must learn, Francisi, if you are to be of the greatest assistance to us.

"I should inform you also that I have already sent Father Nimsky to Paris. I have asked him to work with the Russian

[136]

émigrés, and particularly with the old aristocrats, so that when they are restored to their old places in Russian society—"

"Restored?" asked Francisi.

"Yes, this communism shall be wiped out soon enough. Another Congress of Vienna shall return them—"

"You don't seriously believe that, *eminenza?*"

"Did I solicit your opinion on the question, Francisi?"

"It is not a matter of faith and morals, *eminenza.*"

The cardinal shook his head and walked toward the window. "The question that really concerns you and me now," he said, "is how to maintain a check on Ulanov. Though I am stuck with him, that hardly means I am bound to let him venture out alone."

Francisi did not reply. The cardinal was proceeding with his own game, and the archbishop had lost track of the *règles de jeu.* Besides, he felt affronted by this terrible aloofness which did not admit mistakes even in the privacy of his inferior's company. This distance established for good and with no hope whatsoever Francisi's sense of despair in dealing with the Secretary.

"Francisi," said Pacelli, barely looking at him, "bring me Father Marais."

"You have changed your mind, *eminenza?*" Francisi was too surprised for subtlety.

"Changed? Changed? I am sending you, Archbishop, to pick up young Father Marais at his Jesuit residence. Nothing is changed."

"When?"

"Now."

"It is past midnight, *eminenza.*"

"I will call the superior of the house immediately. Father Marais should be ready when you arrive. I shall call for my chauffeur."

"Just bring him here?"

"Yes. No explanations are necessary. All will be made clear in due time." The cardinal then turned and walked into another room of the papal apartments.

When Francisi reached the basement, car and driver were waiting. Speeding through the deserted streets of Rome, they quickly reached the entrance of the Collegio di San Roberto Bellarmino. The archbishop, just as he raised the knocker, found the door opened for him. "Archbishop Francisi?" said the rector. Francisi nodded. "Very good, Excellency, we were waiting for you. Father Marais is in the chapel."

Together the two men walked down the dark soundless hall and into the chapel. A single vigil light glowed red inside the lamp that swung on a bronze chain from the ceiling above the center of the sanctuary. Halfway down the length of pews knelt the cassocked Marais. Francisi took a moment to pray for relief from the confusions of the evening, tiptoed up the aisle, genuflected beside Marais's pew, and beckoned to the French Jesuit.

The rector accompanied them to the door, which was instantly closed behind them. Before they entered the car, Marais gestured with his hand, holding up a finger as a signal of slight hesitation. "May I ask you, your Excellency, where I am going? I don't mind obeying an order, but I would appreciate knowing what the order is."

"So unlike a young Jesuit," said Francisi.

"I've been through a few things recently, your Excellency. From now on I want to ask straight questions and get honest answers."

Francisi found himself liking the young man. "You are being called to the papal apartments, to speak to Cardinal Pacelli."

Marais thought for a few seconds. Then he said, "They have already chosen Ulanov . . . I am sure of it. I can't possibly be the cardinal's selection. He doesn't particularly like Frenchmen—and, besides, this is no hour to announce to someone that he has been chosen for anything."

"Astute enough, Father," said Francisi, ready to reciprocate trust with trust. "You are quite right, you are not the selection— though I doubt that his Eminence would appreciate my supplying you this information."

"You needn't worry, I won't betray your confidence. Besides, we are obviously both outsiders."

"I wish you *were* the selection," said Francisi, laying a hand on his young confrere's shoulder. "I really do."

Marais smiled. "For two strangers, we have certainly gotten to the point very fast, have we not?" The sound of Francisi's laughter echoed along the empty street. "You must not be a regular archbishop, your Excellency. They are usually very cold."

"I am not an archbishop with a diocese, that is true. Nevertheless, I am ordinarily distant if not, I hope, cold. Ah well, events tonight have left me incapable of any show of common sense."

"So Alexander has shown his true colors," said Marais.

"What's that? You possess some recent information about Ulanov?"

"Only *suspect*," said Marais. "There is no evidence, really." He sighed. "So it is out. Is that why they are sending for me?"

"Yes."

"Did he tell them, or did they find out?"

"He expressed his views to the Secretary, after the consecration."

"That would be Alex. When it comes to socialism—"

"Yes, yes, that came out! What else do you know?"

Marais hesitated; frowned; shook his head.

Francisi breathed an exasperated sigh. "You could be his substitute, even now, if there is any further material so serious as the other. Pacelli would have to refuse to send him."

"You don't like him."

"I've never hidden that fact—from anyone, including Ulanov. I have opposed him at every turn of the road."

"In that case you are better than your superior."

"And your own feelings?"

"For me it is not a question of 'liking' Ulanov. He is—let me leave it at this—strange!"

"You are not very helpful, Father Marais."

"I am sorry. I have only my suspicions."

"No, I believe you have more. Much more."

"Nothing that would stand up. If what he has said so far has not stopped his appointment, your Grace, then I doubt that any long-winded recital of mine involving what might be called bizarre incidents would shake his Eminence *or* the Pope."

"But you," said Francisi, "you believe they are more than bizarre, do you not?"

"Yes, but it would take a good deal of time and a sympathetic audience to communicate the . . . flavor, you might say."

"Y-y-yes," Francisi conceded, still unwilling to let a powerful lever escape his grasp. He felt sure that somewhere in the French-man's experience there was something . . . But the hour was ever later, and his charge overdue. Most of all, his own inner exhaustion restrained him from further pursuit of whatever he might find in Marais's story. In any case it would most likely not affect Pacelli's decision.

"He is a lucky man," said Francisi.

"How well I know!"

The two of them got into the limousine, and within minutes reached the Vatican palace.

Just before they entered the building, Francisi turned and gestured toward St. Peter's. Marais looked at him, puzzled. "The crosses—yes, see all the crosses," the archbishop explained, "and churches like this, only smaller, all over the world, and within them at this moment, priest, brothers, sisters, working, praying, for one end and one end alone—the service of Christ. On every continent . . ."

"Yes?"

"That is the real stuff of which the church is made, the workers of the vineyard. Why, why can't *they*"—he pointed over his shoulder to the Vatican palace behind them—"be as coherent, as humble as the rest?" He shrugged. "I'll allow you one answer to a question. Whom and what do you think the enemies of the church will concentrate upon in their impartial annals? The mistakes of our leaders or the thousands of poor, obedient, and chaste missionaries who died for love?"

"We already know," said Marais, regretting only a little that his present state of mind did not allow him to pursue this line of discussion. He never had cared too much to defend the church in her own right. The church either did or did not live up to her ideals, and he tried to live up to his, and when she went wrong she would suffer the penalty as he himself would. Yet the church was like the air he breathed; sometimes it was very good and sometimes bad, but in all instances necessary and fundamental.

"We must go," said the archbishop, and together they ascended the long winding staircase.

The door to the papal apartment stood slightly ajar, in exactly the same position as the archbishop had left it. Francisi and

Marais entered to find Cardinal Pacelli kneeling on the floor without support for his knees, hands folded on the desk, his back half turned to them.

Francisi's exhaustion prevented him from waiting upon the cardinal's devotions. He tiptoed quietly and respectfully toward his superior and stood beside him. The cardinal did not move.

The translucent whiteness of the skin, the cast of the features in the upturned face stopped Francisi for an instant. Surely, he thought, the man was a mystic. And, surely, the graces he received were addressed to causes and not to lesser persons like the archbishop.

Francisi finally coughed. The cardinal turned halfway around, jerkily, as though just awakened. His eyes still did not meet Francisi's. After a few seconds of reflection he raised himself to his feet, and, extending two fingers for balance on the edge of the desk, said in a barely audible voice, "Bring in Bishop Ulanov."

Francisi proceeded to the chapel, where not a moment was wasted: the Jesuit turned as he heard the footsteps, left the pew, genuflected, and walked down the hallway a few steps ahead of the Archbishop.

By the time they entered the room, Cardinal Pacelli was seated behind his desk and Father Marais was standing in front of him. Marais turned sideways, as it to afford Pacelli a view of his guests. "It seems an eternity since I've seen you, Alexander," he said.

Ulanov looked at Marais, shocked, then faced Pacelli.

"Bishop Ulanov," said the cardinal, "will you agree to neither praise nor denounce socialism when you are in Russia? Will you use the formula, 'What belongs to Caesar, render to Caesar, and what belongs to God and the church, render to God and the church'?" The questions were not so much asked as intoned, as if Pacelli were chanting the epistle at high mass.

Perhaps because he had dreaded the worst, Marais's substitution on the mission, Ulanov answered readily. "That is acceptable, your Eminence."

"Thank you," said Pacelli in that same monotone. "Now there have been two small changes in plans. You will go first to

Moscow, it is safer. Secondly, you will be accompanied by Father Marais."

Ulanov's head jerked back as though his face had been slapped. He turned to Marais and back again to the cardinal. "I don't need anyone, your Eminence. It is—it's best if I travel alone."

Cardinal Pacelli stared at the Jesuit for a moment, then said, "He has been appointed by the Holy Father as your companion."

"Frankly, Father Marais is not always well," said Ulanov. "And Russia is known to be inhospitable. Also, I am someone who travels best alone. There is less chance to be apprehended if one travels singly. You increase the hazards..." He turned to Marais almost pleadingly, "Tell them the truth, Paul, that you are not very well."

"I have never been seriously ill, Alexander."

"Your constitution is not rugged enough for this journey. You have a delicate appetite, you—"

"I prefer particular foods, that is true. But I really don't think I *need* them. You'll just have to take my word that a gourmet can survive on ordinary fare."

"Please, Paul, this is no time for heroics. Our mission will be paralyzed if you fall sick. No one will think any the less of you if you tell them that you are not strong enough for this."

"What is wrong with you, Alex? Wiry Frenchmen like me can go on a lot longer than big bears."

"His medical records," said the cardinal, "indicate that he is in sufficiently good health to have no trouble surviving the rigors of a Russian city in wintertime. After all, he is not being asked to trudge on foot from Rome to Moscow. Your protest is duly noted but overruled, Bishop Ulanov. Father Marais will be your constant companion on this trip. His passport will be ready shortly, and those who must be informed will be told of his presence.

"As to the journey being dangerously complicated by this addition, I disagree. Two heads are better than one, and should attract no more—perhaps less—attention than a single traveler."

Francisi watched Ulanov, astonished. The American, whose composure had not broken once during any of the evening's proceedings, including the argument with Francisi, was near to panic now. The small streams of sweat running along his neck struck the archbishop as so inappropriate in this cool smooth-skinned man that he searched for some reason to interfere and again test his opponent under these new circumstances.

The conference, however, was at an end. The cardinal stood up. "Wherever you go"—he pointed first at Ulanov and then at Marais—"he goes. You are to be inseparable companions. All decisions in all your undertakings must have the assent of both parties. Father Marais has the power of veto over any of your decisions, Bishop Ulanov. Your rank as bishop qualifies you as superior but not as sole judge. Tomorrow you both begin training as telephone repairmen. I shall give my blessing before you depart, five weeks hence ... Oh, yes, and you, Father Marais, will be given a special code in order to countersign the bishop's messages. Other instructions will be supplied you privately. And Bishop Ulanov, you shall take an oath tomorrow to respect the prerogatives of Father Marais. Remember, both of you, the vow of silence—you are to speak to no one, absolutely no one, about this mission. Yes, well, you naturally understand all this."

With that the cardinal turned, and, moving more slowly than Francisi had ever seen him walk, made his way into a tiny back corridor. Was he retiring even at that hour to confer with the Pope on this or related issues? The archbishop had no way of knowing.

None of them moved to leave. Each was caught up in a web spun only partly by himself. The whole of it now went so far beyond their individual roles that they were at a momentary loss to gather in the strands.

And how, in God's name, was any one of them to control the others?

BOOK
III

The Mission

8

In the late afternoon of the first of August 1934, Bishop Alexander Ulanov and Father Paul Marais sat warming themselves in the sun's dying rays, on a bench beside a lean-to barn in the countryside near the Polish city of Pinsk. Awake only a few hours and refreshed by a generous peasant meal, they welcomed this last opportunity to relax before the final leg of their journey into Russia.

So far, they were holding to schedule. Through the Alps and into Austria and then on through Czechoslovakia and into Poland, they had encountered no problems in their disguise as truck drivers. The cardinal had thought it wiser that they not travel by train. Warsaw, Brest-Petovsk, and the entire area west of Pinsk were honeycombed with Soviet agents. Any slightly unusual movements on the part of two Russian travelers might attract fatal attention.

Last night, they had surrendered their truck on the outskirts of this city most accessible to Russia. At the prearranged rendezvous spot on a deserted farm route, an old peasant and his son were waiting for them. The younger man drove the truck away from the scene. The old man hurried them under the produce in his wagon and transported them through the darkness for more than six uncomfortable hours to this farmhouse. Upon their arrival, he had insisted that they sleep in his own quarters.

As soon as the two lay down on the soft straw-packed mattress, they fell into a deep sleep, the first they had enjoyed in forty-eight hours. This part of the journey had required two days and nights of continuous driving, not part of the original plan. The Vatican diagram of the inconspicuous side roads they were to take on the trip had proved inadequate. Frequently they had found themselves in dead ends far from any sign of habitation, and even where the maps might have been correct at one time, some natural catastrophe had intervened to remove the thin reality from the face of the earth. In other places a swamp had finally conquered the bare strip of road that constituted an insult to its rank domain.

It occurred to Marais that had Ulanov not been able to speak Polish, any one of the country people, suspicious of strangers and not too kindly disposed toward Russian-speaking intruders, might with little guilt have relieved the travelers of their truck.

During the entire sleepless journey Marais had made it a matter of honor never to complain, knowing that Ulanov would seize upon any opportunity to insist upon his colleague's unfitness for the rigors of this mission. And so the oddest part of the journey thus far had been that Marais laughed at their misfortunes and professed delight at seeing so many off-beat facets of the Central European countryside, while Ulanov cursed their bad luck with maps and the impossibility even of dozing on such roads as these.

Ulanov's determination to meet their time plan exactly seemed to Marais nothing short of demonic. Marais frequently reminded his colleague that, after all, their contacts would not leave the prearranged spot for a few days; that the Poles were famous for virtues like fidelity. Ulanov continued to drive through Czechoslovakia and then Poland as though an hour's delay in reaching Pinsk would spell certain disaster.

More puzzling than this fanaticism was Ulanov's attitude toward Marais. There had been no show of friendship since that night in the papal apartment—and yet, Marais knew, there was another element here. Ulanov seemed to have decided to adopt a mask of distance, and, behind that façade, to be continually calculating. The month and a half that had elapsed since the consecration should have dissolved by now his unhappiness over having a co-apostle. Yet the American never let a day pass without a remark or two about the uselessness of having two where one sufficed. Yes, Marais concluded, it is I who have shaken him, and in a way I couldn't have imagined before. But why?

Everything about the trip would be so much easier were Ulanov only decent enough to cooperate. Together they could render this adventure almost enjoyable. As it was, Marais had to assume that his associate would remain quite fixed in his antagonism.

"When a Frenchman is quiet for so long, it's a sign of madness," said Ulanov.

Marais, still welcoming the quiet, said nothing.

"You see, you must be going mad," said Ulanov. "You did not even answer me."

"The Greeks have a saying, Alex—"

"They always did. Yes?"

" 'According to the outcome of deeds should we judge who is mad, who is wise, and who is not.' " Marais turned as he spoke, smiling at his colleague. "I know that when the deeds are finished, when the outcome is judged, if anyone is seen as mad it will be you and not me—for I do not challenge God, the gods, superiors, common sense, institutions as you, my friend. And somewhere there must be a reckoning."

"Words, words, words. A European disease."

Marais thought for a moment, then said, "Do you remember, Alexander, a place called the Slaves' House in Rome? You were almost destroyed, and you almost finished someone else. What was his name? Oh, yes, Nicholas. Your brother."

Ulanov got up from the bench. "You have no right to drag up every peccadillo of the past. Is nothing too trivial to go unrecorded in a narrow soul?"

"Your temper doesn't throw me for a loss any more, Alexander, not the way it used to. You'd better know that now. Besides, what happened that night wasn't trivial."

"Did you tell anyone those fantasies of yours about that evening? Francisi, or Pacelli?"

"I did not."

"I don't believe you, you know."

"I never—"

"Then *why are you here?*"

"Did I appoint myself?" asked Marais. "No, you were chosen to go alone. Obviously, I said nothing to anyone—if I had, you might not have been selected. So why am I here? Because you and you alone missed your signals with the Secretary of State. You alienated him and he has no certainty whatsoever that you will follow his orders.

"Ever since that night you have acted as if the mission has gone wrong just because I am with you, as if some stranger had been foisted upon you. But it is I who trained with you for three years and am as well equipped as you for this adventure. You should be happy, but instead— Well, you can be damned now so far as I am concerned."

At this outburst, the anger went out of Ulanov's face. He grasped Marais by the shoulders. "Paul, listen to me. Please go back. Please."

The plea was incredibly heart-stricken, almost tender. Ulanov seemed for the first time a desperate ally, as though he were thinking more of Marais than of himself.

"But I mean to help, Alex," said Marais. "Can't you see that?"

"Listen to me, Paul! You can't help, your appointment came too late. I already have plans—"

"What 'plans'?"

"I've worked out things myself, how to survive on my own, it's no good if there are two. It ruins everything."

"How can that be, Alex? There was only a few hours' difference. You couldn't have planned much between the time they consecrated you and the time they summoned me."

A fierce joy suffused Ulanov's eyes, so that for an instant he seemed captured from within by an unnatural vision. "No, no, don't you see? I was very sure I would be selected, long before the night they called me. And I believed that only one person would go. So I had a good deal of time to work out my own approach to making it through Russia and getting out without trouble. But now . . ."

"What kind of a plan do you have that is so inflexible it can't accommodate two as well as one?"

Ulanov swung his arms, the clenched fists and forearms coming up close to Marais's face. "What's the use if you're still going to be hanging around my neck? Would it make any difference if I explained all the details to you? Would you go back if you saw how your presence is going to kill everything?"

Marais did not answer. He had entered the dialogue wholeheartedly, moved by the warmth of Ulanov's plea, and hungrier than he knew for his friendship and the chance to lay to rest whatever misunderstanding lay between them. Now, despite his partner's sincerity, he felt that he had not so much dispelled that enmity as been victimized by it.

"Have you no faith in me, Paul?" asked Ulanov.

Marais sighed. "Faith," he said, "is a two-sided matter. You know very well I can't go back. You too must trust, Alexander."

Ulanov turned to an odd distraction. He began to inspect his coveralls and then his work shoes. He knocked away some mud from the soles. Finally, after fingering the collar of his blue denim shirt, he looked up at Marais. "If you were your own man," he said, "if you were independent, if I could be sure of that, then I would show you. But as it is—well, it's hopeless to tell you anything." On that note Ulanov fell silent, and, indeed, appeared to sink beneath the weight of an unbearable depression.

Marais walked a few paces around the farmyard, trying to bolster his battered sense of reality with the sounds of field and barn, then returned to stand for a long moment in front of the bench. "You had better come to your senses, Alexander," he said finally. "Or I will code a reply that will put an end to this mission once and for all."

Ulanov shook his head as if the Frenchman were beyond comprehension.

"You've got a point of view," said Marais, "and you mean it. I've got one too, and I mean it. I find you as strange as you find me. Your argument only succeeds if you leave out a half dozen important factors, and you insist on leaving them out—something, perhaps a lot, is missing. Well, now you must deal with

[151]

reality, and that's *me*. If I returned to Rome, suppose I did, the cardinal would have some way of stopping you in Moscow before you even got started—which means you need me, don't you understand? If it weren't me, it would be somebody else who might be completely antagonistic to you, but in any case there has to be someone else because he *will not* let you go alone!"

Marais stopped, thinking that he had articulated the logic of his thought very well indeed.

Ulanov kicked stones along the feet of the bench. "You don't know what you're talking about. So clever-sounding, so altogether clever—and so useless. God, man, if you only knew what you have let us in for!"

With that he walked away a few paces, again swinging his arms back and forth in frustration. When he returned, he seemed calmer. "You've talked to me about cooperating," he said carefully. "Well, how about sharing this 'code' business?"

"I can't do that, Alex."

"I see. A weapon over my head."

"Never that. An added precaution for the Vatican."

"Nonsense—suppose you die? Am I ruined?"

"You know to mark an X on the letter. That's all. They'll know. *Marais est mort.*"

"And the mission? Does it cease then?"

"Yes."

"My God, it's as though they thought I'd kill you or something."

"Not at all!" said Marais, laughing.

"Suppose you get too sick to countersign my reports? What then?"

"You're a terrible pessimist, Bishop Ulanov! You had better not let me get *that* sick."

"Finished again, is that it?"

"Correct!"

"And how can Rome finish the mission? There is no one of any importance who communicates back except ourselves. Only our messages count."

"Wrong!"

Ulanov, caught short by Marais's reply, was quick nonetheless. "You see, I was never told that. They informed you but not me."

"I don't know who those people are," said Marais, "but I know *that* they are."

Ulanov turned and walked across the barnyard, alternately kicking at the rut-holes and the pieces of straw in his path.

Marais congratulated himself. He had not lied, since he did not *now* know which persons could stop the mission. They would identify themselves to Marais, and then he would know. As for the details regarding the transmission of the code, he was to review what Ulanov had written back to Rome. If he agreed and wished to add something more, he was to write in regular ink using a peculiar twist for certain letters of the alphabet to signify the veracity of what was written. If he disagreed with Ulanov's report, he would disagree in invisible ink and insert the last letter of the saint for the day on which he was writing within a word near the signature.

Originally Marais had regretted that he could not share these simple mechanisms with Ulanov. He felt that the bishop, as the leader of the mission, deserved the sense of being as completely trusted by his superiors as possible. Certainly Rome could have taken greater pains to convince Ulanov that the assignment of Marais to the mission constituted a protection for him and not a guard on his actions. As it was, Marais was left with a very discontented bishop for a leader—a leader who, unfortunately, had betrayed such madness in his reactions toward the Frenchman that Marais now felt a satisfying identification with the authority which gave him the ultimate responsibility for the mission.

As he watched Ulanov pacing in the yard, he could not help concluding that his colleague was badly frightened. The arms folding and unfolding behind his back, the sudden turns of his head, the stones kicked forward or to the side—all were evidence that something more lay behind his distress than injured pride.

"We're leaving soon," Ulanov called. "I'm going to meditate."

The Frenchman waved at him, more troubled than ever. He had experienced such torments during his own daily hour of

[153]

mental prayer over the last six weeks that he resisted beginning now. Seeking a pleasant pious thought that would not unleash demons, he contemplated the great disparities between himself and Nimsky and Pacelli and Francisi, the convergence of whose lives came from a force so outside personal choice. He praised God for the hundreds of temperaments and thousands of characters in the scattered cultures of the world, all accommodated under the Dome.

At this point the deepest part of his imagination surfaced and placed before him an undeluded blood-streaked Jesus wearing a crown of thorns. Marais flinched. Until his involvement with Russia, he had never had such visions. It had all begun with the Slaves' House, Nimsky, and the old woman. Now each morning these sad eyes appeared to haunt him with a nameless demand. The required hour of meditation could pass without distraction as he knelt, begging from those remorseless eyes the secret of his life—"What service do you wish of me?" he asked at the end of each of these meditations. At times he found himself thinking of Indochina, of the French Jesuit missions there. For all his pleas to heaven, the thought of the East made him recoil. Still, there was consolation in the thought that at least the face of Jesus now appeared to him. He knew what he was not, and had some intimation of what he had to be.

Marais leaned over a pail of cold water at one end of the farmyard, noticing peripherally that Ulanov had returned to talk to the farmer who was their host.

Over and over Marais threw ice-cold handfuls on his face, half soaking the top of his head. He removed even his blouse and undershirt and continued to bathe arms, shoulders, and chest with the water, rubbing his hands vigorously as though to annihilate by this rough ritual his sense of fear. With due care he clothed himself again, solemnizing his act of leave-taking, and walked to the wagon.

The farmer sat under an ancient wooden canopy rigged above his seat and extending back over half of the wagon so that it covered Ulanov and Marais. The driver was to take them over the border along a little used road and then partway through the

[154]

Pinsk Marshes, a vast stretch of watery terrain extending north-ward into Russia. Between 1872 and 1897, eight million acres of it had been drained at heavy cost, but the enormous tract so near the Polish border had hardly been dented. This forbidding, barely inhabited area offered a safe though slow route into the country-side around Kietsk, where they would skirt Nesvizh and then proceed farther north into the suburbs of Minsk.

Ulanov and Marais were reasonably well equipped for this trip of some hundred and thirty-five miles. They had a lantern and enough oil to last two weeks; they had fat rolls of cheese and loaves of bread. These few conveniences along with a stack of recent Soviet magazines and newspapers were enough to keep the routine from becoming intolerable. The periodicals served, also, to channel the tension between the two Jesuits into theoretical arguments as to what a particular article signified in terms of Communist Party tactics.

Again and again Marais was surprised by Ulanov's grasp of Soviet affairs. At the Russicum, they had all talked grand theory—Marx, Lenin, and Trotsky, or men and events remote in Russian history—intellectual discussions from which Marais usually emerged, at least in his own mind, as the superior. On this journey, however, Ulanov amazed him by his intimate knowledge of the actual workings of the Soviet government, of the relation between leaders in Russia and in the International, of the subtle arguments and intrigues between major figures through the last twenty years both in Moscow's domestic hierarchy and in Germany, France, and Italy. To Marais's repeated queries as to where one could possibly gain that kind of practical knowledge, Ulanov gave the same answer. "You must keep your ears open, and in the right places." He admitted that such material was rarely published in books or periodicals, which suggested that Marais's long hours in the library had been all but worthless in assessing live events.

Marais was happy, even at this late stage, to be given so many facts whose existence he might otherwise never have suspected. He had further reason to be grateful. Ulanov's attitude toward him, while far from what it had seemed before their break, turned friendly enough. That unexpected boon compensated Marais for the rigors of this journey, which resembled nothing so much as a forced march in the wilderness.

The days were steaming in the marshes; the achievement of sleep a minor triumph with the insects rising from stagnant pools on either side of the road to descend as living clouds upon the lone wagon. Even the driver's atrocious-smelling ointment offered little in the way of defense.

In his own time the driver unloaded a long wooden rod, which he inserted into a socket hole beneath his buckboard. At the end of the rod, above the horse's head, he hung a burning can of resinous substance which gave off thin black plumes of smoke that served to discourage the attacking hordes. In addition, he had outfitted the flanks of his horses with a blanket of very fine material that resembled a cross between gauze and wool. Between the tar pot and the covering, the horses, at least, were well provided for.

Ulanov upbraided the driver in Polish time and again—had they but known what faced them, they could surely have provided for it better than this. A tar pot, pole, and socket on the rear end of the wagon would have protected the priests. The farmer defended himself by declaring that he had never carried passengers in the back before, nor would he ever again. Had it not been for the request from his Jesuit cousin in Warsaw, the payment he had received, and the chance to renew acquaintance with close relatives near Pinsk, he would never have made such an absurd voyage.

These intense arguments in vociferous Polish did not end with the first driver. Their guide at the completion of his stretch turned out to be a kinsman of his who lived in the midst of the most inhospitable regions of the marsh. Obviously, in this network of relatives, everyone knew which members of a clan were trustworthy and which were not. They had also kept the knowledge of this terrain to themselves. Only the Poles, who had lived on the margins of the swamp for centuries, knew how to maneuver here. And there was never any fear that they would defect to Russia. Religion and nationality formed an impenetrable barrier to assimilation by Moscow. In this way, the Vatican had a ready-made underground route all the way to Minsk.

Yet when Marais thought about the human links supporting the grand designs of his superiors back in Rome, he could not help but laugh. The Vatican knew where conditions were favorable, the Vatican issued directives; but in the end it was an old man, driving a slow cart and two horses through a desolate unmarked swamp, who held the balance of their mission in the reins between his hands.

Marais's impression of these fragile underpinnings struck him particularly one quiet evening just before sunset when they halted somewhere in the middle of the Pinsk Marshes. Their coachman informed them that he had arrived at the end of his contracted part of the trip. While he unyoked the horses, the travelers looked around them—except for the carefully packed, scraped dirt and the large clearing in which they stood, there were no signs of human habitation. In the dim light neither of them could see a landmark distinguishing this particular spot from the boring stretches they had traversed for days. Through patches of soggy moor a billion curving reeds thrust their way up from the watery earth.

"I feel abandoned here," said Marais. "I mean, it looks as if God is absent from the planet when you see all this primeval ooze."

"It's useless now, but the Soviets will subdue it."

"Well, maybe so, but I've always thought that the clue to nations and to souls lies in taking into account just this kind of abysmal sight."

"What's important," said Ulanov, "is what will come of it at the hands of man."

"And there's the difference between us," said Marais.

As Ulanov's laughter rang over the swamp, the driver began to call to them.

They hurried to the old man, who led them down a steep embankment and along a narrow built-up track through grassy stalks. The company walked slowly for perhaps a quarter of a mile along this barely perceptible causeway until they reached a

[157]

clearing that stretched before a long thatch-roofed cottage. The candlelight from inside flickered through its windows, which were made of glass.

The driver called out in Polish and knocked at the main door, which was thrown open by a young man who embraced his relative warmly. He invited the priests inside, and, as was the peasant custom, immediately set food and drink before them.

The family included Mathias Maresky, his wife, six children, grandparents, an uncle, and an aunt. The entire clan stayed up long into the night drinking and talking excitedly with their old cousin, hungry for news about the rest of the family in Pinsk and its environs. Ulanov acted as interpreter for Marais, enthusiastically translating the more comical exchanges for his friend's appreciation.

Marais, having realized during dinner that the whole family knew who the priests were and where they were going, had stared at Ulanov and protested in French that such a sharing in the mission's secrets seemed incredibly dangerous.

Ulanov immediately translated these remarks for the family, who obviously had noticed the Frenchman's growing nervousness. They all laughed heartily, and from then on through the evening, Marais became the object of good-natured teasing.

"You have to know whom to trust, Paul," Ulanov said in French. "These people would go to the ends of the earth to protect us, now that they understand the goal of the operation. If we ever tried to play games and exclude them just to honor some bureaucratic requirement, we would be finished! You see what we've been through. We needed help that really can't be paid for, and we still do."

"Does Rome know?" Marais asked again.

"Oh, I think they understand—on one level, anyway. Of course, if you asked them, they might act as if they were outraged, but then you weren't aware that a Jesuit in Warsaw had to arrange for our passage. Look at all the details so far. They hardly fell out of the skies, did they?"

"I suppose not."

"Well, then, Cardinal Pacelli must have told the Jesuit."

[158]

"Yes . . ."

"Then he was the one who allowed him that leeway. I doubt strongly that the priest went off on his own!"

"Yes, but why are *you* so lenient with them? I should think you would be as concerned as I."

Ulanov seemed about to answer, then hesitated. "Because I understand," he said finally. "You must learn to separate the wheat from the chaff in these affairs."

Marais had been coerced by logic into agreeing with the first part of Ulanov's explanation, but this last remark did not carry the same conviction. The more Marais thought about it, the more he felt that his final query touched the heart of the matter. Once you questioned the premise of Ulanov's attitude, his edifice of rationales seemed shaky indeed.

Marais could not overcome the depressing thought that no matter how well he learned to scrutinize his partner's motives, the exercise usually turned out to be worthless. Usually Ulanov had already committed the questionable action, leaving Marais in the inconsequential role of a protester. He could exhaust his brains and voice in logical argument, he felt, without actually influencing one of Ulanov's decisions.

The strain of these concerns in such pleasant surroundings ended shortly after midnight, when the Mareskys took their guests on a tour of the two rooms adjoining the dining room. At each end of these rooms were sleeping lofts reached by ladders; underneath, there were wide bunks a couple of feet above the floor. Brightly painted curtains served as partitions, and in each of the compartments a bright fire was burning, fueled by bricks of peat. The cottage floor was inset with large smooth stones and rocks covered by rugs of heavy wool dyed in brilliant colors. The boards of the dining room table and accompanying chairs had been hewn from fine oak.

"You must be the richest farmers left in Russia," Marais said when he had taken it all in. "How is that possible here?" He gestured toward the dismal expanse surrounding the house. The family laughed and led him outside. Along the wide shelves of a rock cave near the house lay rows of fish and dried duck and other birds, perfectly preserved. Sacks of potatoes lined the foot of the wall; other edibles were stored in earthen jars. Most remarkable of all, Marais saw large cans of milk.

The Maresky family kept their visitors in suspense about the provenance of these goods until the following morning, when they escorted the priests a mile or so into an area completely hidden from the public road. Marais could hardly believe his eyes. Amid the desolation of those hundreds of surrounding miles, he saw an oasis of abundance. Clear streams ran around and through a large pasture on which goats were grazing. Another big field had been given over to potatoes and vegetables.

As his hosts explained, the streams gave them a good supply of fish, and, in the fall, there were ducks to be brought down from the great flocks flying overhead on their yearly migration. In the spring, there were other fowl. The insects were not troublesome in this area, thanks to a vagary of the wind, and the fresh water. Half a mile farther on, outcroppings of rock had enough grassy substance on them to support a few score sheep.

"After the summer is over," said Mathias Maresky, "myself and Jan take a wagon of salted fowl and fish in to Pinsk. And our relatives look out for us. They help us get good trades—lumber, vegetables we don't raise—and new books."

"But how did your children learn to read without going to school?"

"My parents, that's their job."

"But how did *they* learn to read?"

"From their parents."

"They were here too?"

"Yes."

"My God!" said Marais. "How far back do you people go?"

Mathias smiled. He was obviously enjoying working his listener up to each surprise. "My great-grandfather was a German-Russian officer in the Tsar's army," he explained. "He was an engineer, and they commissioned him to survey this area. That is how he found this place. When he left the service, he returned here with a wife from Pinsk."

"But why? Why out of all the possibilities in Russia or Europe did he come here?"

[160]

"He never told anyone."

"But you stay?"

"What other place could we love like this? After a few hours in Pinsk, I want to come back home. The city is not for me or my family." He called to his two oldest children. "Father Marais is feeling sorry for us."

Marais protested, but since everyone was laughing, he decided he had stumbled into a family joke.

Anna, the eighteen-year-old, gestured about her. "We live with the seasons here—and, Father, we do everything ourselves. I can't envy the people in the city. They don't have the pleasure of beginning and finishing things for themselves. Compared to us they seem prisoners."

"Don't you ever get lonely, then?" Marais asked.

"We have each other," she said.

Her brother Jan put an arm around her. "There is nothing more to seek than what we have right here," he said.

"No horizons?" asked the priest.

"They are all here, there—our own sky."

"But the girls will have to leave for other places. You don't have enough to support that many people."

"I am prepared to go within the next two or three years," said Anna. "But here will always be home."

"She won't be far away," said Mathias. "There is a young man from a well-to-do merchant family in Pinsk who met Anna on her last visit in the city. He wants to marry her."

"And if she doesn't visit us enough, I will go and fetch her myself," said Jan.

Marais shook his head. "You people are almost unreal. I come from a society where families barely imagine such affection."

He looked at the children, who met his gaze without evasion. They waited patiently for some further comment from the educated foreign priest, but he could find nothing to say, nothing to give them that they did not already possess. He wondered: were the Mareskys a sign of the future or a relic left over in a by-wash of the past? As he looked down from the top of the knoll over the quiet of this incredible oasis, he caught sight of Ulanov waving in the distance, calling him to resume their journey.

Before they set out, the priests heard the confessions of the family, and Ulanov said mass in their dining room. The Mareskys were fervent in their participation, and the bishop, touched by their piety, took unusually long over the meditational sections of the mass.

For an encounter that had been so brief, Marais found the parting difficult. The children gave each of the priests a woven vest to help them through the winter in Moscow. In return the Jesuits could only give them their blessing and a promise of masses for their intentions.

Marais's spirits had improved remarkably during his overnight stay with the Mareskys. He felt exhilarated by the existence of such hope and happiness in this country, by the triumph over odds so terrible.

The old handicaps would still be with him, but the frame of mind in which Marais now viewed them had changed. If there were to be continued difficulties along their way, further embarrassments and evasions on Ulanov's part, he would simply have to *cope* with them. He would reprimand Ulanov when necessary; he would learn how to anticipate his companion's violations. Above all, he must not use them as an excuse to terminate their assignment. This Polish family just inside Russia had shown him how possible it was to survive amid a plethora of specters. Their relatives and the many others who knew about them all these years had not revealed their whereabouts to the authorities. Evidence of hope abounded in this world if one had the eye to see it.

Marais's spirits hardly diminished during the next phase of their journey. The remaining section of the Pinsk Marshes seemed nowhere as threatening as they had before the stay at the Mareskys'. The priests were prepared, this time, for the mosquitoes, and they were better equipped with blankets and food. Mathias Maresky pushed the horses along quickly, chatting about the future of the swamps, how to stock fish, how to raise children, how to treat various illnesses; even about the future of communism.

Finally the time came to take on a new driver. The parting from Maresky was difficult for both of the priests. "We will make it our business to see you on our way out, Mathias," said Marais. "We'll share the good news with you and the family."

"You don't have to do that, Father. It might take you out of your way."

"Mathias," said Ulanov, "you are a real part of this mission. We owe you more than you realize, and it would be the smallest repayment of our debt to let you know the result of our labors. In the conversion of Russia your name will not go unmentioned."

Maresky seemed surprised at their praise. "What kind of Catholic would I be," he said, "if I didn't offer what I have to my priests?"

For the next two hours neither Marais nor Ulanov spoke. The "miracle of the marshes," as Marais thought of it, had endowed him with such a sense of happiness and potential that he finally began to joke with his companion over his own inflexibility back at the cottage. Ulanov reciprocated with an astonishing show of camaraderie. Marais had never seen his friend so exuberant, and though he could not understand why his quasi apology should beget such *bonhomie* from Ulanov, he welcomed the change gratefully.

It was but a short step to envisioning the two of them, Father Marais and, yes, Bishop Ulanov, traveling as heroes—and brothers—through the vastness of Russia. Marais chuckled at the notion, then laughed out loud at himself, a laugh that turned finally into an outburst of pure joy as he realized that for the first time since beginning the mission he was, even if only in fantasy, viewing it as a success.

9

By evening of the next day, having ·skirted Dzerzhinsk, Marais and Ulanov entered the White Russian region of Byelorussia. The city of Minsk, their intermediate destination, signaled the end of their dependence on horses. The driver brought his cart close to the railroad yards, where he waited, dozing on a side street, until the moon was visible. He then made a slow circuit around back streets and pulled up alongside a loading platform for the Moscow freight cars.

At the cue of a whistle he was joined by three countrymen, who quickly loaded two large boxes on the rear of the wagon. Marais and Ulanov eased themselves into the open end of these crates, which were half filled with straw under which they were told to hide. The men nailed on the extra side and moved the boxes out onto a large roller, and in a few minutes they felt themselves hoisted into one of the freight cars of the night train for Moscow.

Marais lay in his new house for what he judged to be half an hour before he heard groans and the voices of the same men. From the little Polish he could comprehend, they were struggling with some exceptionally heavy equipment. In another ten minutes the side of his box was removed and Marais was asked to step out. Large engines were put into half of his and Ulanov's boxes, which were then turned to face outward. Their nails were loosened at the front. Presumably, if either box should happen to be inspected, the government agent would pry off the convenient side, glance at the engine, and be satisfied.

The sliding door of the car was pushed nearly shut, leaving the two priests a narrow open shaft from which they could peer out of the shadows into the yard.

"On our way . . . on our way," said Ulanov, repeating these few syllables with an almost mystic fervor.

"It's a historic place, Minsk," said Marais. "Did you know that centuries ago—"

"Who cares?" said Ulanov. "It's not relevant." His tone, less rude than his words, conveyed only dismissal. "History bores me. It is now, what we must do *now* in this different world—with the living, with machinery, industry, society—that matters."

Marais could only sigh at this barbaric rejoinder. "Ah, well, it would take a speech to show you otherwise, Alexander."

"Not Alexander. Dmitri—from now on!"

"I forgot."

Ulanov shook his head. "We can't afford even one of those mistakes, Josef."

"I understand, Dmitri. But you missed my point before. How can a Christian, a Jesuit priest, call history a bore?"

Ulanov pointed through the open slot of the car door. "Here you are," he said, "in Russia, about to penetrate the heartland of the most mysterious country in the world. Who knows what will happen? Because of me, you will go into the history books, and you rattle on at such a moment about *old* history." He edged closer to the door. "We are on our way to Moscow, you and I. This time two nights from now, we shall be there. Think of that!"

"Why does your mind work in either/ors, Dmitri? Why do you never put anything together?" With that Marais gave up the argument.

"If our information is right," said Ulanov, "we should be in Smolensk in the morning, lay over in the yards during the day, and then tomorrow night start off again. We were fortunate to catch this train—they had almost given up on us here, we are so far behind schedule. Those damnable swamps! You had better pray that they haven't forgotten us in Moscow, or we may be in very serious trouble."

[166]

"I will pray, Dmitri, but I've never seen you so worried. I must say, it surprises me."

Marais, who had not intended a great deal by this remark, was surprised when Ulanov agreed with it. "Of course I'm worried, why shouldn't I be? You're incapable of bothering about details, and the Vatican was not all that helpful. Both of us know that Rome hasn't been able to protect *anyone* in Russia so far."

"But Alex—I'm sorry, Dmitri—for weeks you've acted as if you were confidence itself. And now, suddenly—"

"Suddenly, as of this moment, we depend on our wits, on our own and no one else's. The others never came back, do you understand? And they, no doubt, followed orders to the letter. It wasn't enough!"

"Are you afraid, then?"

"Only a fool would be unafraid, facing our odds. Of course I'm afraid. Up to a point. But I'm not paralyzed, if that's what you mean, and there's a big difference."

Marais did not know whether to feel better or worse after this answer. That Ulanov had a healthy respect for the Russian authorities and could be expected to use maximum caution came as a welcome surprise. On the other hand, the intensity of his friend's anxiety was disconcerting. "Why did you never discuss this with me before? That façade you kept up . . . You never showed the least strain, you—"

"My emotions were needed for other purposes," said Ulanov. "I thought and did everything that would ensure success. It's the only way. Prepare completely while you can, and then—then, you go into battle. Well, 'then' is now, and there is no longer any more to do or think, and the worries begin to get through."

"It's strange," Marais said. "Had you ever talked this honestly in Rome, it is just possible that I might not have come. Not until this instant did I realize how much *your* confidence buoyed me up all along."

"Odd that I should have been my own enemy," Ulanov said in that curious detached way of his. "Anyway, you were never forced to think how really dangerous, how nearly hopeless, this mission is."

[167]

"And still *you* never considered backing out?"

"I was meant for this work," said Ulanov. "This is the beginning and end of my life—here, now!"

"My God, do you really believe that?"

"With my heart and soul. And after this performance, it will probably all be over for me, a dénouement."

"You identify your whole being with one affair, with one task! It sounds monstrous, Dmitri. And the way you see your own personality, as though it were merely an external instrument . . ." He stopped, knowing he was not being listened to.

The bishop turned and walked back to the barely visible crates in the compartment. For the next ten minutes he paced about in these tight spaces while Marais, more anxious than ever in the company of one so restless, silently prayed for the train to start up. Just as he was becoming convinced that something had gone wrong, their helpers reappeared.

This time the leader, who handed up to Ulanov and Marais two large packages, spoke in Russian. "Take care, that's all you will have to eat until you get to Moscow." He then hoisted himself up and through the car slat. "The train leaves in about a minute. Do not move out of hiding unless the train is moving. And you must keep this door closed unless you are sure it is past midnight and that you are traveling in the countryside. If the train begins to slow down, go back into the boxes. And when you arrive in Moscow, be patient. It may take some time, but on no condition leave your hiding place. One of our people will come for you. They work there too but they will have to wait, perhaps, until they are sure. Now your blessing, Fathers, and God be with you."

Each of the priests bestowed a benediction on the man, who then jumped from the car, and, with his co-workers, helped slam the door shut. A few moments later the train slowly got under way, and the travelers stumbled through the darkness back to their crates. Marais found that for the moment his quarters were not impossibly cramped. He had to bend his legs only slightly, and even then there was leeway to move. Once he had fastened the box from inside, he found that he did not dread the confinement as much as he had feared.

[168]

For a while, Marais indulged himself by remaining in darkness, breathing in the sense of quiet his resting place afforded him—especially welcome after all the arguing with Ulanov. His mind flitted from one distraction to another, triggered by the most bizarre associations. His father, his childhood, speeches in Paris after this epochal mission was over, the newspapers, world authority . . . Then, repenting such grandiosity, he summoned humble images of himself—serving outcasts in exotic locales; a whispered legend of sanctity as he wandered in the hills half starved and difficult to find like Père Marquette or Jogues.

Marais could not tell how long he had spent with these fancies, for the darkness had easily destroyed his sense of time. He turned on his flashlight and began reading some recent propaganda on the rise in Soviet iron and steel production. Tiring of these statistics, he turned to his collection of recent ideological pronouncements by various party committees. Having read over this material and dozed for what might have been two hours, he was startled to hear knocks on the side of his crate. At his superior's signal, Marais undid the clasp locks that bound him inside and helped Ulanov push the car door back a couple of feet or so.

From then until the first intimations of sunrise they stood and watched the rushing landscape. They spoke very little, though they shared the coarse-grained bread and cheese with which the workers in Minsk had supplied them, and swapped the bottle of crude wine for which Marais had very little liking. The Frenchman assumed that Ulanov too was so overcome with the sight of Russia that he could do no more than silently breathe the air of this dark countryside, a symbol of vastness they could hardly imagine. For historical reasons the marshes of Pinsk had never struck Marais as being really Russia. Only now, as the turning wheels carried them into the heartland, did he feel the full weight of his Slavic appointment.

At the first hint from the horizon that the darkness was lifting, they closed the car door and retreated to their crates. Now began the long vigil during which neither of them would move from his hiding place. Marais found a kind of zigzag position in which he could lie with minimal discomfort. The wine

[169]

and the small streams of air filtering through the cracks of the box helped to ease his already exhausted body into the waiting arms of sleep.

His return long afterward to consciousness came as suddenly and without apparent transition as it had departed. The satisfying heaviness with which he awoke indicated that he had slept into the late afternoon. Hearing voices in the background, he realized that the door of the car was open and the train at a standstill. It surprised him that he had not awakened with these changes. Presumably they were in the railroad yards of Smolensk, which meant they were on schedule and would avoid running short of food or missing their contacts in Moscow.

Marais nudged from his rations a few slices of cheese cut the previous evening and a large piece of brown bread. This sandwich and a few swallows of wine constituted as fine a repast as he could desire in the circumstances. His single complaint through the next few hours was his legs' growing lack of aptitude for this box. Despite frequent and ingenious turns and twists, they ached. When he was ready to let them grow numb rather than move once more, he felt the jerks and jolts of the train that meant they were under way at last. Now he could wait for Ulanov's knock. As expected, it came quickly—the bishop was a half too large for comfort in these crates.

Together Marais and Ulanov spent the long hours much as they had the previous night, violating the strictures of the loading foreman in Minsk. "These rules, they are only good as long as *you* use *them*," Ulanov said, laughing.

Marais felt in no mood to quarrel with this commonsense casuistry. The long period spent in the wooden box had sapped any desire to obey a rule that promised another three hours in the crate.

As they stood by the door and looked out at the darkening countryside, Marais and Ulanov avoided discussing any of the crises that might greet them on their arrival in Moscow. They were so dependent now on their unknown friends there that speculation could only unnerve them.

Marais's own thoughts seemed affected by the rhythms of the train wheels as they turned in their senseless ba-room, ba-rom, ba-room, ba-rom, on and on, moving them ever closer to the Soviet capital. With the clangor of these repetitions came the image of faces, sometimes purgatorially limned; bunched together in a tableau of heads, young and old, pleading for relief from their fate. At other times Marais thought he saw a perverted transformation of the same figures; as they, pale and bizarrely clothed, mocked *him*.

The moment one of these hallucinations struck Marais, he would force himself to the sanity of conversation. Ulanov, for his part, awarded the landscape unbroken pensive gazes from time to time.

As the morning began to give her preliminary signs, the two priests relieved themselves over the side of the freight car, then removed from the car floor the telltale scraps of their last meal.

Ulanov gave Marais one final instruction. "Keep in mind that this next stretch is the most difficult part to predict. The train will probably stop over at a junction or two, or get delayed for some reason outside of Moscow. It hardly ever goes straight into the depot. So we have to be extremely careful when we climb out of these crates. The train's jerks and jolts could be deceptive—don't trust them. Someone may have hitched a ride between two close stations and be standing at the door. Under no conditions are you to get out of the box until I give you a signal."

"But how will *you* know when to get out?"

"I won't be positively certain myself," said Ulanov. "But I do have an instinct for these kinds of situations, and if worse comes to worse, I—well, I'm physically more able to take care of an unwelcome guest than you are."

"You wouldn't kill him!"

"Never," said Ulanov. "Just knock him out, bind him up, gag him so that he doesn't get in our way."

Seeing Marais's expression at this description, Ulanov grasped his arm. "You don't have to worry yourself about these details. I'm capable of handling any trouble like that—believe me. Even two of them would be no problem."

"I believe you. I've seen you in action."

"Oh yes." But Ulanov's eyes reflected only the dimmest

recollection of the cafe brawl. "Then all is agreed," he said. "Wait for my signal, no matter how long it takes."

"I'll wait. But please try not to overdo it."

Following this agreement, the priests retreated to their boxes. In addition to the voices and faces that continued to arise whenever Marais felt the rhythm of the train wheels, he found himself quite nervous at the prospect of Ulanov's assaulting a state representative. He finally resorted to conjuring up such hideous torments as could have been wracking him and were not. This stratagem together with his tiresome reading material finally succeeded in putting him to sleep.

On awakening, he followed his usual routine of eating lightly and then reading. Again he felt that he had slept for many hours; taking into account the time that had elapsed before he fell asleep, he figured that it must now be nearly six o'clock in the evening. The train was not moving.

For a period that seemed to last three or four hours, Marais heard no sounds. Just as he was starting to suffer the panic symptoms of claustrophobia, Marais felt those heavy jolts which served notice that they were under way. The momentum of the train seemed to pick up as the minutes went by.

Expecting Ulanov's knock at any moment, Marais waited and waited, until he could bear neither his own eagerness nor the numbing pain for another moment. Slowly and carefully he undid his clasps. Through practice he had mastered the knack of escaping from the box without making any more noise than could be masked by the train's progress.

As he sat in the dark, listening, he grew confident. He was still debating the virtue of an unauthorized emergence from the crate when he heard a small cough that he thought he recognized as Ulanov's, followed a few seconds later by a low-keyed exchange of voices. As he listened, his hearing more acute than it had ever been, he could pick up the cadence though not the words. He grew more willing to take a risk—yes, he was almost certain, one of the speakers was Ulanov. The thought ran roughshod over every restraint, and Marais began to crawl out of his box, moving as stealthily as possible between the other crates until he could obtain a vantage point from behind one of them.

What he saw destroyed the remainder of his equilibrium. Without a glimmer of doubt, there they were, the two of them by the open slot of the door. Ulanov and his brother, Nicholas, talking as quietly and amiably as any two friends might in the world.

Marais moved swiftly from behind the box. "So this is what you have been up to. You said to wait for a signal—is he it, Alexander?"

"Dmitri is my name here," said Ulanov.

"And who is this? Don't I remember you, sir?"

"It's Nicholas," said Ulanov.

"What is *he* doing here?" Marais was shouting. "Where did he come from? My God, Alex, *what have you done?*"

"Calm yourself, Josef. I told you when we started out—"

"You told me nothing. You had a vow of silence to keep."

"Damn that nonsense!" Ulanov shouted back for the first time.

"Damn the vows?"

"I didn't mean it exactly that way. No, not all of them."

"You took him with us, didn't you? You hid him all this time. Where? How?"

"Let me explain!"

"More lies? No! Liar! Liar! Liar!"

Ulanov grasped Marais by the heavy collar of his workshirt. "Don't call me that," he said, and shoved the Frenchman away from him.

Marais leaned against the side of the crate, breathing hard as he stared at the equally shaken Ulanov. "So he has been with us all these hours and days. In one of those boxes."

"Yes, he has."

"All the way from Minsk!"

"That's right."

"And you never once—wait, how is that possible? How could he have gotten on board this train at Minsk? Who would have known to help him to get into these boxes? I don't understand!"

"Yes you do," said Ulanov.

"Of course, *you* did. Who else? The Pope?"

"No sarcasm, Josef. I don't like it."

[173]

"Really? You have violated the most sacred rule of our mission, you have betrayed me, and now you are upset with my sarcasm?"

"I told you I had a plan!" Ulanov was shouting again. "Did you think I was going to surrender it—the plan which was necessary and could save my life and everyone else's life—just because you happened to be sent along, on some whim of Cardinal Pacelli's? Do you really think that changed anything?"

"That's not the point, your plan! You were sworn to faith, to silence."

"Are you a complete fool? Those kinds of things are secondary. If you can, you do. If you can't, you don't."

"You broke your vow."

"I explained it to you," said Ulanov, walking toward his brother. "I carefully explained to you the first night we got on this train, in the most honest way anyone could, what the lay of the land was. We were walking in like sheep, like all the others before us. You called me 'worried,' but you didn't know half the problems we faced and you still don't. You depended on me, but on whom was I to depend? I know my weaknesses, which is more than I can say for our superiors. I knew what we needed."

"So *he* is your plan?"

"Yes, he is." Ulanov gestured at the silent Nicholas.

"The last I recall," said Marais, "you were beating him half dead and bloody in the Slaves' House—that little incident that you find so hard to remember."

"Of course we remember," said Ulanov, turning again to Nicholas, whose deprecating smile changed for just a fleeting second to a glare. Just as suddenly, the threat vanished. "We have our disagreements, like everyone else," Ulanov continued. "He was drunk that night—upset, hurt. Well, Nicholas tends to be a bit anticlerical, but that's not the worst of moral deficiencies, is it?"

"What does he contribute to this mission?" Marais asked, as calmly as he could. Ulanov's conciliatory approach, he knew, must have a thin crust.

"The tactical brains, the security, the protection we need to go about our work in peace."

[174]

"And who is he to be able to provide those services? By what right does he do those things any better than you or I?"

Ulanov and his brother both laughed.

"Why don't you just explain yourself honestly?" said Marais, embarrassed and hurt.

"Do we have to go through all this, Alex?" The younger Ulanov's first words of the evening struck Marais as equally contemptuous of his brother and their mutual adversary.

"I think we owe it to Paul—Josef," said Ulanov.

"We owe him nothing!"

"He is my partner," Ulanov reminded him.

"I don't want our life story washed out in public. It's none of his business. Besides, you told me you were in charge here, remember?"

"It appears that you've said a few different things to different people," Marais said quietly.

"I can't stand this bickering," said Ulanov. "Look out there, the two of you—look out there, we're in Russia! We have enemies all around and there are only three of us, and we are quarreling among ourselves. Josef, Josef"—he approached Marais—"I realize my brother irritates you, but that is just his way. He says what he thinks straight out and he can sound terrible, almost mean, but he's loyal and trustworthy and—smart! Smart as a fox! You understand what I'm talking about. Some people we both know are all honey on the surface, but inside they're treacherous and cowardly. But Nicholas is as tough, as faithful a man as you have ever seen, and he's brave and—"

"Dmitri!" Marais held up his hand like a stop signal. "Will you tell me, please, why is he here? What exactly does he supply?"

"I will, I will!" shouted Ulanov. "Nicholas has been to Moscow four times already." He smiled at his colleague's surprise. "Yes! Now you can see how valuable a man he is. I say that not just because he is my brother. Nicholas has been a steelworker for many years. Most of that time he spent in America, but for the past three years he has been working around Europe."

"The same month that you arrived in Rome, he came too?"

"Perfectly right! Now, as you know, I am a socialist. So is Nicholas. On a number of occasions he has traveled as a member of workers' organizations, with steel unions and other groups, to Russia. He has a fine understanding of what goes on there, and what is important, he knows how their secret police operate. He has contacts that put him above suspicion. And I can vouch for his cleverness at spotting the least sign of danger—something that is far beyond our abilities, but second nature to Nicholas. This is why I have chosen to take him with us. We need him! What does the Vatican really know about these matters?"

He paused to assess the effect of this explanation. Marais believed that Ulanov's motivation in this affair had been rendered truthfully enough. It also occurred to him that he had rarely seen Alexander work so hard to convince another person of the reasons behind his actions. As for Nicholas, he had turned his side to the others and was gazing out the open slot at the evening landscape. To judge from the set of his profile, he was thoroughly disgusted with his brother's appeal in his behalf.

"You people haven't got all night to discuss this, you know," he said. "The way this train is going we'll be in Moscow within a few hours. They must need the equipment on board pretty bad." Nicholas delivered this nonchalant warning without ever turning around, speaking with that air of weary cynicism which, to Marais, epitomized the entire character of the fellow.

Marais, who knew that he could never think very well when confronted with a *fait accompli* of this sort, now felt himself cornered by the arrangements Ulanov had already put into effect.

"What's wrong?" asked Ulanov. "I have explained everything, and you still seem troubled. It will be all right, Josef, I promise."

"You have done things you had no right to do," said Marais, shaking his head.

"The others didn't come back. I have told you, over and over—"

"You never confided in me. You alone have been the judge of what is necessary and unnecessary, of what are useless and useful rules."

"For the last time, don't you see why I had to do it this way?"

"It is clear what you wanted to do, it isn't clear that the situation really required it. And then, I wonder if there will be other choices you make without conferring with me? What other orders of the Vatican will you set aside?"

"I promise that from here on in you will be a party to every decision."

Marais stared at Ulanov with all the coldness he could summon. The break between the two of them caused by the sudden introduction of Nicholas into the plan was, the Frenchman knew, irreparable. From here on, he and the bishop would be wary partners. He would watch carefully every action of the brothers. He would never accept anything, if it could be helped, on their word alone.

"You accept my promise, then?" asked Ulanov.

"Yes."

"You will not sabotage the mission."

"No."

Ulanov clapped Marais on the back, then turned to his brother. "I told you Josef would understand," he said.

This constant use of an unaccustomed cover name increased the French Jesuit's feeling of alienation.

"He doesn't seem happy about it," said Nicholas.

"I don't know you," said Marais.

"I know my brother," said Ulanov. "Better than I know any soul in this world."

"I suppose that's sufficient," said Marais, intentionally leaving a lacuna to be filled.

"My brother and I have been very close, Josef. I will tell you"—Ulanov gestured expansively—"that all through those years in the seminary, not a visiting day passed but Nicholas came to spend it with me, and when I was sent to Rome, he joined me there, too."

"Have you no family of your own, Nicholas?" asked Marais.

"I've had enough of this sentimental stuff," the younger brother muttered.

"We were orphaned," said Ulanov smoothly. "When I was fourteen."

"No more of this! It's our own business, Alex. *It belongs to no one else.* That's our oath—right, brother?"

"All right. But remember, I am Dmitri—to you, too."

Nicholas reacted to this precautionary remark as though it were an insult. His pockmarked face showed an intense emotion that nearly became tears of rage when he turned back to face the landscape. Ulanov, as far as Marais could observe, either did not notice or did not care. He merely walked away, munching his bread and cheese.

Marais tried again to assess the situation, from every conceivable angle. No matter how he interpreted the facts, he could not reconcile himself to the soundness of the third man. Willing to credit Nicholas with cleverness, survival instincts, knowledge, and experience, he nonetheless found him too crude—or too brutal. Nicholas seemed to be full of undigested lumps of emotion. In many ways, Marais thought, the brother is half savage.

He conceded, on further reflection, Nicholas's strange loyalty to Alexander. And yet, might not the Jesuit be blind to his brother's weaknesses? Perhaps he was too close to notice the immense distance that separated them. In his lack of sensitivity, Nicholas mirrored the Jesuit himself. Since both of these family members lacked some human center, how did they relate to each other?

Somehow, this question now seemed critical. And where, after a bond of so many years, was Alexander's influence on Nicholas?

Ulanov had been pacing about the car, presumably making some assessments of his own. he finally approached Marais. "There are a few suggestions I would like to make, Josef. First, that we take the lodgings Nicholas can obtain for us in Moscow. I believe he is right when he says that if we live in the quarters given us by our contact, we will fall into the old traps."

"I don't know," said Marais, who recoiled from the prospect of further dissension and of making further concessions.

"Well, we need an answer one way or another. It is within your jurisdiction to overrule me if I follow Nicholas's advice on this point."

"I need time to reflect."

"There is no time."

Nicholas snapped his fingers to call their attention to a red light in the distance. "You see that beacon out there? That

[178]

means we're less than a hundred miles from Moscow. You'll have to close the door and get inside those crates in a few minutes."

"Well, what's your answer, Josef? Quickly, we have to—"

"As usual, you give me no choice." Marais cut off his colleague before he could repeat the demand. "From here on," he said, "you will kindly make your requests a couple of hours—hopefully a couple of days—before we must act. Is that understood?"

"I take it that the answer is yes?"

As Marais nodded, he noticed that Ulanov gave the brother a congratulatory wink. The gesture infuriated Marais. "Tell me something, *Dmitri*," he said. "How can Nicholas make these arrangements when he is closed inside a crate like we are?"

Nicholas answered for himself. "I won't be inside that crate. I'm jumping from this train as soon as it slows down. I put in a few phone calls to some steel friends of mine, then I get back to you at the railroad yard. And when the time is right, I tell your contact people that we've had a change of plans. Does that satisfy you?"

"How will you know our contacts?"

"They'll have to show themselves, won't they? They're scheduled to do the same thing in Moscow they did in Minsk, only the other way around this time—get you out of a box and into a truck. I'll tell them where to take us. If worse comes to worse, I'll show them this." He pulled out from his pocket, handling it as he would an old wrench, the pectoral cross that belonged to Ulanov by virtue of his bishopric—the gleaming valuable cross that was a gift of Cardinal Pacelli.

"How much have you really told him?" Marais asked Ulanov.

"Everything."

"So that's how he got on board at Minsk. All of this was arranged in *Rome*."

"I thought I had been through all this with you before. You must not have been listening."

"And what will Nicholas do in Russia—or have you managed to already consecrate him a bishop besides everything else?"

"Your attitude remains hostile, Josef, despite the complete

[179]

honesty with which I have explained every detail. You persist in regarding my brother and my transactions with him as the work of enemies, you attack every improvement we make as though it were some sort of betrayal. I can't have this, I swear!" Ulanov delivered his ultimatum with such force that Marais knew he could push no further. He decided to retreat under a cover of protest.

"You yourself admitted that Nicholas has never made a good impression, and you're his brother. Well, suppose you were an outsider—just imagine what you would think! He acts toward me, your partner in this mission, as if *I* were an enemy. This completely unauthorized person treats a delegate of the Vatican like dirt, and over this kind of behavior you exert no control whatsoever except to berate me. Who in the world could assimilate these shocks one after another, within the space of an hour?"

Nicholas placed himself between Ulanov and Marais. "You don't like my manner and I don't like yours, that's what it amounts to, doesn't it? Well, who cares? I've got a job to do. That's all that counts, and you listen to me, mister—before we're finished, I'm going to save your life and his life, do you get that? I made myself a promise and it's going to be kept. I'll get myself killed before either one of you gets caught. That's *my* mission. The two of you will never see the inside of a prison. That's what I swear to you, and you got nothing more to ask of me than that!"

Nicholas had leaned over Marais, intimidating him not with a physical threat but with the force of his words and tone. Though liking the man as little as ever, Marais found that the strength of his convictions, the intensity of his "promise" went a long way toward ameliorating fear.

"But what will you do in Russia? May I ask you that without offending you?"

"Sure," said Nicholas, that half-surly grin creasing his features. "You see this packet? Well, it's got all sorts of things inside. I got me a visa and a letter from some Italian communists and something else from the Steelworkers' people in the United States. I'm supposed to get an education on how they plan production from central headquarters and what they do to get the individual plants to shape up, a lot of that kind of stuff so I can impress the workers back home. I have a blank check to travel around. Meanwhile, I'll be looking after you fellows a lot of the time so you don't get yourself killed."

"And they didn't ask you to join the Communist Party?" asked Marais.

"Oh, sure, they asked me, but they're more interested in sympathizers. Working-class types, you know what I mean? I qualify for a useful stiff ... Well, that's it! Did you hear those whistles a minute ago? They're pushing this heap, and we're getting close. Okay, now, into those boxes." He gave Marais a heavy clap on the shoulders, said, "I'll see you soon," and pushed the Frenchman into his crate.

With a number of starts and stops, Marais's last stay in his own crate lasted, at a guess, three or four hours. Marais was as surprised by the amount of time elapsed as he had been by the abrupt conclusion of the conversation with Nicholas. Even Alexander-Dmitri had acceded without protest to the brother's urgent directives. Yet the trip from that point had taken so long that Marais now questioned the speed with which he had been dispatched into the crate.

He had also worked his way through confusion to a few simple resolutions. Ulanov obviously had been close to Nicholas for years, and knew how to use him. Therefore, since Ulanov could be trusted on essentials, an indirect act of faith in Nicholas seemed not unsound. Marais would make no scene in Moscow, nor would he write any upsetting notes to Rome. He would await further developments and hope that he had seen the worst.

Then other, more immediate, fears began to play on Marais. He heard the slamming of the freight car door, the heaving grunts and the pounding of boxes around him. From the workers' talk, he gathered that the crates were to be transferred to another train going farther east; perhaps to Magnitogorsk or Kuznetsk. His dread of what could befall his half-false box mounted. Surely the lighter weight would be noticed. And how could he be sure those husky voices outside belonged to friends?

A number of boxes were removed before his own was given a shove. It was even tumbled on its side, and then Marais felt the lighter vibrations of being moved along a swaying ramp. The sensation of expecting at any moment to crash through that wooden underpinning, in company with the heavy motor beside him, was terrifying. Marais was so busy swearing to be content with Ulanov if he ever survived this ordeal that he hardly noticed when his crate was settled on the ground.

He laid his ear alongside the frame, piecing together what was happening from the fragments of conversation he could make out. An agreement had been reached for a nearby truck to transport the crates to another part of the yard where they would be unloaded alongside a boxcar for shipment to the East. Afterward the truck was to pick up parts from a certain depot and then deliver them to the new terminal point. These crucial parts had to be shipped with the motors. A rough-voiced fellow, perhaps a foreman, approved these arrangements and apparently signed papers identifying the drivers and their official purpose. Immediately after, Marais felt the box being loaded onto a truck.

Judging from the terrible jolts, the truck was rumbling at great speed across cobblestones. Then, suddenly, it halted. In another moment Marais heard the knock signal on top of the box. He undid the clasps and slid with a sigh of gratitude out of his wooden prison. As soon as he joined Ulanov and Nicholas, they jumped down and ran behind the corner of a dark hangar. The truck, once they had left it, started off again.

"So far, so good," Nicholas whispered, then put a finger to his mouth. They waited perhaps a quarter of an hour before the truck returned. It stopped beside them for a few seconds, then roared off again once the three had climbed over the tailguard.

They sat close together inside the vehicle. A piece of heavy tarpaulin hung down over half of the truck's rear, and though it flapped most of the time, it gave them adequate cover. The sun had not yet risen, and nobody was on the streets—if people were there, it was impossible to see them without street lamps. Then, just as Marais was adjusting comfortably to his invisibility and the good fortune of being transported through darkness, he heard staccato whistle bursts from either side of an intersection. As the truck stopped, Marais's body froze in chill fear. The others seemed just as stricken. Nicholas, who was sitting knees up opposite Marais, gripped his head between his hands as though ready to scream over this accident of timing.

The driver and his assistant could be heard answering two men who were questioning them about their destination, the cause of this late-night movement, and why they had not repaired this vehicle, which was disturbing the neighborhood with its noisy exhaust. They then asked for the mandatory documents, and, after an agonizing pause, dismissed the driver with a warning to overhaul his machine or face charges if he entered this sector again.

The truck proceeded without delay to leave these men behind. Its rear occupants smiled painfully at each other, each of them aware that they had almost been finished before they began. But when Marais laid his finger across his throat to signal that he knew how bad the situation had threatened to be, Nicholas shrugged his shoulders and turned once more to peer from the rear of the truck into the darkness.

Marais understood why Nicholas could not acknowledge such a near tragedy. He would have been the one primarily responsible for it. Nor would he want the French Jesuit to meditate too long on the lesson to be drawn from this experience—that Ulanov's brother could be catastrophically wrong in his calculations.

Marais tried, nonetheless, to take an optimistic view of things. Once the three were established, there would be no more of these terrifying night rides. Besides, the Ulanovs also had been badly frightened by this encounter. The trio would live as retiring an existence as the humble workmen they were supposed to be. Should petty authorities question them, their excuses would also be in order—soon they would have jobs. The police would probably be content to determine their place of employment without pushing the question of antecedents too far. Hopefully, then, they had passed through the worst at the very beginning.

When the truck stopped without warning and went into reverse, the three men slid up to the tailguard. "We're here," said Nicholas after a quick look at the building in front of them. "Jump!" As soon as they were clear of the vehicle, it rumbled off. Marais realized that he had lost the opportunity of meeting the driver and his assistant who had risked their lives for their cargo, and the thought depressed him. "Come on." Nicholas pulled at his arm. "We've got to get out of this street."

They entered the two-story wooden frame building from a side entrance, climbed the stairs, and proceeded a few steps down a dimly lit corridor where a door stood ajar. Nicholas withdrew a flashlight and probed the room. "This is the place, all right," he said, closing the door behind them. Rummaging around, he found a kerosene lamp which was conveniently filled and lit it immediately. "Welcome to Russian life, fellows. This is it for the next few months."

Marais looked around the room—it was only a few square feet larger than his bedroom as a child. "All three of us will live here?"

"And like it, too! Do you know how hard it is to find a place to live in Moscow? People kill for space."

"After the crates, it is quite acceptable," said Ulanov. "Congratulations, Nicholas. And you must thank your friends for us. They've provided us with all the conveniences."

Marais could see bunks along the walls, a couple of screens, a table and lamp, two well-worn chairs, and a wood-burning Holland stove; but he failed to notice any sign of those other items necessary for "convenience."

"Where is the kitchen?" he asked somewhat plaintively.

"There's one on this floor," said Nicholas. "Everybody uses it. You can store your food in there, but I wouldn't advise it. They'll only steal it. Anyway, if you want to, you can boil some water for tea in there. I guess you already know there's very little hot running water in the Soviet Union. Maybe Stalin has it, but I wouldn't bet on it. If you want it hot, you boil it.

"Look, you've got it easy compared with what you could have had. Up until this year everyone carried a ration card with little colored coupons that let you have only so much of this and so much of that for the whole month. But the new Five-year Plan—"

"Yes, I know all about it," Marais said, as much to forestall a lecture as to demonstrate his knowledge. "After all the emphasis they've been giving heavy industry since 1928, *this* one is supposed to be for the consumer."

"That's it," smiled the other. "So be happy!" He put his hand upon his brother's shoulder. "I told you I would be indispensable, didn't I?" he said softly. "Remember, Alex?"

"Dmitri!"

"Who cares, Alex or Dmitri. I was just trying to shake up your sidekick, Josef, see if he could take it. He's a rich man's son. He's got to get used to the hard life. The working people have to live it, and they don't have the benefit of prayers, either."

While he talked, Nicholas kept his hand on the bishop's shoulder in a posture that may have been their way years before. Marais had never seen anyone so slyly affectionate with Alexander; the gesture seemed a violation of that loneliness and distance Ulanov so carefully cultivated.

Marais's intuition was clearly correct. Brother or not, Ulanov looked at Nicholas as though the other's arm threatened disease. The remoteness of the Jesuit's eyes even discomfited Nicholas, though he seemed determined not to notice it.

To Marais, the byplay was intriguing. Despite the years together, Alexander and Nicholas were not friends, and they both knew it. But then, how *did* the bishop perceive his relation to Nicholas, his only flesh-and-blood attachment on earth?

"I'm going to be doing the shopping for us," Nicholas was explaining. "If I can't an old lady I know will go out, how's that? That will save time."

"Very good," said Ulanov.

"And if I don't cook, she will."

"Nicholas is an excellent cook, Josef," said Ulanov. "It's one of his many talents. I can't cook an egg. By the way, I assume this woman is trustworthy?"

For some reason this question made Nicholas laugh.

"What's wrong?" asked Alexander.

Nicholas shook his head as though his amusement were purely personal. "Sure she is! Absolutely. I thought I was the expert in those things. You wouldn't know the right people to trust if you fell over them, Dmitri."

Bishop Ulanov, his question answered in the affirmative, ignored the self-inflated end of his brother's response.

"How were you able to make all these arrangements on such short notice?" asked Marais.

"Connections. Money."

[185]

"But you know so much about this house."

"I always stay here when I come to Moscow. People know me. I paid the workers who used to live in this apartment a hundred rubles to bunk in with someone else for six months. They jumped for it." Nicholas folded his arms. "You satisfied now? I told you everything."

Marais lay down on one of the bunks. "I'm too tired. I must sleep."

"When do we report for work?" asked Ulanov.

"In a couple of days. You can rest up till then, but don't hang around the halls or neighborhood if you get up late. People will ask questions about you, especially since you're new. I'll get the word out quick that you're telephone repairmen. They'll like that. And remember, you lost your wives and children in an accident. You still haven't gotten over it, so that's why you're not taking out any of the Russian girls. You fellows are too old not to have families, so you have to play the grief bit strong, you hear me? I'll get you phony pictures you can put on the tables, nice smiling women, children . . ."

The astute hints from Nicholas penetrated Marais's inner haze of fatigue. These were the kinds of details that never occurred to the Vatican, but misstepping on any one of them apparently could spell disaster for the priests.

"Just a few other pointers and you're on your way," said Nicholas, obviously enjoying his role as coach. "The two of you speak like guys who got out of college, and that's a problem. People will wonder what you're doing repairing telephones, so you, Josef, you were a teacher once but then you decided to get away, switch jobs. Alex—Dmitri—you can't use the same excuse. Maybe you can change your Russian, shift into more of that rough stuff we learned as kids. Talk more like me if you can. It'll help." Nicholas laughed at some funny association. "You can also tell them your father was a rich bourgeois who gave you good schooling but you've disowned him and become a worker. That will get you off the hook if you forget and start sounding like some intellectual character.

"In the morning I'll give you a list of the names of people on this floor, and one downstairs that you shouldn't talk to if you can help it. And if you have to say more than hello, be real nice and careful, you understand? Some of them are troublemakers, or else they repeat whatever they hear."

Nicholas stretched and yawned, satisfied that he had covered the basics. Marais felt the onset of a warm and novel sense of security beginning to expand in his mind, driving out the old demons of fear, and it wasn't long before this breath of hope mated with the night's exhaustion to bring on sleep.

10

Two months after his nighttime introduction to Moscow, Marais could hardly believe that he had known terror. Nothing that had happened in the sixty days following his departure from the train station in a crate remotely matched the fright of that evening. Never again had he heard the harsh sound of a police agent's voice. No careening rides occurred in the early-morning hours, nor, as it turned out, were there many more restrictions to assimilate from Nicholas's repertoire.

Marais, relaxing now on a bench inside one of the small houses dotting the Park of Culture and Rest, was even tempted to consider his first experiences as unreal. He enjoyed such easy rapport with his fellow workers, and the cover job taxed his energies so little, that he was seriously considering Ulanov's suggestion to extend their stay by six months. Their real work, the baptizing, confirming, and ordaining of Catholic Christians, showed so much promise that considering the lack of threat it seemed sinful to go home on schedule.

Marais gazed at the few pieces still remaining on the chess board in front of him. Since early morning he had been playing one "visitor" after another. This large area, which had been bricked in as a building, served as a perfect place to meet candidates for the sacraments. They could sit and mumble to each other for an hour or more in a corner without attracting attention.

Looking down at the half-completed game, Marais impulsively

moved his rook to a stronger offensive position on the board. He felt chagrined that he was interested in winning—the game was supposed to be no more than a cover, and haphazard moves would be perfectly understandable.

A voice interrupted his concentration. "Are you Josef?"

Marais looked up. "Yes. Can I help you?"

"I am Leonid," the old man said softly. "May I sit down?"

Marais gestured to the seat opposite him.

"Sergey told me that you are a priest. I wish to make my confession. Is it convenient?"

"I was waiting—for you."

"I expect so."

Marais waited in silence for Leonid to muster up the courage to begin.

"I could win this game," the penitent murmured, studying the board.

"You inherited a bad position," said Marais.

"Even so . . ."

"Perhaps afterward."

The old man raised his eyes to meet Marais's. "Bless me, Father, for I have sinned."

Marais closed his eyes and made a small sign of the cross with his fingers on the table.

"It is fifteen years since my last confession. There were no priests, you understand. I might have found one, but I was afraid . . . of the police, yes, but more of myself." He paused on the brink of the abyss.

"Now you are more afraid of how death shall find you. But God already knows."

"I have lived in sin for many years with . . . with a woman. She is not my wife. Not in the eyes of the church."

"Were you married before you met this woman?"

"Yes."

"And is your wife still alive?"

"Yes."

"Why did you leave her?"

"A terrible woman. No one liked her at all."

"You had quarrels."

"I drank a lot then."

[190]

"And now?"

"I gave that up when I met my present wife."

"You have a civil marriage with this woman?"

"Everything legal. The divorce first . . ."

"Was your first marriage in the church?"

"Unfortunately."

"Have you had sexual intercourse with this second woman?"

"Not so much any more. I'm seventy-eight."

"You knew that such cohabitation was mortally sinful?"

"Everyone says so."

"Are you sorry for your violation of God's law?"

Leonid started to cough, and Marais saw a couple of chess pieces fall; the queen and the bishop, lying on their side. "It's so long ago." The old fellow was scratching at his scraggly beard. "It must be almost thirty years I am with Katerina." He seemed to be puzzling over the priest's question. "I can't find it in me to remember the first one. God help me, her face is gone from my head altogether. Though not her tongue."

It was Marais's turn to put his hands wearily across his eyes. The divine law that had to be honored and made so much sense on paper seemed oddly irrelevant at the moment. Marais struggled for some way to open the sacrament to the old Russian without brutalizing his feelings.

"Katerina is a good woman," said Leonid, obviously torn between what he needed and the betrayal that would surely be asked in return. "We . . . we've had a good life together. I love her very much. I never tell her, of course. That wouldn't do. She's liable to take advantage, you know how women are. But, she knows."

"I understand what you're saying." Marais laid his hand on the old man's arm, not looking into his eyes. "Tell me, Leonid," he said finally, "is it possible that you were in any way responsible for the breakup of your original marriage?"

The old man took his time pondering the implications of the question. "I suppose you could say that I drank heavy and then I beat her up a bit. Of course, she had it coming."

"Wouldn't you say you're sorry about those acts?"

"Oh yes, Father. I was very headstrong in those days, a violent brute of a man. You wouldn't have recognized me."

Marais pondered whether this admission wasn't equivalent to repentance over his divorce. The penitent was contrite over acts that led up to it; then, logically, he could be said to be contrite over the final act. The priest could not insist on Leonid's disowning a faithful love of thirty years, but every tack he could think of ended in forcing the issue.

"In the eyes of the church," Marais said, "your present relationship is no real marriage. You understand that?" The old man nodded with a dutiful appearance of regret. "And she accepts that you manifest true sorrow for what you have done?" The penitent nodded again. "But before I can give you absolution, there is another requirement that you must satisfy." Leonid's attention flared instantly. "You must not have sexual intercourse with this woman again."

The Russian pursed his lips and bit on them, weighing the cost of such an assent. He took at least a minute to deliberate. Then, "It's a deal," he said.

Marais looked at him in astonishment.

"What I mean is . . . I think I can manage that."

"You would be committing a mortal sin if you make love to your wife, exposing yourself again to eternal—"

"No, no, I understand, Father. A man can't have everything in this world. All in all, it's very fair."

After Leonid had confessed a few remaining venial sins, Marais gave him absolution by making the sign of the cross with his fingers over the old man's heart. "Do you feel better?" the priest asked.

"Very much relieved, thank you, Father." He stroked his beard again as a prelude to a thought. "It's odd," he said, "how a few minutes like this can make all the difference to heaven or to hell."

Marais managed not to smile. "Leonid, it's a question of attitude!" he said sternly. "And attitude can come in a minute, or a year, or never. The time is irrelevant."

"I suppose so," said the old man. "By the way, if something happens in a man's sleep, is he responsible for it?"

"Not too much, I shouldn't think," Marais said before he realized what the Russian had in mind.

"I'm sorry I can't stay for a game of chess, but things seem

too good now to take a chance of spoiling them. *Do svidaniya,*
Father."

"Yes . . . goodbye," Marais said slowly.

The old man left very quickly, and, in time, Marais began to
doze a bit.

Neither of the Jesuits had anticipated that their activities
would leave them exhausted. Work began at eight in the morning,
and, since no one checked on the telephone workers, they were
able to leave the job about four thirty. With this schedule, their
real job—consuming five, six, or seven hours each evening—could
be handled without undue strain. They devised excuses to take
many Saturdays off, and the use of the weekend enabled them to
rendezvous with Catholics outside Moscow.

Cardinal Pacelli had proven as good as his word. The meeting
with the original contact and the chain of human links worked
exactly as planned. Yet had it not been for Alexander-Dmitri's
extraordinary personality, Marais doubted that they would have
achieved a quarter of their present success. For some reason,
Ulanov inspired a remarkable trust and enthusiasm among the
underground Christians. These Russians believed in him as they
did in no other foreigner, and in few of their countrymen.

And so, Marais thought, Ulanov's prophetic statements about
himself were being verified. He indeed seemed to have been born
for this mission.

In fact, Marais had to admit that Ulanov's election increasingly looked like the most fortunate decision ever made by the
Vatican. Faced now with the actual work in Russia, he realized
how wrong it would have been for either him or Nimsky to have
been chosen as the leader. Whatever could have been in his mind
these few short weeks ago for him to be so mistaken?

Marais put his hand over his eyes and let himself drowse for a
moment. Since the middle of the week he had been experiencing
sudden bouts of dizziness and sweating. A vague fatigue had
crept into his bones so that he ached to sleep. Still, today of all
days, he could not allow himself to give in to this minor aggrava-
tion. "It is a touch of influenza," he told himself. "I will get to
sleep a little earlier, and the trembling will be gone in the
morning."

Sergey Cherbasov, his contact, was late, but Marais would wait another half hour if necessary. He trusted no one on the mission so much as he did the "Great Bear." He had promised to come today; that was enough. Something very important must have come up to delay him.

Marais felt a proprietary interest in Sergey. It was he who had pushed the Russian forward for rapid ordination over Ulanov's objections. It was not that the bishop objected to anything in Sergey's character; he had simply asked for time to reflect. This was the first time in their relationship that Marais had wanted to act immediately and Ulanov to wait. Marais's confidence took a leap with this triumph, for each week that went by further revealed the wisdom of the choice. Sergey's deep voice and giant frame, almost as tall as Ulanov's, served to augment his effectiveness in working among the Russians. They listened to his slow shrewd judgments with a respect otherwise reserved only for Ulanov, and in fact it was Sergey's support of Ulanov and Marais that had won the two Jesuits such early success.

The Frenchman stood up, restless. His legs were numb, and he stomped on the stone floor in an effort to restore circulation. A few of the chess players at other tables turned around and glared at him. Marais nodded back an apology and moved quickly out of doors, where he paced back and forth in front of the chess building. "He probably stayed another hour to coach that soccer team of his," Marais muttered.

He was of a mind to luxuriate in this resentment when he spotted Sergey in the distance and started to hurry toward his friend. He stopped short—Sergey had paused to look behind him twice within the minute—and waited around a corner of the building. "What's wrong, Sergey?" he asked when the Russian was at his side. "I saw you turning and thought it better to retreat."

"I'm sorry I'm late." Sergey gave him a quick rough embrace. "It may be nothing, Father Paul, it just caught me off guard. Give me a moment." He laughed, his hand resting on the Frenchman's shoulder.

"Sergey, I won't collapse, I promise. Stop protecting me."

"You've become so strong these past weeks, Father Paul, I don't want to start up the old fears again and probably for nothing at all."

[194]

"That's behind me now. I'm not convinced any longer that the G.P.U. is waiting to pounce on us at any moment. I realized that's the best way to call attention to ourselves."

"Well, then . . . After I finished coaching the junior soccer team this morning, I went to pick up a paper. I was reading it, going down the street, when I realized it was yesterday's edition and decided to go back. Just as I turned around, I caught sight of Nicholas Ulanov about a block away, looking in my direction. I ran through the crowd to meet him, but when I got there he was gone. I didn't know what to make of it. Then, as I was on my way here, I thought I saw him two more times. He was so quick I couldn't be certain."

"But *why?*"

Sergey shrugged. "Perhaps he doesn't trust us."

"He trusts no one except Alexander, you know."

"I don't know that *I* trust *him*. Were it not for his brother, I would not allow him to move among our people. Nicholas is a low fellow, Father Paul. It makes me very uncomfortable to see him at my back."

"Maybe Alexander told him to watch us. But why?"

"We shall ask when we see them tonight. Nicholas had better have a good answer or . . ." Sergey cracked the knuckles of one enormous hand.

"Nicholas," Marais said quickly, "has a great deal of curiosity about the two of us. He likes to know what's going on, but he has no information about where *we* go twice a week. You haven't told Alexander, have you?" .

"You told me not to. I never understood why you couldn't tell your own bishop, but I have followed your wishes."

"Rome ordered it for security purposes. The bishop knows that these arrangements exist, but that's all he knows. Nicholas made some overtures along these lines a few weeks ago. He was sure he could help with our mysterious security operations. I refused. He insisted, of course. He said I might be jeopardizing everyone without knowing it, and since he was the expert in this area, he wanted to inspect our procedures."

"You noticed he picks the very day we're going to the station to follow me?"

"Perhaps he hasn't given up the idea yet."

[195]

"But I lost him, I'm sure of it. Still, we'll be careful on the way."

Using a variety of precautions, the two priests took longer than usual to get to the terminal. When they arrived, they hurried along the platform to the Leningrad train. Halfway down its length they spied the car with a small white flag attached to a rod alongside its boarding section. Sergey stationed himself along the wall, while Marais went on alone.

"It's all right," said the conductor as Marais opened the door of the car's first compartment. "I'm alone this trip." The old man pulled a small piece of paper from the lining beneath one of the seats. "Here it is, Father."

Marais broke the seal and read the brief message: "Since you are doing so well in Moscow, you can proceed whenever you wish to explore openings in Leningrad and Byelorussia with contacts previously designated." The single initial "F" represented the sender. Marais looked for other code marks inside the words and found them.

"Do you have anything for us?" the conductor asked.

"Not this time, Ivan. Probably next week."

"You sound out of breath. Is anything wrong?"

"We were being particularly careful. We thought someone might try to follow us."

"Our lives rest in your hands, Father. Take no chances! Are you sure there is nothing I should report?"

"Not yet. *Gospodi*, Ivan."

"*Gospodi*, Father."

Marais left just as the steam rose hissing and curling in clouds around the wheels. Together he and Sergey walked back down the platform. "I always feel calmer after I've made contact with Ivan," Marais said.

Sergey smiled. "He makes me feel that things go well both far and near."

They were moving inconspicuously through a side aisle of the terminal when they heard a chuckle behind them. "I said you fellows didn't know how to handle an operation like this, didn't I?"

The two spun around at the sound of the familiar voice. "Where in God's name did *you* come from?" asked Sergey.

"I never noticed him!" said Marais.

"I've been tailing you all day, Father Cherbasov." Nicholas seemed to enjoy addressing Sergey by his new title in a slightly mocking tone. "You're a terrible spy, you know that?"

"Why have you been trailing us? No one gave you any such permission. This is—"

"I'm doing you a favor, you know. You should never allow anyone to shadow you like I did."

"I was positive I had lost you. No one could have stayed that close to us."

"I could. You people are lucky I'm not a real spy. If I was, you'd be dead now. Besides"—Nicholas grinned as he delivered the *coup de grâce*—"that idea of getting in the car with the white flag on it is dumb. I saw the whole thing from down here. If you're going to exchange a message with somebody, you should never meet him face to face. You drop your stuff at a spot agreed on. He comes by and picks it up, and then you come by later on and get his material, understand? You can use a wastepaper basket for that if you have to.

"And as long as you guys are listening, for a change, I got another suggestion. You're too big, Father Cherbasov, to keep coming in and out of here every week without attracting notice. Josef"—he looked at Marais—"you look pretty average, but sooner or later they're bound to catch on to you too. You got to distribute the responsibility among more people, you understand? I don't mind you being this dumb if it was only yourselves. But I don't want me and my brother paying for your mistakes."

With that Nicholas walked away.

Sergey and Marais sat down on a nearby bench.

"Can he be right, Father Paul? Is it possible we were such fools?"

"Don't talk like that, Sergey. I know this man."

"He saw everything."

"He's a trickster. Whatever he's done, there's a trick behind it."

"And what will you do about our arrangements here? They are compromised, and I am responsible."

"We can always change these things later. But, look, it isn't so

[197]

bad as it seems. I doubt that you had much to do with Nicholas getting here." Sergey brightened a bit. "Yes," Marais went on, "I think he may have trailed you to the soccer field and on the street, but you lost him. He gambled at that point, you see. He already had some idea from Alex that our rendezvous was connected with the railroad station. He decided that today might be the day. So when he was left behind, he came here and waited for us. It was easy for us to miss him in the crowd. We were already late. Then, a little peek around the corner of that door and he figures out the signal. In any case, you were not responsible."

"But the contact is ruined!"

"If Nicholas wanted to ruin us, he wouldn't have let us know he was here. He didn't have to. I think he just wants to be in on everything that happens. It could be he doesn't trust us, or maybe he's looking out for the bishop's interests. He thinks that you and I have too much power."

Sergey threw up his hands in exasperation. "I can't get used to this sort of thing. When our people say something, that is what they mean to say. If someone acts as strange as this Nicholas, we either keep him away from us completely, or we dispose of him. The faithful and the spy. There is no in between."

Marais, feeling he had achieved his goal of calming his friend, wanted nothing more than a little rest before tonight's big meeting. "I feel tired, Sergey," he said.

"Come to my apartment, Father Paul. My wife will take care of you."

"I still can't get used to the idea of a priest having a wife. It's a wonderful dispensation you have. Perhaps Rome will give us—no, I can't go."

"Too exciting." Sergey laughed. "Bad thoughts, Father Paul?"

"If I go to sleep at your place, your wife is too kind to wake me up. I'll sleep on until tomorrow."

"And why not? You're not needed at the gathering tonight."

"Yet I must be there. This is the first general assembly of underground Christians in years, a historic occasion, Sergey. Most of these delegates have never laid eyes on me. If I don't establish my own contacts with them, I will be more dependent than ever on Alexander. Besides, he and Nicholas will use my sickness as a weapon."

"What scandalous competition among professed Christians and priests!"

"Can I rest at the warehouse? If we go there directly from here, I can sleep for a few hours and I won't have to travel for the meeting."

"There won't be anybody around at this hour. I know where some bedding is hidden."

The two trekked across Moscow to a section dominated by old commercial buildings. On Saturdays the area was completely deserted. Tonight, at seven o'clock, groups of the faithful would begin entering a warehouse at ten-minute intervals. Alexander would offer mass, and a small celebration was scheduled afterward. Sergey, who had once worked in the building, had made most of the arrangements. To Marais, the safety and quiet of a fifth-story loft was very appealing.

When they reached the warehouse, Sergey found hemp sacks and cotton stuffing for Marais. It took him but a few minutes to fall asleep on this makeshift bed behind some large boxes. His last thought involved a sudden recognition of the packing crates around him. Such objects, once so grim a part of the mission's history, now seemed the homiest of protections for an undisturbed nap.

He awoke much later to find Sergey poking him. "I've already let you sleep too long," he whispered. "The bishop has finished the gospel and is into his sermon."

"I'll be right there," said Marais, who did not really mind being late for Ulanov's mass. His intention was to see and be seen at this convocation.

Sergey had left a bowl of water and a towel beside him. Quickly Marais tried to dissolve the webs of sleep over his eyes by putting his entire face into the water. He shuddered, but in a moment or so felt surprisingly refreshed. As he rubbed his arms and neck, he remembered a scene so vivid he could not be sure it had occurred only in a dream. While he had been sleeping, a haggish face resembling the old woman who had followed him in Rome seemed to lean over him, peering intently at his face. She had poked at his ribs with a stick she carried.

Marais squinted in an attempt to penetrate the cloudy veil of his memory. For all his mental effort he was unable to find that bridge crossing over from a dream scene to a real one. The floor gave no evidence of a visitor. Marais, pronouncing the old woman a fantasy conjured up from the past, smoothed his clothes and combed his hair carefully for his appearance before the community.

Opening the door to the larger loft space, he made his way through the boxes and into the clearing. At least a hundred people, most of them kneeling, were gathered in a circle around a large table piled with loaves of bread, bottles of wine, and small sliced hams. The mass had been kept informal, as a safety precaution. The altar and the proskomidy table that usually stood at the side of the sanctuary had been combined. There were no candles, incense, or crosses in evidence. The only obvious sign of religiosity was the stole that Ulanov had draped about his shoulders. If the need arose, the small squares of bread cut for communion could be consumed instantly. The hams were for the celebration afterward.

Surely disappointed with the quiet imageless ceremony in the loft, the worshipers had been given permission to sing the old ecclesiastic responses. Marais hoped that the heavy resonating chants might satisfy some of the people's nostalgia for the rich ceremonies of their youth.

Ulanov seemed to be nearing the end of his sermon. "Though we are small in numbers," he was saying, "small as the early Christian community and hiding in these our own catacombs, we bear a light that will yet brighten the darkness if we but have the faith to keep it burning. After 1917, there were great resentments in Russia about the Orthodox church—and great hope in salvation from the state. When this hatred and exaggeration dies away, there will be a birth of fervor in Mother Russia such as the world has never seen. It is then that your years of patience will bear fruit.

"So I beg you, brothers and sisters, to bring in Catholics you know who are still loath to step forward for whatever reason, whether in fear of being informed upon or in despair over what so few can accomplish. Tell them how well we have survived. Tell them that we are such a close-knit band of brothers that betrayal is unthinkable. And remind them how few were the Apostles and the disciples of Christ. How incredibly small were the band of communist revolutionaries. A thousand people burning with devotion for truth must prevail regardless of their adversaries' numbers.

"We are particularly interested in approaching disenchanted members of the Orthodox church. They furnish an indispensable ally for the creation of a new Russia. Marching together with us, they assure the survival of the humanity of God on this planet. Such is our mission, and theirs."

Ulanov looked around, gazing down at half-second intervals upon each of the groups as though sealing with these visual interchanges a bond of some sort inscribed from eternity. Then he spun around and moved in front of his chair. The position obviously symbolized in the congregation's imagination his place before the traditional altar. Sergey, who stood beside him, recited the ektene of supplication, which was periodically interspersed with the congregation's chant for mercy, *"Gospodi pomiluy."* Ulanov took them on through the little ektene and the cherubic prayer, the great entrance and offertory, until he came to the consecration of gifts, praying over the loaves and the bottles of wine while Sergey moved continually a large handkerchief over the table. Finally the bishop bowed his head, and, pointing to the square of bread, said the words: "Take, eat, *this is my body,* which is broken for you for the remission of sins." Sergey had poured a cupful of wine from one of the bottles; Ulanov, pointing at it, pronounced the words, "Drink of this, for *this is my blood* of the New Testament which is shed for you and for many for the remission of sins."

Marais recited silently from memory the rest of the celebrant's prayers. "Again we offer to thee this reasonable and unbloody worship, and we entreat and pray and humbly beseech thee, send down thy holy spirit upon us and upon these presented gifts."

Quickly Ulanov moved through the epiclesis and commemora-

[201]

tions until he reached the fractioning of the host and the holy communion for himself and the congregation. Then he circulated from communicant to communicant, Sergey by his side, distributing on a spoon the small squares of bread dipped into the mug of consecrated wine.

When he had finished, part of the congregation was chanting in the dark bass rhythm of traditional Russian, *"Blashosloven hryadey vo imya Gospodne, Boh Gospod' i ya visya nam."* Blessed is he who cometh in the name of the Lord, God the Lord hath revealed himself to us.

In the moment of silence following this response, a loud creaking sound reverberated around the loft. Heads turned to the rear, but the lookout in that corner vigorously shook his head. Again the creaking began, and this time it was followed by footsteps from behind stacks of crates; ever so slow, halting for a few awful seconds before they resumed, never deviating in their direction toward the gathering. The bishop and his co-celebrants did not move; nor did the congregation. Somehow the single steps seemed more eerie than dangerous, the kind of threat that promised to end in relief.

The creaking began again, and then, from around the box, she stared at them—an old woman with a stick. She was no dream figure, Marais knew; she was real, and she was mad. She never flinched before the crowd, but her eyes moving from left to right took them all in as though each of them was to be remembered for his guilt.

"I heard you all, hee, hee . . . from upstairs. You thought no one else was here, but I heard you." The voice crackled with delirium. "Enemies of our government, that's what you are! I could hear the singing, those terrible songs from the old days. The people must be told about this."

She limped nearer the table. "Ah, the bread, the wine . . ." She lifted her cane, jabbing at the loaves, and as she swung it over the table she knocked two of the bottles to the floor. She smiled and poked the end of the stick among the pieces. "Well, you won't get rid of that smell so easily." She glared at Ulanov and Sergey. "And you must be the priests—oh, I remember you"—she pointed at the Russian—"I've seen your picture before, you're a soccer player. I save all the old newspapers in the attic upstairs. Ah, you'll be a beautiful catch for the authorities. They'll give me a reward for this."

"You don't know what you're saying, *babushka,*" Ulanov said as he approached her. "We were just having a party for old times' sake. There's no harm in remembering the childhood songs. We're loyal comrades, like yourself."

"We'll see about that."

Marais was puzzled by the old woman's cruel pleasure in a discovery involving people she did not know. A senile lame recluse married to a principle of impersonal revenge . . . it made no sense, yet she was holding a hundred people in terror.

"What are you going to do?" asked Ulanov with a smile.

She smiled back at the bishop. *"You're* going to stay here."

"But what will you do, *babushka?*"

"I'm going to find a friend of mine who works for the police. He lives around the corner. He'll be very interested in these goings-on here."

"That will take you an hour," said Ulanov. "We'll be gone by the time you come back."

"Run away? Won't matter." She pointed at Sergey. "I'll remember his face from the papers. He's a player." With that, she began to hobble away.

From the other side of the room, Nicholas moved quickly to intercept her. Obviously she had not noticed him before. Nor had Marais; Nicholas must have been observing the whole affair at some distance from the others, standing behind a crate. Certainly he had not received communion.

Now he laid a hand on the old woman's shoulder and grinned down at her. "We can't allow that, Grandmother!"

The old woman began to tremble. "Who are you?" she shouted. "What right have you to touch me?"

"We don't want you to talk about us, Grandmother!"

"Very well, if you really don't want . . . It's a party, but . . . I promise." The old woman did not look up as she mumbled the words.

"I don't believe you."

[203]

"Who are you? You? You're no man of God. You're not like these people." She turned from him, pleading, addressing the congregation. "I promise! I was only fooling... A silly old woman's joke, you believe me, don't you?"

The worshipers did not respond. Having no more than the slightest understanding of what was involved, they seemed paralyzed, watching a drama that was external to them.

Nicholas put his arm gently around the woman's shoulders; gently pushed her in the direction of the boxes.

"What are you going to do?" Ulanov asked him.

"What do you suggest?"

"I don't know."

"She is probably harmless," said Sergey.

"If it wasn't for you, we could take that chance," said Nicholas. "You're the one she recognizes." He grinned down at the trembling old woman, who listened for the decision about her fate. "No," he said, "I think Grandmother here will turn you in—if not today, then tomorrow or the next day. That's your life, isn't it, Grandmother?" As he spoke, the old woman became hysterical, understanding more quickly than the assembly what was happening. She ran over to the bishop. "Please protect me, he means to hurt me! I can see you are a kind gentleman, and you wouldn't let harm come upon one who is old enough to be your mother."

"Of course not! There is no danger of that." Ulanov seemed genuinely solicitous of the old woman. "I knew you were joking."

"I meant no harm at all... to any of you." As she turned toward the congregation, sighs of relief from some of the members mingled with protests from others.

"You play unfortunate jokes," said Sergey.

The old woman extended her hands and lowered her eyes in a gesture that was not so much an apology as a vague excuse of weakness or ignorance. "Fathers, your blessing..." she implored, going down on her knees before Ulanov and Sergey.

The two priests, unable to decide whether they were the objects of cunning or repentance, did not move. As the congregation grasped the implications of the situation, whispers swept through the hall.

It was Nicholas who moved forward. "Give her that blessing, Alexander. It's too late now, you've already told her what she wanted to know. Besides," he smiled at the celebrants and then down at the old woman, "she's entitled to make a request."

The petitioner shuddered in her kneeling position. Bishop Ulanov's hands described the lines of a cross above her head. "May God, Christ, and the blessed saints forgive you all the sins of your past and grant you the graces of a happy journey to an eternal life with them. We pray that death may find you prepared and obedient to the divine will."

In the terrible silence that filled the loft after this blessing, Marais could feel the heavy fear.

Ulanov seemed totally unmindful of the reactions around him. He helped the trembling old woman to her feet. She was quaking even as he escorted her gently over to his brother. "You will be quite all right now. I think it is best if Nicholas takes you back."

The woman was confused. She believed in the bishop's kindness but she did not understand what he was saying, or how he could hand her over to such a man.

Ulanov had remained so calm, had let everything proceed so easily, that Marais too was confused. Would the old woman be allowed to go free? Was the bishop really unconcerned? And Nicholas, who had said nothing since his original accusation—was he intuiting his brother's thoughts, or vice versa? There was a subterranean movement to the whole scene that Marais either could not or would not bring himself to grasp. The rest of the worshipers continued to watch anxiously the drama around the altar table. Sergey had not moved since the beginning.

"You are a dear sister," Ulanov said quietly to the woman, "dearer now than ever." He turned her around to gesture toward the congregation. "There is not one of them who will ever forget you. You will be remembered in a way that was hardly in the realm of possibility fifteen minutes ago. We are all your friends now in the spirit."

The gnomelike creature looked up at him in an odd transformation of that malevolence she had exercised on her entrance. She seemed to welcome, with a mixture of old cunning and new simplicity, the immortality the Jesuit was conferring on her. He had either mesmerized her or caught her in a secret vulnerability.

As Ulanov returned her to Nicholas she gave a sharp jerk, but Nicholas had a strong grip on her arm. "Don't worry," he said, "I'll obey his orders to the letter." Still reluctant, she nonetheless allowed herself to be led around the corner of stacked crates, back the way she had come.

Ulanov quickly began the *Zaamvonna molytva,* the traditional prayer behind the ambo: "O Lord who blessest them that bless thee, and sanctifiest them that trust in thee, save thy people and bless thine inheritance. Protect the fullness of thy church, sanctify those who love the beauty of thy house. Do thou honor thy divine power . . ."

When he had finished, the people sang the *Budi imye Hospadne* chants, slowly gaining strength with each "Blessed be the name of the Lord from now and unto ages." As they began the third of these, Nicholas returned quietly to his place. The congregation's singing started to falter and might have stopped entirely had it not been for the robust performance of Ulanov and Sergey, whose vigor forced the laggards to pick up the tempo.

Ulanov had the congregation sing another response, the *Slava Otsu,* before he finally dismissed them. By that time, the din of their own voices rising louder and louder had almost reassured the members that all was well. It was only in the silence of their individual partings that Marais watched the return of terrors.

11

The next morning Nicholas cooked a late breakfast, which the others managed to eat in silence. It was only as they sipped coffee afterward that Ulanov finally spoke. "I'll have to start picking up the pieces from last night's disaster. I'm going to spend the afternoon making calls. First, I'll see Sergey and ask for his suggestions."

"You might have to comfort *him* first," said the younger Ulanov. "The way he looked last night, he won't be in any condition to think about his flock."

"What are you going to do, Josef?"

"I don't know yet," said Marais. "I feel completely tired. Probably just rest here in bed for a while."

"You aren't going to visit down the hall, I hope?" Nicholas asked him.

"I might," Marais said tiredly. He often dropped in on the Belenkovs in the evenings.

"You shouldn't, you know. You're not supposed to get that close to anybody, it's dangerous. You talk to him, Dmitri, while I clean up the kitchen."

Ulanov shrugged. "Tell me, Josef, what do you find in these Belenkovs?"

"Dmitri, you're not your brother. Perhaps you can appreciate the relief of spending an evening with a simple warmhearted family."

"No, I really don't understand."

"In the mission we're priests, we're always being treated with right reverence. I like to get away from that kind of thing. These people don't know who I am, so I'm treated just like another worker. There's no strain and a lot of fun."

"I really am unenlightened, Josef," Ulanov said. "A priest on a mission like ours should hardly need diversions so soon after coming. Isn't there enough excitement for you in our work?"

"Before I left Rome," said Marais, "Archbishop Francisi asked me to make my own assessments of the Russians. He didn't want me to come back with mirror images of our own thinking. He wanted realistic information on what is happening among the ordinary people, not just those who are already Catholics."

"What can you have learned from these Belenkovs that I haven't told you?"

Marais laughed. "What these people are tells the story."

Ulanov raised his eyes to the ceiling, but Marais went right on. "The old couple are actually the grandparents of the two young people you see around. The couple's own son and daughter-in-law were killed by the White Russians. When they were in their fifties, they took over the care of the orphans, cut off their roots in the country, and came to Moscow so the children would have better educational opportunities. The old man puts in long hours at shoe repairing, and his wife works as a maid in one of the ministries. The four of them have lived, slept, studied together in that same small room for eleven years, and still the old people couldn't be happier if they inherited a palace. Why? Because the granddaughter is in medical school and the grandson is halfway to his engineering degree."

"That's the will of the socialist people!" said Ulanov. "I told you all about that before we ever came to Russia. If you had listened to me, then you wouldn't need—"

"There are some implications to this, Dmitri, that you may not like. The ordinary people talk about their jobs even when they relax in the evenings. They and their friends can go on all night about the latest leaps in Soviet production—a new building in the neighborhood, a new machine in their factory, an improvement in curing some disease . . . The truth is, the Soviets have accomplished what the church declared to be impossible. They have actually built a godless society with its own morals. And the whole thing has incredible roots among the people. It doesn't look like it's going to collapse.

"I know"—he waved off the beginning of an objection from Ulanov—"I heard what you said last night about spiritual hunger. But if these people ever get around to aching for the world of the spirit, it's a long time off. They love the world of matter and technical achievement. They even measure their deprivations by that new standard. You know what old Belenkov told me the other night? 'Did you ever think,' he said, 'that a poor uneducated peasant like myself who can barely scratch a few letters or read any lines of a book, would live to see the day that his grandchildren would be a doctor and an engineer in the capital of this country? So then what difference do the sufferings of my wife and I make when our young state is moving ahead so fast for the sake of all the people, for our own flesh and blood and not just a few rich men?'

"There you have it! The state is a soul, not just a piece of external machinery. We're talking a hopeless language to these people. Archbishop Francisi and the Vatican won't like it, but that's what I'll tell them. And *that's* what I learned from the Belenkovs."

Ulanov walked to the window and gazed out for a long moment before he answered. "You lose heart too easily, Josef. An intellectual's weakness. If we keep faith with our vision, we can change the odds against us. If we believe, then they might believe. But nothing shall change if we waver. We are a force in the balance. What you have said is true enough, I won't deny it. But your interpretation of the facts is false. You surrender hope. To what? I say, these people will eventually hunger for something spiritual. We have no choice but to keep to one course— unite Christ and socialism."

Marais sighed. "You force your will on things with an abstraction that's detached from the way people—and history—operate," he said. "Civilization is evolving, a new spirit has been born that

[209]

will affect everything, even religion. If you don't recognize its future, you will be an obstacle to truth. My feeling is that it is necessary for us to keep alive the memory of the Christian spirit so that something shall be there from which the new world can spring. Very different from your attack—you believe in Christ-as-is, and you force the issue! And you seem to be compelled into pushing harder and harder these current abstractions."

"Isn't it odd that they suspected me in Rome?" said Ulanov. "Because it's you, if they could hear you, that would turn their hair gray. No, Christ as God shall not be superseded and neither shall the church as we understand her today, and socialism and the church shall make their peace. That is what the world needs and that is all she needs. And *you* don't need to spend time with the Belenkovs—particularly that girl you seem to enjoy so much!"

"Quite a change of subject. What brought this on?"

"Practical matters, Josef! She is very pretty, and you are not so strong you couldn't make a slip."

"Don't worry."

"I do. Who can spend so much time relaxing with outsiders without the pressure of his disguise breaking down? You're a telephone repairman, do they still believe that?"

"Yes," said Marais, relieved at the nature of this objection.

"Everywhere I turn, Josef, it's you who are unenlightening. And you're supposed to be the spiritual director of this mission. Now, for the safety of the mission, will you please stay away from that family? You have learned what you say you had to learn. And if you find that they suspect anything, let me know—immediately!"

Marais jumped up from the bed. "Wasn't one killing enough?"

Ulanov stared at him. "I never intended that, I . . ." he stopped and put his hands to his head. "You shouldn't remind us of terrible . . ." He turned away from Marais and moved toward the door. "I must join Nicholas. Be well . . . until tonight." Quietly he opened the door and left.

Marais's own anger quickly died. Still unable to reflect on the tragedy of the night before, he let his mind drift to Sonya

Belenkov. She *was* extraordinarily attractive, and she went to great pains to seek out "her Josef" no matter who was around. The way she looked at him left no doubt how she felt.

Yet it had all happened so quickly that Marais was chagrined when he finally recognized the situation. Now he did not know how to extricate himself except by absence or formality.

Surely he had been a fool to view her ambitions for him as disinterested. She had pressed him to try for a position more compatible with his education and intelligence. His excuse of a bourgeois background served him well for a while, but Sonya was not discouraged. She urged him to publish a denunciation, the standard document that allowed offspring to publicly disown their parents as exploiters.

He pretended to be furious at this suggestion, a stratagem which put Sonya in a quandary. She admired his loyalty; she grieved over the waste of his talent. Her own position as a future doctor was not responsible for her desire to advance Marais; skilled workers and scientists received almost identical incomes, and there was no social problem in a female doctor's being married to a telephone technician.

Marais did not need Ulanov's warning to know that he must limit his visits to the Belenkovs. It was not a question of fearing the bishop's denunciations in Rome. He could defend himself there. He was not sure any longer that he could defend himself against Sonya Belenkov.

He had to admit that this kind of relationship was entirely new to him, and that with it had come new feelings. At first he had called it fondness and then, later, base temptations for which the girl should not be held responsible. He had attempted to exorcise this response with certain spiritual exercises. But in Sonya's presence their power tended to dissolve, and quite rapidly at that.

Marais felt the onset of the fatigue that had plagued him most of the week. The shivering started again; he pulled the blankets up to his chin and then added a few more. He had to hope that sleep would again cure him of this debilitating pain. Hours later, waking in the darkened room, he felt the same shakiness. He rose

[211]

from the bed with great effort, found the bottle of whiskey kept under Nicholas's mattress, and drank himself back to sleep with a large glass of it.

The next morning, he found he could not get up. Ulanov left him to report to work. Marais slept through the entire day except for a half hour at noon, when their cook woke him to swallow a bowl of broth. By evening his throat was so sore that he could hardly eat or drink, and the utter weakness he felt was beginning to paralyze him. Even Ulanov was sufficiently frightened by these new developments to go for Sonya.

The girl never even paused to close the door behind her. In one motion she seemed to enter and be sitting beside Marais on the bed. Whatever concern she felt was translated immediately into action.

Her fingers, sensitive and sure, pried his lids wide apart while she watched the movement of his eyes. Forced to gaze into hers, Marais felt as though he were whirling within hazel depths. Her sharply defined lips and brows, usually so expressive, were perfectly still; the clear eyes hardly blinked. She probed his mouth; felt his neck; held his feet and toes up to the light. She grasped him firmly under the arms and pulled him up. After listening to his heartbeat with a small stethoscope, she took his pulse.

Finally the palm of one strong hand pressed a spot over his liver while two fingers tapped the back of the resting hand. Marais winced a bit, and Sonya moved both hands to various positions in the same region, tapping and tapping again.

"Well, what's wrong with him?" Ulanov asked her.

Despite the Jesuit's impatience, she did not answer him. As she stood up, wordlessly assessing Marais from a distance, her finely arched brows drew together. Ulanov peered at her nervously. Though nowhere near the Jesuit's size, Sonya seemed to Marais to be more than Ulanov's equal. Tall and muscular, she was yet unlike most of the Russian women, who were prone to heaviness. Her real sisters were the Swedes, and in some ways, the girls of Munich. Marais gazed back at her, fantasizing for a moment their walking together in Paris, her fine honey-colored hair stirred by a small breeze. The two of them would catch every passing eye.

Sonya broke the spell. "There are no obvious possibilities. The

[212]

combination of symptoms is not quite like anything I've seen. There are some indications of mononucleosis, but I can't make a positive diagnosis."

"But we have to do something for him," said the Jesuit.

"We have to send him to the hospital."

"That's impossible!" Ulanov paced to the door and back.

"Why are you so afraid of a hospital? Josef needs rest, extensive tests—the best professional attention. That's the only place for him to get it."

"We can't afford that." Nicholas spoke for the first time.

Sonya stared at him.

"If Josef goes into a hospital, he's finished. It will take them no more than a couple of days to get his files. Once his background is discovered he can forget his job, forget supporting his parents. They'll stop him from getting work anywhere in Russia."

"That's preposterous!" Sonya looked at him as though he were a tsarist relic.

"I'm telling you a fact!" Nicholas shouted.

"Our socialist state does not do such things."

Nicholas walked up to her. "You look pretty sure of yourself. But you're young and there are some things you don't know yet."

Sonya smiled.

"Here, look!" Nicholas spread cards in front of her. "I'm a worker. I sit on workers' councils. I know the rules. You don't, you're not a real member of the proletariat. If you want, I'll show you the written directions the party gives us. I'm telling you, he'll be finished if they find out who he is, and they don't care if his parents starve to death. We can't allow you to take him out of here. You've just got to take care of him in the apartment."

Even Marais was touched by the younger Ulanov's concern to protect him. Perhaps that is the most he is capable of, after all, Marais told himself. I expect too much. He is good for what he is supposed to be good for . . . In his weariness Marais let this sentiment fall away as he lay back listening to Nicholas's manipulations of Sonya.

Sonya finally settled for a urine sample from the helpless

Marais and gave him two tablets she had stolen from the operating room. She had friends in the hospital; through them she would be able to procure more pills and a laboratory analysis. Marais, seeing the terrible chance Sonya was taking with her career by treating a patient in these circumstances, felt more depressed than ever.

The next day he was so weak that he felt willing to risk the hospital for the sake of a cure. In the late evening Sergey came with an elderly internist, a trusted member of the congregation who tentatively diagnosed Marais's sickness as infectious mononucleosis, going into hepatitis. "Although," said Dr. Tsailov, "it's odd that there's no sign of jaundice as yet." He returned a few hours later with the necessary medicines and gave instructions to Sonya, then signed a sick-pay form so that Marais's absence at work should bring no further examinations.

For the next three weeks Marais slept alone in the room to prevent the infection from spreading. The mononucleosis had left him so weakened that fifteen hours a day were usually given over to sleeping. He could not read, and his capacity to sustain a serious thought seemed limited to a few minutes. What he regretted most was the loss of contact with the community. After the first ten days, Sergey dropped by in the evenings to keep him abreast of the phenomenal growth of their membership.

Despite the ordination of Sergey and two others, there were not enough priests to keep up with the work. Hundreds upon hundreds of Christians were coming forth to renew their relationship with the church. Sergey was concerned over the screening of these large numbers—it seemed illusory to hope for perfect control where so many were involved.

Still, he remained optimistic. The precautions so faithfully observed should prevent any state infiltrator from deeply penetrating their ranks. A general roundup could only be carried out by an unthinkable defection from the inner circle.

Sergey, as the sole messenger left in communication with the train conductor and therefore with Rome, gave Marais the Vatican's messages. The Frenchman's superiors were delighted to hear of the mission's progress and were praying for Marais's speedy recovery. Giving assent to one of his suggestions, they commanded Ulanov to consecrate Sergey bishop. The Frenchman's pleasure surpassed that of his protégé. Illness had exposed Marais constantly to the shame of his lost place in the work of the mission, but now, with his authority vindicated, he anticipated a speedy return to the field.

On a night three weeks after the onset of his sickness, Marais decided that he was indeed regaining his health. The early part of the evening had been pleasantly spent with Sergey, to whom Marais had given one more message written in invisible ink to be delivered to Rome. In it he requested that Bishop-elect Sergey be allowed a share in all their decisions. Marais considered this piece of politics the consummate move in his and the Vatican's strategy of constricting Ulanov. It was for the good of the mission, yet it seemed ironic that the request should be made just now, when Marais felt that his relations with the brothers had become tolerably pleasant. He even believed that he at last understood Nicholas and his limitations.

Ulanov arrived not long after Sergey's departure. For the first quarter hour he was unusually exuberant. He seemed to be thriving on his demanding schedule; it was as if an expansive spirit had taken him over, leaving him unmindful of the rigors of work. Marais regretted in this happy atmosphere having to inform him that Rome had ruled in Marais's favor in the matter of the bishopric.

Ulanov was silent for a long moment, then finally asked if he might wait two months. When Marais not only refused but invoked the possibility of a censure from Rome, Ulanov promised to comply within a fortnight.

Marais was surprised at Ulanov's restraint. Perhaps the bishop felt compassion for his stricken colleague and was unwilling to interfere with his recovery. Certainly some inhibition was controlling him; he paced about the room for minutes on end, fingering here and there some object or other.

"Do you not think," said Marais, "that it is sinful of you to want to be the *only* bishop?"

"I have nothing against Sergey," said Ulanov.

"Then what's on your mind?"

"It's this damned code you use, invisible ink and all that

trickery. It forces us into being enemies, no matter what we feel."

"I have my orders."

"Another absurd tactic of Rome's. They didn't know what they were talking about—divide and conquer, that's all they were interested in, don't you see?"

"You want something, Dmitri. What is it?"

"I want to centralize these functions."

"In your own hands, that is."

"In both of our hands."

"No."

Ulanov sighed and closed his eyes. "I am the bishop and the superior of this mission and yet I never know what is being said about me or what recommendations are made behind my back. You have the last word, and I have no way of replying or even of defending myself."

"Come, come, Dmitri! Have you ever yet been forced to defend yourself? Even once?"

"It's the principle of the thing! The threat of it, the distrust implied by this tactic is intolerable. You see the messages last when they go out and first when they come in. No matter how much I like you personally, I'm telling you these Roman machinations are a divisive technique that does the mission no good. They destroy my self-confidence, they prevent me from sharing spontaneously, as I would like to, every thought and feeling I have about the mission."

Marais shook his head. "Nobody is a law unto himself, Dmitri. We all tend to go off on our own or to forget limits in the excitement of the moment. It's always better if there are two."

"But that's exactly what I am asking, two to share—not this one-against-one arrangement they have imposed on us."

Marais laughed. "There would be no two to share if I did not have my own rights in this mission. I really don't think I would see you again, Dmitri, if I handed these secrets over to you. In short, I understand your grievance but I can't give you the code or the ink materials."

"Is that final?"

"Yes."

"Very well. Suppose you get worse, then what? After all, I warned them that you were not up to the Russian winter. I deserve to—"

"I would have to get very sick indeed not to be able to write or hear a report. And that's my last word."

"Nicholas will be very upset with this decision of yours," said Ulanov. "And we need him."

"You should not have confided these details to Nicholas."

"You have no sense of gratitude! Nicholas has saved your life and mine, and you still treat him as an outsider. But that is how it is with people like you."

"I too have risked my life and my career for you and Nicholas," Marais said as Ulanov put his hand to the door latch. "If I had reported his presence to Rome, there would have been no mission. But people like you are never content. You pretend to forget and then you raise the stakes." He turned his face to the pillow.

"Do you have any objection if I make a quick visit to Leningrad?" asked Ulanov.

Marais sat up. "Surely you have enough to keep you busy here!"

"Underground Catholics in Leningrad have sent inquiries on the mission—they are anxious to meet us. I want to assess their needs, get acquainted with some of their people. Anyway, it would only be for a week. Think it over, and I'll talk to you soon."

As he turned again to go, there came a series of tentative knocks at the door. "Yes?" said Ulanov.

"I am Mikhail . . ." The voice was apologetic. "Sergey told me where to find you."

Ulanov looked at Marais. "You don't mind?"

"No, let him in."

Ulanov opened the door to admit a short husky man in his mid-fifties, cap in hand. He glanced first at the priest on the bed. "I'm sorry for your trouble, Father." Probably a former peasant, thought Marais.

The man fell on his knees before Ulanov and kissed his hand. It made no difference to him that the bishop wore no ring. Alexander bent over quickly and pulled him to his feet.

"I . . . I am Mikhail," he repeated.

"Of course, I remember you from our services."

Mikhail pointed to the door. "My children . . ."

Ulanov moved to the hallway and beckoned. A tall slender boy looked around shyly as he came through the door, followed by a younger girl, perhaps sixteen years old. She smiled sympathetically at Marais. Another girl, even younger, made a point of walking in the footsteps of the others without glancing up. Ulanov himself ushered in the fourth child, who hardly came up to the waist of the Jesuit. He was the liveliest of the quartet. He climbed up on the bed to take a look at Marais. "Are you a bishop too?" Marais and Ulanov laughed as the father, embarrassed, scooped the boy up and stationed him alongside the other children, who stood shoulder to shoulder at Ulanov's right side.

Mikhail touched each of them in turn. "This is Vladimir, Marya, Anna, and our youngest, Boris." The first three knelt, one by one, and kissed Ulanov's hand. The bishop's distaste for this ritual was obvious, as was his impatience to know why they were all there. "Well, now," he said to Mikhail.

"We are sorry to disturb you, Excellency."

"I'm here to serve you."

The man twisted the cap in his hands.

"You have a problem?"

"Yes, yes, Excellency."

"Did you tell Father Cherbasov?"

"We wished to see you."

"He can advise as well as I."

"For myself, yes, I would not mind Father Cherbasov. But my children, they will not listen to anyone but you. They have heard your sermons, they have seen you on the streets. You are for them the voice of God. I can understand their feelings. You are for all of us someone—"

"Yes, yes," said Ulanov. "But what is it you want?"

"Our family is very divided, Excellency."

"You are quarreling?"

"We do not have much peace any more."

"For some reason the children are against you?"

The peasant nodded, his eyes on the floor. "They wish to do things that I do not think are wise," he said.

"And what things are these?" Ulanov turned to the oldest boy, who may have been seventeen or eighteen.

Vladimir stood very straight. "My brother, my sisters and I want to witness to the faith," he said. "Like you do, your Excellency."

The Jesuit seemed puzzled by this soldierlike avowal. "Is it a vocation to the priesthood that upsets your father?"

The boy shook his head. "My sister, my brother, and I very much want to do what you do."

"We want to spread the faith," young Marya burst out.

"We want to talk about Jesus Christ to our friends," said Anna.

"It doesn't seem right to keep what we know to ourselves," Marya explained. "Remember, when you told us about the salt of the earth and light kept under a bushel?"

Boris, who had been playing with some of the books on the windowsill, stopped for a moment. "What's everybody so excited about? They say the same thing in school about the state. That's more practical, I think."

"Hush, Boris," said Marya. "Don't take any notice of him, Bishop. He's still impressed with school."

"I *like* what they teach us," said Boris.

"You're not old enough to know what you're saying," said Anna.

Boris shrugged and returned to the books.

"Bishop Ulanov," said Vladimir. "Our father does not think we should say anything—anything at all."

Mikhail looked up at the Jesuit. "I . . . I am afraid. It is dangerous."

"No, it isn't, Father," said Marya. "You keep saying the same thing, over and over."

"You must warn them, Excellency. I beg of you. They are only children, they do not know."

"We know which students might be interested and which ones are tattletales," said Marya.

"I feel so strange not telling my best friends," said Anna.

[219]

Marais couldn't help smiling—she seemed more concerned for her relationship to her school chums than for the faith.

"Wait," said Ulanov. "Your father is right. You must be very careful."

"Your Excellency, please tell them to *stop completely.*" Mikhail was near tears.

"Jesus died for sinners," said Vladimir. "We can take a chance."

"I would not deny you that," said Ulanov.

The three older children let out a shout and grasped each other's hands.

"It is not as simple as you think," said Ulanov. The children stopped still. "You must not say anything directly. You must not come out and try to convert your friends openly or give them copies of the gospel. Do you understand?"

"But what shall we do if we don't do that?" Vladimir asked.

"Your father is right in one respect. You never know who you're talking to in Moscow. Your friends might innocently talk to their parents and then there would be trouble from the government."

"My beautiful children, you would all be dead." Mikhail looked down at his two girls and young Boris. "Tell them that, Excellency."

"It is . . . possible."

"You came here to Russia," said Vladimir, challenging his hero. "*You* took a chance."

"But not foolish chances. God does not ask that. You must be like a general. Plan, wait, be patient. Talk to your close friends about the reasons for a Creator of the World, about sin and grace in an easy way. If after two or three years you are still friends and even closer, and they give evidence to you of wanting more, then you may begin to mention Jesus and the church and the gospels. When they are ready, do that, but not before."

The father shook his head. "I don't know."

"Mikhail, you must not be so concerned for life and happiness that you deny any spiritual heroism to your children." Ulanov went over and placed his hands on the man's shoulders. "God runs the world. If he wishes, we will be. If he doesn't we perish. I can see you have lost some trust in him. We have all survived because he wishes it. He has great plans for a Christian Russia, and we must see ourselves as part of that plan. He is looking over us, his first army of missionaries."

Marais stared at Mikhail, who seemed to have strengthened physically with each of Ulanov's pronouncements. "I understand, Excellency," he said. "You are right, I have lacked faith. I shall support my children, for that is what we are here to do, is it not, to save our own souls and those of our family and those we may meet?"

"Well said, Mikhail." Ulanov grasped his shoulders hard, then turned to the children. "And now you, Vladimir, Marya, Anna, and you, Boris"—he tousled the boy's hair—"remember what I said. God is with you, if you don't tempt him. You understand? No one breaks good news suddenly to anyone. You must try them piece by piece without letting on, and, then, after they have shown you their mettle, reward them."

"I will make sure that everyone follows your instructions, Bishop." Vladimir spoke the words like a new recruit, his jaw set to meet any ordeal.

"Come now, and I will bless you all together."

The family knelt in a circle around Ulanov, who raised his hand. "May the Father, Son, and Holy Spirit come upon you and guide you in your apostolic work. May their strength and wisdom dwell with you in abundance and give you the grace to withstand whatever the enemy throws up against you. May they grant you the grace of perseverance to carry through to the very end what you have so courageously begun. Amen."

"Amen!" the children responded—all except Boris, who laughed. "I don't understand anything you said. But I understand Father Lenin and Marx."

"You will soon understand." Ulanov lifted him up and swung him in a great arc. The boy loved the fun of it.

"We will teach him about Christ," said Marya.

"If we have to break his head," Vladimir added.

The Jesuit put his arms around the children, two on each side, and walked with them into the hallway. When he returned, he sat down in the chair for a moment. "A remarkable family," he said.

"You really aren't afraid for them?" said Marais.

Ulanov smiled at him. "You heard my advice, Josef. If they follow it, they will be all right. Besides, they really are God's elect—I sensed it. That puts them beyond ordinary dangers."

"And young Boris? He's being indoctrinated."

"They'll bring him around. The family is stronger than the state. Why do you raise such problems? That's all I hear from you these days . . . no word about our success."

"It's your incredible success with the people that makes me sensitive to little problems. I can't believe that everything goes as well as it seems."

"So that's how the French waste their energies." Ulanov stood up, laughing, and left the room.

After Ulanov's departure, Marais slept until he was awakened by Sonya.

"It's time, Josef."

"Wouldn't it be healthier just to let me sleep?"

"A massage will stimulate your muscles and you'll have a much better sleep. Besides, I thought you liked it."

"Of course, of course. But why must it be at such inconvenient times?"

"Turn over."

He obeyed, and her strong hands immediately dug into his shoulder muscles; pressing and easing, pressing and easing. Soon, Marais was gasping. "Isn't this too much for you after a busy day?" A pair of thumbs found just the right cords in his neck, exerted pressure and moved down the spinal column. "Sonya! Isn't this too much for *me?*"

"Sometimes, Josef, I think you like to be sick."

Marais gave her a pained expression as he turned over on his back. He had difficulty in following Sonya's shifts from professional to personal opinions. She could swing to one pole or the other at a moment's notice, while he remained ever in a middle area.

"Why are you so far away?" Sonya put one hand on the pillow and bent over him.

"I just am."

"That's no answer."

Marais, wanting to avert his eyes, found himself impaled on

[222]

small pins. What was worse, she was grinning at his embarrassment.

"Were you to answer such a question directly," she said, "you wouldn't be Josef." She laughed.

Marais looked up at the ceiling with a groan.

"Don't be so dramatic," Sonya said. "It isn't that serious."

"But I never know what to say to you!" he said.

"Just say whatever comes into your mind. I'm your friend, am I not?"

"Of course you are."

"Not just your doctor?"

Marais glared at her. Immediately the shrewd watching expression vanished, and she smiled at his playfulness.

"I have to admit," Marais said, taking advantage of these quick changes, "that I have had very little to do with beautiful professional women."

"You don't mean 'very little.' You mean 'nothing.' "

"Be a stickler."

"That doesn't make you any different from the rest of Russian men."

"Well, then, I must bring this problem up to my brothers at our next drinking session."

"See how you evade coming to terms with personal attention?"

"I don't follow you."

"Yes you do, Josef."

Marais shrugged. Young as she was, Sonya possessed a confidence that never failed to surprise him. Even her beauty seemed to be of a piece with her feelings. Vibrancy, he thought. Clarity. The clear skin and hazel eyes; the well-defined features and long, loose-limbed body—even the fine hair, neither controlled nor quite free—somehow fit her perfectly. As for her mind, well, she was no intellectual, but her candor and quick intelligence attracted him enormously despite the probing and the danger.

"Am I taxing your strength, Josef?"

"Not really."

"Well, try to keep it up for a few more minutes. You still have a rubdown coming."

As she reached for the alcohol, Marais turned over once more.

The icy liquid splashed over his back, and those incredibly strong hands went to work rubbing it in. Marais, slipping into a state of perfect relaxation, conjured up the faces of Francisi and Cardinal Pacelli.

Well, what did you expect? Marais asked them without moving his lips. I have to do the best I can. The edge of this apology quickly wore off, and with it, the necessity to appease his conscience. Images of Sonya's face, her body, her touch, her quick movements floated before his eyes. He felt so close to her in one moment that he could envision himself embracing her the next. There it was, the free and simple act of pleasure; if only he could exist in the physical order and no more. If only he were not what he was—a Jesuit priest on a mission.

"You may turn over," said Sonya. As he did, she looked down at his body, and moved quickly to the edge of the bed. Casting his own eyes down, Marais saw that he had an erection; it was visible through his pants, and he had been totally unaware of it.

Sonya knelt beside him. Marais, mortified, tried to rise; tried to speak. "Shhh," she whispered, and kissed him very gently. Marais held her face lightly, his fingers more sensitive than he could believe. She sat beside him then on the bed, bending over; her face lying on his. For a long time they stayed this way. Marais caressed her hair, and the softness and the weight of it flowing through his hands were as though he had found the most secret and delicate part of her being.

Then, holding the length of her body against his, he could no longer keep the tears from rolling down his cheeks. Their unity was a threat he had escaped, but far more, a promise denied. He held her even closer to overcome the sadness.

How long they might have remained there together, unmoving—what might have happened if either of them *had* moved— Marais was never to know. He began to feel a strange tingling sensation; nerves vibrating in his right cheek, tightening at the rear of his mouth, or, perhaps, at the top of his throat. He groaned and Sonya sat up immediately; he grasped his head with his hands as the pain reached his temples and both sides of his face started to tremble.

Sonya stood for an instant, transfixed by Marais's look of

[224]

agony. Then she rushed out the door and down the hallway, returning in a few seconds with her brother. Marais could hear her ordering the boy to run to a neighbor's phone and call Dr. Tsailov.

Marais remembered his eyes growing heavier and heavier as they lost all ability to focus before he passed into unconsciousness. When he awoke, the old doctor and Sonya were sitting beside him on the bed. Perspiration glistened on their foreheads and necks. They seemed exhausted, but a small smile of triumph relieved their somber expressions when they saw him open his eyes.

"Can you move your head?" asked Tsailov.

Marais tried and found he could manage a small nod.

"Then answer my questions that way, yes or no. Is your sight normal? Good. Are you in pain? No? Excellent. Can you make any sounds? Well, that is to be expected. Can you move the extremities, fingers, toes? Ah . . . Can you feel my pressure on them? Excellent . . . Has anything like this ever happened to you in the past? I shouldn't have thought so. And your mind? Do you feel it impaired? How? Reflective abilities, seminormal, you think? Of course . . ."

He turned to Sonya. "This is the most peculiar attack I have ever seen. There are no signs of a coronary attack nor of a stroke. I am sure of that. Of course, we will check it more carefully tomorrow, but neither will show up."

Ulanov stepped forth from the shadows behind the bed and bent to lay a hand on Marais's shoulder. "I am sorry, Josef, I am so sorry. We will do everything possible for you, you can count on that. Already Dr. Tsailov, here, has probably saved your life with his needles and body massages."

"And don't forget Sonya," said the doctor. "If she had not been with you, young man, you would almost certainly be dead. She's been massaging you and stimulating your respiration since this paralysis seized you."

In this short interval Marais had almost taken for granted his sudden seizure and, for the moment, lay as if entranced by the reactions of those around him. Ulanov's tribute touched him, and it even seemed understandable that he would not refer to Sonya.

"Will he be like this very long, Doctor?" asked Ulanov.

"I don't know. If I can't diagnose what has happened to him, I have no way of predicting the outcome. The prognosis, let me tell you straightforwardly, Comrade, is very uncertain. As it is, if I had not been trained in Germany many years ago, I could not have used the techniques I employed on our friend Josef. They are not ordinary procedures in Moscow."

"As far as I'm concerned," said Sonya, "you saved his life. Besides, I trust your opinion." With that she bent and kissed the patient lightly. "Josef is very important to me, Dr. Tsailov. He's been a wonderful friend to me and my family."

The doctor chose to answer something in her remarks that may not have been intended. "We have a far more serious worry here than propriety, yes?"

"Do you mean to say," Ulanov broke in on them, "that Josef could stay like this for the rest of his life?" His belated arrival at this possibility struck dread into the heart of Marais, who had not thought of it either.

"That is a terrible question to ask in front of Josef," said the doctor. "I can guess and say no, but that answer, however comforting, has no value until I know what it is we must counteract. Now let us think . . ." He walked over to a chair opposite the foot of the bed, and, settling down, stared at his patient. Finally he said, "Many years ago, before the Revolution, I saw a number of cases like this when I traveled in North Africa. They were the results of highly venomous snake bite. I have also seen cases of paralysis resulting from poor canning procedures. There are some limited similarities—"

"Just what are you suggesting?" asked Ulanov.

"Sonya," the doctor ignored the bishop, "what are some basic questions that occur to you?"

"I . . . I can't think, I'm—"

"No, no, my dear. You are a medical student."

Sonya threw up her hands. "How could this happen in these surroundings? He was given the best of care, he was not exposed to any disease. There is no possibility of mononucleosis or hepatitis leading to paralysis . . ."

[226]

"Go on."

"Perhaps a constitutional disorder of some sort?" said Ulanov.

"No," said Sonya. "His symptoms and what we know of his medical history almost certainly rule out such a diagnosis."

"And what does that leave us?" asked the doctor.

Sonya looked at him a moment, then said reluctantly, "Some substance ingested, I should think. Or, he took—"

"Precisely!" Tsailov walked over to Marais's bed. "Did anybody supply you with food, drink, a capsule, other than Sonya, myself, or the cook? No? Very well." He glanced about the room. "Who does the cooking?"

"Sometimes I do." Nicholas Ulanov stepped forward from behind his brother.

"And who are you?"

"Nicholas, that's who. I'm a close friend of Dmitri and Josef there."

"I can vouch for him," Ulanov said quickly.

"Have you done the cooking recently, Nicholas?"

"I suppose the last time was about ten days ago."

"Then who did?"

"A woman I know."

"How well do you know her?" asked Tsailov.

Nicholas smiled. "Pretty well."

"Who hired her?"

"I did. You're talking like a detective, you know!"

"Look at this man." He pointed to Marais. "*Someone* is responsible for this serious, almost fatal condition."

"I don't understand how you get that."

"It should not be difficult, even for you. Other possibilities being ruled out, there is a high probability that this man has been poisoned."

"I can't believe that!" said Ulanov.

"Why would anyone wish to poison poor Josef?" said Sonya. "He is so kind. He's only a telephone repairman. It's crazy, it makes no sense!"

The silence following this unknowing cry was unanimous, since no one could rise to the emergency. Sonya looked around her. "You all know something, don't you? You're not telling me the whole truth. Josef was in trouble, and you all knew. What is it, Doctor?"

Ulanov answered for him. "Josef comes from a wealthy family," he said. "They did harsh things to the poor, years ago. A few of that generation have sons who want revenge."

"It must be reported to the government," said Sonya.

"No, no, they would only fire Josef from his job, and his parents would starve to death. You know the state hates educated bourgeois—sons or fathers."

"But something must be done! If they can sneak in here and bribe a cook to poison Josef, he is not safe from them anywhere."

"We don't know for sure that anybody poisoned anybody," said Nicholas. "One of my jobs is to protect my friend there, and I just can't believe that the old woman I hired put something in his soup. I've known her off and on long before I met this fellow. She cooked a lot for me and my friends, and nothing ever happened to us."

"What else could cause this? Perhaps you'd like to tell *us!*"

"How can I say, I'm no doctor. Maybe he's got a kidney problem, a liver problem . . . anything. You just don't know what it is."

At this, even Ulanov looked disgusted. He stepped to the bed and stared at Marais, obviously considering seriously the possibility that poison had been administered to his colleague.

From his bed, Marais felt the first stirrings of rage.

The doctor was looking out on the street from the far window, calming himself after the exchange with Nicholas. The situation was complicated by the presence of Sonya, the only one in the room not privy to "Josef's" true role. Her presence, quite obviously, was constricting the others' ability to react wholeheartedly to their own logic. If it was true that Marais had been poisoned . . . well then, he knew, their entire mission must have been found out. He intuited also that some piece of the puzzle was missing, and that the others were being forced by Sonya's presence to arrive at the missing piece in the isolated recesses of their own thoughts.

[228]

Dr. Tsailov turned around finally and addressed Nicholas, very politely. "During these last two weeks," he said, "I have given Josef a number of medical checkups. We are positive he has no such disease as you suggested."

"It had to come through food? This . . . thing he's got?" Nicholas was at last showing a trace of nervousness.

"I'm almost certain."

"The doctor is on our side, Nicholas," said Ulanov.

"No one's arguing that. But, look, I've hitched around a lot of places and seen a lot of guys put down with one thing or another—bad, they looked real bad—and the doctors would all say they were done for and you could bury them on the spot if you wanted to, understand? These white-coat boys are wrong a lot more than they're right, I seen it a hundred times. Look, I haven't gone off crying about Josef, not that I don't feel for him but because I think if he was meant to die, he would have died. He's got better than a fifty-fifty chance to pull out of this. Believe me, that's the way it happens. It's a fluke, what happened to him. Something in the water, the food . . . he was weak, anyway."

The bishop stared at his brother for a long moment. Then, "I don't follow you, Nicholas. We've just heard the medical opinion. It's from a trustworthy man and it leaves only *the cook*."

"No, dammit, no. What would be her motive? I swear to you there, Josef." Nicholas walked over to the bed and held up those great arms of his. "I would strangle her on the spot with these hands if I found out that she intentionally—"

"Ah, wait!" said Tsailov. "Who said it has to be intentional?"

"But I thought that poison—" said Alexander.

"You led us to believe . . . yes, you did, Comrade Doctor—" said Sonya.

"Yes, well, I thought of a number of factors in the background of the case, you understand"—he gave a nod to the Ulanovs and Marais—"that made me very prone to suspicion, and, when I concluded that poison was involved, I assumed there was foul play. But, of course, that need not be. Not necessarily."

"I did not think that peasants would do something like that," said Sonya. "They don't use poison to kill, and I don't think they would travel a long way to revenge themselves on an innocent son. At the worst, they might beat him up if he came back."

As she finished, a tangible wave of relief spread through the room. Here, then, was the flaw into which they had been led by overcharged suspicion. The word "unintentional," Marais thought, held their peace of mind within its syllables.

Nicholas uncorked a bottle of cognac from his little satchel and passed the liquor around to Ulanov and the doctor.

"Each of us was too nervous, Sonya," the bishop said a moment later. "That's why we jumped to such a conclusion. Certainly you can sympathize with our position."

"Yes, of course. But he is still lying there, Josef is no less paralyzed than before. Poison, meant or not meant, and he only half lives!"

"My hunches have been pretty good so far, haven't they, Comrade?" Nicholas edged up alongside Sonya. "Well," he said, "if we had money I would bet ten thousand rubles to your hundred that our friend has just had a bad shock and he's going to pull out of it. You'll see, he'll be good as new in a couple of months. If he isn't I'll give you all the money I've saved anyway. That's how positive I am, Comrade."

Sonya, who clearly liked Nicholas no better than his opinions, could not help being moved by this conviction. "Of course we shall see, Nicholas," she said, then turned to Tsailov. "But what are we going to do now?"

For the last few minutes the old physician had seemed anxious to interject a remark and at the same time reluctant. Sonya's question forced the issue. "I don't like to have to remind you all that I said paralysis *could* be the result of an unintentional act. It could also have been intentional. We do not yet know which, Nicholas, and so I want you to get this cook."

"Now? It's the middle of the night."

"We must find out what we can while the evidence is obtainable."

Nicholas looked at his brother.

"He's right," said the bishop. "We must be sure. Besides, she is only a few doors away. Tell her it's an emergency."

"And you, Sonya," said the doctor, "I want you to go with him and inspect her kitchen. Wrap up the last pots she used and bring them back."

Marais knew that if anyone could noiselessly enter the old woman's building and persuade her to come with them at that hour, it was Nicholas—who, as it turned out, needed but ten minutes to verify the Frenchman's faith in his abilities. Yet for all they obtained from the old lady, they might have saved themselves the bother of rousing her on this wickedly cold night. She said that she had cooked the last meal no differently from before for the man who was now so sick. She answered each of their questions in an unimaginative few syllables; no one could coax her into the slightest amplification of her response.

Sonya, on the other hand, brought back evidence both tangible and encouraging. She had found the woman's cooking utensils—two of which she had with her—unbelievably dirty, as was her kitchen; probably capable of spawning and transmitting any number of infectious diseases.

"Now, doesn't that take care of our worries?" Ulanov said with a wave to the group. Turning to Marais, he looked stricken. "Forgive me, Josef. I didn't mean *all* of them."

Marais, feeling the weight of his body's paralysis and the effect of the doctor's needles climb irresistibly into his brain, could no longer attend to the discussion. The last words he remembered were the doctor's—he had fired the woman, he would have the contents of the two pots chemically analyzed, he was installing his own wife as cook . . . As though an iron door had closed, sealing the prisoner from the outside world, Marais's mind shut down.

12

During the following weeks, Marais's frame felt anchored in boots three feet deep in heavy soft snow on the Siberian wastes. He would awaken from time to time and stare at whoever stood before him; he would listen to their remarks, but he could not bring himself even to nod. And as Sonya and an elderly woman he had not seen before poured spoonfuls of hot liquid down his throat, he felt no emotion whatsoever, not even gratitude. Frequently he was gone again before they had finished.

The doctor brought in several specialists, none of whom could decide on the reason for Marais's paralysis. They made frequent references to his prior illness. They were sorry they had not known him then. His siege of hepatitis had left him weakened; quite possibly subtle reactions had developed undetected by Dr. Tsailov. The consensus was that if he lived, he might improve; that he remained alive was a hopeful sign. Polyneuritis and other such terms were favorite expressions.

Marais listened to the words. He understood them. They were spoken softly at the foot of his bed; they became imprinted in his memory. He was not stirred by them.

Ulanov had appeared several times during the first week, and then asked Marais if he had any objections to his leaving for Leningrad immediately and journeying to a rendezvous point with Byelorussian Catholic representatives.

"He hears you," Dr. Tsailov told the bishop, "but he can't respond."

Finally, Ulanov removed from their hiding place behind a wall board the names of all the members in the Moscow congregation. It had been the Frenchman's right to hold these secret documents, but Ulanov explained that in his present condition Marais was hardly responsible enough for the task. Marais had meant to burn them; now they passed from his possession without resistance. Afterward, Nicholas asked in Alexander's behalf for the invisible writing materials and the code. Since there was no way for the patient to honor this request, the brothers departed empty-handed.

Sergey came every day. When he heard from the doctor that Ulanov had removed the documents, he seemed upset that Marais had never informed him of their existence. They were too valuable, he said, to be in the hands of Bishop Ulanov, who had so many duties that he left the details of the mission to Nicholas.

Sergey never failed to accord the patient a great deference during this first month. Even though Marais had no way of replying, questions were addressed to him with respect and an almost extravagant kindness. During the following three weeks, Sergey's attitude gradually changed. He became more demanding, he spent some of his time shouting at the patient. He seemed to expect something in return for these demonstrations—at least, he waited for minutes on end as if the helpless Marais really had within himself the power of an answer.

Dr. Tsailov often watched these harangues, never restraining Sergey. And on certain occasions he cooperated openly with him, during an exercise in which both of them moved Marais's fingers, trying to force them to point at letters on an alphabet chart and frame words in response to the questions they asked him over and over. Initially Marais was bored by this annoying stimulus, with its alternating voices repeating endlessly the same childish questions. On the second and third day of this routine he began to experience a sense of resentment, building at last into a violent desire to throttle the perpetrators of this outrage.

Although this anger did not force speech, as Sergey and Tsailov had surely intended, Marais did notice improvement in his finger movements. He soon found himself venting his irritation on the alphabet chart, and in a surprisingly short time could point to letters as quickly as some men speak.

[234]

One night in the seventh week of Marais's confinement, Nicholas appeared. He strutted around the room for a few moments. "Terrific," he said. "The whole thing—terrific! Do you know where we've been? Not just to Leningrad, we went to the northern Ukraine."

Marais motioned to the optical board with its huge black letters, leaning against the wall.

"Hey, this is a great idea, Josef. But you still can't talk? Too bad. We thought you might have beaten that by now." He held the board up alongside Marais, who rapidly pointed out the letters: "How did you manage all that traveling?"

"The brothers Ulanov—what a team we are!" Nicholas punched the air. "Move, move, move—nothing to hold us down."

Marais tapped at the board: "Do you mean me?"

"Oh, you know I didn't mean that. It's just that I could push Alex faster when I had him to myself."

"Sounds like you did just that."

"More than anything I had planned. I still can't believe it myself. And would you have loved Alex's performance! He's incredible, once he gets going. He met fellows who represented groups all the way down to the Black Sea and out to the Urals. He told them they were the hope of the country, the hope of the world. They were different guys once he talked to them, I tell you. They're convinced the ground for souls is as fertile as the Ukraine, that Russia's going to change, that the state's religious policy can't last much longer. He even got *me* excited. You know, I never suspected there were so many believers still around. Some of those gatherings Alex talked to looked like real conventions. He could be right after all, there just might be millions and millions of Russians waiting to rise up and demand that the government give them back their God."

"I'm delighted," replied Marais, who was in fact finding it difficult to assimilate the import of their extraordinary trip. Nicholas's enthusiasm obviously reflected his brother's, but the Frenchman longed to hear the original voice. "Where is Alexander?" he tapped.

"He got delayed, but he should be showing up here in a couple of days. He sent me ahead to straighten out a few details he forgot when we set out so fast... By the way, he's been praying for you every day at mass. He wanted you to know that."

"Thanks, I'm much improved," said Marais's fingers.

Nicholas seemed at a loss to know how to conclude his report. He paced around the room a few times, then stood at the foot of Marais's bed.

"Anything else?" Marais tapped.

Nicholas waited for a long moment, then clicked his teeth. "I guess it can wait," he said, and left the room without another word.

Late the next night, Marais awoke with a terrible jolt. His head was being twisted away from his shoulders; he felt the pressure of enormous hands about his throat. The mouth that opened and shut in that mad face so close to his own pronounced the words slowly: "So help me, Josef, I'm going to strangle you if you don't give me that invisible stuff and the code. My brother is sick over the way he's been treated. He likes you all right, but he doesn't deserve to be insulted this way by anybody. I'm here to make sure that it doesn't go on, you understand? Now I'm going to hold up this board and you spell out the letters of those words I want to hear from you, Josef. I don't think you're as sick as you think you are, or maybe you're bluffing. I don't care, but you just better cooperate."

Nicholas went to the foot of the bed and held up the board with its enlarged alphabet. "Where are the materials? Where are the materials? The materials? In what? I-N . . .?"

Marais lay perfectly still.

"I'm warning you," said Nicholas. He dropped the board and walked around the bed toward Marais, removing his jacket and thrusting his arms toward the Frenchman's neck. Marais saw the rippling cords of the arms, the great hands closing in near his head, and, in the terror of that instant, his throat emitted a croaking gasp, a loud gurgling sound as though he were already suffocating. Nicholas struck him an open-handed blow on the forehead.

Marais heard voices next door, women's voices, and just as Nicholas's massive arms reached for his throat, Sonya and the

[236]

doctor's wife came through the door. They screamed, pummeling Nicholas about the chest and head with each shriek. He threw them off, which only encouraged them to scream the louder. Marais watched Nicholas's face as he assessed the carrying power of the women's cries, and, then, rushed from the room.

Sergey came soon, with four men. "I've sent out an order among our people to capture Nicholas, to do whatever they must to get him off the streets. He is a madman. We are fortunate he acts only in behalf of his brother and not the state. But he is a menace to us with this unpredictable behavior of his. From now on, two men will be stationed in this room in eight-hour shifts."

Marais nodded, as if he were too exhausted to care.

"Listen to me, Josef, try in the name of Christ to push yourself. The community needs you, and Dr. Tsailov says you *should* have made more progress. We all know what you've gone through, but the doctor sees improvement in your finger movements, in your color, in your blood analysis. Try, if not for your own sake—for ours."

Sergey might have spared himself the speech, for Marais's encounter with Nicholas went a long way toward releasing him from his torpor. In the next few days, a certain ease gradually asserted itself inside his skull, enabling him to *feel* the impact of words addressed to him.

"Perhaps there is something we can thank Nicholas for, after all," said Sergey. "Now let's see about these movements. Concentrate—you can move your fingers well. See if you can move your arms and hands. If your head is working, maybe they are too."

After a half hour's trial and error, Marais succeeded in finding a labyrinthine route connecting his desire to the hand so that he could grasp an object. Within a few days, his improvement was so apparent that Sonya, the doctor's wife, Sergey, and Tsailov all went about the place laughing and talking in those normal tones of voice they had not used for so long. Marais could not yet talk, but he could form syllables to produce a kind of breathy whisper.

Just before sunrise, on the fifth day after the incident with Nicholas, Marais awoke with a cry whose shrillness startled the guards and quickly brought Sonya and the doctor's wife from

[237]

their quarters next door. Marais, panting heavily, mouthed the syllables, clear enough in the thick silence of the room: "Get Sergey."

Within half an hour, Sergey was standing before him, still half dazed from his own broken slumber, waiting with some irritation for an explanation of this summons.

Marais did not care. A dream had come to him, he explained in whispered fragments; a dream that was beyond anything in his experience. Bodies careening about in space, turning upside down and sideways above a house and fields, their limbs and torsos purple and blue and gray. Each head dangled from its neck, twisting in a different direction from the rest of the body. The wide eyes set in white faces stared out and turned on Marais with an utterly tortured expression.

Sergey rubbed his eyes. "You called me to run this distance so early in the morning just to relate a bad dream, Josef? Nightmares are to be expected after the illness you've been through. It's the strain of recovery, don't you see?"

"You fool!" Marais gasped. "I have had so much time to ponder. I . . . I who have done not one foolish thing during all these weeks of sickness! You must listen to the rest, I am not finished."

He began to explain that he had not awakened immediately after the dream. He had lain there for some time in a semiconscious state, like a powerless spectator reviewing these mutilated figures; trying to ask them a question or to decipher the landscape. He had wrenched his eyes from the figures and focused them down, closer, ever closer, to the ground—to the sight of sheep, small sheep in a rough place—and then the name of Pinsk sounded like an awful gong inside his head, and he had screamed.

Marais had momentarily exhausted his last reserves of strength. Sergey stood at the foot of the bed, totally alert now.

"Can you get out of Russia?" Marais whispered.

"Yes, to Riga in Latvia. I know a way."

"Then go there. Go and telephone Archbishop Francisi in Rome. You will ask him to investigate Pinsk, the farmhouse . . . to find out if the people are well or not. We *must* know. If Francisi finds bad news, ask him what he makes of it, what we should do . . . You must also tell him about Nicholas . . . That is my confession."

"He does not know this man is *here?*"

"One thing after another came up. Finally it meant the mission . . . I could not tell Rome . . ." Marais stopped, then began again in a whisper so low that Sergey had to lean over him to catch the words.

"We kept Nicholas under control, didn't we? He has been helpful in a thousand ways . . . I'm sure he has saved our lives."

"We're also sure he tried to kill you only a few days ago!"

"That was something different . . . for his brother."

"An odd distinction to make in your circumstances," said Sergey.

"Never mind that . . . Will you go and tell Francisi what I have done?"

"For a *dream* I would never consider taking such a risk. But with Pinsk, the chance to retrace our steps—"

"We must *know* . . . Please, I can't talk much longer." Marais sank back into the pillow. "Those people, the Mareskys . . . those beautiful people, they can't all be dead, mutilated . . ." His voice trailed off as he saw once again the broken doll-like bodies floating over their homestead.

"You understand," said Sergey, "that I must weigh a number of things here, that as bishop of the community, I can't charge out—"

"But you must!" Marais's painful whisper had the force of a shout. "I will send another—"

"In the name of Christ be patient! Can't you see I am listening? I am straining to see the merits, I *do believe* you are on to an important event, however it came to you. But there are problems you don't know about. Alexander is due back tomorrow evening, and I must be here when he arrives. We have not found Nicholas yet. He is hiding from us somewhere, but he will undoubtedly see his brother as soon as he can and try to sell him a bill of goods on what transpired in this room. I must get to Alexander first with the details and the witnesses, then convince him to get rid of that maniac.

"You are not well enough to argue with Alexander, and above

all we must act privately, for otherwise the community would be damaged by our dissension, perhaps irreparably. Most of them see Bishop Ulanov as a hero if not a saint. Should I be forced to denounce him, it would divide our people and then think what would happen—the fights, the backbiting, perhaps the informing. It's too dangerous even to contemplate."

"You could delegate someone else."

"No, I want to be the one to take the risks. It is a treacherous route, with government agents all along it, but as a player and a coach I have traveled often enough in that part of the country to know it well."

"You can't have everything," Marais whispered. "If you want to go, then you go at once and leave Nicholas to us. When did you plan to capture him?"

"As soon as he sees Alexander."

"Your men can do that—"

"Yes, they can, but Alexander will try to persuade you to deliver him. He is very convincing, and you are not strong enough—"

"I will take care of Nicholas until you return ... Please, Sergey, a few more moments and I will be unable to speak at all. You will go to Riga?"

"Yes."

"When you call Archbishop Francisi, give him the code words, 'Alpha and omega, twelve plus one. Christ and the twelve Apostles, including Judas."

"Alpha and omega, twelve plus one."

"Ask only for Francisi at the Vatican Secretariat, do not speak to Cardinal Pacelli. Francisi knows all about Pinsk ... Wait in Riga for him to telephone his report, it will take them a few days to find out the answer. But insist. You will not leave Riga, until they satisfy you. Anything you want to tell him about the mission is up to you. Go ... go, and God bless you."

"I will start at once. *Gospodi,* Father."

As Sergey left the room, his men returned to guard Marais.

On the following day, Nicholas—who had joined his brother, as predicted, only a couple of hours after the arrival—was captured immediately. Just as predictably, Alexander stormed into Marais's room that afternoon and demanded that Sergey's people give Nicholas back his freedom.

When Dr. Tsailov described the attack that had led to Sergey's command, Ulanov apologized for Nicholas's headstrong action. He also reminded Marais that the question of the code had always been a grievance between them. His brother, who no doubt had been drinking, had in a fit of rage overreached himself. Marais should consider that he was unable to execute his powers at the time. In those circumstances, to whom should the code be delegated but to his partner?

"Bishop Ulanov," said the doctor, "he would have *killed* Father Marais if my wife and Sonya had not prevented him!"

"Nonsense, he was only trying to frighten Josef. If Nicholas really wanted to kill someone, do you really think the person would ever know it? He would be dead before he could feel it. Believe me, my brother may have forgotten his strength, but he was roughhousing with you, Josef. You can take my word for that . . . Now, this Belenkov girl—*there* is a scandal. I warned you against allowing her or any other stranger here."

"Sonya helped to save this man's life," said the doctor. "She has done more than could have been expected of any *stranger*."

"But that is the whole point. She is not one of us, and at any moment the secret could slip out. You could talk in your sleep, Josef, and then where would we be? Or your wife, Doctor, could forget that the girl was present and call this man 'Father.' A thousand things could go wrong in these close surroundings. In any case, Father Marais knows the rules of the order, which are in force in Russia as much as in Europe or America."

"And what may these rules be?" asked the doctor.

"A Jesuit may not converse with a woman for more than twenty minutes in a room. In any case the door must remain halfway open and in full view of any passerby, and the subject matter must be spiritual, and the locale must be designated by the superior of the place."

The doctor threw up his hands. "This man is a fine priest with a high sense of propriety. Had he behaved as you suggest, Bishop, he most certainly would have attracted suspicion. There is another answer—a worldly one but nonetheless to the point. For several weeks, my patient has been incapable of such physical activity as you impute to him."

"I impute nothing. Of course not, but there are dangers—"

"Nonsense! For the last time—" The doctor, turning to Marais, found him wearing the closest semblance to a grin he could manage. "Hm . . . well, perhaps, Father, that is the best answer you can give to such madness."

Marais beckoned to the doctor and Ulanov. "Congratulations, Alexander, you do not change despite your travels. You have tried very hard to distract us from the issue . . . Now!" He forced the word from deep in his throat to halt a further tirade from Ulanov. "Now . . . nothing will be done for two days. Then you will come back here and report to me, as you should have, on your travels. That is essential—you, not your brother! You will not complain or remark to the community on Nicholas's absence. If you do, he will die, and you yourself will be taken out of Russia at once by Sergey's men. The good of the community has prior claim on all of us."

Marais lifted his fingers in a gesture of dismissal even as Ulanov stood before him, as stunned at the content of Marais's speech as the fact that he could speak above a whisper. At Marais's signal, the doctor summoned the guards, who held the door open for Ulanov's departure.

Marais felt that events had worked into his hands. He did not feel strong enough yet to engage Ulanov in a long argument, but time was in his favor. Two days from now he would be even further improved. Nor had Ulanov's conduct really shocked him. He felt sorry that his colleague, for all his magnificent gifts, could let himself be cheapened by such misplaced affection.

Forty-eight hours later the bishop returned to demand again his brother's release. For the first few minutes, neither priest spoke. Ulanov looked down at Marais with contempt, obviously infuriated by the notion of waiting upon a lesser man, a nonworking invalid. His giant figure, arms crossed as he leaned against the wall, was a portrait of the outraged hero.

"I presume you're going to apologize," Marais said finally.

"For what, in the name of Christ?"

"Very well," said the Frenchman.

Ulanov moved over to his bed. "You provoked me beyond the limits of endurance. My brother's arrest"—he waved a warning finger—"is vengeance upon me and me alone!"

"You must know better, Dmitri, and your interpretation of it only tells me what is in *your* mind, not what happened. But if you persist . . ." Marais glanced toward the door beyond which the guards were stationed.

"I want Nicholas free!"

"Why? Why? What is he to you that no matter what he does, you—"

"Such a useless man," said Ulanov, "hoarding the little hurts of the past, waiting until others risk their lives in the field in order to seize power behind their backs."

"All right," said Marais. "You won't tell me about your brother, so tell me about 'the field.'" Marais extended the muscles of his face to form a smile. "I have as yet heard only from Nicholas of the marvelous things you did."

Ulanov, taken aback by this disjunctive request, sat down in a chair and was quiet for a moment. He leaned back, his eyes raised to the ceiling as though recreating in that blank space the scene of his triumphs.

"Our trip can hardly be believed," he said, "unless you were there. As much as I myself believed in our destiny, I was unprepared for what actually happened. In Leningrad they came in scores of small groups. From every sector of society! I mean there were factory workers as well as the intelligentsia. At first I thought that many of them were just curious or nostalgic. But no, that's not what happened. They were all of them starved for the good news we brought.

"It was impossible to satisfy them. They wanted to hear more . . . then more. My voice went so hoarse some nights that I swallowed half a pint of honey to ease the soreness. Of course, it was impossible to communicate anything near what I wanted, but then the main thing was the visible testimony of hope my presence supplied. They saw the miracle of religious freedom coming closer.

"Often half the night went by while I did nothing else but baptize, confirm, hear confessions. There were many days when two masses had to be said in different apartments.

"In between times—both in Leningrad and in Byelorussia—I met with Orthodox representatives. They're so disenchanted with their own church that they're willing to discuss our doctrinal differences. Imagine how the Holy Father will welcome *that* development!

"I have told them all that the church is by no means opposed to socialism, that it's only a question of ousting the vicious atheists in Moscow. I believe they were very much reassured.

"As for the White Russians, I can't say enough for their spiritual future. They are among the most religious people in the world. It is imperative that we make an extensive visit to Byelorussia soon.

"I must tell you that we had several narrow escapes from the secret police. If it hadn't been for Nicholas's ingenuity, I don't know where I or many others would be now. His bravery is incredible! I won't tax your strength with a recital of what he did—perhaps later . . ."

Marais had remained perfectly quiet through this extraordinary monologue, knowing some of the content from Nicholas and knowing, certainly, that the bishop would close his account of the trip with praise for his brother.

"Remarkable achievements, Dmitri," he said. "Congratulations." Marais was indeed impressed, not only by the achievements but also by the fervor and eloquence with which Ulanov had recited them. Anything connected with the mission field brought Ulanov alive. There he was free of triviality or competing with his peers. "You may be the greatest missionary since St. Paul," Marais went on. "Well, maybe St. Francis Xavier."

"Thank you, Paul," said Ulanov, and extended his hand. "Now do I get what I want? Oh, by the way, where is Sergey?"

Marais knocked on the wooden sidepost of his bed. "On a mission to the sick. The rest is none of your business, Dmitri."

[244]

The guards entered to escort the outraged bishop from the room.

"You will get what you want," called Marais, "when you tell me what Nicholas is to you that he makes you blind! Goodbye!"

In two days Ulanov returned, and with no preamble began in an excruciatingly slow manner to explain his feelings for Nicholas. The Frenchman had never intended to torment his Jesuit brother by forcing him to this kind of awkward confession.

"When I was a senior in high school," Ulanov was saying, "both of my parents were killed in an accident. There were no relatives around, or even good friends, so I went to work in a steel mill to support Nicholas. I worked there four years while he got through high school. It was only at the end that I realized most of my labor was useless. Nicholas just couldn't get anything out of education.

"Both of us became socialists. I was influenced by the union organizers, and Nicholas was influenced by me. The hard thing was to avoid being recruited by the communists, but we escaped that pitfall.

"For years I had wanted to become a priest and especially a Jesuit. I had read about their intellectual influence, so when the time came and I was free of my responsibility for Nicholas, I went to Baltimore to see the provincial. It was difficult getting in but I made it and I've had no regrets. The order is the perfect place for me."

"Then how is it that you've made no close friends among the Jesuits?"

"I've kept my own counsel. You'll find I was as friendly as others deserved."

"And what is Nicholas that he deserves what you give him—*him alone?*"

"I don't know why," said Ulanov, "but I feel a great guilt about him. He has faithfully visited me during my years in the novitiate, philosophate, theologiate, and yet mentally he's no more improved than the day he left high school. It must be my doing! I've failed him, but I've tried to make it up by my loyalty to him. And he has proved very able in his own way. He's a skillful technician, he handles mechanical details extraordinarily well. He's good at manipulating the practical angles of any situation.

"Of course, at times, his love is childlike. It can be embarrassing. His faithfulness is so total that I sometimes feel imprisoned by it. Still, it's a small price to pay for such loyalty."

"It's strange, Dmitri, how passionately you act and how dispassionately you talk."

"I have my way, you have yours."

"I hardly know any more after the facts than I did before."

"You're looking for mystery where there is none."

Marais shook his head. "But I've known you for a long time. You are mysterious. And yet, lying here, listening to you, you really do make it sound as if you are the simplest of men."

"Don't waste your brain on general impressions, Josef. They're created out of nothing. This idea of me as the lone wolf, for example . . . just because I don't talk as much as the others. As I told you, I had to hold back on some intellectual opinions. I could not explain what I believed indiscriminately, I had to wait until the right time. Of course, my background was different too, wasn't it? The factory, my Slavic origins, my hopes for the people of the world—all of these separated me from others . . ."

Marais's dissatisfaction was enormous. He had observed Ulanov's subtle maneuverings in Rome and on the trip; the calculations that amounted to lies, the self-will, the talk of visions! Yet he did not know how to press the attack further. Ulanov had disarmed him. All was simplicity! The relation of facts with no compunctions, no self-criticism—no perspective or perception when it came to his brother—left Marais without a lever.

"I have no desire to debase myself as a ransom for Nicholas," Ulanov said.

Marais tried to be generous. "It's I who have forced the issue."

"Maybe so, but I wouldn't have told you about Nicholas unless I thought you had a right to it. Nor does your power worry me. It just so happens that you're the only human being alive who's ever been so involved with Nicholas and me. For good and bad, you have become part of things. Besides, you were

[246]

attacked by Nicholas—to have my brother in Christ threatened by my flesh and blood tears me apart. And the scandal! I despise any spreading of gossip to the crowd. Bonds like ours should never be violated! So now Nicholas is owed a little less loyalty and you are owed a little more."

"But if you're that upset with Nicholas, why have you been pushing me so hard for his release?"

"I must be the one to deal with him. The way you have arrested and then imprisoned him hurts me to the quick. You've compounded one evil with another just as bad."

"You're more disturbed by Nicholas's tactlessness than by what he did!" Marais was finding himself unable to follow Ulanov on any point.

"I believe in secrecy. It goes far beyond Nicholas's behavior."

"I think you would be a greater man without your passion for secrecy. It makes you strange sometimes. And, I sometimes think it has made you mad."

"If we had not shared so much together, Josef, I'd never discuss anything with you. Your attitudes are stupid."

Marais could not resist giving vent to a sudden intuition. "You would not discuss it if you thought I was going to live."

Ulanov could not bring himself to look at Marais.

"*I am not going to die,* Alexander."

"I did not say you would."

"But you believe it."

"There are so many hardships left. It's possible . . . and I would be responsible."

Marais let the silence following this remark continue just enough to increase Ulanov's discomfort. Then, "You can have Nicholas. On one condition. For the next ten days two guards must accompany him at all times. Explain to him that he has been given a sort of parole. If he violates it, Sergey has the right to expel him and perhaps yourself."

"I doubt that he can," said Ulanov, "but I will bind Nicholas to those conditions. You must rest, I promise you won't be disturbed by us." He gave Marais a small wave in farewell and entered the hallway without looking back.

[247]

Though Ulanov's reserve had barely been penetrated, Marais was sure that the session just concluded would have a temporary effect. The next six days bore out his optimism. Nicholas, Marais heard, was more subdued in his dealings with the community. The bishop had returned to his regimen of work after the disquieting interruption.

For himself, in the long lonely hours of convalescence, Marais worried and prayed over Sergey and the family at Pinsk. His dream had by now become obsessive. Coming so soon after his own near-fatal paralysis, those floating clown figures with their corpse-like rigidity brought his mind nightly to a cliff's edge where he was stopped only by the thought of God's mercy.

As he waited for Sergey to return, he imagined every conceivable disaster that might have befallen him. The route presented so many dangers; there was a good chance that Sergey, even now, lay in a cell, a prisoner of the secret police. So tormenting were these thoughts that Marais asked for stronger drugs to find sleep.

During the afternoons, the doctor and Sonya's brother exercised Marais. Leaning on their shoulders, he could manage to walk slowly around the room for forty-five minutes. Dr. Tsailov's presence also served as a buffer between the priest and Sonya, who had become more protective of Marais since his second attack.

She spent an enormous amount of time with the patient. He had tried on a few occasions to remonstrate with her over skimping on her studies, but she became so irritated with him that he had to give up. When he tried to encourage her to go out and enjoy herself with other young people, she reminded him that she would make up her own mind on those kinds of questions. Every so often, male admirers from the medical school would drop by the Belenkovs', but she managed to discourage them within a few minutes. Her handling of them was pointed enough to leave no doubt about her feelings.

At the same time, Sonya allayed many of Marais's forebodings by taking advantage neither of their closeness nor of his sickness. Re-creating that one long moment when he had held her, the priest had dreamed up all sorts of possible promises and predicaments. None of them came up. Instead, Sonya treated him as her closest friend. She shared with him childhood recollections and half-comical gruesome stories from the medical school. She outlined her plans for the future. Many an evening she and her brother sang old Russian folksongs to him.

Marais, for his part, talked about the great cities of Europe. He had already told them that as a young wealthy boy he had traveled a great deal in the West. His descriptions held an almost endless fascination for all the Belenkovs. They asked a hundred questions about the customs in Paris, Munich, Rome, and Marais was happy to indulge his own reveries. For all the anti-imperialist indoctrination they received in school, Sonya and her brother had a natural curiosity that could not be stifled. In Sonya's case it seemed to go further than this. She almost identified with the flavor of the places Marais talked about. She amazed him with her ability to mimic the mannerisms of people she only knew through his conversation. Sometimes the eerie sensation came over him that he had actually visited these cities with Sonya.

Luckily Dr. Tsailov was an excellent chess player, and their competition offered Marais a distraction from such fantasies and their source.

The doctor had feared that Marais, during his sickness, would give up in the midst of a delirium the secret of his identity. This had not happened—although, the old man told him, Marais had called for Sonya and even reached out for her. Oddly enough, hers was the only name he invoked. The doctor assumed that the priest had resolved beforehand not to call on Christ and thereby cause suspicion, and credited Marais's Jesuit discipline for the achievement of remarkable control. Marais knew there had been no such resolution. After all his years in the order, a beautiful woman had reached something deeper than his prayers.

As the days of waiting for Sergey lengthened, Ulanov began to return to his old ways. He was growing more persistent in his inquiries about Sergey, and had cornered the doctor two or three times for information. Marais, realizing that the truce with his partner could not last much longer, worked hardest at excluding from his mind the terrifying thought that calamity had struck

Sergey. If it had, what would he do with Alexander and Nicholas? These fears had more power to paralyze him than any sickness. Dr. Tsailov, distressed that Marais's worries might impede his progress, wagered his wife, his practice, even his hidden little art collection that Sergey would return.

And he was right. One night as they were moving pawns and bishops around the board, the door opened to admit a harried-looking Sergey, his coat whitened under an inch of snow. The shadows cast by his shoulders covered the far wall like the wings of a great bird. As he bent toward the fire, the silhouette seemed to flap in motion. Still half out of breath, he asked Marais, "How are you? I was worried that you might not be alive when I got here."

Marais and the doctor looked at each other. "We've already buried you," said Tsailov.

"You didn't! Have I been given the last rites?"

"*In absentia*," said Marais.

"The community wept more tears for you than for Lenin." The doctor shook his head appreciatively at the memory.

"You should see the tombstone they bought you. Oh Lord, the expense. They spared nothing." Marais touched his forehead. "How will we ever explain?"

"And it's not as though you could use it for anyone else," Tsailov added. "Your name has been chiseled on it."

"I wasn't gone that long!" Sergey shouted.

"Your countrymen are very impatient people," Marais answered.

"And pessimists, besides."

"I knew it, I knew it. They love a tragedy!" Sergey pounded his fists on the stove.

"You've lost your one chance to be a legend," said Marais. "Dying in the snow somewhere in the very prime of manhood, watching the wolves close in. Now you'll just dodder into old age."

"The stories they're circulating about your accomplishments are incredible," said Tsailov. "How are you ever going to live up to them?"

"Maybe I should go back and die, is that what you want? Good Jesus, after all it took to get here!"

Marais, unable to contain his laughter another moment, burst out with all the pent-up tension of weeks. He buried his head in the bedclothes.

"You ungrateful illegitimates!" Sergey's voice rose like a battle cry. "For a kopek I'd bury the both of you. Then we'd see who gets a tombstone."

Dr. Tsailov recovered first. He bustled around the Russian, removing his coat. "Where have you been, you big oaf? You frightened us half to death wondering about you."

Sergey laughed. "Remember your manners, Doctor. For better and maybe for worse, I am a bishop!" Then he gave Marais a curious stare and said, "I hope you'll always remember that you were so happy to see me."

"But—you are *here!*" It was all Marais could say or think.

The Russian embraced his friend and then moved to the Holland stove. "It must be the coldest winter in history. Where is the brandy?" The doctor went to his pouch and handed the bottle to him. Sergey took a great swallow, then turned, his back to the fire, and studied Marais over the bottle. "Is he well?" he asked the doctor.

"Progressing marvelously."

"That is excellent news, I—"

"Sergey, what is it?" asked Marais. "Something has happened, hasn't it—to *you?*"

"Well, something is happening tonight out there. The streets, the stations were infested with secret police. I can spot the lice at a mile. They are looking for someone. I don't see how it could be me, but I was careful. It took me six hours to get here from the outskirts."

"Well, you are safe now," said Tsailov.

"Maybe. That depends."

"On what?" asked Marais.

"On you," said Sergey. A long pause ensued while Marais tried to gather the sense of his remark. "There is much to tell you and much for you to decide." He swigged the brandy, swallowing

[251]

again and then again before he finally spoke. "I arrived in Riga all right, after a lot of changes in my plan. But I got there, and I did exactly what you told me to. I asked the Vatican for Archbishop Francisi. They always wanted to give me Cardinal Pacelli's office, but I finally got Francisi and related your premonitions about those people in the Pinsk Marshes and my own feeling that it might be wise to review our steps. It took a while to convince him. We had to work through an interpreter, and sometimes I do not think your archbishop understood. At first, he wasn't sure Pinsk was that important, since your visit there occurred before the real part of your mission."

"Fool!"

"He is no fool, this Francisi. And, he has a point. Pinsk is not Moscow, it is not even Minsk. The archbishop said his investigation would require higher approval, that he would have to show that the results were vital to our mission. This was much more of a problem than you and I had really discussed."

"So you didn't find out—that's what you're leading up to, isn't it? Put off by the damned bureaucrats!"

"I have not finished!"

"Then why must you go through these ridiculous statements of theirs? What are you trying to tell me?" Marais's hoarse voice cracked.

"My story will be brief enough. The archbishop knew he would be called upon to explain the proposal coherently. Of course, it helped a great deal that his opinion of you is so high—though he did ask me if I thought the sickness had affected your mind. I reassured him on that point and then I told him that we Russians also wished an answer about these Pinsk people. As their bishop I insisted that the Vatican investigate the matter.

"Poor Francisi! He must have thought for sure that the mad Russians were dancing on his head. Still, he had to admit that a request from the Muscovite bishop would have the highest priority, could not be turned down unless it ran contrary to an established policy at the Secretariat."

"And you got it through?"

"I'm afraid so."

As the last words dropped, Marais drew himself erect in the bed.

"Archbishop Francisi," Sergey went on, "told me to wait in a certain rectory while he worked on getting the investigation approved by his superior. He called me the following night and explained that although Cardinal Pacelli saw no merit to the idea, he had capitulated to Russian eccentricity because he heard we do terribly suicidal things when we are unhappy.

"Francisi explained that the cardinal naturally found it difficult to honor a Russian bishop named Sergey. For him, *the* Russian bishop has always been our friend Ulanov, and the cardinal apparently remains in a state of ecstasy over his selection of Alexander and sees the mission's success as the start of a new world tide."

"Did you tell the archbishop about Nicholas?"

"Yes, I did. You told me I was free to—"

"What did Francisi have to say about it?"

"Please, you must allow me to tell these things chronologically. I had not said anything immediately to Francisi because, as our proverb has it, 'two hands working at the same time and all the pots are spilled.' I waited, you see, until he called me back that night to inform me that he had not only permission but a plan. He is quite capable, your Francisi—"

"Very," murmured the Frenchman.

"When I had one bird in hand, I told him about Nicholas. He was dumfounded. The interpreter told me, in fact, that the archbishop could not speak for some minutes. When he could, he was furious. He could not believe that you had concealed this detail from the Vatican, nor could he understand why you had done so."

"I had my reasons. They were good ones, there would have been no mission otherwise."

Sergey went right on. "Francisi told me that he needed time to get what we wanted in Pinsk. He said he would speak to me again in three or four days, and then he asked me what I thought about Nicholas."

"You gave him the truth, I hope?"

[253]

"Yes, I did. I told him everything I could remember, how dependent Bishop Ulanov was on his brother, how Nicholas took care of many of the mission's details, its problems ... And that I did not like him, this crude unspiritual fellow."

"And what did he say to all that?"

"Well, that part is rather odd. He ended our conversation by saying that he had a Jesuit friend named Father Dillon in America whom he must try to locate at once. And then he hung up."

"And did he call you back?" asked Marais.

"Of course! Four days later!"

"Get to it, man. What happened?"

Sergey went on, but slowly. "Archbishop Francisi went to Warsaw and found the Jesuit priest who knew the family. Together they went to Pinsk. There it appeared that something suspicious might have happened, because this Maresky, the head of the family, had not been seen in the market. He and his sons were long overdue, and a great discussion was going on among the relatives as to when they should make an attempt into the marshes—the weather had been terrible. It was then that Francisi hired an airplane and got the original helper of the mission who first took you and Ulanov through the marshes. He put him into the front seat with an experienced pilot, because the old man said he would be able to find the farm from the air—and he did ..."

"Go on!"

"They circled over and over. The place looked bleak enough, barren, yet that is what one would expect in the wintertime there I should think. But the old man said no, there was definitely something wrong. He and the pilot spotted the outlines of a truck, though it was covered with snow. They did not know what to think until several men came running from the house and began firing rifles up at the airplane, and the pilot decided very courageously to take one more low sweep over them since he did not believe they could really hit him and he needed a closer look at these men. Well, he got it, and he got his passengers away safely, but he said he was sure the men below were wearing army uniforms."

[254]

"Then they were *captured?*"

"Obviously."

"My God!"

"Of course, we don't know how or what for. The problem could have been their private agricultural work, which is outlawed. But then why would the soldiers have stayed there? It is possible that the authorities thought they were at the center of some illegitimate circle of producers—not likely, but possible."

"They are dead, dead, dead ... My beautiful people, their lovely garden in the wilderness—"

"I am sorry, Josef. I have already wept my own tears for this family of friends."

"My dream, then, was true."

"I'm afraid so, but we can't be absolutely sure."

"Was it connected with the mission?"

"How can we ever know?"

"Jesus, we have *killed* them!"

"Stop! If they are martyrs, they are martyrs. There is more I have to tell you, and if you dissolve on me I swear I won't put the information into unstable hands."

Marais held up his hand to Sergey for patience, while he worked through some of the images of death as they converged in his mind. The Russian, despite his exhaustion and impatience to finish his story, endured the long silence Marais needed to come to terms with the tragedy he had intuited weeks ago. "Whatever does it all mean?" Marais said finally.

"They are asking you to decide that."

"Who is 'they'?"

"The Vatican. Francisi ... Here is a note that was delivered to me before I left Riga." Sergey pulled a stiff folded paper out of the unsealed envelope and handed it, open, to Marais:

Dear Father Marais,

Certain tragic circumstances and disquieting irregularities surrounding the mission have come to our attention. We are unable as yet to assess their import. We are, however, asking you to do so.

[255]

We leave it up to you to decide whether, given such difficulties, this might not be an auspicious time to return to Rome along with Bishop Ulanov. A total review of the situation and a report of progress up to this date can then be discussed in less pressing conditions than are now available to you. There is no reason to feel that further work in Russia would be hindered by your return. Your visit here can simply be understood as a mutual briefing, and a vacation between missionary labors. Surely you can use the latter, inasmuch as you are not yet recovered from your mysterious illness, which has also disturbed us.

I emphasize that Cardinal Pacelli and I leave you free to decide what you will, that the choice of remaining or returning belongs to you. Bishop Ulanov has other, more general, responsibilities, but in this matter he shall defer. He and his brother are obligated to obey your final orders on the subject.

In any case, a representative of ours, a priest well known to you, shall await you at a rectory in Riga. He will escort you to Rome in the eventuality that you do choose to leave Russia. The address of this particular house shall be supplied you by Bishop Sergey. The code word for the authenticity of this message, one that Bishop Ulanov will recognize, is 'B-12.'

> Yours in Christ,
> Archbishop Francisi with
> the concurrence of the Secretary
> of State

Marais finished the letter and then reread it, breathing heavily.

"You can take days to decide," said Sergey. He began to unpack his bedding material from the knapsack he carried. "I will lie here, if you don't mind."

"It is also too late for me to go home," said the doctor. "Perhaps I can lie on one side of this bed."

"Of course," said Marais. "We shall all need sleep, for we are leaving Russia tomorrow night or the night after." He held his hand up to signal the end of discussion, but Sergey had already crawled from his mat to a position alongside the bed.

"Wait and think," he said. "Wait, can't you, till morning?"

"No," said Marais. "Francisi is right. We must straighten things out. What more is there to say? My health is improving." Marais closed his eyes and his brain to their remonstrations. Sometime between the reading of the letter and the doctor's request to stay overnight, his mind had clicked into a fixed position. He who always wavered between opposites in behalf of reason had made his most crucial choice with a suddenness transcending argument. His intuition as to how the balance of their mission weighed was identical to Francisi's. That was enough. Another good man had shaken his head over these occurrences and wanted them back. They were going to Rome. *Dictum erat . . .*

13

Nor did Marais change his mind on the following afternoon, when he awoke to find Alexander and Nicholas talking with Sergey and the doctor. Sergey, noticing that Marais was looking at them, shrugged. "Your brother in Christ," he said, "has remarkable instincts. He sensed that something was happening here and he appeared an hour ago."

"What's happened, have you told him anything?"

Sergey held up his hand to forestall the objection. "First, I asked Bishop Ulanov his code number. He gave it to me. It was the one we expected, and then I read him the letter, which he concedes is genuine."

"He also told me your . . . decision," said Ulanov.

"I thought it was best for me to tell him," said Sergey.

Ulanov was furious at being talked about as if he were not there. "Who gave you the right to keep this assignment a secret?" he cried. "I presume you are the one responsible for these contemptible tactics!"

"I am," said Marais, "but then you went to Leningrad and half the way to Byelorussia when I was unconscious. Besides, you weren't here at the time."

"Very convenient, wasn't it? Do you realize what you are doing?"

"We're going back. You, I, and Nicholas."

"Not if he doesn't want to," said Nicholas. "My brother doesn't have to take those kind of orders."

[259]

Sergey moved closer to Nicholas. "You have a great deal of nerve to talk like that to someone you tried to strangle. You are very lucky to be here, fellow, lucky even to be alive."

Nicholas studied the much larger Sergey, estimating, perhaps, his chances in a fight. Then he walked away.

"You have fabricated a web of innuendos," said Alexander. "It was set up for Francisi and Pacelli to write back this kind of letter! Suppose I had gone and done the same thing, called Rome behind your back, then we would have a different story. You're a petty man who will stop at no end to ruin our success."

"And after all our work," said Nicholas. "And it was my brother who did it all. You . . . and you"—he pointed to Marais and then to Sergey—"wouldn't be anybody at all without him, now you turn on him."

Sergey made an effort to respond calmly. "It was a legitimate mission," he said. "I told no lies. I simply gave an honest report and asked for advice."

"But name one thing that would have upset them so much?" asked Alexander.

"I name Pinsk!" shouted Marais. "Did you hear they are gone?"

"Yes, yes, Sergey told me. Very well, let us assume they did not move to Minsk, that they were captured by the army. I am sorry about the people, but what does it mean?"

"It means that we might be in trouble," answered Marais. "That by now someone may have broken those people and be trying to destroy the mission. The only clues needed are the two of us. They wouldn't know anyone else. This retracing of steps is standard strategy for people in our position, and now that we have performed the operation, it has turned out negative."

"So you concluded that's what the Pinsk disappearance means," said Ulanov. "Did you ever stop to think that there could be another interpretation?"

"Such as?"

Alexander beckoned to Nicholas, who shook his head at Marais. "You see, that road those people lived on is an open way into Russia. It wasn't much of a route to get in there—too tough for almost everybody, so the Soviets hardly bothered to guard it. They figured the swamps and the insects and the narrow road would do the job. But the local officials must have heard a rumor that a few strangers made their way through the swamps. They put two and two together and figure that this family who lived in the middle of the marshes out there had helped the strangers and maybe a lot of other people to get in. The government probably thought that's how the family survived, making a living by serving as part of a pipeline in and out of the Soviet Union. And that's why you got the army there now and not a bunch of secret service agents in plainclothes. It's the army that protects borders, you understand?

"Look, I'm not saying those people haven't been sent to Siberia. But I'm willing to bet they're not there because of something religious. They were accused of aiding foreigners, Poles most likely, to get into the country illegally. That's why nobody's on our track. You jumped to conclusions right off the bat, see? And now you get everybody excited back in Rome with your suspicions. But the chances are you're just plain wrong and this whole letter—with you ending the mission and sending us back—is built on a cockeyed idea."

"There you have it!" Alexander jumped in to conclude the case. "Admit it, he's being reasonable—and shrewd."

"He's shrewd, all right," said Marais. "But we are going back, Alexander. That decision is irreversible."

"You are destroying the greatest mission since the Jesuits went to China. That is how history will judge you—as I have."

"We can always return to Russia," said Marais.

Ulanov turned to face Sergey. "And what will you tell the people?"

"That you received orders to report back to Rome," said Sergey. "And that you intend to return to Russia."

Alexander fell quiet with the realization that all the exits had been closed. Nicholas, however, was not so easily silenced. "Suppose my brother and I refuse to go?" he demanded. "What could you do—you in the bed there?"

"Let me answer for him," said Sergey, stepping very close to the smaller man. "I would have you convicted of attempted murder and then disposed of tomorrow. Alexander could say your requiem mass, and then I would have him escorted, conscious or unconscious, to the border. Does that answer your question?"

"There's no need to talk like that," said Ulanov. "I am a Jesuit and a soldier of Christ. I do not disobey orders, however foolish they may be. I am confident that Nicholas and I can account for ourselves in Rome. Together, and with little help from Father Marais, we have accomplished what the Apostles might envy."

"When do you wish to go?" Sergey asked Marais.

"Tonight."

"How is that possible?" asked Nicholas. "You can't count on me to help you, and how are you going to manage getting out of here without me on a few hours' notice?"

"We can do it," said Sergey. "I have been up since noon, and I've already talked with a trusted man. Some of our people have contacts with truck drivers making deliveries to cities west of Moscow. They told these men that they would drive the trucks for nothing, that they just wanted to visit relatives en route and the drivers could take a vacation and get paid for it at the same time.

"We've picked two trucks that have to travel together to a point not too far away from where I have friends. They live in a collective, but there is an abandoned cabin in a woods nearby where they can shelter us—the others won't know—and then slip us across the border. Meanwhile two of my men will accompany us, and they can make the shipments. The doctor and I will make our way back ourselves. I know a safe route."

"You surprise me, fellow," said Nicholas. "I would never have figured you to get to Riga and back without getting caught, and now you're going to try it again."

"It was close last time, I admit." Sergey stared at Nicholas as if scrutinizing him for some meaning beyond his words.

"Very well, we are ready then," said Marais, cutting through what he considered a haze of incidentals.

"My man will bring the trucks around in front of the house here, and we'll smuggle you out in a basket," said Sergey.

"Gentlemen, gentlemen," the doctor burst out. "I have said nothing through all of this discussion. It was none of my business, but Father Marais's health is most certainly my affair. Ordinarily, no physician in the world would permit a patient to travel in his condition—do you realize how easily he could contract pneumonia? The weather out will be brutally cold, I—"

Sergey stopped him with a tug on the arm. "The men are bringing heavy clothing," he said. "Besides, we will have to sit three abreast in the cabin of the truck, so we'll keep each other warm."

Tsailov walked over to Marais's bed. "Do you realize, Father, that you will have to sit up in a pounding truck for many hours? If you can just wait a few weeks—"

"I relieve you of all responsibility," said Marais. "One week is too long to wait. Anyway, you will be along to take care of me."

The doctor threw up his hands at his patient's stubbornness. Sergey, satisfied that all the details had been agreed upon, opened the door. Two of his men were standing there. He asked them to bring in food for the group and then pack up the Ulanovs' belongings. "I don't want you going anywhere, Nicholas," he said. "We might not be able to find you when the time comes."

Marais turned over for a nap to prepare himself for the long journey. It was not long before Sergey announced in a loud voice that it was time to leave. Marais rose quickly from the bed, and two of the men came inside to help him into a large basket. They were reaching for the cover when the door opened and Sonya walked in, smiling. As she watched the faces of Sergey and the Ulanov brothers, she understood immediately that she had intruded on something very important. Her smile faded; Sergey covered his eyes with one hand. "Bad luck," he said, too low for Sonya to hear.

Her eyes finally moved to Marais, sitting in his basket, shielded by the bodies of two husky men. "Whatever are you doing, Josef? What is this silly thing?"

"It's all right, Sonya. I'm . . ."

Sergey moved quietly to her side. "It's a makeshift conveyance, just to get him outside without attracting attention. He needed help, so I brought along some friends of mine to give us a hand."

"Why must you take him anywhere? He's still not well, you know that."

"That's just it!" said Sergey. "Josef needs to have a rest, that's why we're taking him away—to a special sanitarium in the Ukraine."

"I don't believe you."

Dr. Tsailov stepped forward from a corner of the room. "It's on my advice, Sonya. Josef must leave Moscow."

"And why has such a decision been kept from me? Together you and I helped to keep him alive—and you can move him so far away without *telling* me? Why am I not trusted, why?"

"I had no choice," the doctor said. "I did not want a scene. And I was right. Just look at yourself, how you are reacting: A 'doctor' that is too close to her patient is . . . ruined."

Sonya half closed her eyes and leaned a little closer to Dr. Tsailov's face. Her lips parted in a trace of a smile. The doctor retreated from a gaze that seemed to hold each of his words up before him and then quietly let them drop like glass. Content with this effect, Sonya released Tsailov from his embarrassment and contemplated, one by one, the others behind him. Except for Nicholas, each man acted as though he were on inspection. Marais was ready to intervene when Sonya anticipated him.

"May I talk to Josef?" she asked, scanning the group. "Alone?"

Unable to look at each other for fear of betraying more of their secret, the men moved quickly—and with obvious relief, Marais thought—into the hallway. Sergey left the door ajar, but Sonya pushed it shut.

She lingered, her hand on the knob for a few seconds, and then walked back slowly to the chair farthest away from Marais. The Frenchman climbed out of the basket, feeling ridiculous, his breathing somewhat labored from the effort. He sat down on the edge of the bed.

The silence of the first few moments lengthened into a minute and then settled into a duel.

"I would assume that you really didn't want to see me again,"

Sonya said finally; a pained conclusion, not an opening. "You didn't have to run away like this, you know. That's what really hurts, that you thought . . ."

Marais was confused by the different complaints. "I care very much for you, Sonya," he began.

"It certainly seems so."

Marais winced. "That approach isn't going to help."

"A little honesty might."

Marais reflected for a moment on Dr. Tsailov's defeat and realized that Sonya could never be deceived by excuses so far from the truth. Still, he could not break his vow to Pacelli. He could hardly confess to being a Jesuit. He searched his mind for an answer that would come closest to the real one.

Sonya got up from the chair and walked to the window. Her figure, seen from the back, caused a dry ache in Marais's throat. Her lithe frame, the strong curves of flesh generating unfinished lines inside him, assailed his senses with an invitation that was actually painful.

Still, her body was only the entrance to the woman, and it was the woman with each of her differences of feeling that held out a promise. Oddly, Marais felt no strain with what he had come to think of as the "true" priesthood. His depression was due to what his Roman ordination entailed—celibacy.

"Of course, if you don't want to, Josef, you don't have to explain," Sonya said without turning. "It's not as if you made any promise, or even that we were . . . well, lovers. It's just that friends should share, and I thought we were friends."

"We are more than friends," said Marais.

"Well, then?" Sonya spun around with her hands out-stretched.

"I will explain, Sonya. But please be . . . quiet. I'm —"

"I know you're sick. But so am I, now."

"I knew this would happen. That's why I tried to leave Russia without seeing you."

"Leave Russia?" The waves of soft hair rose and fell as she leaned toward him.

"You wanted the truth."

"But Russia is your home!"

"My mother is Russian. I'm from Europe."

Sonya had begun to walk to him and then stopped. Marais saw the suspicion in her eyes, the look of a doctor discovering the first malignant symptom. She leaned on the back of the chair and waited.

"I'm a Christian, Sonya. A serious one. That's what I could not reveal. I came to Russia to spread the good word, and my life depends on secrecy. I'm going back for a while, but only for a while . . ."

Marais stopped, hoping desperately that she would find the new information so startling that all her energy would be used in coping with the facts.

Sonya sat down on the chair, her eyes never leaving his. "A foreigner? A believer?"

"In time I would have told you."

Her face reflected every nuance of her reaction, which apparently changed every two or three seconds. "It sounds hopeless," she said finally. "What a terrible risk to run for . . . for a belief like that! And you are such an intelligent man."

"I believe in Christ."

She shrugged. "I'm not for or against, I don't know anything about him. But who sent you?"

"A Christian organization."

"And if you were caught?"

"Death."

"Oh, Josef," Sonya got up and walked over to him, touched his face. "You are crazy," she said. Then she put her hand to her forehead. "I can't think. I never heard of anything like this."

"I never expected you to help me in this situation," Marais said.

"You never—what? What's wrong with you, Josef? Is this what your Christ tells you about women?"

"I've thought so long about what you would think if you knew," Marais protested.

Her anger dissolved as quickly as it had appeared. "Did you mean that?" she asked softly.

"Yes."

"I believe you," she said. "And do I look broken?"

[266]

"No."

She stared at him so that Marais felt caught in an involuntary bond. For an instant he could not believe that he would never see her again; for an instant, all else in the world besides her was unnatural—history, beliefs, friends, the outside.

Sonya spoke as though she had lived with him through the same dream. "I'm going with you," she said.

Marais felt jerked about, cruelly. He did not try to speak. He stared at the door, which had been pushed open a crack. Sonya had not noticed.

"It's no use protesting. I can take a chance too. I will only need a moment to pack. You need me."

"Sonya, no! I'm coming back, there's no reason— '

"Are you sure?"

Marais could not reply. She had touched the single wound he could not bear to face. Once he left Russia, he would not be back.

"I'm right, aren't I, Josef? You can't be sure of returning. That's why I have to go with you, don't you see? Now don't try to stop me, it's decided. Just give me ten minutes!"

She turned to find Sergey pushing the door all the way open. She stepped to one side; the big Russian stepped too. It was then that Marais knew, before it happened, what Sergey was going to do.

The blow to the chin was delivered with expert dispatch, and Marais could see that no mark or hurt had really been left. Ulanov and the others pushed into the room, and the doctor administered an injection to make sure that she slept for several hours. Marais, too distressed to allow himself the smallest protest, simply knelt over Sonya and reordered the strands of honey-colored hair that partially covered her face.

Looking up, he caught an odd look on Ulanov's face—he was puzzled, yes, but also wistful.

Marais stood up and climbed back into his basket.

As they were about to go down the staircase a familiar figure pushed the street door open. It was Mikhail; bundled in a heavy overcoat, his head shielded by a snow-covered astrakhan.

[267]

"Where is his Excellency?" The man sounded as if he had been running for blocks.

"For God's sake, just say Dmitri," one of the guards warned him.

The Jesuit moved quickly from the rear. "What has happened, Mikhail?"

"That's what I want to know. They say you're leaving."

"And where did you hear such a thing?"

Mikhail pointed at one of the guards. "His brother-in-law knows my wife . . ."

"Yes, I am going."

Mikhail dropped to one knee and grasped the Jesuit's hands. "And what about *us*? All of us? *How can you leave us?*"

Marais, waiting for Ulanov to answer, wondered if his colleague would cast the blame on him.

"I must return to Rome," the bishop was saying. "Those are the orders given Josef and myself, and explained in messages that will reach you all once we are safely out. But it shall only be *for a while.*"

"And what shall become of us while you're away?" Mikhail's voice echoed down the hallway.

"I have left you your new bishop, who—"

"My family and I put our trust in *you.*"

"I am no more than God's instrument, don't you understand? A spark igniting his work, and once that fire is lit it is sufficient to itself."

Mikhail did not seem to be listening. "Our hope is concrete when you are here," he said. "Everyone—my children, too—will say you have abandoned us."

"I am coming back!" said Ulanov.

"When?"

"In a few weeks. I am coming back, and bringing with me greater resources than ever for this mission of ours."

"We are so afraid you won't keep your word. Something will happen."

Ulanov's giant hands grasped the man's shoulders. "It is a holy promise," he said. "I vow to you that nothing imaginable in the world will keep me from seeing you again."

Mikhail stared at the Jesuit. The force of Ulanov's oath had gone so far beyond even this urgent occasion that the Russian seemed transformed by it. "I believe," he murmured. "I believe *you*."

"You will tell them all what I have said." Ulanov was relentless in his attack on distrust.

"Yes, and they too will believe for they know Mikhail and his word as I know my bishop and his."

The group remained for an instant longer in the grip of Ulanov's farewell to the faithful; then they began to move rapidly around the old man. Even Ulanov had left him brusquely, and when Marais looked back Mikhail was still standing at the top of the stairs, a forlorn figure for all his faith in the Russian bishop.

BOOK
IV

The Truth

14

Many miles passed on the road that evening before Marais felt his depression begin to lift. He had spent the first few miles of their journey inside the basket, in the rear of a truck. Once they were well clear of Moscow, he had entered the cabin of the truck to sit between the driver and Sergey while the doctor lay in the boxlike sleeping chamber above and behind the seats. In the truck following behind them, Alexander and Nicholas shared the cabin with Sergey's driver.

The snow along this major road was thickly packed, but the two trucks still moved slowly. The fear of skidding into a rut or even a ravine was enough to stifle any sense of adventure on the part of the drivers. The chill wind that blew through the window pane sent tremors across Marais's chest and down his arms. It threw gusts of snowflakes in front of the driver, causing him sometimes to drive by instinct alone, and the tension gripping the group hardly alllowed them the relaxation of sleep.

Sergey had insisted that they create an extra cushion of time for themselves by making the hazardous night journey on this road to Smolensk, one of the better highways they would be using. "It's not that the Russians are pushy about time, they aren't," Sergey had told them. "We have about three weeks to get this trip done, but you never know when we might need a few spare days for some reason."

Deliveries and pickups would be made in Smolensk, Vitebsk, Pskov, and Novgorod; after which the drivers would return to

Moscow. For the trio going to Rome, Pskov, lying near Estonia, would be the point of departure. Outside this city they would meet Sergey's friends for help across the border.

After the first night the group never again attempted to travel in darkness. Conditions were difficult enough in the daylight hours without compounding the risks. Despite this welcome change, Marais experienced day after day a progressive fatigue. The long hours in the bumping truck as the bitter Russian winter seeped through layers of clothing were taking their toll.

Had the weather, however cold, not been clearer and warmer than any of them expected at that time of year, Marais might not have made it. His fits of shivering and the extreme pain the truck's jerky motions caused him were taking their toll. His fever had climbed dangerously, and although the doctor did everything he could to help, the crowded truck gave him little space to work in.

They arrived at the small cabin in the woods to find that the place had been repaired and a fire lit by Sergey's friends who lived in the collective nearby. Dr. Tsailov could not promise the others that Marais would pull through. He had brought all his medical supplies, but there was a limit, he pointed out, to their usefulness once a patient arrived at this critical juncture. They would simply have to pray that Marais's body had enough residual strength to fight what he now diagnosed as pneumonia.

At the same time, one of the drivers fell sick from a kidney attack. Apparently the strain of the long trip had exacerbated an old problem. The doctor prescribed a rest of ten days before driving again, leaving Sergey with the problem of how to handle the remainder of their schedule, the delivery to Novgorod and the return.

Nicholas volunteered to fill the sick driver's place. Sergey, not wanting to leave the two Ulanovs alone in the cabin with the semiconscious Marais, approved the request but added that he himself would accompany Nicholas and split the strenuous chore with him. Alexander was predictably angry at being relegated to the company of the doctor and to the task of "protecting" Marais and the Russian driver.

The plan called for the two trucks to deliver and pick up

[274]

shipments at Novgorod before returning to Pskov. They would have a longer trip home, but at least their duties would be fulfilled so that the drivers back in Moscow would not have to confess the switch that had taken place.

The journey, round trip, was estimated at three hundred miles. Allowing for minor delays, the trio calculated that they should be back at the cabin within a week's time. Alexander bid farewell to Nicholas and Sergey, and the trucks departed.

When Marais finally felt able to sit up and talk a bit, eight days had passed. And so the first discussions he heard which he could follow with any clarity were the anxious dialogues between Ulanov, the doctor, and the Russian driver over the delay in their comrades' return. Every possible theory, no matter how wild, was put forth. Cheery shows of confidence in the abilities of Sergey and Nicholas alternated with drawn-out periods during which no one spoke for fear of invoking a dread fate just by mentioning it.

By the morning of the tenth day, Ulanov seemed desperate. Caged by his inaction, he paced the floor of the cabin's two rooms ceaselessly.

The doctor himself consumed so much energy in the care of his patients that he usually rocked in a chair content to rest and, now and then, pray for the overdue members of the party. His great solace was Marais's recuperation. "Look at him, he's coming back, he must have the constitution of an elephant," he would say to Ulanov.

On the afternoon of that tenth day a truck rolled up before the cabin. Ulanov and the doctor ran out into the snow and brought inside the man who had driven his vehicle—alone. There was no sign of Nicholas and Sergey. Were they coming? A way behind him? The man did not know.

"Well, then, what *happened?*" Ulanov was pulling at the front of the fellow's coat. The man explained that there had been a long delay at one of the plants in getting their shipment aboard, that Sergey and Nicholas's truck had suffered a small breakdown which took two days for repairs. Finally, on their way back from Novgorod, they had driven up a steep incline so circuitous that the driver, who happened to be in the lead truck, lost track in his mirror of Sergey and Nicholas behind him. When he arrived at the top of the incline he drove on for some time, then noticed that they were not following him and waited. They did not show up, so he turned around and came back to find them.

He was terrified that they might have suffered an accident and gone over the side of the hill. But there were no tire marks on the slope other than his own, which meant that they had not even attempted to climb the road. At the bottom, he saw from the markings that the truck had turned around and gone in the opposite direction. The driver was stunned. He followed the tracks for some ten miles, but never came within sight of them. He waited awhile longer and then decided to return by himself. That was it. That was the story.

Ulanov spent the next half-hour hearing and rehearing the driver's report until the man could not repeat it once more. It was not that there was a question in anyone's mind but that the events had happened exactly as told. The peasant driver was the very soul of honesty, without the wit or imagination to distort any detail no matter how slight. He had seen what he had seen, and only that much.

"Christ Jesus in heaven, tell me. What is this damned madness? They're gone! Where? What for? Swallowed up by the earth? In hell's name . . . somebody speak."

No one could.

Finally he dressed in outdoor clothing, took a week's rations from their supplies, and announced that he was going to borrow the truck and hunt for their missing comrades.

Marais and the doctor appealed to Ulanov's common sense. "Wait a few days," said Tsailov. "Wait and then see if Father Marais is well enough to be moved by sled the twenty-five miles to the Estonian border. Our first priority is to rescue ourselves, is it not? Perhaps, in the meantime, the other two will appear." Ulanov listened without comment, then moved to the door. Soon the truck was out of sight.

For the next five days the four men in the cabin lingered in a depressing limbo of expectation. Marais spent most of this enforced leisure sleeping while the others played cards hour after hour. The doctor used up a good deal of his medicine giving the two drivers sleep-inducing needles. By now the group had surrendered all hopes for the arrival of Sergey and Nicholas. Their discussion and evening prayers centered about the return of Alexander.

Marais himself still protested that it was possible Ulanov had found Sergey and Nicholas. His private fantasy went considerably further. He envisioned absurd scenes in which the trio were drinking together and laughing, the mystery surrounding their appearance cleared up by a simple, enormously funny detail that had never occurred to their friends back in the cabin. Even now, in Marais's imagination, Alexander, Sergey, and Nicholas were making their way back.

Marais held on to his daydream for days. Whenever it was threatened by the others' fears or by his own premonitions of disaster, he would invoke the fantasy with renewed faith.

Finally the doctor came to Marais with disturbing news. The peasants had informed him that blizzard weather would soon be upon them, perhaps in less than two days. Once the storms and extreme cold came, they might last as long as four weeks. Unless Marais wished to wait out this period, he would have to try to cross the border within the next thirty-six hours. Tsailov was of the opinion that even with the help of the heavy clothing the peasants had provided Marais and the unnatural warmth they were presently enjoying, the trip at this very moment would be arduous and risky. Later, it would be impossible. The kind of weather the Russian farmers were predicting would kill the Frenchman within hours, and the burden of transporting him fifteen miles through mounting snow drifts would be beyond human endurance.

"In any case," said Tsailov, "I'm afraid I cannot accompany you. The trip to Estonia could be hazardous, and anyway there is little I can do for you in those conditions. I don't know just how the two drivers and I will get back to Moscow, but we'll manage it somehow. You must concentrate on conserving what resources you have for the journey ahead."

Despite the old man's kindness in not pressing his problems upon him, Marais felt responsible for his and the two drivers predicament. Two trucks were missing. The drivers whose place had been taken back in Moscow would surely face reprisals. And, then, this threatening blizzard could strand the three in the cabin. The peasants could not hope to keep their activities secret or supply them with food indefinitely. What had already been given them by the farmers was remarkable, but to strain it to further limits . . .

Marais asked the doctor to cut the lining inside his fur coat. "There are hundreds of rubles there—no, take them out, I won't be needing Russian currency. The least I can do is to provide our friends a few months' sustenance, or some leverage from which to negotiate a return."

Marais gave half the money to the two drivers and half to the doctor. The gratitude of the group—despite the fact that Marais had hardly touched their fearful problems of transportation and accountability for the trucks—made him all the more ashamed of his inability to help those who had served him. His dream of the meeting of Alexander, Sergey, and Nicholas could no longer be summoned as the hours for definite action drew near. For a long time Marais lay with his face turned to the wall in mounting depression. And yet he would certainly leave. For all his misery, he would get to Rome, and quickly.

The notion of departing without Ulanov proved less hard to accept than Marais had anticipated, perhaps because he felt sure that Ulanov was alive and would return. He had no such confidence in Sergey and Nicholas.

Despite a sleep troubled by bodily discomfort and unresolved spiritual torment, Marais heard nothing during that night. He almost screamed on awakening to find Ulanov asleep on a rug near the fire. He opened and closed his eyes, then peered again at the huge slumbering figure. The rest of the group were still asleep, and the evidence of glasses around the fire indicated that Marais was the only one who had not been roused by the bishop's return.

Ulanov woke within the hour, walked over to Marais, and said simply, "I couldn't find them. Nobody has seen them, it's as if they had disappeared off the face of the earth . . . And how are you?"

"I am much better."

"Do you still want to leave?"

"Yes."

"Then the time is now, the doctor says. I heard the blizzard was coming, which is why I returned . . . The truck is for them." He waved toward the drivers.

"I thank you for that. I know how you must feel."

"I gave you my word. And now would you give me permission to go back to Moscow with them?"

"I can't, Alexander."

"Very well." Fatigue and depression appeared to override Ulanov's desire to argue. "Then let's get this foolish trip started and over, so that I may return to Russia from Rome at the earliest possible moment. And this time by myself."

"That's up to them—and you," Marais said without rancor. "Tell me, did you find *no* clue to the whereabouts of Sergey and Nicholas?"

Ulanov shook his head. "I traced the truck into Novgorod, but there the markings got confused. I spent days looking for the truck, and asking at places where they might have stayed. I even went beyond the city to find out if anybody had seen such a truck on the road . . . How could they have vanished like that in a small city? And *why?* I . . . I have given up trying to find an answer . . ." Seeing his face, Marais could not remember having felt so sorry for his partner.

"The mission," said Ulanov, "has been such a success, and here in the last few miles before our vindication, this has to happen. We operated so well together and now Nicholas is gone and your friend Sergey as if, just before the feast, they were not meant to go in for the palm."

"You don't think they could have had an argument in the truck?"

"No, if they had a disagreement, even a fight, they would have brawled in the snow. One of them would have knocked the other out, and that would have been the end of it. The one who was left would have driven the truck back. Besides, I made Nicholas swear that under no circumstances would he get involved in anything physical with Sergey. In any case, the truck never stopped that long."

[279]

The next half hour, spent gathering provisions, was a welcome distraction. The three men from the collective had no sooner arrived than they began to be anxious about time, so the partings were brief. Marais repeatedly embraced the doctor who had saved his life through the months and risked his own life for him. "The only consolation," he told the old man, "is that your trip back to Moscow will be made without the burden of me!" Marais blessed Dr. Tsailov and promised to remember him forever in his masses.

The plan called for two of the commune farmers to pull Marais's sled for an hour or so, alternating with another team in hopes of making sufficiently good time to avoid the storm. They would take a narrow back road, then cut through a small forest and over some hills for the last few miles of the journey into Estonia.

After two hours on the road, Marais stopped noticing anything. He dozed or daydreamed through the vicissitudes of the trip. The day had proven to be one of the mildest in recent weeks, and yet the cold and the wind taxed his energies to their limit.

Ulanov and the three peasants worked heroically to guide Marais's sled so as to prevent his suffering any sudden jolts, but the deep tracks they made with each step in the snow left him sweating and grunting. Marais had never anticipated that this forced march would be so difficult. It was he who had commanded it over Ulanov's wishes, and now it was Ulanov who was saving him—without the American, quite obviously, there would have been little hope of making the frontier. Ulanov suffered the punishing labor cheerfully and even encouraged the others to sing or hum as they trudged along. Marais told Ulanov that he would not forget his heroism when they got to Rome; Ulanov, typically, hardly noticed the praise or promises.

Marais could never manage to recall how they were able to traverse so many painful miles in that black night and cross the Russian border. In an hour they found a parish church and rectory in the Estonian countryside. The startled pastor and curate could hardly bring themselves to believe that their night visitors were who they were. Even when the pastor permitted the weary band to enter the parlor, his motive seemed more to be

Christian charity than any real belief in their identity. Eventually Ulanov rode on horseback with the curate to a house where the one phone in the village was located.

They finally managed to get their call put through to the rectory in Riga. The identification of Ulanov and Marais having been assured both by the man who answered and even by the auxiliary bishop of Riga, the curate prepared to apologize to Ulanov for his lack of faith. But before the auxiliary bishop left the phone, Ulanov asked him the name of the man to whom he had first spoken. "Despite the terrible connection," he said, "I think I know that voice."

The name of the priest, the auxiliary bishop informed him, was Father Saul Nimsky, S.J. "Well, put him back on the wire," said Ulanov. "He's a friend of mine, and he never identified himself."

"I'm sorry, I can't do that," said the auxiliary bishop. "Good night, Excellency." He hung up the receiver.

The next afternoon Ulanov told Marais about the odd incident. The Frenchman, who had slept the eighteen hours following the escape, could only stare at his partner. In any case, Marais was for the moment cherishing the simplest, most miraculous fact of all—that they were actually safe, that Ulanov, at least, was alive. Rather than deal with Father Saul Nimsky's incomprehensible behavior, he drank his hot broth, ate some bread, and returned to sleeping on and off until the following morning.

The voice of Nimsky had instructed Ulanov that he was not to travel until Marais was fit. Arrangements would be made for their passage to Tartu in Estonia, from which they might ride by train to Riga. Five days passed before Marais felt he had enough strength to face again the bleak rigors of the winter. A closed in sleigh pulled by four horses was placed at their disposal, and, eventually, a car.

The curate stayed with them, helping Ulanov with his patient as far as Tartu, where they stayed overnight so as not to strain Marais. The next day, with additional help, they took the train for Riga. Arriving in the late afternoon, they found no one waiting for them on the platform. Bishop Ulanov required the assistance of a porter to help Marais to a waiting room, where the two priests sat for a quarter of an hour before the auxiliary bishop's chauffeur arrived to escort them to the rectory.

They had hardly moved into the hallway when they met Nimsky. He looked at them for a moment, then began to push by them.

"Do you believe this?" Marais shouted at Ulanov.

"His mind is gone," said Ulanov.

"Oh, no." Marais's voice rose in fury. "He recognizes us."

Finally Ulanov grabbed him by the arm. "It's us, Saul! What has happened to you? Why weren't you at the station to greet us? Say something, for Christ's sake!"

"I cannot."

"You . . . can't?"

Marais, who did not have the strength to raise his voice, beckoned to Nimsky. "Dear Saul, what is the meaning of this? We have been through the fires of hell. We are alive, escaped. Your friends . . . made it . . . a triumph. We have succeeded."

"I am to escort you to Rome, brothers in Christ. Now for some supper." Saul Nimsky walked away, and a servant helped Ulanov to bring Marais into the dining room.

The meal they ate that evening was consumed in the strictest silence. As for the courtesies always extended a visiting bishop, that of a *Deo gratias* meal—conversation, a toast—none occurred. Not only was the politeness of a small feast usually given a guest prelate not granted; the food and style of service was that of a penance meal.

Ulanov and Marais, famished, continued to eat after the others left. "What can you make of this?" Marais asked finally. His senses had been assaulted for so long by unexpected events that he now looked to his partner for some rational orientation in this upside-down world. "I was under the impression that we had achieved the impossible."

"So was I," said Ulanov.

"But they are going out of their way to—insult us! Instead of sending a car to Tartu, instead of welcoming us at the station, we have this sort of thing. Instead of a thousand greetings from the Vatican, we get silence—"

"I happen to have noticed, Paul," said Ulanov, turning a salt shaker around and around in his palm. "It's probably all due to your letter."

"No, no ... That's impossible. You're taking advantage." Marais felt that he could not bear estrangement from his friend at this point.

"You should never have sent that letter," persisted Ulanov. "Somehow these fools have misinterpreted—"

"But you understood that Cardinal Pacelli was still your friend," said Marais. "Sergey said that you stood very well in his favor. And remember, Alex, it is Pacelli who commands the Secretariat of State, not Francisi. It is Pacelli who must have sent Nimsky, and given him instructions."

"Yes, I thought that the letter contained an implication from Pacelli that he was friendly—otherwise he would have signed it himself. But then these people's actions, the way we have been treated ... that must be Francisi's doing." Ulanov hit the table with the salt shaker as though his conclusion was a fact.

"No, it's not Francisi's style. Besides, he doesn't have this kind of power. Please be reasonable, Alexander."

"I don't know what else to think! Three weeks ago we were still beloved and now ... well, I watched him operate, that archbishop friend of yours, and he could easily have carried out these arrangements in his devious way. Pacelli may not know that any of this is going on. The chances are that he became overworked with affairs in Europe and delegated to Francisi the details of our return. He's our liaison in Rome, so isn't that likely? Then there's the fact that Nimsky has been here for almost four weeks—since the time you received the letter. Now what, I ask you, has changed since then?"

"Well, we lost Nicholas and Sergey."

"I didn't ask you that. Losing Nicholas is my own private Calvary, but it isn't their business. In fact, they *don't even know* about the disappearance of my brother and Sergey, do they? The Vatican gets its information through the train conductor, and neither he nor anybody in Moscow knew about the disappearance. So nothing has changed so far as the Vatican is concerned. Nimsky came here with this attitude. He was strange on the

[283]

phone the night we escaped from Russia, and that was days before the doctor and those drivers could have returned to Moscow."

"But Francisi spoke well enough of me to Sergey," Marais pointed out. "Why would he want either of us treated this way? And Nimsky—he has always been so cheerful and our friend for so long. He isn't easily brainwashed by anyone."

"Ah, but you were tricked," said Ulanov. "Francisi was furious with you about Nicholas and many other things, and did not let on. He wanted us both back, you see. He hates this mission, I swear he does, and your letter criticizing me was his opening and he took advantage of it. He didn't appear to get angry with you, he encouraged you—"

"There is something wrong with your explanation, Alexander. I have told you over and over that no offense mentioned to Francisi could merit this kind of punishment, that he personally would never inflict—"

"He has."

"No, you are blaming the loss of your brother on our journey, and it is Francisi and I who are responsible for the journey."

"Enough!" shouted Ulanov.

"Very well, very well. Why don't you telephone your Pacelli?"

Ulanov was taken aback for the moment.

"Yes!" said Marais. "There is no reason on earth why you can't call Rome and complain to Pacelli about this ridiculous situation. We shall know soon enough if Francisi or Nimsky or even I am to blame."

Ulanov mulled the notion over, nervously tapping the salt shaker with a spoon. Finally he rang a bell, and, with the assistance of the waiter, they made their way from the dining room down the hallway to the auxiliary bishop's room. There Ulanov had to insist on his rights with the greatest severity before the superior of the house, unable to locate Nimsky in his room, would allow him the use of the telephone.

The auxiliary bishop seemed in fact to be both frightened and repelled by Ulanov's presence, and this reaction of the small pious man frightened Marais. It seemed to him that he and

Ulanov were surrounded by some mystery, some strange defilement that others witnessed while it remained invisible to themselves.

It took some time for the call to the Vatican, but finally the Secretary of State himself was on the wire. "Your Eminence ... your Eminence, this is your servant Bishop Ulanov. We are alive!" Ulanov's voice shook with a nervousness that he barely managed to contain in front of Marais, as he narrated in an unstoppable flow the beginning of the Christian tide in the Slavic heartland inaugurated by their mission.

"We have baptized, we have confirmed, we have ordained, we have consecrated ..." And, finally, he ended his peroration to the Secretary of State with a moving tribute: "We owe all this accomplishment, your Eminence, to your foresight and your planning, your encouragement and your prayers, without which we could not have been the apostolic instruments of providence. For the mission has been a triumph." Here, for the first time, he paused.

And as he listened, Marais watched shock displace nervousness. Slowly Ulanov put the receiver back in its place, slowly turned to Marais. "I never did tell him about our treatment here—"

"But what did Pacelli *say?*"

"He said to come back to Rome at once, and to obey Father Nimsky without question."

"That was all?"

"All."

"Did he congratulate us?"

"No."

"Did he have *any* comment on the mission?"

"No."

"Was he upset? Angry?"

"No emotion at all."

"That's impossible! They can't do this—"

"I told you, Francisi poisoned his mind! It is the only explanation."

"You're mad. Francisi is the last person whom Pacelli would allow to influence him. He—" Marais stopped, knowing the

[285]

objection to be useless. The door of the room had begun to move slowly, widening from a crack to a full opening as the little auxiliary bishop entered.

"Are you finished? Yes? I will show you to your rooms." The man's manner made it clear that he would not indulge in conversation with them. He addressed himself with a show of energy to the task of guiding the sick man toward his cubicle, passing the darkened chapel on the way. As Marais turned his head to pay his respects to the presence of Christ in the tabernacle, he was startled by a figure whose vague outline seemed familiar even in the shadows.

"Is that Father Nimsky?" Marais pulled the group to a sudden halt.

"Yes, it is," answered the auxiliary bishop.

"In all the years I've known him," Marais said to no one in particular, "I never saw Saul pray in a chapel except during the absolutely required times. It wasn't his style."

The prelate replied almost involuntarily and without looking at the Frenchman. "He never did until a week or so ago. He used to go out all the time to see the sights of Riga. But now he spends all day and half the night before the tabernacle. He never leaves except to eat or sleep."

"Oh my God! Why? What has happened?"

"Please come," whispered the auxiliary bishop, pulling Marais forward.

Once in his bed, Marais took the last of the pills Dr. Tsailov had left him. The center of his being felt as though it were collapsing from the weight of unanswered questions. "Is Pacelli trying to disown us?" battled with "Wait and see what they mean." And yet, Nimsky's embrace of extreme prayer had frightened him most of all. Faced with hopeless conflicts everywhere, Marais could sense himself retreating to the lowest level of his wounded body, into fatigue, into the heaviness of his impairment. The drugs completed his withdrawal and descent.

15

The next morning, Nimsky and Ulanov and Marais were driven to the terminal and escorted aboard the train, where two compartments had been reserved for them. The missionary partners shared one of the rooms; Nimsky had his own. Marais, who had gone through the routine of being transported with the barest consciousness of these events, was asleep before the train pulled out of the station. From time to time on the way to Warsaw he would awaken to find Ulanov reading from a pile of magazines and newspapers he had procured somewhere.

The bishop's attention seemed so riveted on this material that he might have been looking for a clue to their destiny in recent news reports. The conversations they held were inconsequential. Marais could not rise to the strain of even beginning to worry at the tangle of awful events. As for Ulanov, he seemed to have withdrawn into his own world—where, no doubt, he was busily manipulating elements and forces.

From Warsaw to Vienna, no change occurred in this routine. And on the last leg of their trip, from Vienna to Rome, Marais sank even deeper into the night of slumber. On those occasions when he did lie on the coach seat, staring through the window at the blurred landscape, only pleasant images of long-ago events filtered through his awareness.

As the train drew close to Rome, however, even Marais was caught up in the emotion that gripped the other two. On one occasion when he left his compartment, he met Nimsky in the narrow corridor. He was crying; tears rolled from his eyes, and he grabbed Marais and hugged him in bitterness and desperation. "Why didn't I listen to you after the night at the Slaves' House these months ago? You poor man, you probably don't even remember what you told me then—oh, God! Oh, God, Paul!" He wept, terribly, on Marais's shoulder and then was gone.

On the second occasion Ulanov stood up and made a pronouncement. "I know what happened—yes, I have it! Nicholas and Sergey made up, don't you see? Nicholas didn't want to come back, and Sergey finally accepted him but didn't want to tell you that he had decided to take Nicholas with him to Moscow. Now it all makes sense. Nicholas and Sergey, somehow they became friends on that long trip together!"

Ulanov sat back down, half smiling at the vision of his brother and the other Russian bishop working hand in hand in that faraway Muscovite vineyard from which he himself had been so rudely removed. Marais turned over on his coach bed with a tremor at the reemergence of the woeful subject. Ulanov's wild conjecture had left him more pained than ever.

The end of their journey was as dismal as the beginning. At the train station in Rome, no one was waiting for them. Father Nimsky allowed twenty minutes in order to appease Marais and Ulanov, and then called a cab.

Before the car entered the actual precincts of the papal domain, Ulanov insisted that they get out. For some reason he wanted to walk into Vatican City. Accompanied by Nimsky, Marais and Ulanov walked slowly onto the grounds of the sovereign they had served so far away and at such cost. Marais was able to manage by himself, though his steps were slow. Looking up at St. Peter's, he felt as if he were viewing it from the distance of a lifetime.

They entered the palace and eventually found themselves seated in the office of the Secretary of State. On the way they had seen familiar faces, but none of these colleagues returned the missionaries' glances of recognition. An old saying about the Vatican came into Marais's mind, "They may not know *why* you are in disgrace, but they know *that* you are."

[288]

Marais kept saying to himself, "You are a good man. You have made mistakes but with pure intentions. This whole misunderstanding will be cleared up soon. Very soon! Think nothing else."

Saul Nimsky asked to pray with them in the office of the absent Secretary, and, for half an hour, led them in a meditation on the crucifixion. Then he grasped Marais about the shoulders, holding him tightly for a long time in an almost hysterical farewell. He never touched Ulanov, nor did he glance at him as he left.

Marais lay on a sofa; Ulanov paced about for a couple of hours. Neither of them spoke, and then the door quietly opened and Cardinal Pacelli stood before them. He stood gazing at them, motionless: the incarnation of a judge beyond love or hate.

Finally, just as Marais felt that he must break the spell, the cardinal put a commanding finger to his lips. Even as he enjoined silence upon them, he snapped his fingers. A few moments later, a lay brother entered, wheeling a small table cart with two trays. The cardinal left them without uttering a word; it was the lay brother who informed them gently that his Eminence would return sometime after they had finished their supper to escort them to an audience with his Holiness.

Their shock at this extraordinary message had not worn off when Pacelli returned in another hour. Neither of them had taken more than a morsel or two of the food or even finished the small pot of tea. They had barely spoken to each other. Marais had suspected all along that they and their case would be rapidly brought to the highest courts, but this particular treatment beggared even that preparation. He welcomed the mercy of speed even as he grew increasingly terrified at the thought of what it might mean. The Secretary's gesture to follow him was at least a distraction, preserving for the following few moments a neutral corridor in Marais's brain.

The cardinal finally brought them to the doors of the papal apartment, threw them open, and then proceeded, much more hesitantly, to the chapel. There the two entered alone. As they stared through the gloom, they found the Pope at a table before the altar. The flickering candlelight illumined his Holiness and

[289]

the figures about him with an uncertain glow. Marais and Ulanov walked forward until they stood half in shadow before the tiny table and the Pontiff.

The robed priest and prelates standing a step above them all wore plain black habits. They never moved nor took their eyes from the two Jesuits. Slowly each pronounced his name: "Present, Cardinal Bataille" . . . "Present, Archbishop Francisi" . . . "Present, Father General Ledochowsky" . . . "Present, Father Dillon," and from behind them, "Present, Cardinal Pacelli." And then, finally, "I am present, Pope Pius the Eleventh."

In the silence that followed, Marais no longer saw himself as a figure in this world, for the tribunal before which he and Ulanov stood expelled all notions of censure or debate. This conclave was met on the question of existence.

"We are together at the same hour at which Alexander Ulanov was consecrated bishop six months ago." The Pope's words were spoken in a low and somber cadence. "Would that I had rent my garments and his at that hour . . . and could surrender this throne to the most meager of souls in Catholic Christendom, if I might have been allowed to die then, and, so doing, have aborted that monstrous deed."

The words of the Vicar of Christ himself, the absolute and infallible ruler of the church, fell upon them as though the sky had broken. In this terrible darkness, Jesus had spoken to Judas.

Marais began to shudder. Ulanov's own tremor carried him backward, and he grasped the Pope's table.

"What have I done?" Ulanov cried out; the most agonized voice Marais had ever heard.

"Henceforth," continued Pope Pius, his bearing unchanged by the disturbance before the altar, "thou, Alexander Ulanov, art stripped of each and every function, honor, and permission of the office of bishop *and of priest*. Thou shalt not ordain, confirm, offer mass, or hear a confession. Thou shalt not set foot inside a Roman Catholic church anywhere in this world without the personal and extraordinary permission of the reigning Pontiff."

"Why?" Ulanov breathed the question as though from a deathbed. "Before Jesus, what . . . have . . . I . . . done?"

"In a few hours' time, Alexander Ulanov, you shall be transported to the property of the Jesuit order at Toulouse in France. There, in a house that you alone shall inhabit, you will spend the remainder of your days on this earth. You shall speak to no man nor be spoken to by any, excepting the one person designated by your father general as your confessor, and he shall visit you but once a week. This is the judgment of Pius the Eleventh delivered here in the year of our Lord, 1935, before these witnesses, and who likewise commands his successors in the Chair of Peter to honor this decree so long as Alexander Ulanov does live."

Marais watched, numb, as his companion fell to the floor. No one moved to aid him; no one spoke. The sentence of everlasting banishment hung in the dumb silence of the chapel and froze each listener under its icy weight.

Ulanov grasped at the table to pull himself up. "I beseech my Ho-li-ness . . . your Holiness . . . in the name of our Lord to tell me . . ."

The Pope answered his request as if, as it were, he had not noticed it. "Everyone that you have seen in Russia, everyone that you have spoken to, and everyone that they in their turn have spoken to or whose Catholic feelings they had general knowledge of, everyone who has ever manifested a religious sympathy in Russia in relationship, however indirect, to this mission . . . every one of them—" the Pope rose suddenly from his chair and shouted in the chapel—"is dead, or in Siberia, or in Lubyanka prison, or being tortured, or hunted, at this very moment! The whole of Russia is a catacomb for those whom you have turned over to the hunting dogs of Moscow. Men, women, children are dying every moment of this day and this week, their bodies and minds in unmerciful torment until every name and every house that ever harbored the presence of Christ is purged by blood and sacrifice. The Son of Satan could have had no better work for his father-master than yourself!" The Pope seemed to shout for hearing beyond the boundaries of his chapel.

And then, in the quietest voice that could possibly be heard: "What more despicable fate can be imagined than to have betrayed all those who out of love for you bore witness to Christ?"

Ulanov pressed his thumb and forefinger against his eyes in the moment before darkness descended upon Marais, leaving him blind as to place and time.

"You, our representative, have destroyed the church in Russia. It shall not rise again for many, many years, if ever, and then only through an act of God. We are vanquished now. I die with your deed on my soul. I, too, must answer to God."

Marais heard Ulanov's voice ring out frantically in the chapel. "No, never! I deny it all. They have poisoned you against me, Pacelli, Francisi, lies and lies. I shall avenge these untruths. No one is dead! No one is lost, we have succeeded, I am an apostle! Nothing is lost. No proof . . . where? Where? *How?* Answer me that, any of you. Answer!"

When Ulanov's shouts had subsided, the Pope, who again seemed not to have heard the outcries of his most desperate subject, spoke once more: "The individual known as Nicholas Ulanov, for whom you broke your sacred vow of secrecy, is a communist agent." These last words having been spoken quietly, even calmly, the Pope slowly made his way around the table and through his little chapel.

Marais's blindness had passed; clarity now pierced his spirit like a dagger. The shadow behind every deed of the past months, the specter troubling every one of Marais's unwilling acts and judgments, had been revealed in the Pontiff's final sentence.

After the Pope's departure, Ulanov stood looking from figure to figure for a sign that must follow those words.

Cardinal Pacelli walked forward, bearing in his hands a sheaf of papers. He laid them on the table; three times tried to speak and each time could not force a syllable from his throat. Finally he gestured toward one of the figures on the altar.

The short, black-robed figure in the Jesuit habit came forward.

"I am Father Dillon of the Society of Jesus. I came from America this week, summoned by others here. I have been asked to show you certain pictures from Russia which were

[292]

delivered to the Vatican within the last two weeks, and then to give you my own information on the subject."

The priest with the Irish face had spoken in a homely voice devoid of drama or ill will. He walked over to Marais and Ulanov and held up to them rough drawings of Nicholas Ulanov standing in different poses at different locations in Moscow, pointing out individuals whom the police were seizing from the crowd. In others he was sitting in cafes with people beside whom notations of their position in the Soviet secret police system were scribbled.

The characteristic facial expressions and physical mannerisms were unmistakable. Finally, saved by some cruelty of arrangement for the last view, came the photographs. They seemed to have been taken from second-story windows and from rooftops. Nicholas, arms akimbo, standing in front of a crowd of terrified people, in which here and there Marais saw a familiar face.

Marais suddenly leaned closer to one of the photographs. "Sonya," he whispered.

Ulanov edged in closer. "It cannot be she. She was not involved, she—"

"It is my Sonya!" this time Marais shouted.

As Ulanov began to turn away from the photograph, Marais pulled him back. "They have put her with Mikhail and his children! *What have we done,* Alexander?"

Ulanov stared at the altar.

The small priest returned to the table. "What I have to say will be brief," he began. "These pictures and drawings were sent to Rome through the railroad conductor. It appears that the brother of our bishop neglected to arrest this man immediately. The Vatican presumes that there was a standing order in Moscow for months not to arrest this conductor lest we grow suspicious. In his eagerness to round up all our people, Nicholas Ulanov apparently failed to rescind this order, and our contact remained free. We have, fortunately, managed to save him. He has brought us evidence and many written notes from those who had not yet been arrested but had witnessed the persecution by Nicholas Ulanov. A number of these came through Bishop Sergey's wife, who, before her arrest, delivered them to the railway.

"One is of particular interest. It was passed to her by a friendly nurse. She records that Bishop Sergey died in a Moscow hospital after the most vigorous attempts to save his life on the part of the Soviet authorities. They were too late, for he had been beaten far too badly by Nicholas Ulanov to be able to survive the operation. The authorities, in the nurse's hearing, berated this Ulanov for his disservice to the state, for Sergey's information died with him.

"There is one further note. In a restaurant where one of our Catholics works as a waiter, he heard an intoxicated Nicholas Ulanov tell a party of officials how faithfully he had kept his vow to his brother and the Frenchman to 'spare their lives.' He also admitted being frightened by a badly bungled poisoning of Father Paul Marais."

Father Dillon sat down at the table and meditated for a moment, his hand cupping his chin. "That is all that I have been authorized to tell you."

"Yes, we must end here," the voice of Father General Ledochowski commanded his subordinate.

Father Dillon did not turn around. "There are only two now present who have the right to speak in this chapel, Archbishop Francisi and myself. We threw nets around Father Ulanov, and others broke them."

No one answered him.

"Alexander, my poor Alexander, you have reaped a terrible judgment. The world would say an inhuman one. But you and I know that you would drown yourself in the Tiber tonight if there were no hope of redeeming these deaths."

Ulanov was crying behind the hands that covered his face.

"You broke your oath of silence, your vow of obedience. You thought you knew better than we."

"He was sworn to tell no one!" said the father general. "We chose him for his independence of character, and all along he was bound to this wretched creature!"

"No, no," Ulanov was still crying; the quietest possible sobs that, nonetheless, shook his giant frame from head to foot.

"This is too cruel," whispered Francisi from the altar.

[294]

"Before he goes, he should hear what lies behind this tragedy," said Bataille. "That is kindness, not cruelty."

Dillon ignored the conversation behind him. "You have lived your whole life in a dream, Alexander, though few dreams are meant for this world. You were so far removed from human nature that you were driven all the harder to impose your views. Fellow Jesuits would have seen through this act, so you trusted only a fawning child, your brother, who was supposed to be your slave. That Nicholas Ulanov would work to master you was beyond your comprehension."

"Why . . . *why* did he hate me so?"

Father Dillon waited until Ulanov lifted his head. "You supported him. He thought of you as one he could depend on forever in a harsh world, and you abandoned him for an alien priesthood. Here"—Father Dillon held up a sheaf of papers—"are the statements of witnesses I have collected these past two months in America, in Pittsburgh. They testify that through the years, whenever he was drunk, Nicholas Ulanov ranted against a single human being—you! In his hatred, he became more radical than you. You introduced him to socialism, but he became a communist. Where you embraced the 'God-Illusion,' he worked to destroy it. Lost love became your brother's obsession."

Archbishop Francisi moved to stand beside Dillon. "We know now that Nicholas made a bargain for your lives," he said. "The communists promised to spare the two of you, then, when you had given them all the information possible, Nicholas was to disappear. He wanted you to live with the knowledge of what he had done to you. He saw that as a more exquisite punishment than to have you tortured to death in Lubyanka prison. He kept his word to 'guard your lives.'

"Bishop Ulanov, you may yet achieve redemption for mankind in your life of penance. What none of us will ever comprehend is why God permitted so many to die as a result of your madness." Father Dillon stood up. "Now it is finished. Let us go."

The figures about the altar broke their ranks and began to walk slowly toward the door. Still Marais and Ulanov did not move.

[295]

Father Dillon stood in front of Ulanov, looking down at the Russian bishop as though he were his helpless child. "Come, Alexander, stand up and come with me. It is I who will escort you to Toulouse. It is best for you to begin your purgatory as soon as possible. You have very little time, considering all you must do."

Father Dillon and Bishop Ulanov began to walk together behind the others.

"And what of me?" called Marais after them.

"Oh, you . . . I don't know that they care. To Indochina, I think, so long as you are never seen in Europe. Yes, for life—to the East."